W9-BMW-473

Praise for Elmer Kelton

"Elmer Kelton is a Texas treasure. . . . [He] truly deserves to be made one of the immortals of literature."

—*El Paso Herald-Post*

"Kelton creates a story rich in historical context, character development, and action."

—*Houston Chronicle* on *Texas Vendetta*

"Elmer Kelton, a wily old cloudburst, imbues his Westerns with ancient myths and modern motifs that transcend cowboys and cattle trails."

—*The Dallas Morning News*

"One thing is certain: as long as there are writers as skillful as Elmer Kelton, Western literature will never die."

—*True West* magazine

Forge Books by Elmer Kelton

After the Bugles
Badger Boy
Barbed Wire
Bitter Trail
Bowie's Mine
The Buckskin Line
Buffalo Wagons
Captain's Rangers
Cloudy in the West
Dark Thicket
The Day the Cowboys Quit
Donovan
Eyes of the Hawk
The Good Old Boys
Hanging Judge
Hard Trail to Follow
Hot Iron
Jericho's Road
Joe Pepper
Llano River
Long Way to Texas
Many a River
Massacre at Goliad
Other Men's Horses
Pecos Crossing
The Pumpkin Rollers
The Raiders: Sons of Texas
Ranger's Trail
The Rebels: Sons of Texas
Sandhills Boy: The Winding Trail of a Texas Writer
Shadow of a Star
Shotgun
Six Bits a Day
The Smiling Country
Sons of Texas
Stand Proud
Texas Rifles
Texas Standoff
Texas Vendetta
The Time It Never Rained
The Way of the Coyote

Lone Star Rising
(comprising *The Buckskin Line, Badger Boy,* and *The Way of the Coyote*)

Brush Country
(comprising *Barbed Wire* and *Llano River*)

Ranger's Law
(comprising *Ranger's Trail, Texas Vendetta,* and *Jericho's Road*)

Texas Showdown
(comprising *Pecos Crossing* and *Shotgun*)

Texas Sunrise
(comprising *Massacre at Goliad* and *After the Bugles*)

Long Way to Texas
(comprising *Joe Pepper, Long Way to Texas,* and *Eyes of the Hawk*)

RANGER'S TRAIL

{ and }

TEXAS VENDETTA

Elmer Kelton

A TOM DOHERTY ASSOCIATES BOOK NEW YORK

NOTE: If you purchased this book without a cover, you should be aware that this book is stolen property. It was reported as "unsold and destroyed" to the publisher, and neither the author nor the publisher has received any payment for this "stripped book."

This is a work of fiction. All of the characters, organizations, and events portrayed in these novels are either products of the author's imagination or are used fictitiously.

RANGER'S TRAIL AND TEXAS VENDETTA

Ranger's Trail, copyright © 2002 by the Estate of Elmer Kelton, was originally published by Forge in September 2002. *Texas Vendetta*, copyright © 2003 by the Estate of Elmer Kelton, was originally published by Forge in November 2003.

All rights reserved.

A Forge Book
Published by Tom Doherty Associates, LLC
175 Fifth Avenue
New York, NY 10010

www.tor-forge.com

Forge® is a registered trademark of Tom Doherty Associates, LLC.

ISBN 978-0-7653-7771-5

Forge books may be purchased for educational, business, or promotional use. For information on bulk purchases, please contact Macmillan Corporate and Premium Sales Department at 1-800-221-7945, extension 5442, or write specialmarkets@macmillan.com.

First Edition: July 2014

Printed in the United States of America

0 9 8 7 6 5 4 3

{ Contents }

RANGER'S TRAIL

Dedicated to Nat Sobel, agent, friend, and a good judge of a story

{ ONE }

AUSTIN, TEXAS, JANUARY 1874

The election had gone smoothly except for certain extra-legal shenanigans perpetrated by both sides. Those were a normal feature of Texas politics and came as no surprise. By contrast the aftermath was chaotic enough to try the patience of saints, if there had been any. Rusty Shannon had encountered few saints in reconstruction Texas.

He slow-trotted his dun horse westward along a rutted wagon road skirting the edge of the Colorado River and wished he were back home on the farm where he belonged. On one side of him rode Sheriff Tom Blessing, in his sixties but still blacksmith-strong, solid as a block of oak timber. On the other, Andy Pickard whistled in a country boy's youthful awe and marveled at the town just ahead. His urban experience had been limited to a few small crossroads settlements.

Andy declared, "I had no idea Austin was this big. Must be three—maybe four—thousand people here. I never saw such a place in my life."

No one knew exactly how long a life that had been. Andy had been orphaned before he was old enough to retain clear memories. Rusty's best judgment was that he might be eighteen or nineteen, allowing some leeway on one side or the other. Strenuous outdoor labor and the excesses of Texas weather had given him a mature appearance beyond his years. He had a young man's seasoned face but had not lost the questing eyes of a boy eager to ride over the hill and see the other side. Girls seemed to consider him handsome. Andy seemed to have no objection to their thinking so.

Rusty turned up his frayed old coat collar against a cold wind coming off of the river. He had been wearing that coat for more than ten years, always intending to buy a new one someday when he felt he had a few dollars to spare but always "making do" for one more winter. He said, "San Antonio's bigger. I was there once."

His face, browned and chiseled with premature lines, was that of a man forty or more. Actually he was in his mid-thirties, but most had been hard years spent in sun and wind, riding with frontier rangers or walking behind mules and a plow. He said, "Got no use for San Antonio, though. It's overrun with gamblers and whiskey peddlers and pickpockets."

Tom Blessing declared, "Austin's worse. It's overrun with lawyers."

Andy had seen little of gamblers, whiskey peddlers, pickpockets or lawyers, but he was itching to start. He told Rusty, "You always say I need more learnin'. I'll bet I could learn a lot here."

"Mostly stuff you oughtn't to know."

Andy was well schooled in the ways of nature, but Rusty had worried about his limited book education. Andy had caught a little here and a little there as country teachers came, stayed awhile, then drifted on. Rusty, in his time, had had the advantage of coaching by a foster mother. There had been no woman to help teach Andy. At least he could read a newspaper, and he had an aptitude with figures. He was not easily cheated, nor was he a forgiving victim. Most who tried once never cared to do it a second time.

Andy said, "I doubt I'd get bored in a place like this. Bet there's somethin' goin' on all the time."

In Rusty's view, that was the trouble. His idea of a perfect day was a quiet one. He had finally begun having a lot of those, thanks to the farm. "Most of it you wouldn't want any part of. Country folks couldn't abide the crowdin'. You soon get tired of people trompin' on your toes all the time."

He was here against his will and better judgment. He had planned a journey north toward old Fort Belknap to visit the Monahan family and to bring Josie Monahan back with him as his wife. But Tom had asked him to make this trip, and it was against Rusty's nature to refuse a good friend. Tom had ridden often with Daddy Mike Shannon in old times when there was Indian trouble. He had introduced Rusty to the rangers at a crisis point when Rusty had badly needed somewhere to go. Rusty often said he would follow Tom into hell with a bucket of water. He had, once or twice. Austin might not be hell, but Rusty did not consider it heaven, either.

He wished he had not given in to Andy's plea that he be allowed to come along. He dreaded the temptations this town might present to someone no longer a boy but not quite yet a man. Rusty had taken on the responsibility of a foster brother after Andy's nearest known relative, an uncle, had rejected him. At times, like now, it had been an uneasy burden to carry.

He surveyed the town with apprehension. "Tom, reckon how we'll find your friend amongst all those people?"

"Maybe we'll get lucky and stumble into him. Otherwise, he's likely puttin' up at a wagon yard. We'll ask around."

Tom had been a county sheriff before reconstruction

authorities threw him out of office for having served the Texas Confederate government. The recent election had restored his badge after the former Confederates finally regained their right to vote. Another sheriff, a friend of his, had sent word that he was badly needed in Austin. He had not explained his reasons. He had just said to hurry and to bring help. Tom had immediately called on Rusty, respecting his law enforcement experience before war's end had caused the ranger companies to disintegrate.

Andy had jumped at a chance to quit the farm a while and see the city. To Rusty he had argued, "You're liable to need somebody to watch your back. You made some enemies while you were a ranger."

Rusty suspected Andy's motivation had less to do with protectiveness than with an urge to see something new and enjoy some excitement.

Because it was the dead of winter, Rusty and Andy had little farmwork that could not be postponed. Last year's crop was long since harvested, and this year's planting had to await warm ground. It would have been a good time for Rusty to get his red hair trimmed, then take a several-days' ride up to the Monahan place and ask Josie a question he had postponed much too long. Instead, he found himself approaching Austin and wondering why.

During ranger service that often took him far from home, Rusty had remained at heart a farmer with a strong tie to land he had known since boyhood. Andy empathized but had never been that dedicated to the soil. A tumultuous boyhood had given him a restless spirit. He welcomed any excuse to saddle Long Red and travel over new ground, to cross rivers he had not previously known.

"It's the Indian in him," Rusty had heard people say. "You never saw an Indian stay in one place long unless he was dead."

Andy was not Indian, at least by blood, but when he was a small boy the Comanches had taken him. They had held him through several of his vital formative years. Rusty had found him injured and helpless and returned him to the white man's world. But Andy had never given up all of his Indian ways.

Rusty hoped youthful curiosity would be satisfied quickly. He doubted that Andy would remain contented for long in a city like Austin any more than he was likely to be content spending all his life on the farm.

A squad of black soldiers drew Rusty's attention. He and Andy and Tom had drawn theirs as well. He murmured, "They're studyin' us like we might be outlaws."

Tom muttered in a deep voice, "They're lookin' at our guns. They're always afraid some old rebel may take a notion to declare war again." A few had, from time to time.

Rusty half expected the soldiers to stop them, but they simply watched in stone-faced silence as the three riders passed by and turned into a long street, which a sign on the corner said was Congress. At the head of it, well to the north, stood an imposing structure larger than any other Rusty could see.

Andy's eyes were wide. "Is that the capitol? The place where they make all the laws?"

Tom said, "That's the place. Fixin' to be a lot of different faces there now that we've elected a new governor. Be a lot of carpetbaggers huntin' new country."

Rusty had mixed feelings about the outsiders who had crowded into Texas after the war, hungry for opportunity. On the positive side they had brought money to a state drained dry after four years of debilitating conflict. On the negative side some had brought a bottomless hunger for anything they could grab and went to any lengths of stealth or violence necessary to satisfy it.

Now thousands of ex-Confederates, disenfranchised after the war, had finally recovered their voting rights. By a margin of two to one they had defeated the Union-backed reconstruction governor, Edmund J. Davis. They had voted in Richard Coke, a former Confederate army officer and one of their own. Perhaps that transition accounted for the large numbers of men standing along the street as if waiting for something to happen, Rusty thought. It did not, however, account for so many being heavily burdened by a variety of firearms.

Andy grinned. "Looks like the war is fixin' to start again." War had been a central fact of life among the Comanches, often sought after when it did not come on its own.

Rusty frowned. "I'm commencin' to wonder what we've ridden into." He reined his dun horse over to a man leaning against a cedar hitching post. "Say, friend, what's the big attraction in town?"

The man straightened, fixing suspicious eyes on Rusty, then on Andy and Tom. "I reckon you know, or you wouldn't be here. Did Governor Davis send for you?"

"I wouldn't know Edmund J. Davis from George Washington."

The man said, "A lot of Davis's friends have come to town includin' his old state police. They're all totin' guns. I see that you are, too."

Rusty kept his right hand away from the pistol on his hip, avoiding any appearance of a threat. "We brought our guns because we came a long ways. We didn't know what we might run into, or who."

"Just so you ain't one of them Davis police."

Mention of the Davis police put a bad taste in Rusty's mouth. "I used to be a ranger, but I never was a state policeman."

The governor's special police force—a mixture of white and black—had been organized as part of the state's reconstruction government, replacing the traditional rangers. Excesses had given the force a reputation for arrogance and brutality, arousing enmity in most Texans. Rusty had always felt that a majority were well intentioned, but a scattering of scoundrels overshadowed the law enforcement achievements of the rest.

A new legislature had recently abolished the state police to the relief of the citizenry and the consternation of Governor Davis.

The man said, "Local folks are naturally stirred up about so many strangers bringin' guns to town. Coke has been sworn in as governor, but Davis won't recognize him. Word has gone around that he has no intention of givin' up the office."

"But the people voted him out."

"He's declared the election unconstitutional."

Tom's face reddened. "He can't. That's not legal."

"He claims he's got the authority to say what's legal and what's not. Thinks he's the king of England, or maybe old Pharaoh."

The occupying Union forces had given their handpicked governor dictatorial power. He had instituted worthwhile improvements, particularly to the educational system, yet Texans resented his issuing punitive executive orders from which they had no recourse. Though Davis was a Southerner and a longtime citizen of the state, most former Confederates felt that he belonged to the enemy. He had fled Texas early in the war, eventually becoming a brigadier general in the Union army. The governor's office had been his reward.

Now it appeared that he did not intend to give it up.

Tom said, "We hold no brief for Davis. We voted for

Coke." He glanced questioningly at Rusty. "At least I did."

Rusty nodded. He, too, had voted for Coke because he felt it was time to shed the smothering reconstruction regime so Texas could work its own way back to order and stability.

"Then I'd advise you to either join Coke's militia or take care of your business and move out of town before the roof blows off of the capitol yonder."

Pulling away, Rusty muttered to Tom, "I think I see why your sheriff friend asked you to come and bring help."

"I've known him a long time. I couldn't turn him down."

Tom's loyalty to a friend was such that he had reluctantly left an ailing wife at home to come on this mission. Rusty's loyalty to Tom did not allow him to refuse Tom's request, though he had planned to be marrying Josie Monahan about now. He said, "We're liable to get pulled into a fight that ain't ours. That whole damned war wasn't really ours."

Like the late Sam Houston, Rusty had never favored secession from the Union, nor had he ever developed any allegiance to the Confederacy. One reason he had remained with the frontier rangers throughout the war was to avoid conscription into the rebel army. Even so, he had come to resent the oppressive federal occupation.

Tom frowned. "I wouldn't have asked you to come if I'd known we were ridin' into a situation like this. Maybe you and Andy better turn around and go home."

Disappointed, Andy said, "We ain't hardly seen the city yet."

Rusty said, "We've come this far, so we'll wait and size things up. Then we can go home if we're a mind to."

Initially Tom had harbored reservations about the wisdom of the war, but once it began he had given his loyalty to Texas and the South without looking back. He said, "Davis got beat fair and square. If he was a proper gentleman he'd recognize the will of the people. He'd yield up the office."

Andy said, "The Comanche way is simpler. A chief can't force anybody to do anything. If the people don't like him anymore they just quit payin' attention to him. No election, no fight, no nothin'." He snorted. "And everybody claims white people are smarter."

Andy's sorrel shied to one side, bumping against Rusty's dun. Two men burst off the sidewalk and into the dirt street, wildly swinging their fists. Immediately another man joined the fray, then two more, cursing, wrestling awkwardly. Foot and horse traffic stopped. Onlookers crowded around while the fight escalated.

Andy asked, "Whose side are we on?"

Rusty said, "Nobody's." He saw little difference between the combatants except that some might be drunker than others. He said, "We'd best move on before some fool pulls a gun." He found the way blocked by men rushing to watch the fight.

Faces were bloodied and shirts torn, but nobody drew a pistol or knife. Whatever the quarrel was about, the participants did not seem to consider it worth a killing.

A city policeman strode down the street, gave the situation a quick study, then stepped back to observe from a comfortable distance, hands in his pockets. Shortly a blue-clad army officer trotted his horse up beside the policeman. His sharp voice indicated he was used to people snapping to attention in his presence. "Aren't you going to stop this?"

The policeman did not take his hands from his pockets. "A man can get hurt messin' in where he wasn't asked. Long as they don't kill one another, I say let them have their fun."

"You are paid to enforce the peace."

"Not near enough. Ain't been any peace around here since this governor business came up. You want to stop the fight, go ahead."

"The army is not supposed to interfere. This is a civilian matter."

"And this here civilian is goin' into that grog shop yonder to have himself a drink. If anybody gets killed, come and fetch me." The policeman turned away. The officer watched him in frustration, then turned his attention to the ongoing fight. A couple of the brawlers had had enough and crawled away to sit on the edge of the wooden sidewalk, there to nurse their wounds while the altercation went on. They were not missed.

Andy's eyes danced with excitement as his fists mimicked the movements of the belligerents. He had been in plenty of fights himself, usually instigated by other young men making fun of the ways he had learned from the Indians.

Rusty knew a good scrap when he saw one. This was not a good one. It was slow-footed and clumsy, loud but not likely to produce anything more serious than loose teeth, bruised knuckles, and maybe a flattened nose. He decided the policeman had been right in leaving bad nature to run its course.

Onlookers' comments bore out his assumption that some of the fighters were Davis men. Others supported Coke. The fight slowly staggered to a standstill. The Coke men appeared to carry the victory, such as it was. They moved away in a triumphant group, weaving toward the grog shop the policeman had chosen. Their opponents dragged themselves to the sidewalk and slumped there, exhausted.

The fight had energized Andy. He said, "Some folks take their politics serious."

Tom Blessing nodded grimly. "With good reason. Davis's men tromped on everybody that got in their way. Stole half the state of Texas. Now comes the day of reckonin', and they ain't willin' to 'fess up."

The three rode north up the wide street, Rusty warily eyeing the armed men scattered all along. He saw no reason anyone would shoot at him on purpose, but he had learned long ago that the innocent bystander was usually the first one hurt. The more innocent, the more likely.

They reined up short of the capitol building. Several men stood shoulder to shoulder at the front door, holding rifles. They had a military bearing but did not wear uniforms. Rusty surmised they were former Confederate soldiers who had not forgotten the regimens learned in war.

He said, "Looks like they're guardin' the state treasury."

Tom said, "Too late for that. Talk is that Davis's adjutant general slipped away with it and sailed for Europe." He stepped down from the saddle and lifted the reins for Andy to hold. "You-all better stay here so we don't accidentally provoke somebody into somethin' rash. I'll walk up there and see what the game is." He unstrapped his pistol belt and hung it over the saddle horn as an indication that his intentions were benign.

Andy gazed southward back down Congress Avenue, where substantial buildings lined each side. Rusty assumed he was marveling at the variety of merchandise available here for anyone who had the money to buy it. That was the catch. Texas was just emerging from the economic devastation of war and its aftermath. Not many people other than opportunistic outsiders had much money to spend. Most of what Texans needed, they produced for themselves or did without. But Austin had been something of an oasis, money flowing more freely because of the Union soldiers and the state's reconstruction government based here.

It dawned on Rusty that Andy's attention was focused

on two young women who stood in front of a nearby saloon. It was obvious they were not Sunday school teachers.

He warned, "Don't let your curiosity get stirred up too much. I don't expect we'll be stayin'." It occurred to him that he had taught Andy a lot about plowing straight rows but not enough about avoiding society's pitfalls.

Tom returned, his jaw set grimly. "Governor Davis has got himself barricaded in the capitol basement with a bunch of his old state police. The Coke men and the legislature have got the upper floor."

"A Mexican standoff," Rusty said.

"Maybe not for long. Davis has sent a wire to President Grant. He's askin' him to order the troops in. Wants them to throw out the Coke crowd and keep him in office."

That news troubled Rusty. "If he does, there's apt to be an awful fight."

Andy had no problem with the notion of a fight. "I wish old Buffalo Caller could've seen this." Buffalo Caller was the Comanche warrior who had first captured him and kept him for his own. "He would've given a hundred horses to watch white men battle one another instead of fightin' the People. And it would've been worth every one of them."

Tom declared, "You're white. That's a scandalous thing to say."

Andy said, "Was it to happen, I'd cheer for the old Texans to win. But not too quick. I'd like to see the fight stretch out a while."

Tom shook his head. "Scandalous." He looked back toward the capitol. "I've offered to do my part and stand with Coke. This ain't none of you-all's fight unless you want it to be."

Rusty said, "We're here now. We wouldn't go off and leave you by yourself."

Tom seemed pleased. "You sound like your old Daddy

Mike. But I won't be by myself. There's several of my friends up there from way back. There's a bunch of old rangers, too. Friends of yours, I'd warrant."

Rusty's interest quickened. "Rangers?"

"Yeah, but like I said, it don't have to be your fight. I wouldn't want a young feller like Andy on my conscience. Or you, either."

"We came of our own accord. We're grown men." Rusty glanced at Andy. "*I* am, anyway."

Tom nodded. "There's a wagon yard down yonder. Would you take my horse for me?"

Rusty jerked his head. "Come on, Andy."

Andy led Tom's mount. Rusty guessed there must be a hundred horses in the several corrals to the side of and beyond the large wooden barn. A droop-shouldered liveryman slouched in the big open doorway, waiting for customers. He limped out a few paces and spat a stream of brown tobacco juice at a bedraggled cat, missing by a foot. A bit of the spittle remained in his stubble of gray-and-black beard. He said, "You're supposed to be in there chasin' mice. They're fixin' to carry off the whole shebang, barn and all." He looked up at Rusty. "What can I do for you-all?"

"Got room for three more horses?"

"If there ain't room enough we'll just stack them like cordwood. I expect you-all are in town to see the excitement?" It was a statement, but he made it sound like a question.

"We didn't know about it 'til we got here."

"I ain't takin' sides, you understand, but I hope the Coke people give that Davis crowd a hell of a lickin'. I've had a gutful of them thieves."

Rusty smiled. "Sounds like you *have* taken sides."

"I reckon, but if the shootin' starts I'm keepin' my head

down. I taken a Yankee ball in my leg durin' the war. Convinced me I ain't no fightin' man."

"But you're willin' to take money from either side?"

"I take care of horses, and horses don't know nothin' about politics. I do business with any and all, long as the money is genuine." He extended his hand, the palm up. "And paid in advance."

Rusty took his time counting out the coins, for he did not have enough that he could afford to spend them needlessly. "We'll want to bed down here in the wagon yard tonight. We've got no money to waste on a hotel."

"Hotels are all full, anyway. Spread your blankets anywhere you can find an empty space. And be careful with your matches. You don't want to buy no burned-up barn." He dropped Rusty's coins into his pocket. They clinked against silver already there.

The capitol standoff was good for business.

The liveryman looked behind him as if to be certain he would not be overheard. "Couple of fellers were talkin' back of the barn. They're waitin' for Coke to give the word to make a rush against the capitol and put Davis out on the street. Could be a right interestin' show."

Rusty glanced uneasily at Andy. "Tom could get hurt. He's a shade old to be mixin' in a bad fight."

Andy said, "He's never run away from one yet. That's why they made him sheriff again."

"He ought not to've let them put that badge back on him. I've got a notion to try and talk him into goin' home before somethin' happens. That sick wife of his needs him more than anybody here does."

Andy had not seen enough of the town. "Gettin' kind of late in the day. We couldn't go far before dark."

"We could get out of gunshot range."

Andy resigned himself to disappointment. He patted Long Red's neck. "You better eat your oats in a hurry." He followed Rusty out the door.

Rusty told the liveryman, "Don't turn our horses into the lot just yet. We're liable to be leavin'."

The old man shoved his hands into his pockets. The coins jingled like tiny bells. Reluctantly he said, "I guess you'll want your money back. You still want me to feed them some oats?"

"I wish you would." Rusty was more willing to spend on the horses than on himself.

He saw a crowd of nervous-looking men standing around the front of a hotel as if waiting for someone to assert leadership and take them somewhere . . . anywhere, to do something . . . anything. A familiar voice called his name, and a man pushed through the cluster. Len Tanner was tall and lanky, in patched trousers that hung loose around a waist thin as a slab of bacon. He always looked as if he had not eaten a square meal in a month. In truth, he could put away an alarming amount of groceries when the opportunity presented itself.

Rusty exclaimed, "Len! Thought you were back in East Texas, visitin' your kin."

"Ain't much excitement in seein' kinfolks. Here's where the fun is at."

Rusty had ridden with Tanner during his ranger service. Since the war, Tanner had spent much of his time at Rusty's farm when he lacked something better to do. He was not addicted to steady employment. Tanner said, "There's a bunch of our old ranger bunkies here ready to run the carpetbaggers out of town on a rail. But Coke keeps holdin' back, hopin' Davis will cave in without a fight."

"What if he doesn't?"

"After fightin' the damned Comanches, this oughtn't to make us break a sweat." Tanner frowned at Andy. "Sorry, button, I didn't mean nothin' personal."

Andy shrugged. "I take it as a compliment to the Comanches."

"They're honest enemies, at least. They come against you face-to-face. Carpetbaggers sneak up behind you and kill you with affidavits." Tanner's family had lost their farm to confiscatory reconstruction taxes, though he, like Rusty, had never actively supported the Confederacy. He said, "I know why Davis wants to keep that office. There's some of Texas that his cronies ain't stole yet." His momentary dark mood fell away. "Speakin' of old friends, I'll bet it's been a spell since you seen Jim and Johnny Morris."

"Sure has." Rusty looked around eagerly. "Are those rascals here?"

The Morris brothers had served in the same ranger company as Rusty and Tanner until they went into the Confederate army late in the war.

Tanner said, "Me and them are plannin' on a little sortie tonight. Goin' to aggravate some Yankee soldiers."

That did not surprise Rusty. Like Tanner, the brothers had always gloried in a fracas. If they could not find a fight already in progress they had occasionally instigated one.

Rusty and Andy followed Tanner through the crowd. Two men of roughly Rusty's age shouted his name and pushed their way to him. They could be taken for twins, though Jim was a year or so the oldest. He declared, "Glad to see you're still alive." He gripped Rusty's outstretched hand with a force that could crush bones. "Me and Johnny figured you'd worked yourself to death on that wore-out farm."

"I've come awful close."

Jim turned to Andy, his manner jovial. "You'd be the Comanche button Len's been tellin' us about."

The brothers' being friends of Tanner's did not automatically assure Andy's acceptance. He regarded them with an element of doubt. "Len's been known to lie a little, once or twice."

Johnny Morris grinned. "We've caught him abusin' the facts ourselves. But only when he's awake." He jerked his head, beckoning Rusty and the others beyond the edge of the crowd. In a low voice he said, "Rusty, you're just the man to help us do a little job tonight."

Rusty felt misgivings. As much as he liked Tanner and the Morrises, he remembered times when they had acted first and considered the consequences later, if at all. Events had not always worked to their advantage. "I'd want to hear the particulars before I say anything." He already leaned toward saying *no.*

"The army's brought up a cannon from San Antonio."

Rusty's jaw dropped. He had not considered that the dispute would come to this. A cannon could blow a big hole in the capitol building. He thought immediately of Tom Blessing, standing guard somewhere in or around it.

He protested, "Hard to believe the army would fire on the capitol while Davis and some of his people hold the basement floor."

"No," Johnny said, "but they'd fire into the crowd if a bunch was to try and rush the buildin'. We figure they're just waitin' for Grant to wire them the orders."

"But a cannon . . . what could you do against a weapon the size of that?"

Jim said, "Me and Johnny and Len are goin' to spike it."

Andy demanded, "What do you mean, 'spike' it?"

Johnny explained, "You drive an iron spike into the touchhole. They can't fire 'til they get it out, and that can be hell to do if it's pounded in there hard enough."

Rusty said, "Don't you know they'll be guardin' it? You'll get yourselves shot."

"Len'll distract the guards. Won't take us but a minute to fix the cannon and be gone. You could help him."

The idea was much too simple. Rusty could see a dozen holes in it, most of them potentially lethal. "You're crazy, all three of you."

Andy said eagerly, "Let's do it, Rusty. We can run rings around them soldiers."

"*Four* of you are crazy. You're too young to be mixin' into a thing like this."

"How old were you the first time you rode with the rangers?"

"That was a long time ago. Times were different." It struck Rusty that his foster father, Daddy Mike Shannon, had said the same thing to him once, to no effect.

Johnny Morris turned. "Yonder come some of them brunette Yankees." A small squad of black troopers marched up the street, led by a white officer on horseback, the same one Rusty had seen earlier. "At least they ain't brought their cannon with them."

Jim said, "Washington still ain't given them permission to mix in. That's all they're waitin' for."

The presence of black troops had been a thorn in the sides of ex-Confederates during the reconstruction years. Texans were convinced that the victorious Union intended to humiliate them by putting them under the authority of former slaves. The effect had been more of outrage than of humiliation.

Several in the crowd began catcalling, shouting racial and political insults at the soldiers and their officer. One man stepped out past the others and shook his fist, loudly cursing all Yankees and their antecedents from the poorest foot soldier all the way up to President Grant. His slurred speech indicated that he had imbibed a good measure of liquid courage.

The officer unbuttoned his holster and drew a pistol. He pushed his horse up close and brought the barrel down across the heckler's head. The man went down, his hat rolling in the dirt.

The officer turned in the saddle. "Arrest him. Two of you men take him to the bull pen."

Len swore under his breath. "That old boy was too drunk to know what he was sayin'."

"He knew," Rusty said sternly. "But loud talk is no reason to break a man's skull."

A noisy protest arose from the crowd, but no one made a move toward the well-armed soldiers.

Jim Morris said, "Whatever happened to free speech?"

Johnny replied, "It ain't free anymore. And the price keeps goin' up."

Rusty gave way to rising anger as two troopers dragged the half-conscious man away. He looked into the faces of his friends and saw the same reaction.

Andy demanded, "Don't you think we ought to do somethin'?"

Rusty said, "Like what? The South already lost one war."

Tanner said, "At least you can look the situation over with us. Help us figure out how we're goin' to do it."

"I guess I can go that far. But this is a dog fight, and me and Andy have got no dog in it."

{ TWO }

The liveryman did not get up from his rawhide-bound chair, but he eyed Rusty with regret. "Fixin' to go? I done fed your horses some oats, so I can't give all your money back."

Rusty said, "We're not leavin' town yet."

Cheered, the liveryman pushed away from the chair. "I'll show you where they're at."

Andy lagged behind, nursing his disappointment. Rusty had told him he had to stay at the wagon yard. He saw no need for Andy to take chances by joining Tanner and the Morrises.

The liveryman led Rusty into the barn to a small pen where his horse, Andy's, and Tom's still nuzzled a wooden trough, seeking stray bits of grain stuck in the cracks. Rusty wondered if they had actually been fed as much as he had paid for.

He led his dun out into the fading daylight. As he prepared to mount, Rusty heard a familiar voice. "How's my young Comanche friend?" It was addressed to Andy.

Andy considered his answer, then said firmly, "I don't remember that we was ever friends, Farley Brackett."

Brackett was a large man with a scar from the edge of his eye down to his cheek. War had scarred him even worse on the inside, turning him into an outlaw, at least in the eyes of the state police. As Brackett approached, Andy took half a step back before standing his ground.

Brackett pointed his chin at Long Red. "I see you've still got my sorrel horse."

Andy bristled. "He never was your horse. Your daddy gave him to Rusty, and Rusty gave him to me."

"He wasn't my daddy's to give. He was mine."

Andy stiffened. "So you say, but your daddy's dead. We can't ask him."

Rusty intruded. "You're runnin' a risk, Farley, showin' up in public. The state police don't forget."

"They've had their fangs pulled, but I haven't. Any of them tries to mess with me, he'll get what they gave my old daddy." State police had mistaken the father for Farley and had killed him.

Rusty said, "Anyway, you leave Andy alone. We're not here to fight."

"Everybody else is." Brackett looked back at Andy. "I still say he's my horse. You've just got the loan of him. For now." He walked away, toward the milling crowd that stirred dust along Congress Avenue.

Worriedly Andy asked, "He can't take Long Red back, can he?" Andy thought more of that horse than of any human. Almost any human, at least.

Rusty said, "He's got no claim. His daddy gave me that horse to replace one Farley stole when he was on the run."

"If he tries to take Long Red, I'll shoot him."

Rusty suspected Andy would at least try. But Farley Brackett had shown the reconstruction authorities he was a hard man to kill. "You shouldn't talk loose about killin'. It can lead to more than just talk."

"Just the same, I'm keepin' a close eye on Long Red. Farley had better not so much as look crossways at him."

Rusty met Tanner and the brothers where the three had dropped their blankets near the river. Johnny pointed. "The troops made camp down thisaway."

As they rode, Rusty heard a horse loping up from behind. Andy pushed to overtake them.

Rusty turned in anger as Andy pulled in beside him. "I told you to stay behind."

"That Farley kept hangin' around the stable. I decided the best way for me to keep an eye on Long Red was to be ridin' him."

Rusty knew that was more an excuse than a reason. "All right, but don't be gettin' any foolish notions."

He saw several rows of tents lined in military order. Johnny said, "They got the cannon placed back of the tents."

A hundred yards beyond the tent line stood a set of wooden pens. The troops were infantry. Rusty surmised that the few horses he saw were for the officers. He counted four draft mules. Drawing the cannon would be their job.

He shivered at the thought of such a weapon being fired into a crowd. For that purpose artillerymen would probably load it with scraps of metal and pieces of chain. Those would damage more rioters than a single cannonball.

Tanner muttered, "A mean piece of business. And all on account of politics."

Rusty said, "The whole war was because of politics."

He was not surprised to see two black soldiers standing guard on either side of the cannon. He was a little surprised there were not more. "You think they'll stand by idle while you-all drive your spike?"

Tanner said, "When the time comes I'll see to it that they ain't there."

"You wouldn't kill them? The army would run you to the ground and hang you from the tallest tree they can find. If they didn't just shoot you outright."

Johnny said, "We wouldn't hurt a hair on their heads. Len is goin' to draw them away."

"How?"

"We hoped you'd help us figure that out."

Rusty studied the cannon and everything around it. He saw a stack of hay near the horse pens. He said, "I don't see anybody guardin' that hay yonder. If it was to accidentally catch afire . . ."

Jim nodded, his eyes brightening. "That's the same stunt me and Johnny pulled on some Yankees just before the end of the war. Got away with a bunch of their horses. They didn't need that many, anyway, since their hay burned up. They didn't have anything to feed them."

Andy had listened quietly, but excitement built in his eyes. Rusty sought to head him off. "You're not goin' along with them. You're too young, and it's too dangerous."

"I've been in dangerous places before. My Comanche brother Steals the Ponies could tell you that."

"But he's not here. If he was, he'd be welcome to help. But not you. I didn't spend all these years raisin' you to lose you in a fight that's none of your business."

Rusty expected more argument. Andy simply shrugged and said, "Here come some soldiers to see what we're about. You want to talk to them?"

Four troopers and a white officer were marching toward the five Texans. Rusty said, "I don't believe we've got anything to talk about." He reined his horse around and started back toward the brothers' camp, careful not to move faster than a walk. He did not want to arouse suspicion by appearing to run away. The others followed him. The troopers soon stopped.

Tanner asked, "You reckon they suspect us?"

Rusty said, "They suspect everybody, and have since the first day they came into Texas."

Tom Blessing walked to the wagon yard about sundown, tired and burdened with worry. "Hard to guess what's fixin' to happen," he said. "Governor Coke has got a bunch of his old rangers at his side. Governor Davis has called out the Travis Rifles to help him hold the capitol. Some of them have come over to us, but there's enough left to give us a right smart of trouble. And we still don't know what President Grant will do. If he orders the troops in, with their cannon, . . ."

Tanner declared, "Don't you worry yourself about that cannon. It's fixin' to be took care of."

Rusty frowned at Tanner and looked about to see if anyone might have overheard. Most people around here were strangers. He had no way of knowing which side they were on. He said in little more than a whisper, "The Morris boys figure on spikin' that cannon tonight."

Tom was not relieved. "They're liable to get spiked themselves."

Rusty said, "Len Tanner's goin' to help."

"That's no big relief." Tom nodded toward Andy. "Surely you're not lettin' the boy go."

"He's stayin' here with me."

Tom said, "Good. We're dealin' with people who are used to absolute power. If they got him in their sights, they wouldn't take his youth into account."

Andy spoke up. "If I was still with the Comanches I'd be looked at as a warrior now. I sure wouldn't let a bunch of bluecoats scare me."

Tom said, "They scare *me*. I just hope Grant doesn't set them loose. You know they arrested the mayor today."

Rusty said, "I hadn't heard that."

"Roughed him up some, then turned him loose because it looked like a riot was fixin' to break out. They still haven't got their orders from Washington."

Rusty walked to the door and stared out into the street. Everywhere he looked little clusters of armed men stood waiting, watching. The tension was electric, much like the atmosphere before a thunderstorm. "Wouldn't take but one good spark to touch off the powder. I wish we'd gone back home."

Tom said, "For my wife's sake, I wish we'd never been asked to come in the first place. She needs a woman to be with her 'til she gets her feet back under her. I ain't been able to find one who'd stay."

Rusty kept a disturbing thought to himself. What would become of Mrs. Blessing if a bullet brought down her husband? "We could start home right now. It won't be full dark for another hour."

Tom shook his head. "We finally got back the right to vote. It's time to get off of our knees and stand on our feet."

"No matter what it costs?"

"We're at a fork in the road. One way follows the law. The other twists the law to whatever it wants it to be."

Rusty smiled. "First time I ever heard you make a speech."

"I don't often feel the need, especially with you."

Rusty did not intend to go to sleep so early, but it had been a long day. Soon after he lay down on his blankets he dozed off. He awakened suddenly to the squealing of two horses nipping at one another. He saw that Andy's blankets had been thrown back. Andy was gone.

Damn fool kid, he thought. He's gone to help Tanner and the Morrises.

The stableman was asleep on a steel cot in a small office at the front of the barn. Rusty aroused him to ask when Andy had left. The man sat up, blinking rapidly, swinging his bare feet over the side. His voice was sour. "Don't you people know what the night is meant for?"

"That boy who was with me, did you see him leave?"

The man ignored the question. "Night's a time for rest. If you want your horse, you know where he's at. Catch him yourself. And you can put him back for yourself when you come in. If you're too drunk to unlatch the gate, just tie him to the fence."

"How long has it been since the kid left?"

"I didn't look at my watch." The man scratched his backside. "What kind of a critter is that button, anyway?"

"What do you mean?"

"He come stealin' in and got his horse. I wouldn't have knowed he was here if the horse hadn't snorted just as he passed my door. Wouldn't surprise me none if that boy's got Indian blood in him."

"I'll admit he acts like it."

The stableman said, "Probably snuck off to find him a sportin' gal. I did when I was his age. 'Spect you did, too. I got no quarrel with it as long as they let a man sleep."

Rusty saddled his horse while the stableman returned to his blankets, muttering all the way.

The kid's got more nerve than judgment, Rusty thought darkly. As bad as Len Tanner.

He rode in a long trot to the Morris brothers' camp at the edge of town. He found the fire burned low. No one was there. He was sure he knew where they were, and Andy with them.

Damn Len Tanner. He knew I didn't want Andy to be any part of this.

He rode toward the soldier camp under a dark sky, the moon hidden by a heavy cover of clouds. Unable to see much, he almost rode upon two men sitting on horseback. Johnny Morris demanded, "Who the hell are you?"

"It's me, Rusty. Where are Len and Andy?"

"They've snuck off down yonder to set the hay afire.

While everybody's runnin' to fight the fire, me and Jim will fix the cannon." He showed Rusty an iron rod. Jim carried a blacksmith's hammer across the pommel of his saddle.

Rusty said, "Why didn't you-all turn the boy back?"

Jim said, "His mind was made up. We couldn't have stopped him if we'd hit him over the head with this hammer."

Rusty knew how stubborn Andy could be. "Maybe I can head him off. You-all be careful. Some Yankees are good shots."

He rode down toward the camp. He could not make out the shape of the haystack, but he knew more or less where it should be. He felt a chilly dampness moving up from the river on the south wind. He shivered and pulled his old coat more tightly around him. A couple of fires flickered in the soldier camp. He envied the men warming themselves there.

The cannon guards had a fire of their own. Rusty took that as a good sign. Glare from the flames would diminish their ability to see through the darkness.

He saw a match flare, then flicker out. Andy and Tanner must be having poor luck getting the hay to catch fire. Both were single-minded enough to keep trying, even if soldiers swarmed over them.

A hostile voice demanded. "Who goes there?"

Rusty realized the challenge was directed at Andy and Tanner. He put spurs to the dun horse, urging him into a long trot.

A rough voice shouted, "Who are you? Speak before I blow your head off!"

Tanner's answer was defiant. "I'm Robert E. Lee and I'm here to whup some Yankee sons of bitches."

Rusty saw a quick movement and heard a thud as a

soldier struck Tanner in the stomach with the butt of a rifle. Rusty did not give him a second chance. He rode in, swinging his pistol. He felt the barrel connect with a trooper's head. The trooper fell, firing his rifle by reflex. Tanner wrestled with another soldier but was losing ground. Rusty grabbed a handful of uniform and pulled the man off of him. He swung the pistol but missed.

He heard a shout. "Corporal of the guard! Post number two!" It came from the direction of the cannon. He heard more soldiers running toward him. A rifle cracked. Rusty fired his pistol into the air, hoping to confuse and perhaps discourage the soldiers. "Forget the fire," he shouted. "Get out of here."

The troopers guarding the cannon came on the run, silhouetted against their fire. Rusty aimed a shot in their general direction, slowing them. One discharged his rifle into the darkness but had no clear target. Rusty leaned low to be sure he did not present one.

Andy came riding out, leading Tanner's horse. "Here, Len. Get on him quick."

Rusty heard the whisper of bullets passing much too close. Len staggered. Andy swung around to help lift him into the saddle. The three set their horses into a run.

The firing continued behind them. Rusty said, "You two stirred up the whole Yankee army."

Andy laughed. "Didn't we, though? But we couldn't get the fire started."

Len lamented, "Damned hay was wet. All I burned was my fingers."

Rusty said, "It was a fool notion in the first place."

Andy said, "Only thing wrong with it was that it didn't work."

Rusty did not see the Morris brothers, but he figured they were old enough to take care of themselves. They always had. Andy was young, eager, and still needed watching. Tanner should have known better, but he was inclined to create trouble even where there had been none. He had long maintained that a good fight was more invigorating than a double shot of whiskey.

Rusty led Andy and Tanner along the river until he was sure they had shaken off pursuit by the foot soldiers. Then he circled back in the direction of the Morris brothers' camp. Andy was still laughing.

Rusty decided it was time for the lecture. "Now listen here—"

Andy cut him off. "I know what you're goin' to say, so there ain't no use sayin' it. I didn't have any business bein' out here. But I figured Len needed help. By himself, he was apt to get killed."

"You could've both been killed."

"We weren't, and I had more fun tonight than I ever got followin' a mule across a field. Len, you're lookin' kind of sick."

"Took a rifle butt in my ribs. I'm goin' to be awful sore in the mornin'." He moaned. "Every time a man gets to feelin' smart, somethin' comes along and kicks him in the belly."

Johnny and Jim arrived in camp just ahead of them. "Everybody all right?" Johnny asked worriedly. "What went wrong out there?"

"Damp hay," Rusty said. "Looks like it ruined you-all's plan."

The brothers grinned at one another. "Not really," Johnny said. "Len and the boy set out to draw attention away from us. They sure did that."

"You managed to spike the cannon, after all?"

"The only way it could hurt anybody now would be if it fell on him."

Rusty grunted, surprised but pleased. The troops could do a lot of damage with their rifles if they were called into the dispute, but at least they should not be able to use artillery against the crowd.

He said, "If you-all don't mind a little company, I think me and Andy'll bed down here instead of goin' back to the wagon yard. The stable keeper needs his sleep."

With only their saddle blankets for cover against the night chill, Rusty and Andy lay near the campfire. Rusty poked a little fresh wood among the coals and watched the flames rise up before he stretched out on the ground. He lay awake, replaying the evening's action in his mind.

Tanner was soon snoring. Andy rolled onto one side, then moved to the other, pulling his legs up tightly. Rusty asked, "Can't you sleep?"

"I'm a little cold. And there was too much excitement, I guess. Got my blood all stirred up."

"I'm not havin' much luck myself." Rusty arose to put more wood on the fire. Instead of lying down and rolling up in his saddle blanket, he squatted on his heels and stared into the fire.

"Been doin' some thinkin', too," he said. "How would you like to have a cabin of your own?"

"What do I need a cabin for? There's plenty of room in yours."

"Maybe not for long."

Andy stared at him in puzzlement. "How come?"

"I've been plannin' a trip up to the Monahan farm. Been wantin' to see how everybody's gettin' along."

"Especially Josie?"

"Especially Josie. I'm figurin' on askin' her to marry me."

Andy grunted. "It's about time. She's been askin' *you* long enough."

"Things weren't right before. I never knew what the carpetbaggers might throw at us. They tried once to take the farm, and I was always afraid they might do it again. But things'll settle down now that we've got a new governor."

"We've got two governors. We don't know which one will win out."

"I've got a feelin'. Old Preacher Webb always said if you keep the faith, good things will eventually come to you."

After a campfire breakfast of bacon and black coffee, all five rode up onto Congress Avenue to see if anything had changed overnight. A large group of men had gathered some distance below the capitol building. Rusty recognized several as former rangers with whom he had ridden at one time or another. Tom Blessing walked out from among them and hailed Rusty. He said, "Word has come from Washington. President Grant won't order the troops to help Davis. Told him the election is over, he lost, and he had just as well yield like a gentleman."

Rusty accepted that as good news, but not the ultimate answer. "He hasn't given up though, has he?"

"Not yet, but he must be feelin' like a mule has kicked him in the ribs. He can't call in the army. All he's got backin' him now is a bunch of his old state police and some office-holders who know they're fixin' to be out of a job."

Rusty was still trying to absorb the fact that the troops were not to be involved. That meant they would not have used the cannon even if it had not been spiked. Last night's wild sashay had been unnecessary.

Tanner had waked up with sore ribs and belly from the blow he had taken. He would hurt even more when it soaked in on him that he had taken the punishment for nothing.

Tom said, "We're waitin' for Governor Coke to show up and lead us on a march to the capitol."

"And if Davis won't give up?"

"We'll burn that bridge when we get to it."

Richard Coke was tall and heavyset, his white beard neatly trimmed. He wore a suit well tailored to his bulk and projected a sense of dignity the way a governor of Texas was supposed to, in Rusty's view. In a booming voice he shouted, "Let's go."

Flanked on either side by ex-rangers and Confederate officers Rip Ford and Henry McCulloch, he led the parade of determined men up Congress. In front of the capitol stood a line of well-armed Davis men, appearing just as determined. Coke acted as if he did not see them, never breaking stride. The defenders looked to one another for guidance, for someone to take the initiative and do something. No one did. The Davis men stepped back grudgingly, and the Coke procession marched into the capitol.

A tall, gaunt, defiant Davis awaited them in the hallway outside of his office. The door was closed. He stared sullenly at Coke.

Coke said, "Governor Davis, the new legislature has convened and canvassed the vote. They have declared that I am the rightful holder of this office. I respectfully request that you honor the wishes of the people of Texas."

Davis glared, his gaze sweeping over the men who faced him. "I do not recognize the election as legitimate. But I see that the laws of the state have been trampled underfoot. The rule of the mob has prevailed."

He strode past Coke. His opponents moved aside to let him pass. He did not look to right or left but focused his gaze straight ahead.

An audible sigh of relief arose from the men clustered in

the hallway. One of Coke's lieutenants tried the door to the governor's office. "Locked," he said. "Davis did not turn over the key."

Another lieutenant said, "Break it open."

Tanner and a couple of others put their shoulders into the task. The door splintered. Tanner stepped back, gripped his belly, and grimaced in pain.

Inside the office, Davis's secretary of state still sat at his desk. The lieutenant who had tried the door said, "It's over. You can leave."

The man sat in stubborn silence.

The lieutenant said, "Some of you escort him outside."

A momentary clamor arose as several in the crowd suggested throwing the man out the window, but Coke overruled the idea. "That is the way of the old regime. As of today Texas is steering a new course."

Three men lifted the secretary from his chair and hustled him outside. Tanner did not volunteer to join them. He was still holding his stomach.

The people of Austin, and most of the visitors, celebrated far into the night. Rusty thought of the stable keeper. He wouldn't be getting much sleep.

Tom Blessing sat on the ground near the Morris brothers' campfire, chewing a piece of bacon. He told Rusty, "I'm ready to start home come daylight. You and Andy seen enough of the big city?"

Rusty glanced at Andy, who put up no argument. "I was ready before we came. But now that it's over, I'm glad we were here to see it. It'll be somethin' to tell our grandchildren about someday."

"Andy's too young to be thinkin' about grandchildren. And you ain't even married."

"I'm figurin' on fixin' that."

Tom stopped chewing. He seemed a little perturbed. "You sure bein' a ranger is a proper thing for a married man?"

"I'm not a ranger anymore."

"But you could be again. Governor Coke says one of the first things he plans to do is reorganize the rangers. He'll be lookin' for men of experience."

"I've *had* plenty of experience," Rusty said ruefully. "More than I ever looked for. I'm not sure I want any more like it."

"It gets in your blood, like sheriffin' got into mine. You'll want to study on it before you take to double harness."

{ THREE }

Len Tanner stood with hands in his pockets to keep them warm. He watched as Rusty and Andy lifted blankets, provisions, and Rusty's saddle into the bed of the wagon. The sun was just breaking over the eastern horizon, looking crisp and frosty through a thin blanket of gray winter clouds.

"I don't see why you want to take the wagon," he said. "You'd get there a lot sooner if you rode horseback."

"Josie'll be wantin' to bring all her things," Rusty said.

"How do you know she'll even come? You ain't asked her yet."

"She'll come." Rusty looked toward a new single log cabin standing halfway between the older double cabin and the livestock pens. "I hope you don't mind finishin' the roof on Andy's cabin."

"I got nothin' better to do. And Shanty's comin' over to help me build the chimly." Shanty was a former slave who lived a few miles away. Age had bent his slender frame, but his hands were still those of an artisan. "We'll have the place ready for the button to move in by the time you-all get back."

Andy had been torn about making the trip. He wanted to stay and help finish the cabin, but Rusty had persuaded him that the Monahans would be eager to see him. They had come to look upon him as a member of the family.

Andy saddled Long Red and tied Rusty's dun horse behind the wagon. "Reckon we got it all?"

Rusty said, "If we don't, we'll do without it." He shook Tanner's hand and climbed onto the wagon seat.

Tanner said, "Tell that cute little Alice girl I said howdy."

Rusty grinned. "We'll tell her."

"And watch out for Indians. They may not all know they're Andy's friends."

"I doubt they'll come far enough south for us to see them. They've got their hands full fightin' buffalo hunters."

Rusty had heard talk that large numbers of hide hunters had filtered down onto the Texas high plains from Kansas during the fall and winter. They had decimated the herds farther north in Cheyenne country. Now they were invading the Comanches' best hunting grounds. The Comanches were not feeling generous.

The news had disturbed Andy. His first thought was of his Comanche family and how the buffalo slaughter would affect them. "I thought there was a treaty that said the hunters couldn't come south of the Cimarron River."

Rusty said, "The treaty was with the federal government, on federal land. The federals have no right to make agreements about Texas land."

"I doubt that Steals the Ponies knows where the line is

or that he would give a damn. Land is land. The Comanches figure they own all of it they're strong enough to hold."

"That's what counts, bein' strong enough."

Rusty had not tried to argue Texas's case. Andy had strong feelings where Indians were concerned. Trying to alter his views was like trying to stop a flowing river with a leaky bucket.

Andy looked back as they started away. He said, "I like my cabin, but a good tepee would serve me just as well."

"You won't feel that way when you've got a blaze goin' in the fireplace on a cold night. I hear the reservation Indians have started buildin' houses."

"Yes, but a lot of them put up tepees beside their cabins. They like to sleep next to Mother Earth. She gives them their strength."

"I've spent a lot of my life sleepin' on the ground. All I got from Mother Earth was rheumatism and a likin' for an honest-to-God bed."

They crossed the Colorado River at a ford. The water was higher than it would be in spring, when winter-dormant vegetation came back to life and sapped much of the underground moisture before it had a chance to seep into the river. Rusty pushed hard to keep the team moving forward briskly enough that the current would not pick up the wagon and carry it away.

He had ridden this trail many times, going to or from the Monahan farm or in the course of his ranger duties. Andy had ridden it, too, once when he was almost too young to remember. On that first trip he had traveled northward as captive of a Comanche raiding party. He had ridden again as a half-grown boy, this time heading southward to join his adopted brother as a participant in a horse-stealing foray. Fate in the guise of a fallen horse and a broken leg had dropped him back into the white world. There he had remained, though not willingly at first. He had never completely relinquished the heritage of his Comanche years.

Some people considered him unreconstructed, a streak of the savage locked forever in his heart. Andy had found he could use such people's attitude against them, keeping them at arm's length as a measure of self defense. His friends accepted him as he was. He was not troubled by what others thought.

Andy rode alongside the wagon, talking at intervals, then silent for long stretches. He was especially quiet after they made the first night's camp. Rusty recognized the dark moods that came over him now and then and did not push him for conversation. As they hitched the team next morning, Andy asked, "We goin' by the grave?"

Rusty had suspected this had been heavy on Andy's mind. "We can if you want to."

"I reckon I want to."

The grave was above the north bank of a small creek, just off the wagon track. At one end of a stack of stones a wooden cross had fallen to the ground. Rusty moved the wagon a little beyond and stopped. He got down, but he stood back, letting Andy have his time alone.

Andy dismounted and removed his hat, his head bowed. After a while he wiped a sleeve across his eyes, then straightened the cross. He pulled off a small wad of dark hair. "Buffalo," he said. "They knocked it over, scratchin' their itch."

Many of the stones lay scattered. Andy placed them neatly back over the mound. "Someday," he said, "I'm comin' back and puttin' a fence around this." When he was satisfied with the appearance of the grave, he straightened. Rusty joined him, hat in his hand.

Andy said, "I wish we had Preacher Webb with us. He'd know the words to say."

Rusty nodded. "He already said them, when we first buried her here." He shuddered, remembering.

Andy bit his lip. "I can't quite remember what my mother looked like. I sort of remember her voice, but I can't see her face in my mind. I like to think she was pretty."

"I expect she was, but she'd been poorly treated by the time we found her."

The memory chilled Rusty. It had been his first time to ride with the rangers, though they were little more than a loose band of local militia at the time. They had trailed after marauding Comanches who had killed several settlers and swept away all the horses they could find. They had kidnapped a small boy and his mother. The rangers had found the mother here, dead. The boy had disappeared. He was not seen again until Andy turned up years later, left behind in the wake of another Comanche raid.

Andy said, "I guess a lot of folks wouldn't understand. I don't myself, sometimes. The Comanches killed my mother here. Then they took me as one of their own. Some would say I ought to hate them, but they became my people. They're still my people."

"I like to think we're your people, too, me and Len and Shanty, and the Monahans. Tom Blessing, too."

"You are. Guess there ain't many like me with people on both sides of the fence. Not blood kin, but even better." Andy turned toward his horse.

Rusty said, "We don't have to be in any hurry if you'd like to stay a while."

"I've said all I know to say to her. Stayin' and wishin' won't bring her back. It won't even bring back a clear memory." Andy mounted the sorrel and started out.

Rusty remembered the first time he had seen the Monahan farm. Preacher Webb had escorted him there on his way to join the rangers at Fort Belknap. The place had looked like paradise after a long ride up from the Colorado River. Paradise was lost during the strife of war, but fragments had been regained in the years since.

Andy asked, "You nervous?"

Rusty was. The nearer they came to the farm, the less certain he was of what he should say, how he should approach Josie. In his view, one thing had always stood between them. He had once loved her older sister Geneva, but she had married another. For a long time he had feared that his growing feeling for Josie came only because she had begun to resemble her sister so much. The years had gradually erased his doubt, but he was afraid Josie might not be so certain.

He saw two men working with a young horse in a corral, trotting him around and around at the end of a rope. A boy sat on the fence, watching. He raised his arm and pointed, then jumped down and began running toward the two visitors. One of the men called after him. "Billy!"

The boy seemed not to hear. He cried, "Andy! Andy!"

Andy dismounted and swept the boy into his arms, swinging him halfway around. "You derned little Indian, you've grown a foot."

"I ain't no Indian. But I *have* grown. I'm near as big as you are."

He was not, but the point did not merit an argument.

Rusty said, "Howdy, Billy."

The boy replied, "Rusty," and gave his attention back to Andy.

He thinks Andy's the one that hung the moon, Rusty told himself, smiling. Billy was Geneva's son, and Evan Gifford's. While Rusty had been away serving as a frontier ranger, Evan had come back from the war, gravely wounded. Geneva had nursed him, and a strong bond had developed between them. Rusty recognized Evan in the corral, along with his brother-in-law, James Monahan. Evan climbed over the fence and walked out to meet the visitors. He was smiling, but his voice was stern.

"Billy, we've taught you not to go runnin' off by yourself that way. You don't always know who's comin' in."

Billy said, "I could see it was Andy. Couldn't you see it was Andy?"

"My eyes aren't as sharp as yours." Evan grasped Andy's hand as if to crush it. "Good to have you back." He looked up at Rusty. "You, too. Bring your wagon on up and we'll unload it."

Rusty looked toward the main house, hoping to see Josie come out onto the porch. Evidently she did not know he had arrived.

"Is everybody all right?" he asked.

He caught the serious look that came over Evan's face. Evan said, "Didn't anybody write you about Clemmie?"

Clemmie was the family matriarch, mother of Josie, Geneva, and the youngest sister, Alice.

Rusty felt a sharp foreboding. "Our mail goes astray a lot. What's happened to Clemmie?"

Evan jerked his head in the direction of the main house. "Yonder comes Preacher Webb. It's more his place to tell you than mine."

More than thirty years ago, circuit rider Webb and farmer Mike Shannon had found the orphaned Rusty wandering bewildered in the wake of an Indian battle. Mike had become Rusty's foster father. Webb had been like a benevolent uncle, poor in the world's goods but generous in spirit and rich in friends. He had married the widowed Clemmie Monahan three years ago.

He seemed older now than he actually was. He had lived a strenuous life, most of it in the service of others. Rusty felt a rush of sympathy as the tall, gaunt minister walked slowly toward him. Every step seemed to bring pain. Rusty hurried to meet him, to spare him from having to come so far. He was conscious that Andy followed him, eager to hear about Clemmie. She had become like a grandmother to him.

Rusty was careful how he grasped Webb's gnarled hand, knowing arthritis afflicted him. "It's good to see you, sir. What's this about Clemmie?"

Webb's face was grave. "The Bible tells us that even the just must suffer times of tribulation. Clemmie has had a stroke. Her limbs are paralyzed on one side. She cannot so much as leave her bed without someone to support her. She even has trouble in speaking."

Rusty was momentarily speechless. Clemmie Monahan was a little woman, weighing scarcely a hundred pounds, but she had always reminded him of a willow. Ill winds had bent her more times than was her due, but never, it had seemed, could they break her. It always shook him to see infirmities catch up with people he had considered invincible, like Daddy Mike and Preacher Webb and Clemmie. Such occasions forced him to consider his own vulnerability.

He asked, "Can't anything be done?"

"James fetched a doctor out here all the way from Sherman. He gave her some medicine, but I think it was more to bring the family's hopes up than to fix what's wrong with her. I've lost count of how many times I've prayed over this."

"I wish there was somethin' I could do."

"She'll be cheered that you've come." Webb put an arm around Andy's shoulder. "Andy, seein' you will be better medicine than anything a doctor could give her. She looks on you as one of her own."

Andy said, "I wish I was."

Rusty said, "I wonder what brought this on."

Webb frowned. "Just one trouble too many, I reckon. I don't guess you knew that Alice ran off with a cowboy."

Alice was the youngest daughter. Len Tanner had long had eyes for her. This news would be a sad disappointment to him. "Any idea where they went?"

"We had a letter. Said they got married down at Fort Griffin. James swore he'd go and fetch her back whether she wanted to come or not. He was killin' mad. Clemmie had to talk hard to stop him. That's when the stroke hit her."

"How did Josie and Geneva take Alice's runnin' away?"

"Better than their mother did, but that's not sayin' much."

Rusty could not wait longer without asking, "How *is* Josie?"

"Bone tired. Besides bein' nurse, she's takin' on all the work Clemmie used to do. I've been afraid she'd wind up sick herself. You'll be like a dose of tonic to her."

"I'd have come earlier if I'd known."

"Josie wrote to you. I guess you didn't get her letter."

"Never did." He had lost Geneva because of a lack of communication during the last part of his ranger service. She had thought him dead. Evan Gifford had come along, an answer to her loneliness.

Josie heard footsteps on the porch and came to the door. She stared at Rusty in pleased surprise, then self-consciously reached up to check her hair. It needed combing. She said, "I must look a sight." She seemed to consider retreating back into the house, then stepped out onto the porch and into his arms. He held her tightly and said, "You look beautiful."

"You're a terrible liar."

"I'd have come sooner if I'd known about Clemmie."

He stepped back without releasing her. As Webb had said, she looked tired and drawn. Even so, she was still a pretty woman. Josie's blue eyes glistened. "I wrote you a letter," she said.

"I never got it. I ought to've come sooner anyway."

Webb asked, "Is Clemmie asleep?"

Josie shook her head. "She woke up when she heard Billy holler. She'll feel better, seein' who's come." She kissed Rusty again. "So do I." She led him to a bedroom. Andy and Webb followed.

Rusty wanted to say something that might pretend cheerfulness. Seeing Clemmie lying there even thinner than normal, her mouth twisted by the stroke, he could think of nothing that would not sound flippant and false. "I'm sorry, Clemmie." That was all he could say before he choked.

Her left arm was still and useless. She raised her right arm, and he took her hand. She struggled with her words. "The heart . . . ain't quit beatin'." Her eyes cut to Andy. "How's . . . my Indian boy?"

Some people could call him that and he would take it as a compliment. Others said it and he was ready to fight. Clemmie could call him anything she wanted to.

Andy seemed to have as much trouble with his words as Clemmie did. "I'm . . . I'm just fine." He leaned down and kissed her on the forehead. His face was pinched. Rusty sensed that only a strong will held back Andy's tears.

She squeezed Rusty's hand and looked at her daughter. "Take Josie . . . take her out into the sunshine. Make her smile."

Josie protested, "What if you need somethin', Mama?"

"Warren . . . ," she nodded toward her husband . . . "he can get it. Or Andy." She touched the boy's arm. "You stay with me, Andy."

Andy cleared his throat. "Sure. I ain't goin' nowhere. You want somethin', you just tell me."

Josie seemed hesitant, but Clemmie dismissed her with a motion of her hand. Rusty put his arm around Josie and walked her out onto the porch. They seated themselves on a bench. She took a deep breath and expelled it. "The fresh air does feel good. I haven't had much time outdoors since this all happened."

"Preacher Webb is worried about you. I'm sure Clemmie is, too."

"There's nobody else here to care for her in the things it takes a woman to do. Alice is gone. Geneva's got her own family to see after. Preacher Webb and James do what they can, but the rest is up to me."

"You've got your own life to live."

"I wouldn't have a life if it wasn't for Mama. She always took care of me. Papa would turn over in his grave if I didn't take good care of her."

The family had never entirely recovered from Lon Monahan's death early in the war. Radical secessionists had killed him for his Union sympathies, and a young son had died with him. After many hardships and indignities, the surviving Monahans had found shelter and protection at Rusty's farm on the Colorado River. There they had remained until the war ended.

Then, at least, Rusty had known how to help them. He felt useless now.

He said, "I suppose you can guess why I came."

The look she gave him seemed strangely defensive. "I think I might."

"Things are in good shape down at the farm. They came near takin' it away from me once, but that's over now. I'm askin' you to go back down there with me."

The sadness deepened in her eyes. Tears welled before she turned her head and wiped them away. "For years I waited for you to ask me. Even a few weeks ago, I could've said yes. Now I can't. I can't leave here while Mama's in this shape."

Rusty could not have said the answer surprised him, but it shook him nevertheless. He could have come earlier. Once last fall's crops had been gathered he could have made the trip at any time. But he had waited, uncertain of the future, uncertain he would continue to own the farm when others wanted it and were more favored by the reconstruction government.

"We've built a separate cabin for Andy," he said, realizing how feeble an argument that was, how little it must mean to her in the face of hard reality.

She said, "You can see, can't you, why I can't go with you? Even if I'd gone with you before, I'd have had to come back. There's no debt as heavy as one you owe to your blood kin."

Rusty had no blood kin that he knew of. He had been a nameless orphan, left wandering in the wake of an Indian raid. But he understood what she meant by debt, for since boyhood he had felt a deep obligation to those who had given him a home and selflessly cared for him as if he had been their own.

"Clemmie would want you to be happy," he said. He knew that was another weak argument.

"I couldn't be happy knowin' I hadn't done right by her.

No, Rusty, we'll have to wait . . . wait 'til Mama gets over this stroke, or 'til . . ." She did not finish.

He tried to keep his voice from betraying the disappointment he felt. "You've got to do what you think is best."

She leaned against him. "I wasn't sure you'd understand."

"I understand."

"I always said you're the best man I ever knew, Rusty, except maybe for Papa and Preacher Webb. I'll just have to wait some more. I hope you can."

He could. He had to. In all his life he had loved only two women. One had been lost to him. He would go to any length to avoid losing this one.

"However long it takes," he said. "I just wish there was somethin' I could do for Clemmie."

"The best medicine she could have would be to see Alice come back. Or at least to know she's all right."

"Why wouldn't Alice be all right?"

"It's that man, Corey Bascom. I never did trust him. I don't think anybody did except Alice. James wouldn't have hired him if he hadn't been desperate for help in breakin' horses. I could see that Alice was taken with him, but I never once suspected they might run off together."

"It's hard sometimes to tell what's in young folks' minds." Rusty often had difficulty in reading Andy's intentions. He could be as inscrutable as an Indian.

Josie said, "Alice got a thrill out of havin' all the young bachelors around here come and pay court to her. That's why I can't figure why she settled for Corey. He had an air about him like he was hidin' somethin'. Maybe it was the mystery that attracted her."

Rusty considered a while before he offered, "What if

I was to go and look for her? Maybe I can find out if she's all right and bring her home if she's not."

Josie's eyes flickered with momentary hope that quickly gave way to doubt. "I always felt like there was somethin' a little dangerous about Corey. Nothin' I could put my finger on, nothin' he ever exactly said or did. Just a strong feelin'. He might hurt you."

"There's been others tried."

"What if he doesn't want to be found? What if Alice wants to come home but he doesn't want to let her?"

"I'll just have to persuade him."

Misgivings were strong in her eyes. "It's too much to ask of you, Rusty."

"You're not askin'. I'm offerin'."

"I wouldn't want you to put yourself in harm's way for this family."

"I've been in harm's way most of my life. And you-all and Andy are the nearest thing to family that I've got."

"At least talk to James. And to Evan. They worked with Corey. They'll know the most about him."

"I'll do that. It's best you don't say anything to Clemmie. If I don't find Alice, she'd just be hurt all over again."

Josie remained on the porch while he walked toward the dusty corral where James and Evan were working with a young horse, sliding a saddle blanket along its back, getting it used to the strange new feel. Geneva Gifford stood outside the fence, watching them. Her son, Billy, and a young daughter were beside her. Turning as Rusty approached, she extended her hand. She attempted a smile but could not quite bring it off. She said, "Billy told me you and Andy had come. I guess you've seen Mama."

"I wish I'd known sooner."

He could never look at Geneva without feeling a sense of

loss, though he had gradually come to terms with that loss a long time ago. He had taken comfort in the fact that her marriage was a good one. She had a husband who was worthy of her. Childbearing had matured her. She carried more weight than when he had courted her, but she was still handsome.

She said, "I saw you on the porch with Josie. Did you ask her this time?"

Geneva had always been able to read him as if his thoughts were written across his face in block letters. He replied, "She said no. On account of her mother."

"You can't blame her."

"I told her I'd try to find Alice."

"I'm not sure that's a good idea."

"It's the only idea I've got."

James released the horse and walked over to the fence. Geneva told her brother, "Rusty says he's goin' to look for Alice."

Rusty's relationship with James had always been shaky. Ranger service had put him at cross-purposes with Josie's brother more than once. The end of the war had brought them to a truce, but earlier disagreements had left a lingering aftertaste like burned coffee on the tongue.

James demanded, "What's Mama say about this?"

Rusty said, "She doesn't know. It's best to leave it that way."

James frowned. "In other words, you're not sure you can do it."

"All I'm sure of is that I'll try."

James said grimly, "I wanted to go myself, but Mama wouldn't hear of it. She thought I'd more than likely shoot the son of a bitch. And I would've, if he gave me any excuse."

Rusty pointed out, "He did marry her, at least. He is Alice's husband."

"A son of a bitch, just the same. A good rider but rough on horses. Used his spurs too much. A man rough on horses is apt to be rough on a woman, too." He motioned, and Evan came over to the fence, carrying a coiled rope. "Evan worked with him as much as I did. His opinion is the same as mine."

Geneva told her husband what she had told James. Evan said, "I was always uneasy while Corey worked here. I suspicioned that he planned to steal some of our horses. I never thought that he might steal Alice instead."

James said, "I never was plumb sure that Corey Bascom was his real name. Wouldn't surprise me if he borrowed it someplace."

Most of the aliases Rusty had come across seemed to be simple names such as Smith or Jones or Brown, not unusual enough to be memorable. "You have any idea where he came from, or where he might've gone with Alice?"

James and Evan glanced at one another. James said, "All we know for sure is that Alice sent her mother a letter from Fort Griffin sayin' she had got married."

Evan added, "He told me one time that his family had a stock farm over east someplace. I think he mentioned the Clear Fork. But I guess there's several of those in Texas."

Rusty said, "He could've meant the Clear Fork of the Brazos. It flows past Fort Griffin and spills into the main Brazos farther east."

James grunted. "That's a long ways from here. But if it was closer I'd've gone after Alice no matter what Mama said."

Evan asked, "You want somebody to go with you?"

Rusty caught the misgivings in Geneva's face. "There's

no need in that. You-all have got enough to worry about right here."

Geneva looked relieved. She reached through the fence and clutched her husband's arm. Evan did not argue the point.

Geneva bit her lip. "One thing, Rusty. If you find Alice, don't give her the notion that she caused Mama's stroke. There were so many things that piled up . . . the stroke might've come even if Alice hadn't run away."

James said, "And maybe it wouldn't. Alice hasn't exactly been a sweet little angel. Maybe she *ought* to feel guilty."

Rusty shook his head. "It's not my place to blame her *or* to forgive her. I'll just see if she wants to come home and bring her if she does."

James added, "And don't kill anybody you don't have to. Mama wouldn't like it."

{ FOUR }

Rusty tightened the cinch on his dun horse in the frosty light of the winter sunrise. Andy led Long Red to where his saddle rested on the top rail of a fence. The sorrel's breath made a small cloud in the crisp air.

Rusty demanded, "What do you think you're doin'?"

"Fixin' to go with you."

"I want you to stay here. Make yourself useful to the Monahan family."

Andy lifted his saddle from the fence. "You don't know what you may be ridin' into. You're liable to need help."

"I doubt it. If I do I'll go to the local law. You stay here."

Rusty mounted and rode away, looking back. Andy stood with the saddle at arm's length, watching him.

"You stay," Rusty hollered back.

He had ridden half a mile when he heard a horse coming up behind him. He stopped and turned the dun around as Andy approached. He said, "I told you I'm goin' by myself."

"And I'm goin' by *my*self. I just happen to be travelin' the same direction you are."

Rusty wanted to be angry with him but couldn't. "As I remember it, you trailed after your Comanche brother once when he told you not to. Got yourself in bad trouble." That had been the time Rusty had found him lying helpless, his leg broken after his horse fell.

"I was just a kid then."

"By my lights, you're still a kid."

"But too big for you to whip. Are we movin' on, or do we just sit here and talk?"

Rusty saw that neither reason nor threat would change Andy's mind. He had a stubbornness that Daddy Mike Shannon would have appreciated. "I guess we can argue and ride at the same time. Come on."

He carried supplies rolled up in a blanket tied behind the cantle of his saddle. Andy had brought nothing but an extra blanket. Rusty knew they would have to be sparing of his coffee and flour and bacon. He said, "Keep a sharp eye out for game or we'll be awful lank by the time we reach Fort Griffin."

"You don't know what hungry is 'til you've ridden with the Comanches. They can go for a week on a chunk of sun-dried meat the size of your hand."

"I've done it, but I never liked it."

Fortunately Andy's sharp eyes picked up some antelope that afternoon, and his keen marksmanship brought one down. Antelope would never replace beef in Rusty's opinion, but it was better than fat hogback.

Preacher Webb had told him about an army chaplain he had met in Fort Griffin. "When he wasn't ministerin' to the soldiers he was takin' the gospel to others that needed it. The good Lord knows there's a lot of them that need it around Fort Griffin. The ground over there is soaked in whiskey."

Andy asked, "Is Fort Griffin really as bad as Preacher makes out?"

Rusty said, "From what I hear, one minister isn't near enough."

It was not much of a village. Its main clientele was soldiers stationed at the post on a flat-topped hill just to the south. It catered also to ranchers and farmers of the area and to freighters passing through. Whatever resentment the old Confederates might harbor against Union soldiers, they were never averse to profiting from them.

Rusty had found from experience that a saloon was a good place for information, though sometimes it required a modest investment in goods from behind the bar. He tied the dun in front of a crudely constructed frame building and told Andy, "You don't belong in there."

Andy smiled. "Neither one of us does. Looks like a place where you could get your head stove in for two bits."

"Or maybe less," Rusty agreed. "You stay here while I go ask a question or two."

Andy moved his head in a manner that said neither yes nor no. But he took a position out in front, by the door, where he could hear what was said inside.

The saloon keeper reminded Rusty a little of the stableman in Austin, middle-aged, thin, a red-tinged face indicating that he was quite familiar with his stock. He gave Rusty a piercing study as if gauging his ability to pay. "What's your pleasure?"

"Depends on what you've got."

The barman waved his hand toward a row of bottles along the wall behind him. "You see it. Different bottles, same whiskey. Whichever one you take, you'll wish you'd taken somethin' else. But there ain't nothin' else."

Rusty liked a little whiskey when it came handy, but he had never felt any addiction to it. "I'll trust you. Just pour me one."

The whiskey seared his throat as it went down. He almost choked.

The barman said, "Told you."

Rusty had no wish for another drink. When his throat stopped burning he said, "I'm lookin' for a preacher."

"You ain't dyin'. My whiskey ain't *that* bad."

"The preacher I'm lookin' for would've married a young couple a while back. I'm hopin' he can give me an idea where they went."

"Probably the chaplain up on the hill. Regular preachers usually take a look at this town and decide it's beyond salvation. Young couple, you say? Name wouldn't be Bascom, would it?"

Rusty stiffened. "That's right, Corey Bascom. You know somethin' about him?"

"Enough not to be talkin' much. He brought a young lady to town with him and got the chaplain to tie the knot. Spent the night camped on the river. Some of the boys thought about goin' down and givin' them a shivaree but decided against it. Them Bascoms are mean all the time. They get *real* mean when they're riled up."

"Do you have any idea where they went from here?"

"The family claims land to the northeast. I doubt it's

recorded at the courthouse, but who with any sense is goin' to challenge them?"

"How would I get there?"

"You know where the settlers forted up against the Indians durin' the war?"

Rusty remembered the place. It had been named Fort Davis in honor of Jefferson Davis, disregarding the fact that a military post by the same name existed in mountains far to the west. It had been populated a relatively short time, affording protection to civilians against the Comanches and Kiowas while so many of their young men were away to war.

The barman frowned. "I hope you ain't got trouble on your mind. Them Bascom boys can give you more of it than you can handle. And old Bessie Bascom . . . she's the devil's stepmother. You a lawman?"

"Used to be a ranger. I'm not anymore."

"You'd better not let them know you ever was. They're a grudge-holdin' bunch, and they got a grudge against any kind of law."

"I'm just lookin' to be sure the girl's all right. She needs to know that her mother has taken down sick."

"Just the same, you tread softly around that bunch. There ain't a preacher amongst them."

The barkeep drew a crude map on the back of an outdated fugitive poster originally circulated by the state police. The description on the poster fitted the man himself. He cautioned, "Now, don't you let them Bascoms know I told you how to find them. I was lucky to live through the war. I don't know how much luck I got left."

Andy was waiting outside. He indicated that he had heard everything so Rusty need not repeat any of it. Rusty said, "I'd ought to leave you here, only this is no place for a green young feller like you."

Andy said, "Maybe those Bascoms aren't as bad as he makes out."

Rusty did not attempt a reply.

He had visited the site of Fort Davis while on ranger patrol, so he had no difficulty in finding it. Old cedar picket buildings, thrown up for temporary shelter, slumped in various stages of ruin. A stockade fence, started but never finished, leaned toward its final rest upon the ground. A hungry-looking coyote slunk away at the far end of the quadrangle, its ribs showing through a rough coat. Winter had not been kind.

Rusty said, "Folks here had a hard life. Carried water up from the river in buckets. The men, what there was of them, did their cow huntin' in bunches. Had to watch for Indians all the time. They took care of their farms the same way. There were more women and children than men."

Andy remarked, "The Comanches had just as hard a time of it. If they had ever really wanted to they could've cut through this place like a knife through butter." He spoke with a touch of pride.

The saloon keeper's map was vague. It showed a wagon road leading away from the ruined fort, but Rusty found there were several. He asked, "Which one do your Indian instincts tell you to take?"

"I'm afraid my guardian spirits stayed back at Fort Griffin. I'm not hearin' anything from them."

Rusty chose one at random. "Let's try this."

A couple of miles proved it to be a bad choice. The road showed no sign of recent use. It disappeared where heavy rain had washed it away, taking a deep cut into the topsoil. Rusty decided to strike due east, hoping he might intersect a trail showing more sign of recent travel. He did, after a time, and followed it until he came upon a farmer breaking sod with two mules and a moldboard plow.

He asked if they were anywhere near the Bascom place.

The farmer eyed him suspiciously. "You a friend of theirs?"

"I don't even know them. I'm just carryin' a message." He saw no need to burden the man with details.

"Well, if you don't know them, and they don't know you, it might be better if you don't find them."

"The message is important."

The farmer hunched his shoulders as if to say he had given fair warning. "You follow this road another mile or so, then take the first wagon trail that forks off to the right. Stay with it 'til you get to a long picket house with dirt coverin' on the roof. Better holler good and loud before you ride in so you don't surprise anybody. Them Bascoms don't like surprises. Don't like neighbors much, either."

Rusty thanked him for the information and the advice. He glanced at Andy as they resumed their journey. "Aren't you glad you came with me?"

Andy smiled. "Beats plowin'. They sound like interestin' folks."

If it had not been for Clemmie, Josie, and Geneva, Rusty would not have undertaken this mission. Alice had made her bed, and it might do her good to lie in it a while. She resembled her two older sisters in appearance but not in personality. If anything she was prettier, and she was filled with fun-loving spirit. This in some respects had been to her detriment. It had brought her more adulation than was healthy from starry-eyed boys and young men of the area. As the baby sister she had been petted, sheltered, and catered to more than the others. Too young during the war years to realize fully what was going on around her, she had not had to develop the toughness and steadiness of purpose that marked Geneva and Josie. Much had come easily for her. Rusty could imagine how the dashing manner of a handsome stranger could have turned her head.

In due time he and Andy came to the picket house the farmer had described. Rusty paused for a long look. "I don't see but one horse in the pen. Maybe most of the family is gone somewhere."

"That's just as well. They sound like the kind of folks you'd want to meet one at a time."

The farmer had said the Bascoms did not like neighbors. To Rusty that meant they were probably into some kind of business that did not welcome observation. The chaotic years that followed the war had spawned much of that kind of industry. The state police, often more involved with politics than with law enforcement, had done relatively little to stem such offenses as bank robbery and horse and cattle theft.

He said, "If we ever get the rangers back, this whole country is due for a big sweepin' up."

Andy asked, "Do you figure on joinin' them?"

"Like Tom Blessing said, the rangers is no place for a married man."

"You ain't married yet." As an afterthought Andy added, "Neither am I."

"You're too young to be a ranger."

"How do you know? *I* don't even know how old I am. If I told them I'm twenty-one they'd never know the difference. For all we know, I may *be* twenty-one."

"You're some short of that."

"We don't have to tell them so."

Rusty had not suspected that joining the rangers had even crossed Andy's mind. "We'll talk about it when and if the time comes. The state's broke. It may not have enough money to reorganize the rangers anyway."

"I'm bettin' it will. You saw Rip Ford and Henry McCulloch with Coke when he marched up to the capitol. He didn't pick old rangers like them for nothin'."

Rusty remembered the farmer's admonition to announce himself before he rode up to the Bascom place. He shouted, "Hello the house."

He saw a movement at a window and had a quick impression of a face, though it was gone so quickly he could not be sure whether it was that of a man or a woman. He shouted again.

The door opened. A tall, raw-boned middle-aged woman stepped outside with a double-barreled shotgun pointed in Rusty's and Andy's general direction. The chill wind toyed with her long, stringy hair that showed no familiarity with comb or brush. "I don't know you," she hollered. "You got no business on this property."

"If this is the Bascom place, we're carryin' a message for Alice."

"You're close enough. I can hear you from where you're at. Deliver your message."

Rusty disliked having to shout, but that shotgun did not invite a closer conversation. "It's kind of private. It's about her mother. Is Alice here?"

Rusty caught a quick glimpse of a girl coming up behind the woman in the doorway. The woman shoved her back inside. "You tell me, and I'll tell her what she needs to know."

"Her mother is worried. Wonders if she's all right."

"Of course she's all right. Why wouldn't she be?"

"Her mother's *not* all right. Alice needs to know that she's awful sick."

Alice pushed her way outside toward Rusty, but the woman grabbed her and pulled her back. Alice struggled to free herself. Momentarily distracted by her effort to control the girl, the woman turned the shotgun away from Rusty. He took the opportunity to spur the dun and close the distance. Without dismounting, he wrenched the weapon from her hand. He pitched it to Andy, who caught it and broke it open to extract the shells.

The woman's face flushed with rage. "Who are you to come bustin' in here like this? You've got no right."

"We just came to see Alice and tell her about her mother."

Alice's eyes said she was afraid of the woman. She pulled away. "What's happened to Mama?"

"She's had a stroke. Paralyzed on one side. It's a struggle for her to talk."

"She was all right when I left."

"It happened afterwards. It'd do her a world of good to see you."

The woman's eyes were the deadly gray of bullet lead. "You got no business goin' anywhere. Your place is here with your husband."

"I want to see my mother."

"And ride off with two strangers? I won't stand for it."

"They're not strangers. Rusty and Andy are friends of my family."

"They're men, and you're a woman. A married woman. It wouldn't be decent."

"Decent?" Growing indignation pushed Alice's fear aside. "You call this family decent? You call robbin' and stealin' decent?"

The woman raised her hand as if to slap Alice. "Shut up, girl. You don't know what you're talkin' about."

"Oh, but I do. You think I don't know where Corey and his brothers have gone?"

Rusty saw murder in the woman's eyes. "You shut your mouth or I'll shut it for you. I told Corey he made a mistake bringin' you here."

Rusty felt a strong apprehension. "Alice, you'd better come with us. I already see that this is no place for you."

She hesitated. "I don't know what Corey might do."

"We'll take you back to the protection of your family. There's nothin' he *can* do."

The woman declared, "The hell there ain't. He'll be comin' after you and draggin' you back by the hair of the head."

The girl wasted no more time considering. She said, "I'll gather my things." She went into the house.

Rusty said, "Andy, go saddle that horse yonder for Alice. I'll keep Mrs. Bascom company."

The woman seethed. Rusty was glad she no longer had the shotgun. She scolded, "It's a mortal sin, comin' between a man and his wife. My son and Alice taken the vows before a minister of the gospel and in the sight of the good Lord Hisself. The Book says what God has joined together . . ."

"You don't talk like somebody who'd know much about the Book."

"I know it says an eye for an eye and a tooth for a tooth. You carry that girl away and I'll see to it that my boys take a lot more than an eye and a tooth."

Rusty saw no point in arguing. He let her continue a malevolent harangue laced with profanities the likes of which he had never heard pass a woman's lips and some he had heard from few men.

Alice brought a cloth bag out of the house. Rusty asked, "Is that all you've got?"

"I didn't come here with much. I haven't picked up anything new except bitter experience."

Mrs. Bascom shook a finger at her. "There'll be hell to pay when the boys fetch you back here. And they will."

Alice murmured, "Hell is all I've had since I came."

"You Jezebel!" The woman slapped Alice so hard that a red splotch arose where the flat of her hand had struck.

Alice made an angry cry and drove her fist into Bessie Bascom's face. The woman rocked back, almost falling.

Rusty watched in pleased surprise. Maybe he had underestimated Alice. He said, "Looks like you're your mother's daughter, after all."

Andy led a brown horse up from the pen, a sidesaddle on its back. He boosted Alice up into place. Mrs. Bascom held one hand to her jaw, her eyes blazing from shock and pain and anger.

Alice said, "I've wanted to hit that woman ever since the day I came here."

Rusty asked, "Why didn't you?"

"She'd have killed me, or made me wish she had."

"Well, she can't do anything to you anymore."

Andy still had the shotgun. He pitched it up on top of the dirt-covered roof, raising a wisp of dust. He said, "I hope the law don't get after us for takin' this horse."

Alice said, "It's the one I came here on. It never belonged to the Bascoms."

Rusty said, "Let's git. I wouldn't put it past that old woman to climb up there after that gun."

They rode at a rapid pace for a mile or so, then slowed. Alice looked back with concern. Rusty said, "She wouldn't chase us afoot, not this far."

Alice was not comforted. "You don't know Bessie Bascom. She's liable to take a broomstick and come flyin' after us."

"How long do you think it'll be before her menfolks come home?"

"Hard to say. They've been gone three days. Corey was talkin' about a nice little Yankee bank over east that he said needed robbin'."

"So that's what they do for a livin', rob banks?"

"Part of it. They burgle stores, steal cattle, horses, whatever comes easy to hand. I'm sure now that's why Corey came to our farm in the first place. He had heard about the Monahan horses. But we took a shine to one another, and he carried me off instead."

"Against your will?"

"Not then. I wanted to come with him. But when I got here I found things weren't like he'd been tellin' me. Nowheres near."

Rusty had noticed a blue mark beneath her left eye. "Corey did that to you, I suppose."

"Not Corey. His mother. She reminds me of the wicked stepmothers I used to read about in fairy tales."

"How long has she been a widow?"

"Several years. From what Corey told me, Old Ansel got surprised by the state police and tried to put up a fight. After that the Bascoms declared war against all authority. The only thing the boys are scared of is that old woman. Anybody who crosses her is fixin' to bleed some."

She plied Rusty with anxious questions about her mother and others of the family. He knew her concern was genuine.

There's hope for her, after all, he thought. Maybe she's smartened up. Perhaps this bitter experience would bring out the strength and will that was her rightful heritage from Clemmie and Lon Monahan.

They rode by Fort Griffin but did not tarry longer than was necessary to pick up a few supplies. Rusty suspected that pursuit would not be long in coming. Bessie Bascom would insist upon it.

They rode by the saloon where he had stopped for information. The barkeeper stood out in front, puffing smoke from an evil-looking black cigar. His eyes lighted with curiosity as he saw Alice riding with Rusty and Andy. He asked no questions, and Rusty did not pause to offer any answers. But he noted that the man looked hard in the direction from which they had come.

He figures like I do, Rusty thought. *They'll be coming after her.*

"Let's pick up the pace a little," he said. "We can cover a lot of miles before dark."

Rusty did not ride boldly into the Monahan headquarters. He reasoned that Corey Bascom would expect them to head straight for Alice's home. Though it was unlikely, there was a chance that he and his brothers might have pushed hard and gotten here first.

He watched a while to be sure everything looked normal. He saw Evan Gifford riding a hackamored young horse around and around in a corral. Geneva stood on the porch and shouted for Billy to come home. He climbed down reluctantly and trotted toward her.

Rusty eased. "I don't see anything amiss."

"Let's hurry," Alice said. "I want to see Mama."

As they rode in, James Monahan came out of the barn, a bridle in his hand. Seeing Alice, he quickly hung the bridle across the top of a fence, then trotted to meet the three riders. "Alice!" he shouted. "Baby sister!"

He had every right to be angry with her, and some recriminations might come later, but now was not the time. He lifted her down from the saddle and hugged her as if she had come back from the dead.

"Mama is goin' to be tickled to see you. She's liable to get up and come runnin' when you walk in the door."

"How is she?" Alice asked anxiously.

"Fair to middlin'. She'll do better now." He looked up at Rusty and Andy. "Did you have to kill anybody?"

"Not yet."

"Where's Corey?"

Rusty looked behind him. "Back that way, somewhere. We figure he'll be comin' for Alice. We just don't know when."

James gave his sister a searching look. "When he does, will you be wantin' to go with him?"

"I'd rather kill him than go back there."

"We'll try to see that you don't have to do either one." James reached up to shake hands with Rusty, then Andy. "Fellers, I ain't got words enough to thank you."

Rusty said, "It wasn't much trouble to get her away. Keepin' her may be somethin' else."

"We'll keep her. We've fought off rebel hangmen and Comanche Indians and horse thieves. Corey Bascom ought not to be that much of a challenge."

Alice said, "You haven't met the rest of his family. Especially his mother."

James frowned. "I don't see how one old woman could give us much trouble."

Andy said, "You'll think different if you see her. When she dies and goes to hell even the devil is liable to take out a-runnin'."

Geneva saw Alice and hurried down from her house, throwing her arms around her sister. "Thank God you've come back."

"Thank Rusty and Andy. I wouldn't be here if they hadn't come and fetched me."

Geneva turned to express her thanks to Rusty. She held on to his arm long enough to stir old feelings he had hoped he had put behind him. He was almost relieved when Evan came up to join his wife.

Josie stepped out onto the porch in response to the racket. Recognizing Alice, she came running. She embraced her sister with tears in her eyes. "You're the best medicine anybody could've brought for Mama." When she released Alice she hugged Rusty. "And you're the doctor who fetched it." She looked up at the boy. "And you, Andy." She turned back to her sister. "Come on, let's go show you to Mama."

The family trooped into the big house. Andy started to follow, but Rusty raised a hand to stop him. "This is for the family," he said.

Andy nodded, seeing the rightness of it. "But you're one of the family too, just about."

"Not yet, not 'til Josie and me stand up in front of Preacher Webb. Right now there's no tellin' when that is liable to happen."

{ FIVE }

Corey Bascom was in a dark mood as he and three younger brothers approached the long picket house that had been their home since soon after they had left Arkansas just ahead of some angry horsemen. The bank for which he had held considerable hope had been a disappointment. With the muzzle of a pistol in his face, the bank's president had stammered that local farmers had made only a mediocre crop the previous fall and most of their money had already been spent. The county government should have had some funds on deposit, but the outgoing officeholders had absconded with most of the money. "We've got nothing but a toenail hold," he had said, "and hopes for a better year."

Frustrated, Corey had promised to come back in the fall, after harvest. "You'd better have somethin' here worth the takin'. Otherwise you'd better start learnin' how to play a harp."

His brother Lacey then forced the sweating banker to go to his knees and beg for mercy. It was a bluff, but Lacey took pleasure in his ability to frighten people. He especially enjoyed it when he could make them wet themselves, which the banker did. Corey sometimes worried that Lacey would get carried away and really kill someone. He had come close. So far the Bascom brothers' crimes had stopped short of murder. So far.

Before leaving town the brothers had paused to rob a mercantile store but found its till was as poor as the bank's.

Lacey shot out a window glass as they left. "Somethin' for them to remember us by," he had explained. It was an unnecessary gesture. Nobody ever forgot a visit by the Bascoms.

The only bright spot Corey could see in this whole trip was the prospect of getting back to Alice. He had enjoyed women before, usually with payment involved, but this girl had awakened a hunger in him that never remained satisfied for long. She had been shy and uncertain the first few times, and he had gotten a little rough. He had occasionally been rough with other women but considered that to be his right inasmuch as he had bought and paid for them. He suspected this treatment was the reason Alice had become increasingly reluctant about his attentions as the weeks passed. He had tried to be gentler, but he didn't know how.

This trip had kept him away for four days—and four long, lonely nights. He hoped his absence would have made her more receptive. He would keep working on the gentleness thing and see if it helped.

He saw smoke rising from the chimney and realized he was hungry for more than Alice. Though Ma's cooking wouldn't get her a job even in a hole-in-the-wall chili joint, when a man's belly was empty her beans and cornbread were welcome. Nobody ever complained, at least where she might hear. Though her sons were grown, she felt obliged now and again to take a quirt to one or another of them just as she did when they were little. To Ma they would always be "my boys," to be praised highly or punished severely, whichever the situation called for.

Praise came sparingly. She had come near taking a quirt to Corey when he brought Alice home unannounced. In her view he had no right to get married without her approval, especially to a pampered girl who was obviously a misfit, unlikely ever to find a comfortable place in this close-knit family. Bessie Bascom had tried hard to weld her boys into an insular unit, mutually shielding one another from the rest of the world. To her it had always been "us against them." Anyone outside of the family was a potential enemy, not to be trusted.

She always preached that old Ansel Bascom had died because he trusted others too much. Someone had betrayed him to the damnable state police. He had died with a dozen bulletholes draining his life's blood into the dirt street outside of a two-bit bank that had not been worth the gamble in the first place.

"Never take nobody into your confidence outside of family," she had told her boys again and again. That prohibition included Alice, whom she regarded as a potential Jonah, if not a Judas.

Corey had been reluctant about being away from Alice so long, leaving her in Ma's less than gentle hands, but family needs took precedence over his personal desires. He would make up for lost time tonight. In his mind he was already in bed with her.

He noticed that the Monahans' brown horse was not in the corral where he had been kept penned and fed, handy in case Ma needed to saddle him and go somewhere in a hurry. The gate stood open, which struck him as odd.

Bessie Bascom heard her sons' arrival and came striding out from the picket house. Her long steps and grim face told Corey that something had gone awry. He had expected her to raise hell when she found out how little money they had brought home, but it appeared she was not going to wait for the bad news.

She went immediately on the attack, shaking her finger in his face. "I told you that little hussy didn't belong here. Well, the buttermilk has done been spilt now. She's gone."

Corey swallowed hard. She could not have hit him harder if she had struck him with a club. "Gone? Where?"

She touched her fingers to her chin. "See this bruise? She put it there. Hit me with her fist, she did, then rode off with two men bold as brass. And they wasn't even her brothers. Told you she wasn't no good."

Corey did not care about the bruise. He cared about Alice. "What men? Who were they?"

"She said they were friends of her family. I told her it wasn't fitten for a married woman to do such a thing. I told her it was agin the Book."

Corey struggled to absorb what his mother was telling him. Damn it all, how could Alice just up and leave like that? She belonged to him. She had no right to do anything or go anywhere without his say-so.

"Did they tell you where they were goin'?"

"Back to her folks, they said. But from what you've told me, that's at least two days' ride. That means two nights, layin' out with two men. It don't take much imagination . . ."

The image was too ugly for him to contemplate. He clenched a fist. "Stop it, Ma. She wouldn't do that."

"She did it with you, didn't she? I've heard the two of you many a night, and I've seen you slip into the barn with her in the daytime when your brothers was out workin', like *you* was supposed to be. She's a tart."

"Did you hear her call them by name?"

"I heard her call the oldest one Rusty. The other one was just a big boy, but I expect he's old enough to know what to do with a woman like her."

Corey tried to remember. Rusty. He had heard the Monahans mention that name often. Rusty Shannon, it was. Had an understanding with Alice's sister Josie, as he recalled. He had been a ranger for a long time. Had a farm way down south somewhere. Alice had told him the Monahans stayed on that farm during part of the war, getting away from Confederate zealots who had killed Lon Monahan and a young son named Billy for Unionist leanings.

Corey tried to push his conflicting emotions aside and think. If Rusty Shannon was going to marry Josie, it seemed unlikely he would do anything untoward with Alice no matter how many nights it took them to get back to the Monahan farm. As for the boy, though, he must be the one they said had lived with the Comanches. A boy brought up on Indian ways was something to worry about. There was no telling what he might do.

He demanded, "How long they been gone?"

"Left about this time yesterday. They got a long start on you if you're figurin' on goin' after them."

"Damn right I'm goin' after her."

Bessie nodded. "I told her you would. Told her you'd come draggin' her back by the hair of the head."

"Them Monahans may not give her up easy."

"You better get her back, or else shoot her. She knows too much about our business. If she talks to the wrong people it's liable to cause us a lot of trouble."

"I couldn't shoot her, Ma."

"I could. Wouldn't bat an eyelash. And you'd better be ready to do the same thing. You don't need her. You can buy plenty of women better than her for the price of whiskey."

Corey felt sick at his stomach. He had not dreamed the girl would go off and leave him. "Love, honor, and obey," the chaplain had said. *Obey* was the word that stuck in Corey's mind. She had pledged to obey him no matter what. As his wife she was property like his spurs and saddle and guns, like his horses. A man didn't let somebody run off with what belonged to him and not do something about it.

He turned to Lacey. "You boys go rustle us up some fresh horses. Soon as Ma fixes dinner we're goin' after Alice."

Lacey grinned in anticipation. "You goin' to take a quirt to her, Corey? That's what you ought to do, is take a quirt to her." Lacey had been on the receiving end of many a smart whipping from Ma, and deserved most of them. He enjoyed seeing somebody else get it.

Bessie said, "Lacey, you and Newley and little Anse bring up a horse for me, too. I'm goin' along with you boys to make sure you do the right thing."

Corey had rather she didn't go. She was not a good traveler, always finding fault. He said, "It'll be a hard trip, Ma."

"I've made many a hard trip before. I want to see you

give little missy what's comin' to her. And if you don't do it, by God I will."

Rusty sat on the front-porch bench with Josie and watched as twilight darkened the fields stretching beyond the barn. She laid her head against his shoulder, her fingers firmly clasping his arm. She said, "I've been thinkin' a lot about that farm of yours."

"Ours," he said.

"I remember how it looked when Mama and us stayed there durin' the war."

"It's nicer now. We've fixed it up a right smart, me and Andy and Len Tanner, when Len would stand hitched long enough to help. You'll like it. I'm anxious to take you down there."

"Maybe it won't be as long as we thought. Mama perked up a lot when you brought Alice home. She's got a stronger look in her eyes, and I do believe her talkin' has improved."

"But you don't want to leave her just yet?"

"Not 'til she's on her feet. Preacher Webb is hopeful this will all pass and by summer she'll be back to the way she was."

"Summer seems like a long time off. Me and Andy will have to go back home and get the plantin' done before that."

"But you're not in a hurry, are you?" Her tone was hopeful. "You *are* goin' to stay with us a while longer?"

"I'm waitin' to see what Corey Bascom does. James and Evan and Preacher Webb will need all the help they can get if he and his brothers come for Alice."

"You've already done a lot. We're all grateful." She kissed him on the cheek. "How many times have I asked you to marry me?"

He smiled. "Lately, or altogether?"

"I guess it's been shameless of me, but you know I wanted you. I've wanted you ever since I was a girl."

"That was when you first asked me."

"I just didn't want to let you get away. I knew I had to speak up because I could see you and Geneva had eyes for one another."

"That was a long time ago. Things change."

"Not my feelin's about you. I love you."

Rusty tried to say what she had said, but the words would not come as he wanted them to. He said, "I . . . I've got the same feelin's."

Geneva came out of her house across the yard, her small daughter at her side. Josie's gaze followed her sister as she seated herself in a rocker on the porch. The girl climbed up into her lap.

Josie said, "Geneva's still a pretty woman."

"Yes, she is." Rusty felt uneasy, talking about her.

"I remember when everybody figured you-all would get married after the war was over."

"That was before Evan came along."

"Some feelin's never die. I can't help but wonder sometimes if you just think you love me because I remind you of her."

Rusty thought hard about his reply, for he did not want to say anything that would reinforce her doubts. Only to himself would he admit that the same question haunted him from time to time. The answer seemed clear as he sat here beside Josie, feeling the pleasant warmth of her cheek, the arousing pressure of her body leaning against him. But away from her, he might wonder again.

He said, "Geneva's got her own family, and she's happy. Whatever was between us once is long gone."

She pulled away far enough to stare into his eyes. "I

wouldn't want to find out someday that I'm a substitute for somebody else. Not even my own sister."

"I can't deny that Geneva was the first woman I ever loved. But you'll be the last."

"Show me," she said, and kissed him again. He felt as if the sun was bearing down upon him with all its noonday heat.

She said, "Hold me, Rusty. Hold me like you'll never let me go."

Evan Gifford had been keeping watch and sounded the alarm. "They're comin'," he said, running up from the corrals. "Looks like a bunch of them."

Rusty had seen them from the porch. He squinted. "I count five. You sure it's the Bascoms?"

"That's Corey in the lead. I never saw the rest of his family."

The only rider Rusty could recognize was Bessie Bascom, sitting straight as a fence post on a sidesaddle. She had a determined posture that reminded him of old Captain August Burmeister of the prewar rangers. Rusty was surprised to see her on a mission like this, but after reflection he decided he could have expected it. He had quickly gained the impression that she was mother, father, and supreme commander of her troop.

James and Preacher Webb and Andy came out of the house. James gave the situation a quick study. "I'll stand here and wait for them. I wish the rest of you would scatter the way we talked about." He glanced back at Webb. "Preacher, it might be better if you stayed in yonder with Mama and the girls."

Webb demurred. "Maybe I can talk common sense to them."

"I doubt as they'd pay attention to it. If you're goin' to stay out here with me you'd best fetch a gun. That way maybe they'll be more willin' to listen to the gospel."

Evan trotted to his own house. Geneva came out onto the porch. He waved her back inside and took a position at the corner. Andy moved out to stand beside the woodpile. Checking the load in his rifle, Rusty walked to the corner of the barn and stepped back out of sight. If the Bascoms rode all the way up to the main house they would be covered from all sides.

From his vantage point Rusty studied the faces. He already knew Bessie Bascom's. Her square jaw was firmly set, her eyes fierce like a hawk's. In comparison, her sons looked almost benign. Rusty decided the one riding closest to Bessie must be Corey, for he appeared a little the oldest and had the most serious expression. The others, Rusty guessed, had probably come along mostly because Bessie had ordered it. He doubted the strength of their resolve. Alice was not *their* wife.

One of the Bascoms had an ironic smile as if he found the situation amusing in some off-center way. Instinct told Rusty that this one might bear special watching.

James stepped to the edge of the porch, a rifle across his folded arms. "That's about close enough, Corey."

Rusty had been correct in assuming which was Alice's husband. Corey stopped and leaned on his saddlehorn. He said, "You know what we've come for."

"You can't have her."

"She's mine. We had the knot tied by a sure-enough preacher." He nodded at Preacher Webb, standing beside James, rifle in his hand. "Wasn't no jackleg, neither. Army chaplain, he was. Had the papers and everything."

James argued, "Bein' married don't make her your

property, to be branded and treated like a mare. She's still a freeborn American, with the rights God gave us all."

"Her place is with me. How I treat her is between me and her. She ain't your business anymore."

"She's my sister, so she'll always be my business. *Our* business, this family's."

"She belongs to my family now. And I brought them along to see that she goes back where she's supposed to be. There ain't enough of you Monahans to stop us."

James frowned. "Maybe you ain't seen everybody yet. You're just countin' me and Preacher Webb. You're probably thinkin' a preacher ain't any hand with a gun. You'd be wrong. He can knock a coyote's eye out at a hundred yards. And you know my brother-in-law Evan. That's him over on the porch of his house, carryin' that shiny new shotgun."

All the Bascoms turned to look as Evan stepped away from the corner of his house, bringing the shotgun up into both hands.

James went on, "Now, if you'll look out yonder by the woodpile you'll see Andy Pickard. Raised by the Comanches to be mean as hell. Crack shot with pistol or rifle. If he runs out of shells, he can get you with a bow and arrow.

"And finally, I want you to make the acquaintance of Rusty Shannon. That's him beside the barn yonder, with the rifle. A ranger for years. Brought many a bad man and several Indians to heel in his prime, and he still ain't got enough gray hair that you'd notice it much." He shifted his attention back to Corey. "You still got a notion you want to tackle this family?"

Corey sat rigid in the saddle, his face reddening. He said nothing.

Bessie watched him, looked at James a moment, then turned back to her son. "Is that the best you can do, Corey Bascom, sit there and let them run a bluff on us?"

Corey did not look at her. Grittily he said, "You better count the guns, Ma."

She turned in fury toward her other sons. "You-all just goin' to let this stand? They've got a woman in yonder that rightfully belongs to your brother. Carryin' his seed now, more than likely. Ain't there any shame in the lot of you?"

Nobody moved. They could count, even if the old woman couldn't.

She shrilled, "I'm glad your pa ain't here to see his family tuck their tails between their legs like egg-suckin' hounds." She pushed her horse forward. "If you-all won't do anything, I will."

Rusty saw hesitancy in the faces of James and Webb. If one of the Bascom brothers had made this move they would have stopped him. But though they raised their rifles, he knew they would not shoot a woman.

The front door opened, and Alice stepped out holding a pistol in both hands. She aimed it at Bessie and shouted, "They won't shoot you, but I will. I got cause enough."

Rusty's lungs burned. He had been holding his breath. The air was cool, but he sweated as if he were digging postholes.

Corey said, "Better stop, Ma. She means it." He rode forward far enough to grab her bridle reins. "This ain't worth gettin' killed over."

Bessie's face was flushed with fury. "It ain't her. You can buy better than her in any dancehall from here to Arkansas. But the shame she's brought on this family, that *is* worth killin' for, or even gettin' killed."

"Nothin' is worth gettin' killed for, not money, not

pride, not even a woman. Come on, Ma. We're startin' home." He had to pull on the reins and forcibly turn her horse around.

She cursed her son as she had cursed Rusty the day he had taken Alice away.

Not until they were a hundred yards out did Rusty pause to wipe sweat from his hands onto his trousers, then rub a sleeve across his face. Andy came to meet him halfway to the house. He whistled in relief. "The Fort Griffin bartender was right. That old woman is the devil's stepmother."

Rusty nodded. "You're a good judge of character."

The Bascoms stopped a half mile from the Monahan place, all but Corey. He kept riding.

Bessie shouted, "Where you goin'?"

"I'm goin' home, and I'm goin' by myself. You'd bitch at me the whole way, and I don't want to listen to it."

"You come back here. We got talkin' to do."

Corey kept riding. Bessie hollered at him again, more of a screech than a shout. "Damn you, come back here!"

Corey gave no sign that he heard. Bessie turned to her other sons, her mouth puckered with fury, her eyes cutting like a knife. "To hell with him then. It's up to us to do what has to be done."

Lacey was the next oldest to Corey. He said, "We could slip back in there and pick off them Monahans one at a time 'til Alice gives up and comes with us."

"One or two of us might get picked off, too. No, there's just one thing to do. That girl knows a way too much about this family and our business. If she was to testify in a court, ain't no tellin' what the law might do. So if we can't take her home, we have to see that she don't talk to anybody ever again."

Lacey almost grinned. "You mean kill her?" He had had no use for Alice since she had blackened his eye one day when he tried to drag her into the barn.

Bessie said, "This won't set well with Corey. She turned his head real good. But he'll get over it. So we'll find us a place to rest a while. Come full dark, Lacey, me and you will go back and do what Corey didn't have the stomach for."

Little Anse, the youngest, asked, "You ain't takin' me and Newley, Ma?"

"Two's enough. More than that might attract attention."

Newley Bascom had had a crush on Alice ever since Corey had brought her home, but he had had the good judgment not to let Corey see it. He said, "Seems a waste, killin' her. She was a lot of help to you doin' chores around the place. Couldn't we just grab her and drag her away before they can stop us?"

"I know what you want her for, and it ain't the chores. She ain't worth the risk. Come on, boys. Let's find us a good place to wait for dark."

Rusty sat on the porch bench, staring off into the darkness, wondering if the Bascoms were really gone. He was aware that Evan sat on his own porch, doing the same.

Josie came out and seated herself beside him. He asked, "How's Clemmie?"

"A little worried the Bascoms might come back. But I guess everybody's worried some or you wouldn't be sittin' out here watchin'."

"It doesn't seem likely they'd try, but with people like them you never know. Main thing is to keep Alice indoors so they can't grab her and run before we can stop them."

"You figure they really want her that bad?"

"Maybe Corey does, that's hard to say. I feel like the old woman is mostly afraid of what Alice knows and what she might tell the law."

"I don't understand people like that. They could probably make a good livin' for themselves if they'd buckle down to honest work, probably better than they're doin' now with the risks they're takin' and the trouble they cause to others. Maybe it's the times."

"You can't just blame it on the times. We've always had people like them, good times and bad. By what Alice has said, Bessie and her husband brought the boys up to see the rest of the world as their enemy. They always hated the law. Didn't make any difference if it was Union or Confederate. Most people raise their younguns to be whatever *they* were. The Bascoms always had a wide streak of outlaw in their blood. The old man and the old woman taught the boys to make the most of it. Used the whip on them if they showed weakness."

She leaned to him, and he put his arm around her. She said, "We won't have a whip on the place, you and me. We'll raise our children with love, like Mama and Papa did."

Rusty remembered the kindness of Daddy Mike and Mother Dora, treating him as if he were their own. He said, "I can almost feel sorry for the Bascom boys. They weren't raised up, they were just jerked up. Life's too short to do it that way."

From the direction of the barn he heard the snort of a horse, followed by the sound of hooves. He stood up and grabbed the rifle that leaned against the wall. "Stay put," he told Josie.

He walked partway to the barn, pausing to listen. The horses were quiet again. Hearing no more from them, he returned to the porch. He said, "Just a little bitin' match, I suppose. My dun horse never has quite got used to these here."

Josie motioned for him to sit. "I guess even the horses are a little skittish. They seem to sense when things aren't right."

"What you-all need is a couple of real mean dogs to keep watch on this place."

From inside the house he heard a woman's voice. The words were not clear. Josie said, "That's Mama. I guess she needs me."

Rusty grasped her hand for a moment. "I'm hopin' she won't be needin' you too much longer."

She smiled at him. "Don't go away. I'll be back." She kissed him and went into the house.

Moments later he saw a flash from out in the night and heard the crack of a rifle. A windowpane shattered. Josie gave a cry that made Rusty's blood run cold.

He raised the rifle and sent a wild shot in the direction of the flash he had seen. He heard Alice scream. "Josie! Josie!"

Rusty rushed into the house. In the lamplight he saw Alice holding Josie, trying to keep her from falling. Dropping the rifle, Rusty took three long steps and grabbed Josie. His hand against her back felt warm and sticky.

Josie looked up at him with stricken eyes. She gasped for breath. Rusty lifted her up and carried her into the room she shared with Alice. He placed her gently on her bed and found his hands red with her blood. "Josie!" he cried. "Josie!"

She found breath enough to whisper his name once. The light slowly faded from her eyes. He shook her, trying desperately to find life, but there was none.

He heard Alice sobbing. "Rusty, she's gone."

{ SIX }

Rusty felt numb, kneeling beside the bed where Josie lay. He did not look up as James and Andy rushed into the room. Alice leaned her head against the wall and cried softly, her back turned.

James shouted, "Andy, blow out the light."

The room fell into darkness. From the next room Clemmie called in a desperate voice, barely understandable, wanting to know what was happening.

James bent to touch his sister, then drew his hand away. "My God. They've killed her."

Rusty heard Preacher Webb's quiet voice, offering a prayer. Andy said, "I'd best see after Clemmie." A moment later Clemmie gave a cry of anguish. Her voice seemed clearer then. "Help me, Andy. I've got to . . . got to go to my daughter."

Still in shock, Rusty managed to push to his feet and make room for Clemmie. She limped painfully into the room, her arm around Andy's strong shoulder. Webb moved to help her. She fell across Josie and wept.

James trembled, his voice breaking. "For God's sake, how many more? First Pa and Billy. Now my sister."

Rusty heard heavy footsteps on the porch. Evan rushed in. Though the room was dark, he immediately grasped the sense of tragedy. "They shot Alice?"

Andy was the only one who seemed to find voice. "No, they killed Josie."

Evan sighed, "God help her." He bent down for a look, then straightened. "I heard two horses runnin' away right after the shots. We all expected them to come for Alice, but why Josie?"

Andy said, "They were out yonder a ways. They saw Josie in the lamplight and mistook her for Alice."

Rusty had been too stricken to reason it out, but he judged that Andy was probably right.

Alice saw it, too. She turned, both hands to her mouth as she stared at Josie's still form in the dim reflected light from the moon. "Then she died in my place. Why couldn't it have been me instead?" She seemed about to collapse. James and Webb both grabbed her.

Webb said, "Hold tight, Alice. Some things we are not given to understand. It was not your fault."

"But it was." She made a weak effort to break free of them, then fell back against the gaunt Webb. "If I hadn't been addle brained, if I hadn't run off with Corey, . . ."

Webb said, "You couldn't have known it would lead to this. You couldn't have known what Corey was capable of."

Corey. The name ignited a flame in Rusty's brain. Bessie Bascom had vowed that her sons would take an eye for an eye. The flame built into wildfire. He said, "Corey Bascom will die for this."

Webb said, "You're in shock, Rusty. Wait 'til you have time to think straight."

"I'm thinkin' straight enough. Corey Bascom killed her. I'm goin' after him."

Andy moved to his side. "Not by yourself. I'll go with you."

Webb showed no more inclination to argue. He bowed

his head, his voice breaking. "I prayed for Clemmie, and I prayed for Alice. I never thought to pray for Josie."

James placed his hands on Rusty's shoulders. "Josie was my sister. I've got as much interest in Corey as you have. But let's don't go off half cocked. We need to see her buried first, with the proper words said over her."

"And give Corey a long start? No, I know where he'll go first. I'm not givin' him time to go any farther."

Evan said, "You and Andy may not be enough against that bunch. I'll be ridin' with you."

Rusty argued, "You've got a wife and family to think about."

"This family took me in when I was near dead and gave me a life again. Josie was my wife's sister, and like my own. I'm goin'."

Rusty felt too beaten down to protest more.

Evan said, "But first I've got to break this to Geneva. She's at the house with the kids, probably worried to death. Tellin' her will be as about as hard a thing as I ever did."

Andy said, "I'll go catch up our horses."

James relighted the lamp and turned to Rusty. "You've got your mind made up to go. Nothin' I can say will stop you?"

Rusty found it painful to speak. "I can't do anything to help Josie now. But I can do somethin' about Corey."

"Then I'll throw some grub together for the three of you. You'll need it."

Corey Bascom expected his mother and brothers to return home soon, but they did not show up until near noon of the day after his arrival. He walked to the barn to meet them as they rode in. They were dusty and weary, but his mother had a stern look of triumph about her.

He asked, "What kept you-all? You ought to've been home yesterday."

She fastened accusing gray eyes on him. "We stayed around and finished the job you ought to've done for yourself."

Alarm quickly stirred in him. "What do you mean?"

"I mean your sweet little Alice girl ain't goin' to do no talkin' to the law or anybody, not ever again."

He felt as if his skin were afire. "What did you do?"

"Me and your brother Lacey went back and took care of her."

Corey's jaw dropped. For a moment he could not move. He could only look at her in disbelief. But he knew he had to believe. He felt a fool for not having realized she might do it. She was fully capable of killing anyone who stood in the way of her and the family. He remembered that years ago she had stalked and shot a witness in Arkansas just before the grand jury was to convene and bring an indictment against old Ansel for stealing hogs.

He trembled. "But I loved her, Ma."

"Love!" She spat the word. "Love is what you give to your family, not to some calf-eyed little tart. All your thinkin' lately has been below your belt or you'd have seen what had to be done and done it yourself."

Grief and fury rose together, swelling and spilling over. "Damn you, Ma!" He drew back his hand and slapped her, hard. He had never done it before.

She recoiled in disbelief, then brought up her quirt. She lashed him about the face and shoulders until he grabbed the limber leather end and jerked it out of her hands. He flung it aside and strode beneath the shed where his saddle sat astraddle a rough log rack.

"Where are you goin'?" she demanded.

"As far from you as I can get." He turned burning eyes

toward his brothers. "From all of you." He took a rawhide reata and cast a loop around the neck of his black horse.

She shouted, "Corey Bascom, you turn that horse a-loose. You ain't goin' nowhere."

"How are you goin' to stop me? You goin' to shoot me, too?"

Bessie made a gesture at Lacey. Lacey came at Corey with clenched fists. Corey did not wait for him to strike the first blow. He hit Lacey first in the stomach, taking his brother's breath away, then a second time to the jaw. Lacey went down on his knees and spat blood.

"That's for Alice," Corey said. "I ought to kill you." He saddled his horse and rode away, not once looking back.

Lacey pushed to his feet, rubbing his aching jaw, wiping blood on his sleeve. Newley, who had been morosely silent since the shooting, watched his older brother's departure with concern. "He ain't fixed for travelin', Ma. He didn't take so much as a blanket, and no grub at all."

Newley was a fool, she thought, concerned only about Corey's comfort. Because he, too, had a weakness for Alice, he could not see or chose not to see the threat she had presented to them all. She said, "He'll come draggin' back when he gets hungry enough."

"Maybe not. He looked awful mad."

"Then he'll have to take care of himself. He chose that girl over family." She spread her fingers against a face still reddened and burning from Corey's slap. "First time one of you boys ever raised a hand against me. I don't know why the Lord has let the world come to this. Folks are losin' all sense of right and wrong, the way it looks to me."

Bessie recognized Rusty Shannon and the boy Andy on sight. She did not remember the name of the third rider, though she recalled that he had backed the Monahans when the Bascoms had made their first try at recovering Alice.

She looked around to be sure her three remaining sons were close by and armed. They were. She had put years of training into preparing them for a hostile world, though they had fallen short of her expectations in many particulars. Especially the weak-willed Newley, and now Corey. She stood waiting, the quirt in her hand.

Rusty Shannon had a look of death about him. He reined his dun horse to a stop. The boy Andy pulled a long-legged sorrel in beside Shannon. The third man drew up on the other side, a shotgun across the pommel of his saddle.

Shannon's furious gaze swept over the Bascoms. "Where's Corey?"

Bessie said, "You can see for yourself, he ain't here."

"You say he's not, but you could be lyin'."

Bessie felt a quick indignation. She never lied except when it seemed expedient. This time she didn't have to. "He's gone away. What do you want him for?"

"For killin' a woman."

Bessie felt gratified. She had been a little concerned over the slight possibility that Alice might have survived the bullet, though Bessie had seen the blood gush when it struck her in the back. Lacey's aim had been true.

She asked as innocently as she could, "And what woman would that be?"

"Josie Monahan."

Bessie felt as if a bullet had struck *her.* She struggled to control herself lest Shannon read the dismay she felt. "*Josie* Monahan?"

"That's what I said."

Bessie began to shake in spite of a determined effort to take a grip on her emotions.

Shannon seemed to read her thoughts. "I guess you thought it was Alice. But Corey shot the wrong woman."

Bessie's mind raced as she considered the implications of the mistake. Shannon was clearly in a killing mood. It was a good thing Corey had left. Shannon was prepared to kill him or die in the effort. But there was another complication. Alice might or might not have talked before, but her sister's death would make her eager to tell everything she knew about the Bascoms.

Shannon stared at her with a severity she could not handle. She looked away from his blazing eyes. He said, "I'm askin' you again, where's Corey?"

Newley said, "Corey didn't—"

Ma cut him off short. "Shut your mouth, Newley."

Andy brought his rifle to bear on the brothers, and Evan followed his lead with the shotgun. Andy said, "We'll keep these boys off of your back if you want to go search the house."

Without answering, Shannon rode close to the picket house and dismounted, keeping the horse between himself and the dwelling. Rifle in hand, he walked to the door and kicked it open. He rushed inside.

Bessie said to the other two, "Told him Corey ain't here. He left, and I doubt he's comin' back. Ever."

Andy said, "Won't do him any good. Rusty'll hunt 'til he finds him."

"Shannon ain't a Monahan, and neither are you. What was that Josie woman to you-all?"

"Rusty and her were fixin' to get married."

Bessie had no time or inclination to feel sorry for people outside of her own, but she recognized that this made Shannon a lethal threat. She had seen with Corey how much store a man could place in a woman whether she deserved it or not. The mood he was in, Shannon was as dangerous as a den of rattlesnakes. She hoped neither Lacey nor little Anse was foolish enough to try a move against him, not right now. Shannon could probably kill them both and not lose a minute's sleep over it. She did not have to worry about Newley. At the first shot he would probably turn and run like a dog.

Shannon remounted his dun and returned, his eyes as threatening as before. "Whichaway was he goin' when he left here?"

She said, "You know we wouldn't tell you. Look for yourself. Maybe you can find his tracks." She had little concern on that score. There were so many horse tracks around here that he could have no idea which were left by Corey's mount.

Shannon said, "I'll find him. Consider him dead, because I'll find him no matter how long it takes." He jerked his head at his two companions. They rode away in the general direction of Fort Griffin. That was the course Corey had been taking when she last saw him.

Newley was the first to speak. He had looked relieved when he found out Alice was still alive. "Ma, you let them go on thinkin' Corey done it when it was really Lacey."

She lashed him with the quirt. "Don't ever let me hear you say that again. They'd have killed Lacey as sure as he's standin' there."

"But they'll kill Corey if they find him."

"Corey can take care of himself better than Lacey. He's a better shot. But we stand together, us Bascoms. We take care of one another, and we don't point a finger at any of our own. Now gather close and listen." She looked around as if she thought some outsider might hear. They had let Alice hear too much. "You boys have got a job of work to do. Lacey, you heard what he said. You shot the wrong woman."

Lacey was immediately defensive, raising his hands as if he expected her to take the quirt to him. "You know we couldn't get real close to the house. She looked like Alice, the best I could see in the lamplight."

"You was in too much of a hurry to get it over with and run. So now you got to do it again."

"They'll have that place guarded better than it was before. I might not come back."

"If you don't kill that girl there ain't no use in you comin' back. Time she gets through tellin' what she knows, Texas won't be big enough for any of us."

Newley said, "Let me go do it, Ma."

Her eyes narrowed in suspicion. "I got other work for you and little Anse." She knew about Newley's infatuation. He had no intention of killing Alice. If he had the chance he might carry her away to protect her. "You heard what Shannon said. The only way to keep him from huntin' down your brother is to kill him before he can."

Newley betrayed strong misgivings, as she expected. Little Anse seemed eager. "How do you want us to do it?"

"Any way you can. Trail after him. First chance you get, bushwhack him."

"What about them two that's with him?"

"Maybe they'll split up. Even if not, they don't have the killin' fever in their eyes like Shannon has. Get him and they'll probably give up the chase."

Without enthusiasm Newley said, "We'll do our best."

Newley's best wouldn't be worth a Confederate dollar, but little Anse would give it a good try. "Get at it then. Saddle your horses. I'll be puttin' some grub together."

In the house she paused in her task to look at a tintype on the mantel over the fireplace. It was of old Ansel. She kept it there as a constant inspiration to her sons and a reminder that they had to keep their guard up because the world was against them as it had been against their father.

"You was always weak, Anse," she said. "I've tried to make your boys stronger than you ever was, but I swear sometimes I have to wonder. Maybe they got too much of your blood and not enough of mine."

Rusty stopped once they were out of the Bascoms' sight. "I'm afraid I just made a bad mistake."

Andy said, "I didn't see you do anything wrong."

"I talked when I ought to've stayed quiet. They thought Corey had killed Alice. I let them know otherwise. Now they're liable to make another try for her."

Evan said gravely, "I hadn't thought of it that way."

Andy said, "We'd better get back to Alice before they have a chance."

Rusty nodded. "You two go. The Monahans may need all the help they can get. I'll keep after Corey. Maybe I can catch him before he finds out Alice is still alive."

Andy frowned. "By yourself?"

"He's by *him*self."

"You don't even know which way he went."

"No matter where he intends to go, I'm bettin' he'll stop at Fort Griffin first for supplies. Maybe I can pick up his trail there."

"How long do you figure on bein' gone?"

"Don't look for me 'til you see me comin'."

Andy gave Rusty a worried study. "You ain't slept, hardly, since Josie died. You're worn out. If you do catch up with him, the shape you're in, you may not be a match for him. You could get yourself killed."

"I lost a lot of sleep in my rangerin' days. Never got killed yet." Rusty stepped down and tightened the cinch.

Josie's image came to him suddenly and unbidden. He swallowed hard and turned to Evan. "There's somethin' I want you to do."

"Anything you ask."

"It won't be hard." Rusty's eyes burned. He blinked away the tears that came to cool them. "When you get home, you take Geneva in your arms and hold her like you'll never let her go."

He could hardly expect Corey Bascom to be waiting for him on the street in Griffin Town, but he watched closely just the same. He saw everything that moved. He rode up to the saloon where he had stopped the time he had asked directions to the Bascom place. He found the same dour bartender wiping dust from glasses and placing them on a shelf behind the bar.

The bartender gave him a critical study. "I know you, but you look different."

"I'm huntin' for Corey Bascom."

"I told you the last time where he lives."

"He left there. I thought he might've come this way."

The bartender grunted thoughtfully and went back to dusting glasses. "Any special reason you're lookin' for him?"

"He killed a woman."

The barman stopped what he was doing and studied Rusty with a more critical eye. "*Your* woman?"

"She was."

The man turned to retrieve a bottle from a shelf. He poured a glassful and set it in front of Rusty. "The look on your face tells me you need a drink."

"What I need, I won't find in that bottle."

"But it might help. Drink it."

Rusty took the contents of the glass in two swallows. The initial burn was followed by a healing glow.

The bartender said, "I don't ordinarily mix myself in other people's problems, and I sure don't go around givin' out information on other people's business. But I reckon this case justifies an exception. Corey was in here late yesterday. Bought supplies at a store down the street, then he stopped in here and got him two bottles of whiskey. Said he needed them for the road. Sounded like it was goin' to be a long one."

"Do you know which way he went after he left here?"

"No, swear to God I don't. I never watched him. There's lots of trails out of here. He could've gone south toward the Conchos and Mexico. Could've gone east, toward Arkansas, or even north, toward the Indian nations. There ain't no tellin'. With all the travelers who come and go, I doubt anybody paid him much mind."

The barman poured another drink. "Down this one. For what you been through, you ain't hardly started."

Rusty hesitated, then tipped the glass.

The barman said, "Couldn't nobody blame you if you went and got yourself staggerin' drunk."

"But then I couldn't do what I came for." Rusty paid him for the drinks. "Do you know what kind of horse he was ridin'?"

"It was a black one. That's all I can tell you."

"Thanks for the help."

He went down the street to the general store. The clerk, like the bartender, was meticulous about not minding other people's business. He was evasive until Rusty told him he knew Corey had bought supplies. He admitted, "Yeah, I sold him some stuff . . . coffee, bacon, salt, cartridges, and a wool blanket. I took it he was figurin' on a long trip, but I didn't ask any questions and he didn't offer any information."

"Did you see which direction he went leavin' town?"

"With customers like the Bascoms I make it a point not to see anything they do after they walk out this door. For all I know, he just evaporated."

Rusty recognized the futility of further questions. He walked back out to his horse. He rode around the tall hill on which the army post stood and hit the military road that led southward toward distant Fort Concho. Fresh wagon tracks covered any trail Corey might have made, if he had even ridden this way. Rusty swung back to the Clear Fork and looked at the wagon road that led eastward. It had the same abundance of fresh tracks as the other. The north road toward Forts Richardson and Sill would be no different.

He came upon a pair of heavily laden freight wagons creaking their way down from the north, the hubs badly in need of a greasing. He asked the first teamster if he had come upon anybody riding a black horse. The teamster considered, then said, "A troop of them dark-complected cavalry soldiers is all. Talked like they was lookin' for Indians, but I suspect they wasn't lookin' very hard."

Rusty scouted around until dark but knew his search for tracks was futile. Corey could have put on wings and flown away for all the trace that could be found now. He returned to the saloon, weary and sick at heart.

The bartender knew by the look on his face. "I told you. You ready for another drink?"

Rusty placed two coins on the bar. "A whole bottle."

He rode along the Clear Fork a while until full dark caught him. He unsaddled the dun, staked him on a long rope, then considered fixing a little supper. He had not eaten anything today. He built a fire but decided he was too weary to cook any of the bacon he carried. He opened the bottle and took a couple of long drinks.

He stared into the flames, feeding in dead wood to keep the fire going. The need for sleep weighted his eyelids and the whiskey churned his empty stomach, but he feared the dreams that might assault him. He concentrated on the flames. They went in and out of focus as he turned to the bottle from time to time. An old arrow wound in his leg began to ache. It often did when he was tired.

He kept seeing Josie's face in the flickering coals. He imagined Josie's voice, assuring him they would not have to wait much longer. He dwelled at length on the plans they had made for a long life together. Gone. Torn away from him in an instant.

After a time, from grief and sleepiness and the whiskey, he became confused. Was it Josie's face he saw, or Geneva's? Somehow they started looking alike.

He had loved two women, and he had lost them both.

Sleep overwhelmed him. He sprawled on the ground and fell away into a troubled darkness.

The bottle tipped over. The whiskey trickled out and soaked into the dry earth.

He boiled a can of coffee and forced himself to broil some bacon on a stick for his breakfast. At least the Clear Fork's water was good. A lot of water in the rolling plains was barely fit to drink. He felt better rested, but his head hurt from the whiskey. He wondered at the weakness that had allowed him to drink it. Normally he seldom drank, and on the rare occasions that he did it was more for sociability than for enjoyment.

Josie's image was much on his mind, and he was less alert than he should have been. At mid-morning he became aware that two riders had fallen in three or four hundred yards behind him. He gave them little thought at first because the trail showed signs of frequent travel. But after a time he noticed that when he slowed, they slowed. They seemed deliberately trying not to catch up to him. He sensed with rising alarm that they were waiting and watching for the right place to overtake and trap him.

He wondered who they might be. He considered the possibility that Corey had doubled back to the family place and brought one of his brothers to help.

Under other circumstances Rusty would be content simply to elude those who followed him. The thought that one might be Corey made this situation different. He began looking for a chance to swap places with his pursuers, to employ a double-back trick Indians sometimes used against those who would trail them. Corey might be too shrewd to fall for it, but the chance was worth taking. All Rusty wanted was to get close enough to place Corey in his sights.

He edged into the timber that lined the creek, trusting that it would hide him from the two riders' view. After a couple of hundred yards he crossed the creek and rode back in the opposite direction. He hid himself in heavy foliage and dismounted, drawing his rifle from its scabbard. He placed his hand on the dun's nostrils to prevent it from nickering at the other horses should it feel moved to do so. The dun was not particularly sociable with its own kind.

Through the heavy leaves he watched the two men on the other side of the creek, one leaning from the saddle to observe Rusty's tracks.

He felt a sharp disappointment as the pair came into clear view. Neither was Corey. But they were Bascoms, a couple of Corey's brothers. When they rode past him, he remounted and brought the rifle up high enough that he could place the stock against his shoulder in an instant. He put the dun across the creek and closed the distance. The murmur of the creek masked the sound of his horse's hooves.

He ordered, "Turn around and raise your hands."

The voice startled the two. One of the brothers complied, carefully reining his horse about, then lifting his arms. The younger hesitated.

Rusty shouted, "I won't say it again."

The youngster made a grab at the pistol on his hip, at the same time jerking on the reins, trying to turn his horse around to give him a clear shot. Rusty did not allow him time to complete the move. He fired the rifle. Dust puffed from little Anse's shirt. The impact drove him backward as the horse took fright and jumped to one side. Anse tumbled from the saddle. The horse turned and ran a short distance before the dangling reins became entangled in the underbrush.

The younger brother lay in an awkward heap, just as he had landed. He hardly quivered. Newley Bascom's face seemed drained of blood. He trembled.

"Please, Shannon, don't shoot."

"I won't unless you give me reason. Fish your six-shooter out of the holster and pitch it into the creek."

Newley complied.

Rusty said, "Now the rifle under your leg." Newley tossed it away, too. It made a splash and quickly sank to the bottom.

Rusty demanded, "Who sent you-all after me? Was it Corey?"

Newley fought to keep his frightened voice under some measure of control. "We ain't seen Corey since he left home. It was Ma sent us."

That did not surprise Rusty. "Corey hasn't been back? You're not lyin' to me?"

"I wouldn't lie, not when you got that rifle in my face. And my baby brother layin' there on the ground."

"There was four of you brothers. Where's the other one at?"

Newley was reluctant but finally replied, "Ma sent Lacey out to do another job."

Rusty knew what that would be: to finish Alice. "All right, get down real careful and go fetch your brother's horse."

Newley freed the bridle reins and led little Anse's mount back. Rusty dismounted and picked up Anse's pistol. He started to pitch it into the creek to join Newley's but reconsidered and shoved it into his waistband. An extra weapon might come in handy.

"Put your brother's body up on his saddle. Tie his hands and feet so he won't slide off."

Tears streamed down Newley's face. In a breaking voice he said, "I don't know how I'm goin' to tell Ma about this. She's goin' to take it mighty hard."

Remembering the woman's ruthless nature, Rusty could muster no sympathy. "Tell her it's her own fault, sendin' you-all out to do a dirty job."

Only as he watched Newley lead away the horse with his brother's body tied on it did Rusty succumb to any sense of remorse, and that only because of little Anse's youth. The boy was a member of an outlaw family. Even with the best of luck he had probably been fated to an early death by bullet or perhaps by hanging. It was likely that Bessie Bascom would live to mourn all her sons unless her machinations somehow resulted in her own death beforehand.

He considered what Newley had said about the third brother, Lacey, being sent to kill Alice. That came as no surprise; Rusty had expected another try. He had warned Andy and Evan to keep a close watch. Now he began to reassess his own mission, the search for Corey Bascom. This endless riding was getting him nowhere. He might travel a thousand miles and get no nearer to Corey than he already was. Even if he found Corey and killed him, that would do nothing for Josie except avenge her death. The best thing he could do for Josie at this point would be to help keep her younger sister alive.

He decided to return to the Monahan place. He would not give up his search for Corey, but he would reluctantly defer it for a while. Vengeance would have to wait.

He approached the farm, his shoulders hunched, his body so tired he held himself in the saddle by force of will. The dun horse seemed to falter in its step. It needed long rest and many generous helpings of grain.

James Monahan walked out from the barn. "My God, Rusty, is that you? You look like hell."

Rusty rubbed a hand over his unshaven face. "I've been through hell and out the far side. I'd swear I've ridden this poor horse a thousand miles."

"He shows it. Find any sign of Corey?"

"Not one. He could be in Mexico or Colorado or California for all I found out. How are things here?"

"Grim."

"Is Alice all right?"

"She's feelin' low. Blames herself. Still wishes it had been her instead of Josie."

So do I, Rusty thought with a rush of bitterness, then felt guilty for it. "The Bascoms made any more effort to get her?"

"One. Somebody tried to sneak up to the house a couple

nights ago. Andy challenged him with a shotgun. Whoever it was, he turned and ran. Andy gave him a blast and heard him holler."

"All the Bascoms except Corey know Alice is alive. Far as I can tell, though, he still thinks she's dead." Rusty told about his encounter with the two younger Bascom brothers.

James said, "Maybe losin' that boy will convince the old woman to take what's left of her family and leave the country."

"You ever see a hurt snake get so mad it bites itself? She'll probably be meaner than ever, and more determined. All the way back, I've been thinkin' we need to get Alice away from here."

"Where could she go that they wouldn't find her?"

"My old friend Tom Blessing has a wife who's ailin'. He's been wishin' he could find a woman to help take care of her 'til she's back on her feet. It's a long ways down there. The Bascoms would have no idea how to find her."

"Mama's still in bad shape. I don't know as Alice would want to leave her."

"Clemmie's lost one daughter. What would come of her if she lost another?"

James mulled that over. "Then we'll send Alice away with you whether she wants to go or not."

"Me and Andy can take her out of here after good dark. Even if the Bascoms find out she's gone, they won't have any idea where she went."

"Don't you think you need to rest a day or two first?"

"We don't know how much rest the Bascoms are takin'. I can rest after I get home."

Alice was strongly opposed to leaving, as Rusty had expected her to be. But even Clemmie urged her to go. In a strained but determined voice Clemmie told her, "I don't figure on stayin' in this bed forever. I'll still have Warren and Geneva and James. They'll see after me. You go and see after yourself."

Alice gave in. Clemmie beckoned Rusty to her side and took his hand. Her grip was weak. This woman had been heart and soul of the Monahan family. He hated to leave her now when she was ill.

She said, "I know you're hurtin'. We're all hurtin'. But I've been there before. It passes, with time."

Rusty's eyes burned. "I hope so, because it sure hurts right now. You-all are the nearest thing to family that I've had since my folks died."

"You'll always be family to us."

Preacher Webb walked with him up to the little Monahan cemetery. A bare new mound had appeared beside the grassed-over plots where Lon Monahan and his son Billy had been buried years before.

He felt Webb's comforting arm on his shoulder. As far back as he could remember, Preacher Webb had been around to offer spiritual strength when he needed it.

Webb said, "She's not really here, you know. She's gone on to a better world."

Rusty took no comfort in the words. "I wanted her here, in *this* world. If your God is so merciful, why does He let things like this happen?"

"People have asked that ever since time began. I don't know the answer to it. I just know there is sunlight and there is dark. There is good and there is evil. It's up to those of good heart to try and end the evil."

"I'll put an end to Corey Bascom if I ever find him. And I'll find him!"

"The Bascoms have taken away somethin' precious to you, but don't let them take away your soul. You don't stop evil by doin' more evil. Whatever you do, do it within the law."

"It's been a long time since we've had real law in Texas."

"But we'll have it again. Be a part of it, like you used to be."

"Like in the rangers?"

"Like in the rangers. I hear they're comin' back."

{ SEVEN }

Bessie Bascom had been preparing to milk the cow when she first saw the oncoming rider. So long as she was outdoors, she missed very little that moved. She had watched the horseman now for half an hour, hoping he would prove to be Corey. Her eldest was the only one she felt was capable of lifting the darkness that had befallen the Bascoms. Sure, he was the one who had brought it upon them in the first place, fetching that girl Alice here, making her privy to the family's doings. And sure, he had taken it badly when he thought his brother Lacey had killed her. But she felt he would come around to his mother's way of thinking eventually. He was family. When the chips were down, the Bascoms always pulled together. Her sons had rallied like troopers when old Anse died at the hands of the state police. They would rally now.

She knew the rider was one of her sons. She knew them by the way they sat in the saddle, the same way their father had done before them. In time she became aware that he led another horse. It appeared to be carrying a pack. That was strange. She had not sent the boys for supplies. She had ordered Newley and little Anse out to trail the man named Shannon. She had dispatched Lacey to finish the job he had botched the first time, killing Josie. He had returned in pain, barely able to sit in the saddle. She had spent more than an hour digging buckshot out of his backside while he howled like a hurt dog.

Not until the horseman was within a hundred yards did she recognize him as Newley. Her heart began to race as she realized that what she had thought was a pack was in reality a body tied across a saddle. She went running, screaming. "Little Anse, my baby. Oh Lord God, my baby."

The horses spooked at the wailing and the flare of Bessie's skirts. Newley had to hold tightly to the reins.

Bessie threw her arms over the body and kissed the still, cold face. She wept bitter tears while Newley dismounted and stood awkwardly, his head down. He rubbed his sleeve over his face.

Bessie turned on him. Accusation overrode the grief in her eyes. "What happened?"

Newley took a step backward in fear of her. "Wasn't no fault of mine, Ma. He oughtn't to've tried to draw on that Shannon. It was over before I could move."

"I'm guessin' you never moved at all. I'm guessin' you just sat there."

"Wasn't nothin' I could do. Shannon come up from behind. He had the drop on us before we even seen him."

"But your little brother drawed on him just the same?"

"He oughtn't to've."

"Why didn't you draw, too? You could at least have shot Shannon while he was busy shootin' your baby brother."

"He'd have shot me, too. You got no idee how fast he is."

"Maybe it would've been better. You'd've been spared the shame of bringin' this innocent baby boy back here dead while you don't appear to have a scratch on you."

Newley turned away, tears running down his cheeks. "I'm sorry, Ma. I done the best I know how."

"I ought to take a quirt to you, but it wouldn't do no good. Wouldn't make you no smarter, nor braver. Wouldn't bring little Anse back to us. I'm just glad old Anse ain't here to see this. One son dead. One son gone off to God knows where. Two other sons dumber than dirt, can't even take care of a simple job. It's a mean world we've come to."

Newley drew himself up with what pride he could muster. "I'll go find that Shannon, and I'll kill him."

Bessie was gratified that Newley had that much pride, but she knew pride would soon give way to fear. "No, we'll give your brother a decent buryin' first. Then I'll want you to go find Corey and bring him back here."

"Ain't no tellin' where he's at."

"He's somewhere. You'll find him."

"What's Lacey goin' to do?"

"When he's able to ride again I'll send him back to watch for another chance at that girl. It's your job to find Corey before Shannon does."

Newley brought himself to look at his mother for only a moment, then he cut his eyes away. "Do we *have* to kill Alice?"

"Get them silly romantic notions out of your mind. You know it's her that's at the root of all our trouble. It's like she's cast a witch's spell over this family. Trouble will keep throwin' its shadow over our door 'til we've got rid of her.

"Now go carry your baby brother into the house. I'll be washin' him while you and Lacey dig a proper grave. We'll send him to glory in style. And when the time comes, we'll send Shannon to hell."

* * *

Looking back in the rosy glow of sunup, Rusty saw that the wagon wheels were cutting deep tracks through the winter-brittle grass. The days were warming, but the nights still brought chill enough to delay the green-up. Riding Long Red alongside the wagon, Andy looked back with concern. "Even a blind Apache could follow our trail."

His Comanche upbringing had given him a dim view of the Apache. The Comanche considered himself superior to all other beings, especially the Apache.

Alice sat on the wagon seat beside Rusty. He had not spoken to her and had hardly looked at her since they'd left the Monahan farm about midnight. Dense clouds had hidden the moon. He had counted on darkness to hide their leaving.

He said, "There's other tracks besides ours, freight wagons and such."

He had left his weary dun horse at the Monahans', trading for a bay to take its place. It was tied to the rear of the wagon.

James had said of the horse, "He's a good one. Come to a chase, he's about as fast as anything I've rode in a long time. Got some wild spirit left, though, so you have to stay awake and watch him. Now and then he'll bog his head and pitch for no cause except he wants to throw you off. You'll like him."

Andy kept looking at the back trail, not convinced that no one was following. He glanced at Alice from time to time, his face troubled. Out of her hearing, he had expressed to Rusty his concern that people might question the propriety of her making this long trip with two men. Rusty had said, "You can be her chaperon."

Andy's Indian upbringing had subjected him to a lot of speculative gossip over the years. "I don't care when it's just me," he had said. "I'm used to it. But folks will mean-talk a woman whether she deserves it or not."

"Maybe she does deserve a little of it." Rusty immediately regretted what he said and was glad nobody except Andy had heard. Andy had too much honor to repeat it.

Alice looked back from time to time. "It's goin' to be tough, not knowin' how Mama is gettin' along."

Rusty had fought against his resentment toward Alice and tried to keep it out of his voice. "Your mother isn't much bigger than a banty hen, but she's got a will like iron. If she makes up her mind to get on her feet, that bed won't hold her for long."

He could see some of Clemmie's strength in Alice, though she still had a young woman's voice. He wished she had employed that will against Corey's entreaties and had not gone off with him in the first place.

Perhaps caring for Mrs. Blessing would help keep Alice's mind off of her mother. He remembered a strong nurturing instinct in Clemmie and her two oldest daughters. Geneva had stayed close by Rusty years ago while he recovered from a bad arrow wound incurred in ranger service. Later, Josie had nursed him after he took a bullet in the back. He hoped Alice possessed the same instincts, though he had seen nothing to convince him that she did.

They took a long noon rest. Rusty slept despite pain from the old wound. He was still weary after his long search for Corey Bascom. He suspected that Andy did not even try to sleep, watching their trail for sign of pursuit. Moving on, Rusty felt better for having had a little rest. Andy's shoulders drooped a little.

Rusty said, "You ought to've slept while you had a chance."

Andy's answer was curt. "Somebody had to watch."

"They don't even know we're gone."

"Maybe not. And maybe they do. That old woman has

got an evil spirit sittin' on her shoulder. For all we know, it's tellin' her everything."

Rusty frowned. He had tried for years to turn Andy away from notions left over from his life with the Indians. They still cropped out from time to time. "What does an evil spirit look like?"

"It can look like anything. Most of the time you can't see it, but you can feel that it's there. Did you hear the owl last night, just before we left?"

"There's been owls around the Monahan place for years."

"Not like that one."

One owl had always sounded like another to Rusty, but he knew owls were a symbol of ill fortune, sometimes death, to the Comanche people.

Andy said, "For all we know, that owl could've been the old woman herself, watchin' us. There's some people can do that, you know, turn themselves into somethin' else. I knew a medicine man once who could turn himself into a wolf."

"Did you see him do it?"

"No, but I talked to people who said they saw him go into a cave, and a wolf came out. He could howl like one. I've heard him start, and wolves would answer him."

"That doesn't prove anything. I've known a few white people who could do that. It helped them hunt down wolves."

Andy said nothing more for a while, his feelings wounded a little. Argument over such matters was pointless. Neither he nor Rusty would change his mind.

Alice had held quiet for the most part. Finally she said, "This far south, do we need to worry about Indians?"

Rusty suspected Andy's talk about spirits had prompted her to wonder. "You never stop watchin' for Indians, wherever you are. But the odds are that most of them are still in winter camp north of us. The way the country is settlin' up, they're bein' crowded off of a lot of their old stompin' grounds."

Andy broke his silence. "And losin' their buffalo to the hide hunters. Damn shame, people killin' buffalo for the skin and leavin' the meat to rot. What do they expect the Indian to do?"

Rusty said, "I expect most would like to see the Indians all evaporate, like a puddle of water in the sunshine."

Andy's voice became strident. "Well, they won't. They'll take just so much crowdin', then they'll raise up and fight." He sounded as if he wished he could join them. Over the years there had been times when Rusty feared he might do just that. But Andy had left enemies as well as friends in the Comanche camps. Going back would be fraught with risk.

Alice took in a sharp breath and pointed. "If there aren't any Indians around here, what's that yonder?"

Rusty saw a dozen horsemen moving toward them out of the west. He knew at a glance that they were Indians.

Andy said, "Next time I talk to you about owls, maybe you'll listen."

Rusty did not waste time with argument or denial. He said, "We'll head for that buffalo wallow yonder. Maybe they haven't seen us."

Andy said, "They probably saw us before we saw them. Anyway, that hole's not deep enough to hide us."

It would give them a better defensive position, however, if this meeting turned into a fight. Sometimes a good position and a show of weapons would turn away a hunting party that was out mainly for meat and not for scalps. A war party would be something else.

He took the wagon into the dry-bottomed wallow and stopped. "Help Alice down," he told Andy. "She's too good a target up on this wagon." When Andy had done that, Rusty said, "Look in my saddlebag. You'll find that Bascom boy's pistol. Give it to her."

Worriedly Andy said, "We don't want to kill any of them unless we're forced to. Some might be friends of mine."

"Then they'd better act friendly."

Alice checked the pistol's load. She appeared more determined than frightened. Rusty asked her, "You sure you know how to shoot that thing?"

"Mama taught me to shoot before she taught me how to sew. Said every country girl ought to be able to use a gun because there wouldn't always be a man around to do it for her."

The wallow was not deep enough to hide even the wagon, but its shallow bank would provide cover for a person lying on his stomach and sighting a rifle up over the edge. Rusty said, "Andy, your eyes are sharper than mine. Are they wearin' any paint?"

Andy observed them a minute before answering. They had stopped a hundred yards out and seemed to be considering their options. "I don't see any. Probably just out huntin'."

"But they wouldn't pass up three scalps and four horses if they thought they would come easy."

Andy's expression indicated he didn't like what he saw. "I'm afraid that's just what they're thinkin'. They act like they're fixin' to give us a try." He handed Rusty his rifle. "I'm kin, of sorts. I'm goin' out and see if they'll parley."

Rusty thrust the rifle back at him. "You don't look like anybody that's kin to them. They're liable to kill you before you can tell them you're a cousin."

Andy refused the weapon. "If they're bound to kill me they'll do it anyway. Three of us ain't got a chance against them all." He climbed up out of the wallow and paused to add, "Told you about that damned owl."

He moved toward the Indians, his hands in the air to show he was unarmed. Rusty held his breath. An old image flashed into his mind: the sight of Andy's dead mother many years ago, butchered in the cruelest manner. He made up his mind he would not let that happen to Alice. If he saw they were about to be overrun, he would put a bullet through her head.

Some of the Comanches raised their bows. At least three had rifles or shotguns. Andy began making sign talk, and Rusty caught remnants of his words as he spoke. The Indians surrounded Andy. For a few moments he was out of sight. Rusty checked his rifle again. It felt slick against his sweating hands.

Alice said nothing. She held the pistol ready, the hammer cocked back. Her jaw was set like Clemmie Monahan's.

Andy emerged from the circle of Indians. He walked slowly and confidently toward the wallow. The Indians followed at a respectful distance, offering no overt threat. Andy signaled from fifty yards that everything was all right and motioned for Rusty and Alice to lower their guns. Rusty did, but not by much.

Andy stopped at the edge of the wallow. "Told you it was better to talk than to fight. Turned out I know a couple of them. We used to play at stealin' horses together."

"They're past the age for play-actin'. They look like they mean business."

"They're huntin' for buffalo. First thing they wanted to know was if we are, too. They thought maybe the wagon was for haulin' hides. Seems like there's a lot of white hunters workin' the buffalo range north of here. It's got the People pretty mad."

"Tell them those hunters are mostly out of Kansas. We're Texans."

"They don't like Texans, either."

Two of the Comanches ventured up close enough to look down into the wallow.

Rusty warned, "Don't let them see fear, Alice. If they've got mischief on their minds it'll encourage them."

The pair focused their attention on her. She still held the pistol cocked and ready, though she diverted the muzzle a little to one side. She looked cocked and ready, too, if they made any direct move toward her.

Andy said, "It's all right, Alice. It's not often they see a white woman up close."

She said nothing. Rusty suspected she knew her voice would be shaky, and she did not want to reveal that she was frightened.

Andy said, "They asked for tobacco, but I told them we don't have any. They'd settle for some sugar. You don't find much of that in a Comanche camp."

Geneva had bagged sugar and coffee and salt for use on the trip to the Colorado River. Rusty said, "Give them the sugar, Alice. We can do without it." He liked sugar in his coffee when he could get it, but more often than not he had to drink it straight. He did not consider that a hardship. Through the war years he had gone for long stretches without even coffee.

Some sugar granules clung to the outside of the bag. An Indian wet his finger, ran it through the sugar, then touched the finger to his tongue. He broke into a broad grin.

Andy said, "Alice, you've made a friend for life."

The one holding the bag spoke a couple of words that Rusty assumed were the equivalent of "thank you," then reined his horse around and set off toward the rest of the party in a long trot. His companion followed but did not catch up to him.

Alice finally found voice. "Are they goin' to eat it right out of the sack?"

Andy said, "Sure. Hasn't everybody done that?"

When Andy had first returned from the Comanches he gorged himself on hog lard and raw sugar. The lard evidently made up for some nutritional deficiency. Sugar had been a new and exciting experience. At the time it was still scarce even in the Texas settlements.

Andy went on, "They don't seem as fearsome when you just see one or two up close, do they?"

Alice looked at him askance. "They look scary enough for me."

"You have to get used to them, is all. They're people just like everybody else, except a little different."

Rusty burned to be on his way, but he was hesitant about leaving the dubious shelter of the buffalo wallow until the Indians were out of sight in a direction other than south. He watched them pass the sugar sack around. Apparently there was some dissatisfaction over the fairness of the division, for the last man angrily threw the empty sack at the one who had offered it to him.

Andy said, "See what I told you? They're just like everybody else."

Not until the Indians were out of sight did Rusty motion for Andy to help Alice back onto the wagon. "They may be friends of yours, Andy, but we're travelin' 'til after dark tonight."

Andy said, "I'd worry a lot more about them Bascoms than about my Comanche kinfolks. Them Bascoms ain't civilized."

They paused briefly at the grave of Andy's mother. The

marker was down again, buffalo tracks all around it. Even if Andy carried out his vow to build a fence around the site, Rusty knew the buffalo would not respect the fence any more than they respected the marker. They would rub their itchy hides against it until they knocked it down. If the Kansas hunters kept moving south, that problem would be eliminated over time. He would not mention that to Andy, however. It would just raise the young man's hackles.

Alice knew Andy's background, but she had never been here before. Seeing the grave brought the old tragedy to a reality she had not quite grasped earlier. She offered a prayer, spoken so softly that Rusty could not hear most of it. She asked Andy, "Do you remember any of what happened here?"

"A little." He grimaced. "A little too much."

She reached out and touched his arm, then drew her hand away.

Rusty felt impatient. "We can still make some distance before dark." They moved on.

They reached the farm just at sunset. Rusty said, "It's too late to go on to Tom's tonight."

Alice surveyed the place with keen interest. "You've built it up some since we stayed here durin' the war. Broke out some more land and built another cabin."

Rusty said, "The new cabin is Andy's. I thought he ought to have a house of his own when Josie and me . . ." He did not finish. He cleared his throat. "Wonder if Len Tanner is around. Be like him to've gone off on another *pasear*."

Tanner appeared on the dog run of the larger cabin, stretching his long frame as if he had been napping.

"Howdy. You-all are just in time for supper. All you've got to do is fix it."

The garden showed signs of fresh work. Evidently Tanner had kept himself at least moderately busy. He had no real obligation to do so because he was not a hired hand. He was not drawing wages. He simply had a home here whenever he wanted it, and in return he contributed a share of the work when he was around. He was free to tie his meager belongings behind his saddle and ride off at any time he felt like it, which was fairly often.

Sight of Tanner momentarily lifted the melancholy that had fallen upon Rusty. "Len, I was afraid you'd be off to hell and gone again."

"I would've been if you hadn't got home when you did."

"Where to this time? Thought you'd seen all you wanted of your kinfolks."

"I have. But now I got other things to do." Tanner looked up in surprise at the girl on the wagon seat. "Alice? Is that you?"

"It's me." She gave him a tentative smile. He had flirted with her and her sisters in the past but had shied away from anything more serious than a stolen kiss, which once had earned him a quick slap in the face.

He said, "You're gettin' to where you look more like your sisters every time I see you. How're they gettin' along?"

Rusty had to look away. Andy said quickly, "Josie's dead. I'll tell you about it later."

Tanner's jolly mood was gone. He stared as if struck by a club. "Damn but I'm sorry." He reached to help Alice down from the wagon.

Andy asked, "You seen any strangers around here?"

Tanner set Alice on the ground. "Gettin' to be a lot of traffic around this place. Sometimes two or three people a day goin' one direction or another. Country's settlin' up to where it don't hardly seem the same anymore."

Andy persisted, "These people would likely have asked about Rusty or Alice."

Tanner shook his head. "Nary a soul."

Rusty said, "The Bascoms couldn't have gotten here ahead of us even if they'd known where we were goin'. For all they know we headed north for Colorado, or east for Arkansas, . . . if they've even found out we're gone."

Andy said stubbornly, "That old woman knows."

Tanner looked from one to another, confused but content to wait until someone saw fit to explain.

Rusty asked, "Know anything about Tom Blessing's wife?"

Tanner said, "She's still poorly. Shanty was here yesterday, helped me plant some tomatoes and okry. He'd been by to see the Blessings a couple of days ago."

Shanty was a former slave. His little place lay between Rusty's farm and the Blessings'.

Rusty said, "I brought Alice to stay with Mrs. Blessing and try to help get her back on her feet."

Tanner nodded his approval. "She's a grand old lady. She'll perk up just from havin' the company."

Rusty knew that Tanner had been smitten by Alice for a long time. He was not sure about Andy. He was aware that Andy had been watching women. For a while he had become somewhat attached to a neighbor girl named Bethel Brackett. That involvement seemed to have faded, probably because of his antipathy for her brother Farley.

Rusty told Alice she could have the bedroom side of the double cabin. As she went inside Tanner said, "I told you to tell her hello for me. I didn't mean you had to bring her all the way here."

Rusty told him as much as he figured Tanner needed to

know for the time being. Tanner nodded gravely. "I *am* mighty sorry about Josie. If any of them Bascoms come pokin' around here lookin' for Alice, I'll blow a hole in them you could put a wagon through."

Andy said, "Just a little hole would be enough, long as it's in a place to do the most good."

A hundred times Rusty had imagined himself confronting Corey Bascom. He thought he could probably shoot him in the heart without flinching once. Someday, some way, he intended to do just that.

Tanner said, "Fact is, though, I won't be here. I've just been waitin' 'til you got home. I've joined the rangers."

The word brought Rusty and Andy both to full attention. Rusty said, "The rangers?"

Tanner nodded. "You probably ain't heard. Governor Coke is callin' up a lot of the old hands. The Morris brothers brought the word to me. They've joined up, too."

"Those Morris boys are liable to get you shot."

"I'm too skinny to be hit. I can hide behind a fence post. Anyway, them boys have got their hearts in the right place."

"It's not their hearts that worry me. It's their heads."

Andy spoke up. "How old do you have to be to join?"

Tanner shook his head. "Can't rightly say. If it's the way it used to be, you're old enough now. Got to furnish your own horse and your own gun."

"I have those."

"Don't know what the pay'll be. It doesn't matter much anyhow. I'm used to not findin' anything in my pockets except my hands."

Rusty felt uneasy about Andy's eagerness. "You'd better take a long look before you jump, Andy. It can be a hard life."

"I've never had no featherbed."

* * *

Rusty decided upon the wagon to take Alice to the Blessing place. The things she had hastily gathered from home were already in it. That would save having to pack them on a horse. He left Andy with Tanner to clean up the place. Tanner's housekeeping had been of the lick-and-a-promise variety.

They went by Shanty's farm; it was but little out of the way. Shanty had no real last name, though when he had to put his X on legal papers he adopted the surname of his late owner, Isaac York, who had willed him the farm.

Shanty was in his garden, hoeing out shallow trenches and planting seeds, then covering them lightly. His years weighed heavily upon his thin shoulders. He straightened slowly, with obvious back pain. Recognition of his visitors brought him to the garden gate. He removed his hat in deference to Alice, or perhaps to both of them. Old slave habits died hard.

"You-all git down and come in the house," he said.

His house was a cabin built of logs to replace one burned by night riders who had resented the idea of a black man owning a piece of land in their midst. Firm talk by Rusty, Tom Blessing, and other friends had put an end to that kind of devilment. A few neighbors still did not like his being there, but they had been buffaloed into silence.

Rusty said, "We're headed for the Blessing place. You remember Alice?"

Shanty smiled. "I do, but it was a long time ago, and she weren't much more than a thin saplin'. She's growed into a fine-lookin' young lady."

"Alice is goin' to help Mrs. Blessing."

"The Lord will smile on her for that. I been worried about Miz Blessing."

"But one thing, Shanty, . . . if some stranger should come askin' about Alice, you haven't seen her. You don't have any idea where she's at. You don't even know who she is."

Shanty's smile faded into a frown. "Hard to believe somebody'd mean harm to this young lady."

"They do. That's why I've brought her all the way down here." He explained briefly about the Bascoms and Josie's death.

Shanty nodded sadly. "I'll just act like I don't know nothin'. They generally figure that way anyhow." Long years in servitude had taught him how to tell white people what he thought they wanted to hear or to pretend total ignorance, whichever the circumstances called for.

Rusty thought Shanty looked more tired than usual. That concerned him. "You feelin' all right? You haven't been workin' too hard and gettin' yourself too hot?"

"Work and me been friends all my life. And friends know not to crowd one another too much."

Rusty took the remark as a sign that Shanty thought he had been working too hard and not getting enough rest. "We'll be gettin' on to the Blessings'."

"May the Lord walk ahead of you and smooth the road."

{ EIGHT }

Tom Blessing's dog announced the wagon's coming and trotted to meet it, tail wagging vigorously. Tom stepped out onto the opening between the two sections of the log cabin and shaded his eyes with his big hand. "Git down," he shouted. "Git down and come in."

Alice looked a little apprehensive. She had gotten to know the Blessings when the Monahan family stayed at

Rusty's farm during part of the war years, but she had been only half grown. She had not seen them since. "What if it turns out they've already got somebody to stay with Mrs. Blessing?" she asked.

Rusty suspected that question had been on her mind for some time, but this was the first time she asked it. He remembered the way Tom had answered a question once. He said, "We'll burn that bridge when we get to it."

His comment served only to increase her concern.

Tom raised his strong arms to help her down from the wagon. "Is this Josie?" he asked, smiling. "Lord how you've changed."

"I'm Alice, Mr. Blessing. I've come to stay and help take care of your wife."

"Alice? Then you've *really* changed." He looked expectantly at Rusty. "You left here aimin' to get married. Leave the bride at your place?"

Even after all these days, Rusty still found it difficult to speak about her. "Josie's dead. I'll tell you about it in a little while."

Tom's face fell. His eyes pinched in sympathy. He seemed about to say something to Rusty, but he could not bring it out. He turned back to Alice. "Come on in, girl. Mrs. Blessing will be tickled to see you."

Rusty busied himself unloading Alice's few belongings, placing them in the dog run. He could hear her voice from inside the cabin. It sounded like Josie talking. He leaned against a wagon wheel and stared across Tom's field, but the image was blurred.

Tom came outside in a few minutes. He said, "Alice and the Mrs. are goin' to hit it off real good. It was mighty thoughtful of you to bring her."

"I had a reason. She needs you-all right now as much as you need her. More, maybe." Painfully Rusty explained what had happened to Josie and why he had felt it necessary to bring Alice so far from home.

Tom nodded, his eyes sad. "I reckon this is about as hard a thing as man ever has to take in this life."

"Another hard thing is knowin' that the man who did it is runnin' loose. But he won't stay loose forever. I'm goin' to hunt him down like a hydrophoby dog."

"How you goin' to do that? You've got no idea where to start. He could be ten miles from here or a thousand."

"I'll just give up everything else and hunt 'til I find him."

"That could take years."

"I don't know what else to do."

Tom frowned, deep in thought. "Did Len tell you he's signed up for the rangers?"

"He told me. Andy's itchin' to do the same thing."

"It's not a bad idea. The rangers could be the answer to your problem."

"I don't see how."

"Think about it. You're just one man, lookin' for another man who could be anyplace. If you were a ranger you could put him on the fugitive list. Instead of just one man lookin' for him there'd be a hundred or two, however many rangers there are. And I can send word out to sheriffs around the state to be watchin' for him."

"But I want to be the one who gets him. I want to look him square in the eyes and tell him he's fixin' to die."

Tom frowned. "What's more important, bringin' him to justice or takin' your own personal revenge?"

"The way I feel, I want to do it myself."

"Revenge can poison the soul, Rusty. The man on the receivin' end dies just once, and generally quick. The man out for revenge may die a little every day as long as he lives. Remember after Daddy Mike was killed? You almost let it get the best of you that time."

Rusty remembered. He had been roughly Andy's age. Tom had enlisted him in a frontier ranger company to get him away from home, saving him from killing the wrong man.

Tom said, "Even a justified killin' can eat on a man like slow poison. Say you kill this Corey Bascom but destroy yourself in the doin' of it. Do you think that's what Josie would want?"

"There's no way to ask her."

"Deep down, you know."

"All I know for sure is that I want to see Bascom dead."

"Then at least go about it a right and proper way. Do it through the law."

That, Rusty recalled, was more or less what Preacher Webb had said. It was as though he and Tom had conspired together.

Tom persisted, "You could do a lot of good, bein' a ranger. There's still Indian trouble up north. And what the Yankees called 'reconstruction' spawned enough outlaws to overstock hell. It'll take some strong-minded lawmen to put them down."

"Is that why you let them make you sheriff again?"

"I looked around and didn't see anybody I thought fitted the job. Except maybe you, and you had your hands full with that farm."

"I still do. That's the reason I can't join the rangers."

Tom's frown deepened. "But you'd leave in a minute if you got a lead on Bascom."

"That's different."

The sound of a running horse drew Rusty's attention to the wagon road that led from town. He saw a rider pushing hard, waving his hat. Rusty began to hear his shouting though he could not make out what the man was trying to say.

Tom stiffened. "Nobody's ever come ridin' in that fast to bring me good news." He walked out to meet the horseman. Shiny with sweat, the horse slid to a stop.

The man shouted, though he was close enough that he would not have needed to. "Sheriff Tom, there's been a shootin' in town. And a robbery."

Tom accepted the information with a grave expression. "Slow down, get your breath, then tell me about it."

The rider had the look of a clerk, his shirt white except where sweat had soaked through and attracted dust. His string necktie was hanging askew. He leaned heavily on the horn of his saddle, struggling for air. "Two men. Strangers. Held up the general store. When Mr. Bancroft reached under the counter, they shot him."

"Kill him?"

"I'm afraid so. He was still breathin' when I left, but he looked like a goner." The man pointed. "They rode out headin' west, across country. I followed their tracks part of the way here. They was pretty plain."

Tom grunted. "I ought to be able to cut across and pick them up." He asked for a description, but the one given was vague enough to have fitted Rusty himself, and half the men he knew.

Tom looked back at Rusty. "See what I told you about lawlessness? It's got mighty close to home."

The words popped from Rusty's mouth before he allowed time for consideration. "You want me to help you?"

"I'd be much obliged."

"I'll need to get back home and swap this wagon for my horse. Need to tell Andy and Len, too, or they'll worry about where I'm at."

"I'll swing by your cabin and pick you up after I get a line on them tracks. Want to say adios to Alice?"

Rusty had not had much to say to Alice during the trip.

He knew nothing to say to her now. "You do it for me. I'll be gettin' started." He climbed into the wagon and put the team into motion. Looking back once, he saw Alice standing in the dog run, watching him with a big question in her eyes.

Two men. Robbing stores was one of the Bascom brothers' specialties, Alice had said. He knew it was wildly unlikely that they had been the perpetrators here, but the thought was intriguing enough to set his imagination to racing. He pictured himself confronting Corey Bascom. The thought set his skin to burning with impatience. Flipping the reins across the team's rumps, he yelled them into a hard trot.

Approaching the home place, he wondered that he saw no one in field or garden. Long Red and Len's horse were nowhere in sight. Len's in particular was something of a barn lover, usually found within easy reach of feed. Rusty saw his bay grazing alone, near the shed.

He hollered as the wagon rolled past the cabin, but no one answered. He put the vehicle under the shed. Quickly unhooking the team, he pitched the harness into the wagon instead of taking time to hang it up properly. He caught the bay and saddled him, then hurried up to the cabin to fetch his rifle. He had taken only his pistol to Tom's.

He found no fire in the kitchen. On the table he saw a sheet of paper weighted down by a tin cup half full of cold coffee. He held it so that reflected light from the open door made the penciled message readable. He grumbled under his breath as he read it.

Deer Rusty,

I take pensil in hand to inform you that Me and Andy are gone off to the Rangers. We didnt wait becawz we knowd you would raiz Hell. Dont worry about Andy I will sea that he dont get in no trubbl. With best regards, your verry good frend,

Len Tanner

No trouble. Rusty declared aloud, "Damn that Len." If he was looking out for Andy, who would be looking out for Len? They both needed a guardian, one because he was still young and the other because he would never completely grow up.

Rusty sat down heavily in his chair and weighed the significance of this development. He could go to Andy's ranger captain and argue that Andy was underage. But he had no idea to what company the youngster might be assigned or where it would be stationed. As for age, Andy could pass for his early twenties on the basis of his looks. Rusty could not prove him younger.

This threw a bad kink into his rope.

Tom was not far behind him. He reined up from a hard trot as Rusty walked out to untie the bay. He asked, "Len and Andy goin' with us?"

"They're gone. Went off to join the rangers." As he slid his rifle into the scabbard and swung onto the bay's back he explained about the letter. "I could wring Len Tanner's scrawny neck like a chicken."

"You already told me *he* was goin'. But Andy is a surprise."

Rusty felt too disgruntled to talk about it. "Did you find the tracks?"

Tom nodded. "A couple of miles south of here. They're stayin' off of the roads. Don't want anybody seein' them."

Rusty had a bitter taste in his mouth. "Let's be goin' after them."

He had noted that the young man who brought the message had not stayed with Tom for the long pursuit. Tom explained, "I sent him back to town. The wrong kind of help can get you killed."

Tom led the way, angling southwestward. He cut the tracks in a short time. The fugitives were evidently depending upon fast horses rather than trying to cover their trail.

Tom said, "People noticed them camped outside of town last night but never gave them much thought. There's always folks passin' through. These were probably watchin' to see where business looked the best. Since we don't have a bank yet, the store must've seemed like the richest pickin's. Old man Bancroft was a gentle feller. He ought not to have reached for a gun."

"Maybe they'd have shot him anyway. There are men like that. Didn't get enough killin' in the war. Or didn't go, and now they're makin' up for it."

Tom's face twisted. "Which means we'd better be careful how we ride up on them. Bancroft's funeral is one too many."

"Another one or two would be all right, long as it's the right men gettin' buried."

Tom gave Rusty a long study. "You've got a hard look in your face. I don't know as I like it."

"Been some hard things happened to me. Andy goin' off like that doesn't make it any easier."

"He's not your son. He's not even your brother. Sure, he's still young, but he's shown that he can think and do for himself. I wouldn't mind havin' him with us right now."

"I'm glad he's not."

The trail presented little challenge. A recent shower had left the ground soft so that the hooves had made deeper than usual cuts in it. Tom stopped to study a place where one of the horses had paused to urinate. He said, "They ain't too far ahead of us. An hour or so, maybe two."

Farther on, Tom pointed to a spot where the ground had been scarred slightly. "Looks like one of the horses stepped in that hole yonder and went down."

Boot tracks showed that one man had walked around a little before remounting. Tom said, "Horse must not have broke its leg, but I'll bet it's limpin' some. That'll slow our boys up."

Presently Rusty saw a single rider ahead of them. At first he could not tell whether the person was coming or going, but soon it became clear that he was moving to meet them. He was on a bareback mule, with wagon harness instead of saddle. He carried the long reins looped like a lariat.

Tom said, "That looks like old man Gillis. What's he doin' ridin' a wagon mule?"

As Gillis approached, it was plain that he had been hurt. Blood had dried on the side of his face. A deep bruise had turned dark from his cheekbone up to the edge of his gray hair. Tom said to him, "You look like you'd been thrown off and drug."

"Two men stopped me. Swapped me a lame horse for my best mule. Taken it right out of the harness. When I tried to argue with them they hit me across the head with a six-shooter."

Rusty rode up close to examine the wound. Gillis said, "If I hadn't had this old wool hat on, it'd have broken my skull like an eggshell."

"Looks bad," Rusty said. "I hope you're not goin' far."

"Headin' for my son's place, over the rise yonder. Him and my daughter-in-law will fix me up. But it makes me madder than hell, losin' that good mule. How do they expect a man to farm without a good pair of mules?"

Tom said, "You're lucky you didn't lose more than a mule. They robbed a store and shot old man Bancroft."

The farmer's jaw dropped. "Old tightwad Bancroft? They must've found out he still had the first dollar he ever made. And most of the ones since." He seemed to regret his words. "I hope he ain't dead."

Tom shook his head. "Don't know. But I expect you'll be gettin' your mule back. I doubt your thief will want to ride him any farther than he has to. He'll be lookin' to steal another horse." He pointed his chin westward. "Who lives yonderway past your place?"

"Young folks named Plumley. Moved in last year and broke out new ground." Gillis's eyes widened as he pondered the possibilities. "I hate to think them young people are in danger. That boy's come and helped me several times. And he's got a mighty sweet little girl for a wife. I'd better come with you."

Tom gripped the farmer's thin shoulder. "No, you'd better go on to your son's place and get took care of. Me and Rusty, we'll see after them young people."

The farmer gave him a better description of the thieves than the town clerk had done. One was tall and lanky with a bushy black beard. The other was of heavier stock and had a brownish mustache with a couple of days' growth of whiskers. An instant before the heavier one had clubbed him, Gillis had seen a long, bluish scar on the back of his hand.

"They both had mean eyes," he warned. "I seen eyes like that in the war. A man with them eyes, there ain't much he won't do."

Tom nodded at Rusty. "Then we'd best not give them time for more than they've already done."

It would have been easy to have missed the Plumley farm had the tracks not led Rusty and Tom to it. The cabin was small, without a dog run, and had been built beneath a hill that hid it from the south. A modest field lay below the cabin. Corn plants stood inches high, for the growing season had barely begun.

Rusty pointed. "The corral yonder. I'd bet you that's Gillis's mule."

No horses were in sight. The thieves were probably gone, but Tom was taking no chances. "That cabin has got no window in the back. We'd better ride up on the blind side."

They dismounted fifty yards away and led their horses, pausing to tie them to a tree. They went the rest of the way with pistols in their hands. They paused to listen a minute before Tom pointed to the front door. Rusty noticed that it was ajar and that it opened to the inside. Oldtimers in the days of frequent Indian trouble usually made sure their doors swung outward so it would be more difficult for anyone to force his way in.

Rusty gave the door a hard shove with his shoulder and stepped quickly inside.

A woman cowered against a back wall. She brought her arms up defensively and screamed. "No more. Please, no more." She covered her face.

Rusty's eyes took a moment to adjust to the room's poor light. The young woman was disheveled, her dress torn from shoulder to waist. As she lowered her arms he saw bruises on her face.

Rusty tried to say something to comfort her, but rage overtook him and left him unable to speak. Tom said gently, "We're here to help you, ma'am. We're not the ones who hurt you." He showed her the badge on his shirt.

She buckled at the knees. Rusty caught her before she went all the way to the floor. He carried her to a wooden chair at the table. Tom said, "There's a pint of whiskey in my saddlebags. You'd better fetch it."

Rusty went out and led the horses up to the house. He

fumbled in the saddlebags, found the bottle, and took a long drink before he carried it inside. He lifted a coffee cup from an open shelf and poured whiskey into it. He held it to the woman's bruised lips. "Drink this. It'll do you good."

She choked but got the whiskey down. She began to calm. Tom asked her, "Where's your husband?"

She seemed unable to look him or Rusty in the eyes. Haltingly she explained that her husband had left early in the morning to look for some strayed cattle. He had not yet returned.

In one sense it might have been a good thing he was gone, Rusty thought. He would probably have resisted the thieves, and they would have killed him.

She said, "We just had one other horse. I heard them run it into the pen and shut the gate. When I went out to see what they were up to . . ." She dropped her head even lower.

Rusty walked to the door and stared out, trying to bring his rage under control. Tom comforted her the best he could.

She cried, "My husband . . . what's he goin' to say?"

Tom said, "If he's any kind of a man he'll know you couldn't help what they did. Wasn't none of it your fault. You got any neighbors, somebody we could send to be with you?"

She said she did, a couple of miles southwest. Tom promised, "We'll swing by and let them know. And don't you worry about them men comin' back. We'll stay on their trail 'til we catch them."

Rusty burned inside and knew it was not because of the whiskey. His hands trembled as he untied his horse. "I've seen some bad men in my time. I've known some that would murder a man without battin' an eye and steal anything that wasn't bolted to the floor. But I've never known any that would do a thing like this to a woman."

Tom grunted and climbed into the saddle. "It's a new world. I liked the old one a heap better."

They found the farm Mrs. Plumley had described and told a middle-aged farmer and his wife what had happened. The woman's eyes filled with tears. "That poor girl. Hitch up, Walter. Let's be gettin' over there."

Riding away, Tom said, "With all the new world's deviltry, there's a lot of the old world left. You can still find kindness when you look for it."

Rusty could not reply. He could not shake the image of terror he had seen in the young woman's face. As he reviewed the scene in his mind, her face became Josie Monahan's.

"We've lost time, Tom. Let's be makin' it up."

Dusk came too quickly. Rusty knew they would soon be unable to see the tracks. "They've got to stop sometime. They've got one fresh horse, but the other one has been pushed all day."

"Ours, too. We set off in such a hurry that we forgot about one thing."

"What's that?"

"We haven't got anything to eat."

Rusty patted the blanket roll tied behind the cantle of his saddle. "We're not plumb out of luck. I brought along some jerky left over from our trip down from the Monahans'."

"Jerky." Tom said the word with distaste.

"It's better than nothin'."

"Just barely."

Rusty said, "Indians can get by on it for days. And I ate a heap of it when I was with the rangers."

"Me, too. I always hoped I'd never have to again."

The tracks were hard to see as daylight faded. The fugitives had stopped to water themselves and their horses at a spring some early settler had rocked in but later abandoned. The remains of a picket cabin leaned precariously, threatening to fall over if given a fair push.

Tom asked, "Feel like sleepin' under a roof tonight?" He said it with a touch of humor, but Rusty was in no mood to appreciate it. Hatred simmered for the men they pursued. He said, "That roof would likely cave in on us. Anyway, I'll bet the place is full of snakes."

Reluctantly he conceded that they had no choice but to stop for the night. After watering the bay he staked it on a long rawhide rope so it could graze within a wide circle. Tom did the same, then said, "How about that jerky?"

Rusty unrolled his blanket and took out a bundle wrapped in oilskin. Jerky was strips of meat dried in the sun, usually tasting more of salt and pepper than of beef. Rangers had often carried it with them on long scouts because they had no guarantee of finding fresh game. Though far from sumptuous, it could sustain life until a man found better.

Tom chewed hard. "I've known of men losin' a tooth on this stuff, but I never saw anybody get fat on it."

Rusty realized Tom was trying to jolly him out of his dark mood, but he was not ready to give it up. There was justice to be done. From the description he tried to imagine the fugitives' faces. He could see only one. In his mind they both looked like Corey Bascom.

He said, "I don't understand men like that. What do you suppose gets into them?"

"Hard to say. War soured some of them. Then there's some raised that way by folks that had coyote blood in them. And some are just born with a deep streak of mean.

Somethin' missin' out of their brain or their heart. They're hard to cure."

"There's one way. Kill them dead and bury them deep."

Tom frowned and pulled his saddle blanket around him.

Rusty awakened long before daylight. He rolled onto one side, then the other, trying to find a comfortable position. There was none. He felt as if he would willingly trade a good horse for a cup of strong coffee. He dared not light a fire that the fugitives might see. It irritated him to hear Tom snoring peacefully. He itched to be on the move but knew it would be futile to set out before he could see tracks.

At last Tom sat up, throwing back the blanket. Only the faintest hint of light showed in the east. The first thing Tom did was to look around for the horses. That instinct was deeply ingrained into men used to living along the frontier, where a good horse was always a temptation to the light-fingered breed, white or red.

Rusty said, "They're still where we staked them. I've been watchin' them for hours."

"You didn't sleep much?"

"Kept seein' that poor woman, and then I'd think of Josie. I kept thinkin' of her in that woman's place."

"At least that woman is still alive."

"And probably half wishin' she wasn't. There's not much worse a man can do to a woman short of leavin' her dead."

Tom threw his saddle onto his horse's back and tightened the cinch. "Sooner or later you've got to come to grips with what happened to Josie. Otherwise it'll drive you crazy."

"I'll come to grips when I find Corey Bascom. But those two renegades will do for a start."

Rusty chewed on a strip of jerky as he set out impatiently in a stiff trot. It should have been Tom's place to pick up the tracks, but Rusty did not give him time. Once when they lost the trail, Tom was the one who picked it up. Rusty was adequate as a tracker, but he had never considered himself in a class with Tom and other frontiersmen of Tom's generation. Or even with Andy.

As the sun moved upward toward midday and the morning warmed, Rusty became uneasy. He could not put his finger on the cause. It was instinct, a feeling that all was not as it should be. "Tom," he said, "let's wait up a minute."

"You see somethin'?"

"I feel somethin', like cold wind on the back of my neck."

"You sure you haven't been listenin' to Andy too much? He's always got a hunch about somethin'. Hears voices talkin' to him. The Indian upbringin', I suppose."

"I don't hear any voices, and there's nothin' I can see. But I've been around Andy enough to know I'd better pay attention. Do you suppose those renegades could've doubled back? They could be comin' up behind us."

It was an old Indian trick. He had used it himself on the two younger Bascom brothers.

Tom's expression showed he took the possibility seriously. He drew the rifle from beneath his leg. "I should've thought of that. It's been done to me more than once."

Tom jerked in the saddle, dropping the rifle. Almost simultaneously Rusty heard a shot from behind. Whirling the bay around, he saw a puff of smoke behind a small clump of low-growing brush. Without taking time to consider, he drew his pistol and put the horse into a run toward the shooter's position. He fired three quick shots into the brush.

A heavyset man screamed and staggered out into the open. He stared with wide, unbelieving eyes before he buckled. He pressed both hands against his chest, trying to stop the flow of blood seeping between his fingers.

Rusty caught a movement from the corner of his eye. He swung down from the saddle, keeping the horse between him and a bearded man who raised up from behind another bush. Rusty dropped to one knee and knelt low, sighting his pistol under the bay's stomach. His shot and the fugitive's seemed to overlap.

Startled, the bay jerked the reins from Rusty's hands and trotted away, leaving Rusty exposed. He felt a searing along his ribs as he heard the man's second shot. He winced from the burn but leveled his pistol and squeezed the trigger. He caught the man squarely in the chest. The fugitive gasped and went down.

Rusty heard Tom's shout. "Look out."

The first man was up on his knees, both bloody hands gripping his pistol. Rusty shot him before he could fire. The man hunched, the pistol sagging in his weakening grip. His dying eyes were fixed on Rusty. His lips moved as if he tried to speak.

He could say nothing Rusty wanted to hear. Rusty stared into the contorted face, and somehow it became the face of Corey Bascom. Rage overwhelmed him. He had emptied the pistol. In his belt was the one he had taken from little Anse Bascom. He drew it and fired once, twice, three times.

Tom spoke behind him, his voice brittle. "For God's sake, how much deader do you think you can kill him?"

The fury that had swept over Rusty slowly receded. He stared at the dead man lying almost at his feet. "I must've gone crazy for a minute."

"I never saw you like this. You scared me."

"I've scared myself a little, I think."

"Have you sobered up now?"

"Sober enough to remember that you got hit by the first shot. How bad is it?"

Tom gripped his right arm below the shoulder. His sleeve was red, his hand bloodied. "Missed the bone. But I need to get this blood stopped or you'll be carryin' me home like a baby."

Tom squatted while Rusty cut the sleeve off at the shoulder and wrapped it tightly around the wound.

Rusty said, "I'd better get you back to that Plumley place where you can be tended to good and proper."

"And soon. I can feel sickness comin' on. Before long I may not be able to stay in the saddle." Tom jerked his head toward the nearest of the two fugitives. "Somethin' needs to be done about them."

"Let somebody else come bury them, or leave them for the varmints. They're kin to the coyotes anyway."

Rusty gave Tom a boost up onto his horse. The effort brought a sharp pain to his side and reminded him that a slug had grazed his ribs. The bay had trotted off a little way and stepped on the reins. There he had stopped. Rusty fetched him, then looked around for the horses the renegades had ridden. He found them tied to a bush, out of sight from the ambush spot. He checked the saddlebags and found a considerable amount of money. Loot from the store robbery, he assumed. He tied one horse's reins to the other's tail and led the pair back to where Tom waited, slumped in the saddle.

"Feel like you can make it?"

Tom looked pale, but he gritted his teeth. "I've had a wasp bite worse than this."

Setting out, Rusty reached inside his shirt to feel his ribs. The slight blood flow had stopped. The wound was sore to the touch, but he doubted that a rib had been cracked. He would heal.

They had ridden perhaps a quarter of a mile when a horseman appeared. He approached them warily. He was young, a farmer by the look of him. He eased when he saw the badge on Tom's shirt. "I heard shootin'. You-all catch up to those bandits?"

Rusty said, "We caught them."

The young man nodded toward the two led horses. "One of them is mine. They stole him from my place."

Tom asked, "Your name Plumley?"

"Yes sir."

"How's your wife?"

His face darkened. "Fair, considerin' what they done to her. Some neighbors came to help. I thought I'd try to catch up with you-all and be there for the kill. Since you have their horses, I reckon you caught them already."

Rusty said, "If it's any satisfaction to you they're layin' back yonder a little ways. We didn't have time to bury them. The sheriff needs attention."

"I'll help you get him to our place. Later on I'll take a shovel and do the buryin'. It'll pleasure me to throw dirt on them." Riding along, he brooded in silence. Finally he said, "They don't deserve no Christian ceremony. I'll make sure they won't see Resurrection mornin', either. I'll bury them facedown."

{ NINE }

Approaching a neat row of canvas tents lined beneath the protective branches of huge pecan trees fronting the San Saba River, Andy Pickard felt apprehensive. "We've come a long ways for me to get turned down. Are you sure the rangers aren't lookin' for somebody with more experience?"

Rusty had always said Len Tanner had the faith of the mustard seed, whatever that meant. Tanner declared, "They'll be tickled to have you. How many fellers your age can brag that they've been as far and seen as much as you have? Time I get through tellin' them about you they'll be rollin' out a red carpet and beggin' you to sign up."

That was one thing worrying Andy. Tanner never knew when enough was enough. He could take a good idea and talk it to a slow and painful death. "I oughtn't to've let you get me into this."

In truth, Tanner hadn't used much persuasion. Andy had toyed with the notion of becoming a ranger from the time he first heard they might be reorganized. But the closer he got, the less confidence he felt.

Tanner said, "Too late to turn back. They've seen us already."

Andy was aware that three men were watching them. He tried to brace up his nerve. "Which do you figure is the headquarters tent?"

"The biggest one, naturally. Officers always get a little the best of it."

The best did not look much better than the others to Andy. Most of the tents were tepee shaped, lined evenly where the heavy foliage would provide partial shade in the afternoon. Beyond the tents and between the trees he could see sun reflected off the clear waters of the San Saba. An officer stood before the larger tent, talking to a couple of men. At least, Andy took him for an officer because his stance indicated authority.

The rangers had no official uniform. They wore what they would wear in civilian life as cowboys or farmers or town merchants. Tanner had told him they did not even have an official badge. Some men made their own out of Mexican silver pesos. Others did not believe they needed one. They expected boldness and a serious demeanor to cow most adversaries. The rest would be dealt with according to the demands of the moment.

Tanner said, "That'd be the captain, I imagine."

The officer turned his attention to the two horsemen. Tanner made a poor excuse of a salute. "Private Tanner reportin' for duty, sir. And I've fetched along a recruit you'll be glad to have in the company."

The officer frowned. "That is a determination I'll make for myself. As for you, Tanner, your enlistment started over a week ago. If you expect to be paid for time absent, . . ."

"Couldn't help it, sir. Things came up. But you don't owe me no more than you figure I got comin'." Money meant little to Tanner except in terms of what he could buy with it, usually as soon as he had the cash in hand.

The officer lowered his voice. "I've been notified of your past service record, so I'll overlook your tardiness. This time." He turned a critical gaze upon Andy. "You say I'll want this young man as a recruit. Tell me why."

Tanner dismounted. "I could talk all day, tellin' you why you want to sign up Andy Pickard."

"I had rather you didn't. Just the pertinent facts will be enough."

"Well sir, in the first place he rides like an Indian. Truth is, it was the Indians taught him. And shoot? He can knock a flea off of a dog's ear at fifty yards and never singe a hair. And he's got more nerve than a mouthful of bad teeth. Why, he once slipped into a Comanche camp and—"

The officer raised his hand. "Let him speak for himself. Tanner, you may put your blankets and gear into that farthest tent yonder, then take your horse out and turn him into the remuda. You'll find it on grass west of camp."

Tanner accepted the order with a nod. "Whatever you

say, Captain." He glanced at Andy. "Now, don't you be shy. Tell him everything he ought to know about you. I'll see you after you been sworn in."

The officer watched in silence until Tanner led his horse beyond hearing. "Usually I am suspicious of a big talker, but I am told Tanner was a good ranger in the old days."

"There's a lot more to him than just talk."

"But you are obviously too young to have been in ranger service before. So come into the office and tell me why I should accept you into that service now."

Andy tied Long Red to a rough hitching rack made of live-oak branches. He followed the officer through the open canvas door of the tent the captain called an office. He took off his hat and twisted it in his hands. "First off, sir, Len stretched the facts a little. I can ride, but just about everybody I know can do that."

"How is your shooting eye?"

"Ain't braggin', sir, but I don't generally need two shots. Rusty Shannon taught me not to waste cartridges. They cost too much."

The officer's eyebrows went up. "Rusty Shannon, you say?"

"Yes sir, he's the one raised me, after the Indians. Used to be a ranger along with Len Tanner."

"I've met Shannon. Spotless reputation. I hope he is well."

"Healthy enough, but he lost the woman he was fixin' to marry. It tore him up a right smart."

"Sorry to hear that. But we're supposed to talk about you. What's this about an Indian raising?"

Andy explained that he had been carried off by raiding Comanches when he was small and lived with them until he was around twelve or thirteen. He decided not to go into the circumstances under which he had fallen into Rusty's hands. He doubted the captain would take kindly to the fact that he was trying to emulate his Comanche brothers on a horse-stealing foray. Most people did not like to hear that part of his story.

The captain said, "I'm glad you were rescued. A lot of young people remained prisoners. Grew up Comanche, ruined for life."

Rescued was not exactly the word for it. *Captured* would be a better description, for at first Andy had been an unwilling convert to the white man's road. He had tried to escape back to Comanchería. He judged that this was another aspect of his story best left out. Most white people did not understand how a boy could prefer living in a tepee and following the buffalo with a band of what they considered wild savages most akin to the wolves that also stalked the shaggy herds.

The captain frowned again. "How do you feel about the Comanches now?"

They were still his brothers, most of them, but this was something else the captain would not appreciate. "I've been away from them a long time."

"Part of our job will be to protect settlers from Indian raids. Mainly Comanches to the north, Apaches west and south. If it came to that, would you be able to fight them?" He stared at Andy with an intensity that would not permit evasion.

"I don't know, sir. I guess I could if I had to."

"I need a better answer than that. I can't afford to have men in my command that I could not depend on in an emergency."

"I'll do my duty, whatever that is."

"No matter how difficult it may be for you?"

"If it breaks my back, sir."

The captain chewed his lip in deep thought. "From what

I know of Rusty Shannon he would have made you tough enough to do whatever has to be done, however unpleasant it may be."

"He tried awful hard."

"Very well, there are certain requirements to be met. First, you must furnish a horse."

"That's him, the sorrel I tied outside."

"It may be that the state will furnish weapons in the future, but for now you must arm yourself."

"There's a rifle on my saddle. Got a six-shooter and a skinnin' knife on my belt." Tanner had made sure he brought everything he needed.

"Then it would appear you meet the principal specifications. We need to fill out and sign some papers and administer the oath. Have you ever taken an oath?"

"I swore a time or two to tell the truth and nothin' else."

"The ranger oath is a solemn obligation between you and the state of Texas, taken in the sight of God. I don't know what God's punishment is if you break it, but Texas's punishment can be severe."

"If I make you a promise, I won't back away from it."

"Spoken like a good Texan. Now let's see about this enlistment form. I assume you can read."

"Fair to middlin'." Andy's reading ability was about average, he thought, for most Texans aside from teachers, storekeepers, and lawyers. Schooling was sporadic. Many people living in the country and in small towns had no more than a smattering of formal education. Rusty had seen to it that Andy took schooling whenever it was available.

The captain filled out the forms. Andy ran his finger down the pages, lips moving as he slowly read to himself what was written. He signed where the officer pointed.

The captain said, "You understand that you are being

accepted on a conditional basis? I have the right to dismiss you at any time you fail to obey orders or live up to expectations."

"Any time I feel like I'm not totin' my load you won't have to fire me. I'll quit."

"That's the proper attitude for a ranger of the Texas frontier batallion."

The captain administered the oath after calling up two rangers to stand witness. He said, "There is room for you in the farthest tent, where I sent your friend Tanner."

The two rangers shook Andy's hand and welcomed him into the company. One introduced himself as Sergeant Bill Holloway. He was a tall, broad-shouldered, flat-bellied man of roughly Rusty's age. His face was burnished brown. His pale blue turkey-tracked eyes had a permanent squint brought on by life in the Texas sun. He said, "I heard you mention Rusty Shannon. I rode with him under old Captain Whitfield 'til the war drawed me into the army. Southern, of course. How come he ain't joined up again?"

"He's had some bad luck lately. Got about all his plate will hold." Andy decided to say no more until he had time to size up the company. He had already told the captain more than he intended. Rusty might not want his personal troubles advertised all over the country.

Holloway said, "A couple more things the captain may not have mentioned. No drinkin' in camp."

"I don't drink."

"And no card playin'."

"Never learned no card games."

The sergeant shook his head as if he could not believe. "I guess you don't cuss, either."

"Yes sir, I do. Sometimes it's the only thing that helps."

The sergeant's squinty eyes laughed, and his mustache lifted at the edges. "That's all right. Just do it judiciously."

He turned toward the tent but stopped. "Know any Comanche cusswords?"

"A few."

"I wish you'd teach them to me. Sometimes I use up all I know in English and Spanish and it's still not enough."

Andy untied his blankets and a small war bag of possessions from the saddle. He expected a row of cots inside the tent, but he saw only bedrolls spread on the ground.

Holloway said, "Find you an empty place anywhere. When you're tired enough, the grass will feel like a feather bed."

Andy had slept on the ground during his years with the Comanches and many times since when he was on the move. The Indians had considered it healthy to lie directly upon Mother Earth. A bed put distance between a man and nature, though Andy enjoyed the luxury when he had it.

Holloway said, "A bed just spoils you. Can't take one with you on scout, and the captain sees to it that the nights are short anyway. He'll have you up and goin' before daylight."

Andy said, "I've always heard that beds are dangerous. Lots of people die in them." He dropped his blankets on the ground near the back of the tent, beside the ones he recognized as Tanner's. "How's the food?"

"We have a good cook, blacker than the ace of spades. Old Bo's biscuits would make the angels want to give up their wings and come back to earth."

"Len Tanner will be tickled to know about that."

"I remember Tanner, too. He ever run out of conversation?"

"He hasn't yet."

"He's a man I'd want beside me in a fight, but I wouldn't want to have to listen to him talk about it afterwards."

Andy dropped his saddle on the ground and hopped up

on Long Red's bare back. The sergeant pointed. "You'll find the horse herd out that way. One of the drawbacks of ranger service is standin' your day of horse guard every so often."

It stood to reason that the rangers would be careful of their horses. A ranger afoot was essentially useless. Though Indian raids had become less common, they still occurred from time to time. Comanches and Kiowas continued to steal south from the high plains and the reservations to add to their wealth, measured in horses. White horse thieves had increased even as Indian activity had declined. In a state still short of cash money, horses were a leading medium of exchange.

Glancing back once, Andy saw that Holloway still watched him. He decided serving under the sergeant should be pleasant enough, for in some ways he reminded Andy of Rusty. The captain seemed more businesslike and abrupt, but that was probably necessary for an officer. He could not be just one of the boys and still expect them to jump to his command.

Andy met Tanner walking back, carrying his bridle over his thin shoulder. Tanner said, "Looks like the captain taken you in."

"For forty dollars a month."

"Save it and you'll get rich. If you live for a hundred years." Tanner's face took on a worried twist. "You'll find one of your old friends on horse guard out yonder."

"An old friend?"

"Farley Brackett. He's always wanted your horse. He's liable to take him and ride off."

Resentment stung Andy. Of all the people he might run into, Farley Brackett would have been among his last choices. "If he lays a hand on Long Red, I'll . . ." He could not think of anything severe enough to say. "How'd he ever come to be a ranger? The state police rode some good horses to death tryin' to catch him."

"They weren't tryin' near as hard as they made out. They took care not to crowd him too close. The state police are long gone anyway, and good riddance."

"He shot a couple of them that I know of."

"Scallywags and scoundrels. Most folks didn't see it as a crime. Shootin' state police was looked on as a public improvement."

"Well, if he leaves me alone I'll leave him alone."

"I don't suppose the captain said what time they serve supper around here?"

"I didn't ask. Probably couldn't eat anything now." The thought of Farley Brackett being here had already begun to work on Andy's stomach.

He and Brackett saw each other at about the same time. Brackett and another ranger had the horses scattered loosely, giving them room to graze. Brackett rode over to meet him. His attention seemed more on the sorrel than on Andy.

"Howdy, Indian," he said. "You been takin' good care of my horse?"

Andy could think of no suitable answer, so he offered none. Once, under close pursuit by Union soldiers and state police, Brackett left his own tired horse and took one belonging to Rusty. In return, Brackett's father had given Rusty this sorrel, which Rusty turned over to Andy.

Andy demanded, "With your record, why did the rangers ever take you in?"

"They decided that anybody who had killed two carpetbag state policemen must be all right."

A long scar ran down one side of Brackett's face, result of a wartime saber cut. Deeper internal scars had never healed. Andy had been a reluctant witness when state police cut down Jeremiah Brackett in his own home one dark night, mistaking the father for the son. He could sympathize with Farley's bitterness, but he could not excuse the man's unreasoning violence, or his coveting the sorrel horse.

Brackett's gaze was hard. Andy tried to match it. Brackett said, "I'm surprised the captain accepted you. Did you tell him about your Comanche upbringin'?"

"I did. It's no secret."

"Did you tell him that the first time we get into a scrap with the Comanches you're liable to run off and join them against us?"

"I promised him I'd do my duty. He took me at my word."

"The captain doesn't know you, but I do. If the day comes and you even act like you're fixin' to join your butcherin' brothers, I'll shoot you myself."

"Me and you won't get along. That's plain to see. Maybe one of us needs to ask for a transfer to a different company."

"I was here first. You goin' to turn that horse loose, or not?"

"That's what I came out here for. He'd better still be here in the mornin'." Andy slid from Long Red's back and pulled the bridle down over the ears, then slipped the bits from the horse's mouth. The sorrel hesitated just a moment before turning and joining the other horses. Andy suspected he would not get along with most of them. Long Red tried to dominate whatever company he was in. He would make a friend or two and buffalo the rest of the horses into staying beyond biting and kicking distance.

Andy gave Brackett a final glance but knew nothing more to say. Brackett would be a thorn in his side so long as both of them remained with this company. Andy resolved that he could be a thorn, too.

We'll see which of us hollers *quit* first, he thought.

He walked the three or four hundred yards back to camp. Tanner sat on a crude bench made of branches tied with rawhide strips. He was cleaning his rifle. "I didn't hear no shootin'."

"I didn't do any. But I might if he ever crowds me too hard."

Tanner used a ramrod to push a cloth patch down the rifle barrel. "Maybe it wasn't such a smart idee, me bringin' you along to join the rangers. It's too late to back out, but maybe if I told the captain you lied about your age, . . ."

"I didn't. I told him I don't know just how old I am. So maybe I'm guessin' a little on the high side. That's not the same as lyin'."

"Crowds the hell out of it, though." Tanner shrugged. "Always try to stay where I'll be between you and Farley Brackett. If it looks like trouble is fixin' to break out, I'll have a chance to step in."

Andy disliked the notion that he might not be able to take care of himself. "The man who tries to break up a fight sometimes gets hit from both sides."

"I dodge pretty good."

Andy did not doubt that Tanner would come to his defense no matter the cost. He would not want Tanner hurt on his account. "I'll try to keep my distance from him."

"I ain't the only friend you've got in camp. The Morris boys are in this company. Jim and Johnny are out on a scout."

"Scoutin' for what?"

"Indian sign, horse thieves, robbers, whatever there is. We're west of most settlements here. Good country for them bunch quitters who work in the moonlight so folks don't see what they're up to."

It had taken Andy and Tanner the better part of a week to ride here from the farm, taking their time. They had seen few people the last couple of days. Andy could remember the Comanches bringing their families down from the plains into these limestone, cedar, and live-oak hills to hunt. After white settlement began in earnest they came mainly to raid.

Tanner laid the rifle across his lap and glanced back over his shoulder. "They say there's good fishin' in the San Saba. Catfish so thick they'll crawl out onto the bank to nip at your bait."

Living with the Indians, Andy had spent most of his time in a high, dry country where fish were not plentiful. With Rusty down on the Colorado he had learned to throw a line in the river periodically to vary the menu from venison, pork, and beef. The catching had been all right, but he had not liked the cleaning. It seemed a lot of work for a little bit of eating.

The black cook walked out from the mess tent and struck an iron rod against a dangling piece of wagon tire, signaling time for supper. He gave a wordless holler as if he were calling hogs.

Tanner said, "Let's go see if the boys was lyin' about how good that cook is."

The rangers who lined up were all strangers to Andy, though Tanner knew a few of them by name. No one remained a stranger to Tanner for long. They were a mixed group, mostly young. He saw none who seemed to be nearing middle age. Two or three looked as if they did not have to shave often. That made Andy feel a little less concerned about his youth.

"Fellers," Tanner said, "I want you to meet my compadre, Andy Pickard. Weaned on buffalo milk, brought up by wolves, ripped the hide off of a live grizzly with his bare hands and made himself a bearskin coat. He'd be wearin' it today if the weather wasn't so warm."

Embarrassed, Andy could only stand quietly and look innocent. Sergeant Holloway grinned. "Was that a full-grown grizzly, or was it only half-grown, like that story?"

Andy saw that the rangers were going along with the joke. That eased his self-consciousness. He said, "It wasn't near as tall as Len's yarn. Next time he tells it it'll be two bears."

The grinning sergeant clapped a hand on Andy's shoulder. "Grab you a plate. You never want to miss a chance to eat. There'll be days when you won't get to." He pushed Andy ahead of himself in the line.

Andy decided he need not worry about being accepted. He warmed to the friendliness in the faces around him. He said, "I want to do a good job. Any time you-all see a way I can do better, tell me."

"You can bet on that. This outfit ain't up to strength, so every man has got to pull extra weight to make up the difference." Holloway paused, thinking. "Seems to me I remember some Pickards that used to farm down in the lower country, around Gonzales seems like. Any kin?"

Andy hesitated. "Might be. The only kin I ever met was an uncle. We didn't like each other much."

He did not want to disclose that the uncle had come to see him when he was recuperating from the broken leg that had caused him to fall back into Texan hands. The uncle had rejected him on the grounds that Andy's long exposure to Indian ways had made him unfit for life among white people. Andy had resisted any further attempts to be brought into contact with his blood family. He regarded his real family as a band of Comanches and Rusty Shannon. He also felt an emotional kinship with the Monahans, more than he could ever have with any Pickards who might condescend to accept him.

Holloway said, "You keep an eye on the captain. Watch what he does and learn from it. Sometimes he'll tell you what to do. Other times he'll let you think for yourself."

"Sounds a lot like Rusty Shannon."

"I wish we had Rusty in this outfit. Why didn't you bring him with you?"

"I wish I had." Rusty would be better off in this company than torturing his soul with grief and hatred and hunting for a man who by now might be a thousand miles away. "Right now he's got his own snakes to kill."

After supper Andy heard somebody tuning up a musical instrument. He was a little surprised to find Sergeant Holloway with a fiddle in his hand, adjusting the strings to conform with a banjo held by a young ranger. Holloway had not struck him as a lover of music. Soon the two were playing. Most of the other rangers gathered to listen. Even the captain emerged from his tent and sat on a canvas stool.

Andy found the music pleasant. He tapped his feet to the rhythm.

Farley Brackett ruined his good mood. He said, "I'd've thought a rawhide drum was more to your likin'."

Andy got up and walked to his tent.

{ TEN }

Rusty had never been to Fort Worth before. About the nearest place he had visited had been Jacksboro during his ranger days. He knew that the town had begun with a military post on the Trinity River before the war. It had grown as farming and ranching spread westward and northward toward the Cross Timbers country and the Red River. In recent times it had become an important stopping point for cattle drives coming up from the southern part of the state on their way to the new railheads in Kansas. It was a resupply center for cattle outfits and freighters, for military units on their way west. There was even talk that a railroad would be coming in soon to lessen the need for trailing herds farther north.

Fort Worth had gained a reputation as a wide-open town where a man could do just about anything he was big enough to get away with. If a little short in stature he could make up the deficit by carrying one of Mr. Colt's inventions on his hip or in his boot top.

This was one of several trips Rusty had made on the basis of tips that Corey Bascom had been seen in one place or another. It was said he had been observed playing poker in Fort Worth's red-light district, beginning to be known as Hell's Half Acre. It was a name common to such districts in many frontier towns. Though previous searches had turned up empty, Rusty started each new one with strong hope. Now hope was about all he had left. The long ride had sapped his energy. Only the image of Corey Bascom kept him in the saddle mile after weary mile.

Each failure diminished his strength but increased his determination. To quit would mean that all his effort had been wasted. He had invested too much of himself in the search to give it up.

He rode through the thinly populated outskirts to a chorus of barking dogs and found a wagon yard a short distance from the courthouse. A young man of about Andy's age met him at the barn's open door. "Put up your horse, mister?"

"I'd be much obliged. And I'll spread my bedroll here

tonight, too, if that's all right." He did not want to squander money on a hotel room.

"Sure. May not get a lot of sleep, though. There's two big cow outfits hit town today with herds on the way to the Indian nations. Apt to be a lot of whoopin' and hollerin'."

Rusty shrugged. "I'll just have to put up with it. Town looks a little quiet right now though."

"It's too early in the day. You lookin' for excitement?"

"Mainly lookin' for where the excitement takes place." If Corey was here, he would most likely be found where the action was.

"Wait 'til night. You'll hear it. All you have to do is follow the noise. Or follow a bunch of cowboys. They'll lead you to it."

This would be the drovers' last chance for relaxation and recreation before they hit the Red River and Indian territory. Leaving here they faced a month and more of toil and monotony on the long, dusty trail before they reached the railroad. It stood to reason they would want to let off some pent-up steam and have something to talk about on the tiresome miles ahead of them.

The hostler directed Rusty to a barbershop where he could bathe and have his red hair trimmed. He found a washerwoman to scrub the dirt and sweat out of the clothes he had worn all the way up here. Then he set out walking the dirt streets, locating the saloons and gambling houses where Corey might be. Those he entered appeared to have little business as yet.

A gambler playing solitaire looked up hopefully as Rusty entered. "Interested in a little game, friend?"

"Maybe later. I'm lookin' for a friend of mine. Maybe he's sat in on your game. Name of Corey Bascom?"

The gambler's eyes narrowed. "I know him, but I ain't seen him in a while. You say he's a friend of yours?"

"More like an acquaintance."

"Corey ain't the kind that makes many friends. Nice enough feller, after his fashion, but you got to watch him all the time. He'll cold deck you if you don't."

"That sounds like him. You're sure you haven't seen him lately?"

"No, and I ain't lookin' for him." Suspicion in the man's eyes indicated that he took a dim view of anyone who might be a friend of Corey's. "Even if he's in town he ain't likely to come in this place. He wore out his welcome at my table a long time ago."

Rusty was tempted to ask what Corey had done to earn the gambler's displeasure, but he had not come here to provoke a row, at least with anyone besides Corey.

The gambler said, "On the off chance that he shows up, do you want me to tell him you're lookin' for him?"

"I'd rather you didn't."

The gambler's attitude changed. He smiled thinly. "It's like that, hunh? What's your name, friend?"

"Shannon. Rusty Shannon."

"If I see or hear anything about Corey I'll try to get word to you. Goin' to be in town long?"

"That depends."

"Well, good huntin'."

Rusty returned to the wooden sidewalk and surveyed the street. The buildings were primarily modest one-story frame structures, most of them strangers to paint. A few log houses probably dated back to the town's earliest days. From where he stood he could not see a church anywhere.

A woman in a flimsy gown leaned out of an open window and smiled at him. She said, "Gettin' an early start?"

"Just killin' time."

"Me, too. Goin' to be lots of cowboys in town tonight.

I'm apt to get awful busy. But right now I've got lots of time."

He knew an invitation when he heard it. He said, "Thanks, but you'd better get your rest while you can."

Walking away, he heard her call after him, "Later on you'll get to thinkin' about what you missed, and you'll hate yourself."

He passed a uniformed policeman twirling a nightstick. The officer gave him a nod. Then Rusty heard him address the woman by name. He told her, "Them cow outfits'll be in after a while. You better get ready for a busy night."

"I'm always ready. If you find any of them lookin' for a place to light, steer them my way. It'll be worth your while."

"It always is."

Rusty grunted disapprovingly to himself. He had heard that many city policemen shared in the proceeds from illegal activities in return for looking the other way or even, as in this case, participating. It was against all the principles he had learned in his years as a ranger. But that was Fort Worth's misfortune and none of his own.

He walked into a false-fronted building whose sign proclaimed that it offered the finest in spiritous liquors, beer, and hot lunch. It also offered a billiard table. He heard the crack of billiard balls and looked toward the rear of the room where two young men who ought to be at work this time of the day were engaged in a heated game.

A middle-aged man of ample girth and broader smile approached him. "Howdy, friend. If you're lookin' for the best drinks in Fort Worth you've come to the right place."

Something about him struck Rusty as being familiar. The man gave Rusty a moment's intense scrutiny and said, "Seems to me I ought to know you. Sure as hell I do. You're

Rusty Shannon. Used to serve under old Captain Burmeister in the rangers."

Rusty remembered. "Right. And so did you." He struggled to remember the name.

"Simon Newfield." The man extended his hand and almost broke Rusty's fingers. "Scouted some with you and old Len Tanner. Reckon he's still alive?"

"Still alive and still talkin'." Rusty grinned, old memories coming back in a rush. He looked around the saloon. It was the fanciest he had seen here, or just about anywhere else he had been. "It's a cinch you didn't buy this place from your ranger savin's."

"No, I came into a windfall." Newfield looked around to see if anyone could hear. "Right at the end of the war I captured me a Yankee army paymaster. Took the money in the name of the Confederacy. But the Confederacy folded, so there wasn't anybody I could legally give it to that needed it worse than I did."

"They're probably still lookin' for it."

"I figured it like a loan. I'll pay it back to them someday when I feel like I've got rich enough. Ain't there yet. What brings you to Fort Worth? I never seen you here before."

Rusty lost his grin. "Lookin' for a man."

"Are you a ranger again? Maybe I oughtn't to've told you about that paymaster."

"No, I'm not a ranger. This is a personal matter. Do you know Corey Bascom?"

Newfield sobered. "Lots of people around here know Corey. Some to their profit and some to their regret. I take it that in your case it's regret."

"He killed the woman I was about to marry."

"That's tough. It doesn't sound much like Corey. Robbery and cheatin' at cards are more his style. But I suppose anything is possible when a man has been listenin' to the owls hoot long enough."

"Seen him lately?"

"He was in here two, maybe three, weeks ago. Never saw him lookin' so sour. Got in a game with a man that was better at cards than he was, and better with a gun, too. Seemed like a stupid thing to do, but Corey tried to egg him into a gunfight. The other feller wasn't lookin' to bloody himself, though. He hit Corey across the head with the barrel of his six-shooter and laid him out cold. Said there wasn't any profit in killin' fools and drunks. Corey left town the next day with a knot so big he couldn't put his hat on. I ain't seen him since."

"Any idea where he went?"

"None at all. Never saw Corey act like that before. It was almost like he was tryin' to get himself killed. Doesn't make any sense."

"It doesn't make sense that he'd come here in the open like that. He's bound to know he's been posted for murder."

"That wouldn't make any difference in the Acre. Jesse James himself could come here and not be bothered. The police keep their hands off of this district. It's a sanctuary, sort of, like church."

"Not like any church I ever saw."

"Poor choice of words. The point is, even if you're not the law anymore, it wouldn't be a good idea to let everybody know you're lookin' for Corey. There's some that would kill you on general principles whether they like Corey or not."

"I'll try not to make a show of it."

"Good. Now let's have that drink. We'll toast old times, and better ones."

* * *

While he waited for nightfall Rusty killed time talking with Newfield about long-ago days. Though he did not feel hungry, he partook of the lunch on one end of the bar, boiled eggs, loaf bread, and sliced ham. He washed it down with a beer that would not leave him impaired in the way that whiskey might.

With dusk the crowds began milling. A dozen or so cowboys lined up at the bar. Some moved to the billiard table. Rusty watched them a while, listening to their laughter and loud talk. Most were young, not of an age to be in a place like this. He envied them their youth but wished they were spending it and their money more wisely.

He told Newfield, "I'd better get started if I'm goin' to find Corey."

"Chances are he's not in town. If he was I might've heard. But you won't know 'til you look."

Rusty visited every saloon he could locate, down to a couple of dark dives that made the hair bristle on the back of his neck. Now and then he saw someone who at first glance in dim light looked like Corey but proved not to be. His hopes rose, then fell. Each time they fell they sank lower than before.

He finally returned to Newfield's. The ex-ranger did not have to ask. Rusty knew his face betrayed his disappointment.

Newfield said, "You could hunt every night for two or three months and never find him. You got that much time?"

"No. I ought to be home tendin' the farm. But I've got to look."

"There's no guarantee that he ever will come back here. Gettin' his hair combed with a gun barrel may have turned him away from Fort Worth forever. He could've gone down to San Antonio or maybe over to Fort Smith, even up the trail to Kansas, wherever he might find a card game. If there's paper out on him for murder he might even have sailed to South America like some of them die-hard old Confederates did. You'd just as well try and chase a cloud."

Rusty sighed. "I'll give it another day or two. If I don't find any sign of him, I'll go home."

"I don't like to mess in other people's business, but I'll keep my ear to the ground. If I hear anything I'll let you know."

"I'd be obliged."

"Just don't kill him in here if you can help it, or get killed in here yourself. It's hell to get the blood cleaned up after it's soaked into the wood floor."

Rusty went to the wagon yard and rolled out his blanket on the ground. As the young hostler had said, the place became noisy as cowboys began showing up, full of fun and Fort Worth whiskey. By the time the last of them dropped off to sleep, Rusty had lost the urge. He sat up staring into the darkness and thinking of Josie.

He made up the next day by napping much of the morning after the cowboys departed. At dark he began repeating the rounds he had made the night before. By midnight he had visited every potential place twice. He did not find Corey. He had a strong feeling that Newfield was right. Corey might never come back here.

He decided to give it one more night.

In the late afternoon he returned to Newfield's place. The former ranger came out from behind the bar to meet him, wiping a glass with a white cloth. "Did my boy find you?"

"I haven't seen any boy."

"I sent him out huntin' for you. I got word that somebody named Bascom is in town. Don't know if it's Corey or not."

Rusty's heart jumped. "Where's he at?

"One of the girls from Fat Beulah's house was in here to buy a case of whiskey. She said a man named Bascom is bedded down with a girl over there. Corey used to take a fancy to the women. He knew every sportin' house in town."

"Thanks, Simon. I'll remember you in my will."

"You better write one before you tangle with Corey. He's tricky."

Rusty was out the door and a couple of houses down the street before he realized he did not know where Fat Beulah's was. He stopped a cowboy and asked. The cowboy pointed. "It's that house yonder. But they got a prettier class of girls over at Miss Flo's place."

Rusty examined his pistol before walking up to the house. The low porch was ornate, with freshly painted gingerbread trim. Three lanterns hung from the edge, but they had not yet been lighted for the evening. He peered through the oval glass in the front door before he entered.

A very large woman sat in an oversized rocking chair, darning a black stocking large enough for two normal legs. Flame in a kerosene lamp gave her light to see her work. She looked up at Rusty but did not stand. "Come in. Come in. It's a little early, but what the hell? Never too early for pleasure or business."

"I'm lookin' for somebody."

"We've got lots of somebodys here. Dark, light, one for any preference. What's yours?"

"It's a man I'm lookin' for, name of Bascom."

Her expression quickly changed from welcome to near hostility. "Don't know no Bascom. Most of our customers go by the name of Smith. Now, as long as you're not interested in my girls I want you to get out of here. If you got troubles, take them someplace else."

"Not 'til I find Bascom."

"All I got to do is blow this whistle and half a dozen policemen will come runnin'." She showed him a whistle on a string, half hidden by the pearls around her thick neck.

He grabbed the whistle and pulled. The string broke, but not before biting into her neck a little. He drew his pistol.

She looked at it fearfully but summoned courage to say, "You wouldn't shoot a lady."

"No, but I'd shoot that lamp on the table beside you. Probably start the damndest fire you ever saw." He thumbed back the hammer.

She slumped deeper into her chair. "All right. The man you're lookin' for is upstairs with Cindy Lou, second door on your right. Only don't kill him here, please. It'll give this place a bad reputation."

Rusty hurried up the stairs, knowing it would not take long for Fat Beulah to work up nerve to fetch the police. The pistol still in his hand, he paused at the door, then kicked it open.

A woman screamed. A man sat up in bed, flinging a blanket aside and reaching for a gunbelt hanging across a high-backed chair. Rusty grabbed it first and flung it out the broken door. "Now, Corey . . ."

His finger tightened on the trigger.

He saw then that this was not Corey Bascom. A strong resemblance was there, but the face was not Corey's. He could not stop his finger from tightening, but he tipped the muzzle up in time. The pistol cracked, and a bullet smashed into the ceiling. The woman screamed again and covered her face with the blanket.

Newley Bascom blanched, his body shaking. "My God, Shannon, don't kill me."

Rusty recognized him as Corey's brother, the one who along with younger brother Anse had tried to ambush him.

He found himself trembling a little, too. "I came awful close. I thought you were Corey."

"I'm not. I'm Newley."

"Where is Corey?"

Newley fought to bring his voice under control. "I don't know. I came here lookin' for him. Ain't seen him in weeks."

"I don't know if I ought to believe you or not. I think I ought to just shoot you on general principles."

Newley began to cry.

Rusty felt pity, then disgust. He sensed that Newley was telling him the truth, badly as he wanted not to believe.

But he had to believe. He backed up a step and said, "If you ever do see Corey, tell him he can't go so far that Rusty Shannon won't find him. And when I find him, I'm goin' to kill him." He waved the muzzle at Newley for emphasis. Newley whimpered.

Rusty told the girl, "You ought to give him child's rates. He's not but half a man."

He started out the door. He saw Fat Beulah and a policeman coming up the stairs. He turned back and shouted at Newley and the girl. "Now go on with what you were doin'."

He knew Newley couldn't, not now.

He gave Fat Beulah five dollars for the broken door and the policeman a like amount for his trouble. He did not have the heart to make all the saloons and gambling houses again tonight. He sensed that it would be futile.

Frustration was like acid foaming in his stomach. He just wanted to put Fort Worth behind him. He wondered how far he could ride before dark.

{ ELEVEN }

The captain gave Andy a little time to settle in and begin to feel at home before he sent him out of camp on any special duties. Unlike military service, the rangers did not require marching and close-order drill, but they did encourage target practice. The state offered a supply of ammunition to help make up for the fact that the men so far had to provide their own weaponry. Targets were marked on scrap bits of board and nailed to the heavy trunk of a pecan tree. A bank of earth behind would stop stray bullets, though any shot that missed hitting the board threw the shooter's marksmanship into question.

Andy watched several rangers take their turns. The first board was soon splintered so badly it had to be replaced. Tanner missed centering the target by only about an inch.

Andy said, "Good shot."

Tanner waved off the compliment. "Sun got in my eyes or I'd've hit it plumb center."

Farley Brackett's turn came before Andy's. He hit the target almost squarely in the middle. Turning away, he ejected the spent cartridge from his rifle. "All right, Indian boy, let's see if you can even hit the board."

Riled, Andy resolved to do better. He took a deep breath, sighted down the barrel, and squeezed the trigger. The bullet cut into the edge of the hole left by Brackett's shot. By a tiny fraction it was nearest to the center. Andy noticed the captain watching him with interest.

Brackett looked surprised. Then he frowned. "A target don't shoot back. The trick is to do the same thing when you're lookin' down the muzzle of somebody's gun."

Andy let malice creep into his voice. "Somebody like the state police?"

"I seldom shot at one but what I hit him."

Andy could not argue with that. Burning with bitterness acquired on the battlefields, Brackett had become a terror to occupation officers who attempted to enforce reconstruction laws.

Tanner edged in between the two. He said, "Andy, you stick your right elbow out too far. Let's go over yonder away from the crowd and practice holdin' that rifle."

Andy knew his stance was all right. It was the one Rusty had taught him. But he realized Tanner was trying to get him away before an argument started. "I'd be much obliged for anything you can show me."

When they had moved apart from the other men Tanner looked back over his shoulder. "Ain't really nothin' wrong with the way you hold your elbow if it feels right to you. It don't matter how you do it as long as you hit what you shoot at."

"I usually do."

"I'm just tryin' to keep you from havin' to aim at Farley Brackett, and him at you. One of you is just as good a shot as the other. You'd probably both go down."

"I don't want any trouble with him. But he keeps pokin' at me every chance he gets."

"A smart fish don't grab at bait that's got a hook in it."

* * *

While Andy was taking the measure of the company, the captain had been taking the measure of him. One evening he assigned Andy to night horse guard. "Private Pickard, you will take first watch tonight."

Andy was pleased. He had begun to wonder when or even if he would be given any real responsibility. "Yes, sir. I'll be glad to."

The captain gave him a quizzical look. "You don't have to be glad around here. You just have to do what you're told to, glad or not. And always be ready for the unexpected."

After supper Andy saddled Long Red and checked his rifle.

Brackett leaned against a pecan tree, watching. "Where's your bow and arrow?"

Andy tried not to let Brackett see that his tone stung a little. He pretended he did not hear.

Brackett turned to Jim Morris, just back from a lengthy and uneventful scout. "You know that boy was raised by the Indians? He's a Comanche at heart."

Jim retorted, "I know his heart has got a lot of fight in it. He helped me and Johnny and Len spike a Yankee cannon, with them Yankees shootin' at us the whole time."

That seemed to be news to Brackett. "When was that?"

"Last January, when the carpetbaggers tried to hold on to the state capitol."

"How many of them did he scalp?"

"Not more than five or six. He had to share with the rest of us."

Andy decided Jim could hold his own in a lying contest with Tanner.

Jim said, "They tell me the Comanches called him Badger Boy. He fights like a cornered badger when he's riled."

Brackett appeared impressed, but that did not last long.

As Andy started to ride away, Brackett said, "If any of your red brothers come callin', don't you let them get my sorrel horse, Badger Boy." He spoke the name with derision.

Andy said, "Not them, and not you."

Allowed to spread out and graze during the day, the horses had been brought close to camp and pushed into a fairly compact group that could be watched more easily during the night. Though Indians could strike a horse herd at any time, they favored darkness, when they were hard to see and hard to hit.

Andy had come to rely heavily upon his instincts. Sometimes, though by no means always, he had premonitions about future events. He supposed this resulted from hearing about visions that often came to the People like his foster brother, Steals the Ponies. On several occasions he had sought after visions himself, but they never came. Or if they came, they were so vague that he did not recognize them for what they were. Perhaps he had to be a real Comanche, not an adopted one, for visions to work.

He had no premonition tonight. Nevertheless he was determined to remain alert. He listened to night birds settling in the trees. Indians often imitated the sounds of birds and other creatures in signaling to each other. He did not intend to be fooled. The horses quieted down and began going to sleep, some lying down, others remaining on their feet. Now and then one would snort or stamp the ground or nip at a neighbor that crowded too closely. The one bitten would usually squeal and kick at its tormentor. These were all natural sounds. He catalogued them in his mind so he might recognize any that were not natural.

He had no watch, but Rusty had shown him how to tell time in a general way by the movement of the stars.

The camp routine had kept him busy enough during the days that he had not thought much about the farm. Now, in the long solitude of the night, he thought back on the place where he had spent the years since his return from life with the Comanches. He thought of Rusty and wondered where he was, what he was doing. He wondered if he had made headway in his search for Corey Bascom.

After getting past his initial reticence, Andy had told the captain about Josie Monahan's death. The officer had written down Andy's description of Bascom. "I'll have every man add this to his fugitive list, and I'll send it to the other companies," he said.

Andy had been shown what was called a fugitive book, containing hand-written descriptions of wanted men. The offenses were many and varied: theft of livestock and personal property, burglary, fraud, robbery at gunpoint, assault with intent to do bodily injury, rape, murder. . . . The book was only partially filled, leaving room to add more miscreants to the list. That these pages would eventually be used up was a foregone conclusion. Texas was not a comfortable place for the timid.

No Indians were listed. Few of their names were known. Any found roaming freely within the state's boundaries were automatically considered hostile and in open season, so a listing would have no purpose.

Andy had been instructed to read the book over and over, to memorize the descriptions in as much detail as possible so he might more easily recognize any fugitives he came across. It was considered likely that many were hiding in this thinly settled western country where law was scarce. Local lawmen varied in their diligence, some relentless in pursuit, others tolerant so long as the offenses had been committed elsewhere and were not repeated within their own jurisdiction. In these cases, rangers were the only peace officers likely to bring the offenders to hand.

Andy rode a slow circle around the horses, pausing to

listen for any sound he considered alien. He thought the most effective solution would be to build a corral large enough to contain the herd at night. But this campsite was considered temporary. The company might be moved at any time, so nothing of a permanent nature had been constructed.

Even corraled, the horses would have to be watched. Accomplished horse thieves, red or white, could quietly dismantle a section of the enclosure and put the whole bunch on the move before the rangers could muster an adequate defense.

Eventually Andy's relief rode out to take his place.

He called, "Where you at, Badger Boy?"

Andy recognized Farley Brackett's gruff voice. He replied, "Here." Choking down his dislike for the man, he moved over to meet him.

Brackett said, "Anything stirrin' out yonder?"

"I haven't seen or heard a thing."

"You sure you ain't been asleep? Nothin' gets a man fired out of this outfit quicker than bein' caught asleep on guard."

"My eyes are wide open. They have been all night."

"Glad to hear that. Been worried about my horse."

"Long Red is fine. You worry about the rest of the horses."

Andy turned away. He looked forward to a few hours of sleep before daylight.

He heard a movement of horses behind him, then a shouted challenge. The voice was Brackett's. "Who goes yonder?" He heard the jingle of Brackett's spurs as the man put his mount into a run. Andy turned back, trying to see in the dim light of a half moon. Sound more than sight told him the horse herd was moving. A pistol shot echoed through the trees. He assumed it was Brackett's.

He set Long Red into a lope, trying to circle around and head off the running horses. He heard the thieves holler, pushing for more speed. Andy overtook the moving herd and cut in front of it. He shouted, trying to turn the horses back. He fired his pistol into the air. Some of the animals slid to a stop, then ducked aside, frightened by the shot.

For a moment Andy saw the dark outline of a horseman. He brought his pistol up into line but hesitated. What if these were Comanches? What if his foster brother might be among them? Steals the Ponies had been given his name for good reason: he had earned it.

In a moment the question was moot, for the rider was lost in the darkness and the dust.

He saw a blur as another horseman came at him. He thought this was Brackett but he was mistaken. The man rammed his horse into Long Red. The impact knocked the sorrel off its feet and jarred Andy loose from the saddle. He grabbed at the horn but missed. He hit the ground hard on his left shoulder.

The rider loomed over him, his horse almost on top of Andy. Andy felt around desperately for the pistol lost in the fall. He had time for one terrible thought: that a Comanche brother was about to kill him. He saw the rider's hand come down, steadying the pistol.

He heard a shot, but it did not come from the gun that had been leveled at him. The rider pitched forward over the horse's neck. His body fell across Andy's legs.

Brackett's voice shouted, "Get up from there, Badger Boy. We got horse thieves to catch." Brackett turned and disappeared again, his horse in a dead run.

Long Red had regained his feet. Andy pushed the heavy body off his legs. The Comanche side of him regretted the thought of an Indian being shot, though the white side rejoiced that it had not been him instead. Andy remounted and set out in a run after the horses. He heard a few more shots.

He fired at a shadowy figure which crossed his path but knew he had missed. In a way he was relieved.

He found himself in front of the horses again. They were slowing. He shouted until he was hoarse. Gradually they began to mill. Somewhere beyond sight he heard a few more shots, then the night fell quiet except for the nervous stamping of hooves against limestone rocks, the nervous nickering of horses.

He saw a rider coming toward him from the west and brought up his pistol. He lowered it when he recognized Brackett's voice. "Holler out, Badger Boy." The man and his horse were both breathing hard. Brackett struggled for breath. "Got them stopped did you? I hope we didn't lose any."

Andy said, "I never knew Comanches to give up so easy."

"Comanches? Didn't you get a look at any of them?"

"It was too dark, and things moved too fast."

"If they was Comanches, I'm an Apache squaw. They were as white as me and you. Me, anyway."

Several rangers came up, riding hard. They had had mounts staked in or near camp. The captain was among them. "What happened here, men?"

Brackett said, "Just had a little company. They didn't stay long."

"Did we lose any horses?"

"We can't take a good count 'til daylight. Looks like most of them are still here."

"Indians, I suppose?"

"Not this time. I'm sorry to say it, but there's some white men near as bad as Comanches."

The captain accepted the report with a satisfied grunt. "You did good work, Brackett. You too, Pickard."

Andy said, "Captain, one of them went down back yonder. Private Brackett shot him."

"Dead?"

"I didn't wait to see, sir. Seemed more important to catch the horses."

"We'll pick him up as we drive the remuda back."

Andy gritted his teeth. He had rather take a whipping with a wet rope than acknowledge that Brackett had saved his bacon, but he owed it to the man to tell the truth. "My horse got knocked down. That outlaw was fixin' to kill me. Private Brackett shot him first."

The captain was pleased. "I'll put that on your record, Brackett. It might help make you a sergeant one day."

Brackett said, "I'd've done the same thing for the camp cook. Quicker, maybe. He makes good biscuits."

Tanner and the Morris brothers rode ahead of the horses, looking for the raider Brackett had shot. By the time Andy reached them, they had him. Tanner said, "Looky what we found, Captain, tryin' to sneak off into the timber. He's leakin' some, but he's breathin'."

The man was hunched over, holding one arm tightly against his ribs. Andy did not think he had ever seen him before, though a ragged beard covered most of his face except for his frightened eyes.

Tanner said, "We got no jail to put him in."

Johnny Morris said, "We got plenty of trees to hang him from. What do you say, Captain?"

The man cried out, "Somebody help me. Can't you see I'm shot?"

The captain's voice was grave. "You present us with a problem. As Private Morris said, we have no jail to put you in and no doctor to see to your wound. There seems to be but one answer."

Brackett waved a pistol. "It's my fault, Captain. I was movin' fast and in the dark. Couldn't aim straight. I'll make up for it right now if you want me to."

Andy hoped Brackett was just trying to intimidate the prisoner, but he sounded as if he meant it.

The outlaw sank to his knees. "For God's sake, give me a chance."

The captain made a show of struggling with his decision. "My better judgment tells me to put an end to it. But I might consider an alternative if you'd cooperate."

"Anything. Leave me go and I won't stop 'til I get to California. Maybe even further."

"I'll want you to identify your confederates and tell me where we might be most likely to find them."

"I'll tell you all I know. They run off and left me. I don't owe them nothin'."

The captain pointed his chin at the herd. "Pickard, catch him a horse. He can ride to camp bareback."

The outlaw cried, "I can't ride. I been shot. I think my ribs are busted."

"A little hurting will help you repent your wayward life."

Andy doubted that. The only thing this renegade would regret was getting caught. A while earlier he had been willing to murder Andy. Despite his pleas, he was unlikely to reform. He would travel a crooked road until a better-aimed bullet or a strong rope stopped him for good.

The prisoner grunted in pain with almost every step. Andy mustered no sympathy. Leading the horse, he maneuvered it across the roughest ground he could find.

He wouldn't have lost a minute's sleep over killing me, he thought. What's more, he made me beholden to Farley Brackett.

That might have been the worst offense of all.

Brackett eased over beside Andy. "I been mullin' this thing over. You thought it was Indians, didn't you?"

Andy wondered what he was driving at. "Thought it might be. I couldn't see much."

"Occurs to me you had a chance to shoot this man before he ran into your horse. Why didn't you?"

"I didn't see him soon enough."

"Or maybe you didn't want to shoot a fellow Comanche."

Andy's face warmed. He was glad the darkness kept Brackett from seeing it. He had told the truth about not having time to fire at this raider, but moments earlier he had seen another. He had a few seconds in which he might have fired, but he had hesitated. Brackett was partially right.

He managed a defiant tone. "Believe what you want to."

"I try to give a man the benefit of the doubt, the first time. And I've damned sure got some doubts about you, Badger Boy."

"I suppose you'll tell the captain about them?"

"I'll keep them to myself for now. But I'll be watchin' you."

The prisoner's horse stumbled on a rock outcrop and almost went down. The man grabbed his side and screeched, "Damn you, can't you watch where you lead this horse?"

Brackett said, "You're lucky we ain't leadin' him out from under a tree limb and leavin' you attached to it."

Andy was grateful that Brackett transfered his malice to the prisoner. He settled into quiet meditation over his own situation. Would he have reacted differently had he known from the first that the horse thieves were white? He was not sure. He feared he might have.

The captain had left a strong guard on the horse herd. At daylight they brought the horses into a clearing at the edge of camp for an accurate count. He and Holloway agreed that they were short only three horses. The thieves might have gotten away with them, or they might simply have strayed away from the main bunch during the excitement. He sent part of the company out on a search for the missing three. Then he watched the cook clean the prisoner's wound.

The renegade protested over the fact that the cook was black. "I ain't never let no dirty nigger touch me."

The captain retorted, "That black won't rub off on you. Keep at it, Bo."

The prisoner squalled as the cook poured alcohol into the wound. Bo grinned and poured more. By the time the bandage had been applied and the ribs tightly wrapped, the prisoner had regained some of his lost courage. When the captain began to question him, he refused to answer. "I changed my mind. I ain't tellin' you a damned thing."

"Regrettable. I hope you realize that if you won't talk, you're of no use to us."

"Never meant to be."

The captain nodded gravely at Holloway. "Sergeant, I have a report to write. Would you take charge of the prisoner? See if you can bring him around to our way of thinking." He retired to his headquarters tent.

Holloway said, "Brackett, bring your rope. We're takin' a little walk down to the river."

The prisoner's eyes widened. "What're you fixin' to do?"

"Like the captain said, you're of no use to us, and we've got no jail." He tied the man's hands behind his back with a rawhide string, then took a firm grip on one arm. Brackett grabbed the other. Though the prisoner dragged his feet, they hustled him along. Andy followed at a short distance, curious.

Holloway pointed at a sturdy pecan limb about ten feet

off of the ground. "That one ought to do. Throw your rope over it."

The prisoner blustered. "You're tryin' to bluff me. You wouldn't do this to a man. It's against the law."

Neither Holloway nor Brackett replied. Brackett slipped the loop over the prisoner's head and tightened it around his neck. He pulled the other end of the rope and took up the slack.

The renegade was sweating but tried to show a brave face. "You won't really do this. You ain't allowed."

Holloway nodded, and Brackett pulled the rope. It drew taut. The prisoner choked as his legs straightened. He bent his toes, trying to keep them touching the ground. Brackett pulled until the prisoner's feet were clear by a full six inches. Brackett held him there for a bit, then let him down.

"Got a kink in the rope," he explained. "Need to straighten it out."

The prisoner went to his knees, gasping, his face turning purple. Holloway bent over him. "We forgot to ask if you have any last words for the Lord."

The man coughed but could not speak. Holloway pulled him to his feet. "We'll get it done right this time. Go ahead, Brackett."

As the rope tightened the prisoner found voice. "No! No! For God's sake . . ."

Holloway seemed unmoved. "Tell me why not."

"Get the captain. Ask me anything."

Holloway appeared disappointed, but he turned and winked at Andy. "Don't put your rope away, Brackett. We'll need it if he changes his mind again."

The prisoner was so limp from terror that it took both men's support to get him back to the headquarters tent. A heavy smell indicated he had soiled himself. Holloway said, "Captain, I believe he's come to Jesus."

The captain emerged from the tent, smiling thinly. "He just needed time to consider the error of his ways."

When he quit coughing and regained his breath the culprit became a fountain of information. He said four including himself had been involved. They had planned in the excitement to cut off twelve or fifteen horses and get away with them in the darkness while the rangers chased after the main herd. They had hoped the raid would be blamed on Indians.

He rattled off his accomplices' names without hesitation: Arliss Wilkes, Brewster Pardo, and a boy called Scooter. He didn't know the boy's last name.

Holloway flipped through the pages of his fugitive book. "I find everybody in here except the boy."

The prisoner wailed as the cook rubbed salty bacon grease on his neck, burned red and raw by the rope. The captain told a nearby ranger, "Handcuff him to a chain and lock the chain around a tree. By the time he gets to a real jail he'll think it's the Menger Hotel in San Antonio."

Andy asked Holloway, "Can you do this? Is it legal?"

"Anything is legal if it works, and if you don't let the wrong people see it."

"Somebody is bound to ask about the mark around his neck."

"I'll just say he wears his collars too tight."

The captain chose five men to follow after and attempt to apprehend the thieves. They were Andy, Brackett, Tanner, Johnny Morris, and Sergeant Holloway. "Stay on their trail as long as you feel there's a chance it will be fruitful. Take them alive if it can be done without undue risk to yourselves. Otherwise, shoot to kill. If the rangers are to be respected we must show the outlaw class that we will exact a price for every offense."

Brackett jerked his head at Andy. "Captain, don't you

think this boy is a little green?" Andy had not once heard him say *sir.*

"If so, he will ripen with experience."

By the time the five were prepared to leave, the rangers who had sought the three missing horses returned. One reported, "We found them, Captain. Looks like the thieves didn't get anything except experience."

"With a little luck we'll give them more of that."

{ TWELVE }

It took some circling and searching before Andy found that the three remaining raiders had rejoined one another a couple of miles west from where they had first jumped the remuda. He waved his hat over his head to draw the attention of the other four rangers. Len Tanner had to be sent out to find Johnny Morris, off on a tangent of his own.

Sergeant Holloway said, "Since you found the trail, Andy, we'll let you track for a while. If you run up a stump, somebody else'll take it."

Tanner said, "I'll bet there ain't a better tracker in the company than Andy, unless it's me."

Holloway said, "You may get your chance. We'll see first what Andy can do."

Andy had not expected so much responsibility so soon. He felt a glow of pride, though he knew Holloway was testing him.

Brackett did not allow the glow to last. "Don't you mess up them tracks, Badger Boy. Remember, we ain't trailin' your Indians."

Andy could not think of an adequate retort.

He had left Long Red behind. The sorrel had had a hard run last night and might tire out before this search was finished. The gray he had been lent had a rougher trot than Long Red's, pounding Andy's innards. This was going to be a long, tiresome ride. But at least he was doing something other than following a plow.

The frustrated horse thieves were not experienced at covering their trail. It seemed to Andy that they did not even try. Perhaps it never occurred to them that the rangers would be vengeful enough to follow them inasmuch as they had failed to get away with any horses.

Tanner observed, "They don't seem very smart."

Holloway said, "Most crooks aren't. Very few make much of a livin'. If they'd work as hard at honest labor as they do at mischief they could make somethin' of themselves. They live like coyotes and die like dogs, most of them, dead broke and bleedin' to death in the dirt."

Andy found where the fugitives had camped for the night on a creek. They had built a fire on a flat rock just above the waterline. A couple of drying rabbit skins, covered with flies, remained as evidence of their meager supper.

Tanner said, "Jackrabbit. That's about as far from prosperity as you can get."

Holloway said, "There's misguided kids back East wishin' they could run away and become outlaws. I wish every one of them could see this."

Andy remembered famine times with the People when he had eaten jackrabbit, even rattlesnakes. The thought almost made him feel sorry for the outlaws. But not quite. They had chosen this path. He doubted that anyone had forced them to it at gunpoint. He would reserve his sympathy for people upon whom hard times had fallen without fault of their own.

At midday he approached a small cedar picket cabin, the first dwelling he had seen. Holloway called, "Better hold up, Andy. We'll ride in slow and careful. Tanner, you and Johnny circle way around and come in from the back side."

Andy, Holloway, and Brackett dismounted to present less of a target. They gave the other two time enough to reach their position. Andy said, "Looks like somebody has chopped down an awful lot of cedar." A large area had been cleared around and beyond the cabin. Brush was stacked in piles, probably to be burned when it dried enough.

Holloway said, "I'd figure they're clearin' a field, only this ground has more rocks than soil. I'd hate to try and put a plow in it."

Andy saw a movement and squinted to bring it into focus. "I see a man afoot out yonder. Looks like he's drivin' stakes into the ground. Why would anybody do that in a place like this?"

Holloway shook his head. "Damned if I know. Every time I think I've got people figured out, somebody throws a new puzzle at me."

While the three rode toward the man with the stakes, Andy saw Tanner and Johnny approach the cabin from the rear. Cautiously the pair dismounted and entered, then came back out. Obviously the fugitives were not here. Tracks showed they had passed this way, however.

The man carried a sledgehammer and a long cedar stake, sharpened at one end. Andy saw that he had made a line of stakes stretching to the cabin and beyond.

Holloway raised his hand. "Howdy. We're rangers, on

the trail of three riders that came by here. Did you see them?"

The man wiped his sleeve across a gray-stubbled face to clear away a heavy sweat. His manner was jovial, his blue eyes bright though given a wild look by thick, bristly eyebrows. Andy saw that he wore a heavy boot on one foot and a loosely laced shoe on the other. Perhaps that was the only footwear he owned, or perhaps he had not noticed the difference. "They came by early this mornin' and traded me a couple of tired-out horses for two old skates I had. I sure got the best end of that deal."

"Maybe you did and maybe you didn't. Those men are horse thieves. They may have traded you stolen property."

The man's face fell. "You mean you're goin' to take them away from me?"

"We won't, but if the real owners should happen to turn up, you'll lose them."

The eyes brightened again. "By that time maybe I'll be rich enough to buy plenty more horses. I've got me a gold mine here."

"Gold mine?"

"A town. Don't you see it? A town all my own." He waved his hand toward the line of stakes. "I'll be sellin' lots as soon as I finish layin' out the townsite. Pretty soon there'll be houses all over this place. I'll put in a store and later on a bank."

"But a town has to have people. I don't see anybody except you."

"There's thousands of people back East lookin' for a new home. I've got the place for them right here. How about you gentlemen? Any of you want to be the first to settle in Hanleyville?"

"I take it your name is Hanley?"

"Yes sir, Joshua B. Hanley. *Mayor* Hanley."

Andy looked around but saw nothing to attract people to a site like this, certainly not in any numbers. The ground was unsuitable for farming except in narrow little valleys where rains had deposited soil washed down from the rocky hillsides. It might do for grazing cattle or sheep, but cedar was so thick the grass was sparse. He did not see a spring or creek.

Hanley said, "My daddy fought with Sam Houston at San Jacinto. The Republic of Texas gave him this land grant. He never could claim it because the Indians was too thick out here. They're pretty well gone now. I decided it was time to plant a garden in the desert and build a town where there wasn't nothin' but a cedarbrake."

Holloway did a poor job of concealing his misgivings. "Mind if we water our horses before we go on?"

"There's a well up by the cabin. Dug it myself. Take all the water you want."

The town builder resumed stepping off the lots and driving his stakes. Holloway looked back on him with pity. "I've seen many a 'town' like this, somebody's wild dream. Poor devil'll sit out here waitin' by himself 'til he goes crazy. Maybe he already is."

Brackett asked, "What about those horses?"

"They're not ours. Whoever they were stolen from, there's not much chance they'll ever come this far huntin' them. Leave the poor fool somethin'."

Hanley's description of the fugitives, two men and a boy, had matched the one extracted from the prisoner after his early-morning rope dance.

At midafternoon the searchers came across a limping horse, its head down in fatigue. Nearby lay an abandoned saddle, blanket, and bridle.

Holloway said, "The two horses they've got left are probably the ones they traded from Hanley. One of those'll wear down fast, too, carryin' double. We'll have them pretty soon."

Shortly before sundown Andy caught a whiff of woodsmoke on a warm breeze from the west. He had not seen sign of a human since after they had left Hanley's townsite. It stood to reason that the fugitives had found what they considered a good place to camp. He waited for the others to come up even with him.

Holloway sniffed. "I smell it, too. They can't be far."

Andy flinched at a shot, followed quickly by another. By instinct he was half out of the saddle before he realized the sound came from far away. The shots had not been aimed at the rangers.

Holloway said, "Probably tryin' to get a deer or somethin' for supper. They need it, judgin' by the jackrabbits they ate last night."

The rangers moved into the edge of a cedarbrake and waited, listening. Andy heard nothing else. Either they hit their game with the first shots or it got away and they hadn't found anything else.

Brackett said, "I could stand a chunk of venison myself. Bo's cold biscuits are startin' to taste like horse sweat."

Holloway said, "They'll have to do for now. We'll wait here 'til dark, then close in on them. Maybe they'll have their bellies full and drop off to sleep." He glanced at Andy. "Nervous?"

"Am I supposed to be?"

"Most people are the first time they come up on a situation like this."

"This isn't my first time."

Tanner said, "Andy could tell you lots of stories."

Holloway said, "Another time. I'm fixin' to catch a little nap while I can."

Andy wondered aloud how the sergeant could drop off so quickly and easily.

Brackett said, "I was with him several times in the war. He could go to sleep twenty minutes before a battle or after one. Ain't much that scares him, aside from gettin' old. Bein' a ranger, he may not ever *get* old."

Andy realized that Brackett respected the sergeant. That surprised him. He had not seen Brackett show much respect for anybody.

What'll it take for him to respect me? he wondered.

Holloway awakened at good dark, as if he had planned it that way. He dug one of the cook's leftover biscuits from a canvas bag tied with his blanket roll. He watched Brackett while he ate it. "Horse sweat don't taste too bad," he said. "You just hold your breath and swallow, like it was gyppy water."

He checked his weapons, a silent indication that the others should do the same. He said, "We'll take them alive if we can. If we can't, it's their hard luck. Johnny, you and Tanner circle around. We'll come in on them from this side. Just be careful you don't shoot one another in the dark. I don't want to bury anybody but those horse thieves, and not even them if we don't have to."

The three thieves were either supremely overconfident or not very good at their calling. The rangers took them by complete surprise. They looked at their captors with disbelief for the few seconds the rangers required to take charge of their weapons. One made a grab for a rifle just as Brackett picked it up. Brackett swung it and struck him across the head. The outlaw went down like a sack of potatoes.

Holloway said, "You-all just sit right still and don't twitch an eyebrow. Brackett, you and Johnny put the handcuffs on them."

Two of the thieves were grown men. One snarled at the other, "You said they wouldn't come after us because we didn't get none of their horses. I told you we oughtn't to've built a fire like that."

The other was the one Brackett had struck. Blood trickled down his forehead. "It was you that kept hollerin' about bein' hungry and wantin' to stop and eat."

The third sat quietly and looked frightened. He was a boy of perhaps fourteen or fifteen years. His wrists were so thin that Brackett could not make the cuffs fit tightly.

Holloway asked, "What's your name, son?"

The lad would not look at him, nor would he answer. Holloway tried again without result. He asked, "Son, is one of these men your daddy?"

That seemed to irritate the boy. He exploded, "Hell no they ain't." Then, in a subdued voice, he added, "They're friends of mine."

Holloway asked the men their names, though he already knew from their confederate's confession back at the ranger camp. One said he was John Smith. The other was John Jones. Holloway made a wry smile. "Smith and Jones. I've arrested a lot of your kinfolks in my time."

"We're from big families," the oldest man retorted.

"Of all the victims you could've picked, what made you think you could get away with a raid on ranger horses?"

"We don't know nothin' about no ranger horses. We're just honest settlers mindin' our own business, lookin' for a place to make our homes."

"I don't think you'll need to worry about a home for the next few years. The state of Texas is fixin' to give you one. Maybe I can help get your terms shortened if you'll talk to me straight."

"Straight about what?"

"Whatever I decide to ask you." Holloway turned to the

boy, who by now seemed to have lost most of his fear. "I'm askin' you again, son, what is your name?"

The answer was curt. "Brown. Bobby Brown."

"Jones, Smith, and Brown. You got yourself tied in with some real gallows bait, son. They'll get you nothin' except a hard life and an early death."

"I already had the hard life. Maybe death ain't so bad."

"Don't you believe in hell?"

"Hell can't be no worse than what I've already had. And the devil can't be no meaner than some people I know."

Andy felt a swelling of pity. It was clear that this boy had been badly treated for a long time.

The outlaw who called himself Smith quickly put in, "It wasn't us. We been good to him. Treated him like a kid brother almost."

Holloway's voice had acid in it. "Teachin' him to be like you?"

"Teachin' him how to get along in a hard world. Every boy needs to learn a trade."

"Some trade, stealin' horses."

"We ain't stole no horses. You see any of your horses in this camp?"

"It's not because you didn't try." Holloway studied the boy a minute. "We ought to hang the two of you right here for leadin' this kid astray."

The boy came to their defense. "Wasn't nobody around to take care of me after my mama died. My daddy's in jail. Goin' to be there for a long time. Arliss and Brewster, they picked me up and let me come along with them. Didn't nobody else care if I lived or died."

Holloway almost smiled. "Arliss and Brewster. Not John." He had known that all along.

Smith growled, "Them's our middle names."

Part of a deer carcass was hanging from a cedar limb, a

butcher knife stuck in it. Holloway said, "Well, Arliss and Brewster, I'm grateful to you-all for providin' that venison. We've made do on cold biscuits and air all day." He jerked his head toward the deer. Tanner moved quickly to the task.

After eating his fill, Holloway fetched the fugitive book from his saddlebag. "Arliss Wilkes and Brewster Pardo. Both of your names are on the list. You're wanted for several things besides horse stealin'."

Arliss said, "We get blamed for things we didn't do."

"Accordin' to our information the boy's name is Scooter. But Scooter's not a Christian name." He looked at the youngster. The boy said nothing.

Arliss was the one who had called himself John Smith. He said, "Ain't heard no other given name but Scooter. His last name's Tennyson."

Holloway smiled. "That's more like it. See, it's not hard to talk to the rangers."

"We don't have much choice when you got guns on us."

Brackett growled, "At least we know what names to put on your headboards if you-all give us any trouble. Every man ought to have his right name on his headboard."

Later, chewing on a half-broiled strip of meat, Andy studied Scooter Tennyson. He looked as if he had been brought up in a brush thicket. His hair was a-tangle. Someone had made a bad effort at cutting it, leaving a ragged job that looked more like the work of a butcher knife than of scissors. His shirt was too large for his thin frame. It hung on him like a partially collapsed tent. His trousers, also too big, had patches on both knees and holes in both patches.

Andy let his imagination run free. He could have been in the same situation at almost the same age had it not been for Rusty Shannon. Fate had been kind to him. It appeared that nobody had been kind to this boy.

In a quiet voice he asked Holloway, "What'll happen to the kid when we take him in?"

"The state has got a home for boys like this."

"It's like a junior penitentiary, isn't it?"

"Pretty much, I guess. I've never seen it."

"Doesn't seem right. He's never had much of a chance."

"He's old enough to know right from wrong. Some people set out on a crooked trail earlier than others. He said his daddy's in jail. It's probably in the blood."

"I don't believe that. I'll bet if he was among decent folks a while he'd straighten out."

Holloway's face showed his doubt. "Maybe. You want the job?"

"I don't know that I'm the one to do it. I'm not but a few years older than him. And I've got a job as a ranger."

"I'll talk to the captain when we get back to camp. Maybe he'll see his way clear to do somethin' for the boy. What's your interest in him?"

"Maybe it's because when I look at him I see what could've become of me."

Talking to Scooter was like talking to a post. The boy turned away and made a show of ignoring Andy. His patience strained, Andy said, "I'm just tryin' to help you, kid."

"Don't need your help. Don't need nothin' but a good leavin' alone."

"You won't get much leavin' alone if they put you behind the bars."

"Maybe that's what I was born for."

"Nobody's born for a life like that. They choose it or get pushed into it. Looks to me like you've been pushed. I'd like to see you get a decent chance."

"You a preacher or somethin'?"

"No, I'm just a ranger, and a new one at that. Mostly I guess you'd say I've been a farmer."

"Then go back to your plow and leave me alone."

Andy caught a look from Holloway that said for him to ease off. The boy pulled away from Andy and closer to his outlaw friends. Holloway beckoned Andy away from the campfire, out into the darkness.

He said, "You're wastin' your breath."

"Maybe he hasn't had time to understand the trouble he's in. Once he does, he might be easier to talk to. It took me a while when I was where he's at."

"I tried once to raise an orphaned coyote pup. Thought since I'd caught him young he'd train like a dog, but he never did. He never was anything but a wild chicken-killin' coyote. I finally caught him killin' a baby calf. Bad as I hated to, I had to shoot him."

"There were folks who thought the same thing of me, comin' out of a Comanche camp."

"From what Tanner has told me, some good folks took an interest and set you right."

"Maybe that's all Scooter needs."

"I think you're puttin' yourself in for disappointment, but I'll talk to the captain."

Andy went back and sat down near Scooter, trying to think of an approach that might work. It was Scooter who made the approach. The boy said, "I heard some of what you were sayin' out there. What's this about you and the Comanches?"

Andy took the boy's interest as a hopeful sign. "They killed my folks and carried me off when I was little. Raised me for several years. I was luckier than you. Some good people cared enough to take me in and give me a home."

"I never found no good people except Arliss and Brewster. Arliss was in jail a while with my daddy. He got a notion Daddy had buried money someplace and I might know where it was. But my daddy never had enough money that he could afford to bury any."

"Arliss and Brewster aren't the kind you ought to be travelin' with."

"They're all I got." The boy went pensive. "We come across another feller a few days ago. He was nice to me. Him and Arliss and Brewster robbed a little bank over at a burg called Brownwood. But he didn't cotton to the notion of stealin' ranger horses, nor of goin' farther west. Said there wasn't no banks out there, so he left us. I kind of wished he'd stayed. Seemed smarter than Arliss and Brewster. Maybe we wouldn't have got ourselves caught."

"You were bound to get caught sooner or later."

"I felt kind of sorry for him. Said his wife got shot a while back. He was still takin' it hard."

Andy felt a tingling along his spine. "Who was he? Did he give a name?"

The boy thought for a moment. "Bascom, it was. Yeah, Bascom. At least that's what he told us."

"Corey Bascom?"

"I believe so."

Andy's excitement built. "Did he say where he was goin'?"

The boy looked at him as if he did not believe the question. "I don't never ask a thing like that. Anybody wants you to know, they'll tell you."

So Bascom had been with these two-bit badmen as recently as the last day or two. It was a starting place, at least. Andy could hardly wait to write Rusty a letter. He would do it as soon as he got back to camp.

Sometime during the night he awakened to the sound of a running horse. Brackett shouted, "That damned kid has gotten away."

Andy flung his blanket aside and pulled on the boots he had put beneath it to protect them from dew. He saw Brackett pick up a pair of handcuffs.

Brackett said, "Those cuffs were too loose on him. He slipped them off."

Holloway declared, "Andy, you're so interested in givin' the boy a chance, go see if you can catch him and bring him back. Brackett, you'd better follow along."

Wilkes and Pardo were handcuffed to the trunks of young trees. Scooter had been, too. Wilkes said, "Good for the boy. I hope he gets plumb to Mexico."

Holloway took a quick inventory of the horses. "At least the kid has an eye for horseflesh. He took mine. You'll have to ride hard to catch him."

Andy could not see far in the darkness, but the hoofbeats had told him the boy was headed west. He wished he had Long Red with him. The sorrel had outrun almost everything Andy had ever pitted him against. He had not tested the gray for speed, but he gave it the spurs. He felt the rush of wind in his eyes and ears. Limbs whipped him across the face and shoulders.

Brackett shouted, "You'd better slow down. That horse is liable to fall and bust his leg."

The horse had better night vision than Andy, for it leaped over fallen limbs and cut around trees Andy had not seen. He leaned low in the saddle and gave the animal its head.

He saw the dark shape of the fugitive ahead of him, making a crooked trail through the cedar brush and live oaks. "Scooter," he shouted. "Stop."

Scooter shouted a reply. Andy could not discern the words, but the tone left no doubt about their meaning. The boy was outlining Andy's ancestry in scathing detail.

The chase came to a sudden stop as a low limb caught Scooter across the chest and held him while the sergeant's horse ran on without him. By the time Andy reached him the boy lay curled up on the ground like a wounded caterpillar, gasping for lost breath. Andy demanded, "What the hell were you tryin' to do? You've just added another horse-stealin' charge to your record."

Scooter tried a sharp answer, but he could only wheeze. Brackett went after the runaway horse. It stopped when it realized it had lost its rider.

Andy gave way to anger. "There I was, beggin' the sergeant to give you a chance. Then you pull a stunt like this."

The boy was not as helpless as he had appeared. He jumped to his feet, pushed Andy aside and made a grab for the gray horse. Andy caught his shirt and pulled him away just as the boy's left foot hit the stirrup. He gave Scooter a hard shove that put the boy on the ground again.

Brackett came back, leading the sergeant's horse. He seemed to be enjoying himself. "Looks like that kid's got some badger in him, too, Badger Boy."

Andy's anger subsided. He remembered that he had tried to fight back when he was first recaptured from the Comanches. The difference was that a broken leg gave him no chance of winning. He had tried once to run away, but the weak leg had betrayed him.

"I guess we can't blame him too much for tryin'." He nodded at Scooter. "Get back on the sergeant's horse." He cut a long leather string from his saddle and tied Scooter's hands to the pommel. "I'll bet you don't slip out of that."

The boy tugged at the bonds, then began crying softly.

The last of his anger drained, Andy wanted to comfort him. "Maybe the worst thing you've done is fall in with bad company. They can't do much to you for that."

Brackett said, "He's a horse thief."

"He's just a little reckless about his borrowin'. Seems I remember you takin' one of Rusty Shannon's horses once."

"But I left another one in his place."

"One you'd 'borrowed' from the U.S. Army. Got Rusty into a lot of trouble."

"That was a whole other time. Things are different now. And this boy ain't you. He's somethin' else entirely. Pretty soon you'll be wishin' you'd never seen him."

Andy already wished that. But he *had* seen him, and he could not give up on him, any more than Rusty Shannon had given up on a half-wild kid named Badger Boy.

{ THIRTEEN }

Rusty Shannon leaned on the hoe and looked across the field at the weeds still to be chopped out of his growing corn. It was a job without an end, for before he could get the last row finished, the first would need hoeing again. He missed Andy and Tanner. Andy had always been a diligent worker. Tanner could be, too, when the mood was upon him and he wasn't fidgeting to go somewhere.

Old Shanty had ridden over here yesterday on his mule and offered to help, but Rusty had politely declined. Shanty had work enough of his own. A man of his age and frail constitution needed a lot of rocking-chair time.

"Your eyes show the miseries," Shanty had said. "This old place just keeps you studyin' about the girl you was fixin' to bring here."

"I stay busy, but it doesn't help much."

"Swingin' a hoe don't tie up your mind. Leaves you free to think too much. You need to get away a while."

"I'd be thinkin' about her no matter where I went."

He had left here twice following false rumors that he had hoped would lead him to Corey Bascom. He had ridden for days, only to be left frustrated and sick at heart. So far as he knew he had never been anywhere close to Corey.

Shanty had suggested, "Everybody says you was a good ranger once. The man you been lookin' for could be way down in Mexico by now or plumb out to the California ocean. But there's a-plenty other sinners runnin' loose. They need catchin'. Maybe you'd ought to be a ranger again."

"It wouldn't be the same."

"Sometimes the Lord don't hand us a full bucket. We give Him thanks for what we do get, even if it's just half a bucket."

Rusty recognized Sheriff Tom Blessing's big horse coming in on the trail from town. He gratefully carried the hoe to the turn row and laid it down. Tom usually opened his conversations with either the weather or the state of the crops. He hollered, "Your corn's lookin' good."

"Not as good as the weeds."

Tom dismounted, and Rusty shook hands with him. Tom took another look across the field. "You need to go to town and hire a boy or two to help you."

"I wouldn't want to take anybody away from school."

"School's out. And workin' in the fields will teach them more practical stuff than studyin' about the history of England and all them other places a long ways off from here."

"I'll think about it. How's Mrs. Blessing?"

"Better every day, thanks to Alice." Tom frowned, waiting. "Ain't you goin' to ask me about Alice?"

Rusty thought he probably should. "How's Alice?"

"She's a good-hearted girl. Homesick, of course. And she's still afraid you resent her because she's alive and her sister's not."

At a conscious level Rusty had tried to put such feelings aside, but they still rose to the surface at unexpected times when he was not prepared to confront them. "I know it wasn't her fault. Except for her bad judgment in marryin' Corey Bascom."

"Speakin' of Corey Bascom, . . ." Tom reached into his shirt pocket. "While I was at the post office gettin' my mail I found you had a letter, too. It's from Andy. He thinks he's got a line on your man."

The envelope had been opened. Tom had read the letter. Rusty did not mind. He had far too much privacy out here anyway, living by himself. He hurried to unfold the letter, running his finger along the lines as he read.

Tom said, "They sent Andy and Len to a frontier ranger company camped way out on the San Saba River. That's where he heard about Corey Bascom."

Rusty hurried ahead to the part of the letter that told about a kid who had ridden a short time with Bascom. His hands shook so that it was difficult to read the lines. "Reckon how many days it'll take me to get to that camp?"

"A bunch. It's liable to be a cold trail anyway."

"No colder than others I've tried. At least we know Bascom has been there, or close by." He turned his eyes to the west. "I've never been that far out yonderway." He started walking toward the barn.

Tom rode along beside him. "Me and my boys will keep an eye on the place while you're gone. Can't guarantee to cut all the weeds down, though. If a man could get his crops to grow as good as his weeds . . ."

"To hell with the weeds."

"What about that hoe you left layin' out there?"

"To hell with the hoe, too. I've got some country to cover."

Together he and Tom sketched out a rough map. Tom said, "You've been to Austin, so you know the road that far. From there you'll head west into the hills. I'm a little hazy about the towns, but you'll pass through some German settlements like Friederichsburg. From what Andy says in the letter the camp is west of Fort Mason, close to a settlement called Menardville. Feller told me he saw ruins of an old Spanish mission there. Jim Bowie's name was carved over the gate."

"I'll ask directions as I go along," Rusty said.

"I wouldn't be tellin' everybody my business was I you. There's some wild old boys out yonder. They may get hostile if they find out you're after one of their own kind."

"I take pretty good care of myself."

"You haven't always. I've seen a couple of your scars." Tom thrust his hand forward. "Don't worry about your farm. And don't worry about Alice. Me and the missus never had a daughter before. It's nice havin' one for a while."

Rusty packed a smokehouse ham and a slab of bacon as well as flour and salt and coffee. There had been a time he could usually sustain himself on wild game for days on end. But wherever settlers moved in, the game tended to thin out. He saddled the bay horse and tied his pack onto a fancy-stepping Spanish mule he had acquired at a trade day in town.

Tom warned, "I never trusted them little mules. They can kick so fast you can't see it comin'. They'll break your leg before you can spit."

"I'll be careful."

Tom watched as Rusty rode away. He hollered, "Anything you want me to tell Alice?"

"Just don't let any strangers see her."

In his eagerness he rode far into the first night and had to search in the darkness for a grassy spot to stake the horse and mule and for wood to build a fire. He resolved not to do that again. The road was familiar as far as Austin. He wasted no time there reminiscing about last January's confrontation over possession of the state capitol. He sought directions and nothing else.

He found the topography changed abruptly west of Austin. The road led into rocky cedar-covered hills and scattered live-oak mottes. The land was drier. He wondered at the feasibility of cultivating it. Settlers so far had restricted the plow to valley flats. A scattering of cattle, sheep, and Mexican goats made use of the hillsides, grazing the short grass, browsing whatever parts of the brushy plants were edible.

Looks like a hard place to make a living, he thought.

Yet the first settlement he encountered had a more prosperous look than he would have expected, given the land's meager prospects. The buildings were mostly of native stone, the individual pieces carefully chiseled to fit closely together. The roofs were shingled with cypress, which some artisan had trimmed to just the proper dimensions.

His second night out of Austin he reached the German town Tom had told him about, Friederichsburg. The streets were wide and generous. Most of the signs were in words he did not know, though he could figure out some that bore a passing resemblance to English, such as "Bäckerei" and "Drogerie." He found a tall wooden building with an odd steamboat-looking front. The sign proclaimed it the Nimitz Hotel.

He would not spend money on a hotel room, but he decided to treat himself to the luxury of a dining-room meal. The staff spoke English with an accent that reminded him of the way old Captain—now Judge—August Burmeister talked. After a pleasant supper of venison, gravy, and hot bread, he rode up the Hauptstrasse to look at the rest of the town. Evidently these people had wrung a living from the land despite its less than impressive appearance.

He tipped his hat to a middle-aged woman of generous proportions who was watering a flower bed from a metal bucket that had holes punched in its bottom. Her husband pulled weeds by hand from a vegetable garden beside the stone house. A young girl carried a bucket of milk up from a cow pen in back.

Rusty could see how they prospered against the odds. Everybody worked.

He received directions to the Fort Mason road and left at daylight. The little mule seemed to like Friederichsburg and resisted leaving it until Rusty applied the quirt across its hindquarters. It kicked at him and missed, then gave him a resentful look that said it would exact revenge sometime when he was not looking.

A friendly storekeeper had told him Fort Mason was forty miles away. He also hinted that trouble was brewing between some of the German settlers and a segment of the English-speaking citizens for no good reason that met the eye except that they came out of two different cultures. "Might be a good idea if you take roundance on that town," he said.

Rusty had traveled forty miles and more in a single day when the occasion demanded it, but it was hard on the animals. He decided not to push them. Chances were that Bascom's trail would be cold, as Tom had said. But if it wasn't he would not want to take it up with a worn-out horse and mule.

He camped on the bank of the James River. A German family came along in a wagon, heading in the opposite direction. They said they had found the atmosphere uncomfortable in Mason. "It is for the children that we go," the father explained, his words labored. "It is not good that they see men fight."

Rusty was aware that during the Civil War many German settlers in the hill country had remained loyal to the Union. They had suffered severely for it. Whatever the current trouble was, he suspected it had its roots in the war years and the distrust created between neighbors, even within families.

These people were short of provisions. Rusty gave them most of his flour and coffee, knowing he could replenish his supply in Mason.

He reached the town toward mid-morning. Riding in, he noticed that people watched him with suspicion. It was much like the reception he had received in Austin some months ago when that place was threatened with violence over possession of the governor's office.

The proprietor of the store where he chose to stop spoke with a German accent. He offered no pleasantries but simply sacked up some flour and coffee beans and laid them on the counter. His mistrust was palpable though his manner was civil. Rusty asked, "Where do I find the road to Menardville?"

The storekeeper seemed a little friendlier. "You do not stay here?"

"Just passin' through. Got business at a ranger camp over there."

"You are not here for the trouble?"

"Whatever your troubles may be, they're none of mine."

Leaving the store, Rusty found three men standing in the dirt street, watching him. Their grim faces indicated that their intentions were not benign. Rusty tied his provisions on the little Spanish pack mule, then turned to face the men. "You-all got business with me?"

One appointed himself spokesman. He took a step forward. "We got business with any stranger that drifts into town. How come you to stop at that Dutchman's store?"

"It was the first one I saw."

"Around here these days a man has got to know which side of the fence he stands on. There's them, and there's us. Which are you?"

"Neither. I'm a passin' stranger, and I'm fixin' to pass." He swung into the saddle, feeling angry.

Damn it, he thought, I didn't come all this way to get tangled up in somebody else's fight.

Looking back, he saw that they had caught up horses and trailed behind him. He suspected they would follow him out of town, then challenge him or perhaps even waylay him. He decided to meet their challenge here and now. Reaching down, he brought up his rifle. He turned abruptly and faced them. "I can find my own way. I'm not lookin' for any escort."

The spokesman said, "Just because you talk good English don't mean you're all right. There's some Americans around here sidin' with the Dutchmen. I'm goin' to see what you got on that pack mule and make sure you ain't smugglin' guns."

Dismounting, the man walked up to the pack mule and reached for the rope that held the pack in place. The little mule whirled half around and kicked him on the leg. The impact sounded like a small-caliber gunshot. Grabbing his knee, the man gave a cry of pain and crumpled. The other two got down to see about him while he howled that his leg was broken.

Rusty spurred the bay into a fast trot toward the

Menardville road. The little mule had to trot extra fast to keep up.

He could not remember exactly what he had paid for the animal, but he decided it had been cheap at the price.

He met a horseman wearing a badge and found him to be a deputy sheriff. The lawman asked, "What was the argument down yonder?"

"No argument. Some feller got a little too close to a mule."

He could tell that he had not fooled the deputy. The man said, "Stranger, ain't you?"

"First time I was ever here. Nice lookin' town, but it's got some testy citizens."

"Was I you, I wouldn't linger. Them boys yonder belong to one side. They probably suspicion that you've come to throw in with the other." He narrowed his eyes. "Or maybe that's why you're here."

"I'm just tryin' to find my way to a ranger camp over on the San Saba."

"You a ranger?"

"Used to be."

"You're in luck. Been some rangers in town tryin' to stop trouble. A couple of them are fixin' to report back to camp. If you was to ride along with them, nobody'd bother you none."

"Just point me to where they're at."

"This used to be a pretty good town. Will be again when we get rid of a few rotten apples."

Rusty was pleased to find Jim and Johnny Morris preparing to leave Mason. He had a feeling the deputy did not fully trust him until he saw the welcome the brothers gave him, pumping his hand, slapping him about the shoulders.

The three men who had accosted him made no attempt to follow. He mentioned that to the Morris brothers.

Jim said, "You're in West Texas. A lot of frisky old boys come here when they've wore out their welcome everywhere else. Mason's not the only place that's got a two-bit local feud goin' on."

Johnny put in, "If you think there's some hard *hombres* here, you ought to see Junction City."

"Right now I'm just lookin' for Andy."

Jim said, "I hope you ain't come to take him home. Andy's took to rangerin' like a duck takes to water."

"No, I felt that way myself once. I won't try to get him to quit."

Johnny asked, "Why don't you join up with us? Captain's still got some openin's left, and you can see how bad the rangers are needed out here."

"I have my farm to worry about. And other things."

"We know about the other things. Len Tanner told us."

That was no surprise. Len had never recognized a secret in his life. Rusty explained about Andy's letter.

Jim said, "Yeah, that boy Scooter's still in camp. Rougher than a corncob. Andy's tryin' to work the rough edges off of him, but the kid has got a coyote eye. I wouldn't want him sneakin' up behind me."

Rusty could understand Andy's sympathy for a boy like that. Andy had been in much the same position a few years earlier. "He thinks the boy might give me a lead on Corey Bascom, the man I've been lookin' for."

"The captain's already made inquiries about that bank robbery. Andy talked to them three horse thieves 'til he was blue in the face, but he didn't find out much about Bascom. It's been so long now that I'm afraid you won't be able to pick up the trail."

"I'd like to talk to the boy, anyhow."

"Gettin' him to talk to *you* will be the hard part. He can cuss like a muleskinner, but he don't put out much information."

Sight of the ranger encampment brought back memories, most pleasant, a few painful. It looked much like the wartime camp he remembered far to the north near Fort Belknap. This one appeared better equipped, for the state's Confederate government had always teetered on the edge of bankruptcy. Necessities had been scarce, luxuries not even considered. Postwar Texas was hardly wealthy, but it was better off than ten years ago.

Jim said, "I'll introduce you to the captain."

"I'm much obliged."

Rusty remembered meeting the captain a long time back. The officer said, "Welcome to camp, Mr. Shannon. I hope you have come to enlist."

"No sir, I have other business here."

Sergeant Holloway walked into the headquarters tent. Recognition was immediate, and he grasped Rusty's hand. He said, "Captain, me and Rusty rode together up at Fort Belknap. Chased outlaws and Indians. Even caught a few now and then."

The captain said, "If you have not come to join us, what brings you so far west?"

Rusty explained about his mission and showed Andy's letter. The captain nodded grimly. "I'm afraid you've come a long way for nothing. We interrogated the three prisoners at considerable length before we sent them away to jail. All we got out of them was that a man named Bascom was with them in the bank robbery. He left them before they made a try at our horses. I sent men out to try to pick up a trail, but evidently your man traveled a public road long enough to mix his tracks with a hundred others."

"What about the boy?"

"He is still here in camp, to everybody's regret. Private Pickard thinks he can redeem him. I had about as leave try to redeem a wildcat cub."

"Andy's got a good heart."

"One that outweighs his judgment, I am sad to say. I'd have already sent that young heathen back east to the dubious mercy of the court if Pickard hadn't put up such an argument for him. But the boy has pushed me almost to the end of my tether." The captain glanced at Holloway. "Where *is* Pickard?"

"Out on horse guard."

"Send someone to replace him and tell him he has company." The captain gave Rusty a quiet and calculating study. "This company could use a man of your experience. Are you sure you would not like to enlist?"

"It wouldn't be fair to you. The first time I heard something new about Corey Bascom I'd be up and gone."

Andy arrived at the headquarters tent, riding his sorrel. Rusty imagined he looked older and more mature, but only a few weeks had passed since they had last seen one another. After the howdies Rusty said, "I got your letter."

Andy appeared troubled. "I didn't realize how long it would take you to get it and how long it'd take you to reach here. I'm afraid you've wasted the trip."

"I'd still like to talk to that boy."

"Don't judge Scooter too quick. He looks rough and talks rough, but he's never had much chance to be otherwise. I'd like him to get that chance."

Andy's eyes looked so earnest that Rusty could only go along with him. "All I want to do is talk. Maybe there's somethin' he's forgotten to tell."

Andy led Rusty toward the cook tent. He said, "I hope you weren't mad at me, leavin' sudden like I did. Len was goin' to report to the rangers, and it seemed like a good idea to ride along with him."

"You're old enough to know your own mind. I wasn't any older the first time I joined."

Andy showed him a boy he took to be twelve or thirteen, peeling potatoes for the black cook. A dark scowl showed his opinion of the job.

"Boy," the cook said, "there's too much tater goin' out with them peels."

The youngster flourished the knife as if threatening to use it for a weapon. "There'll be an old darkey throwed out with them if you don't leave me the hell alone."

"Captain says you've got to work if you're goin' to eat. Otherwise he's fixin' to send you where he sent them friends of yours. Be a long time before they see freedom."

"I'd be in better company than what I got here."

"I swear, youngun, I don't know what to do with you."

"You don't have to do nothin', just let me be."

Rusty gave Andy a quizzical look. "You really think you can reform that?"

"You reformed me."

"I don't remember you ever sassed me that bad."

"I'd about forgotten how to talk English. By the time I learned it again I'd smartened up." Andy moved into the cook tent. "Bo, can I borrow your helper a little while?"

"Borry him? You can *keep* him. He ain't much help to me."

Andy introduced Rusty. "Scooter, this is the man who raised me after I came back from the Indians."

Scooter gave no sign that he was impressed. To Rusty he was a freckle-faced ragamuffin in donated ranger clothes so large they swallowed him up. His hair was badly in need of barbering. His eyes were his only outstanding feature. Brown and dark as coffee beans, they seemed to be searching for a fight.

Rusty said, "I want to ask you about Corey Bascom."

Scooter's voice was full of resentment. "I already told them all I know. They've asked me twenty times."

"Didn't he give you any idea where he was goin' when he left you?"

"Didn't even say he was leavin'. Just pulled out. Told Arliss and them it was a fool idea tryin' to steal horses from the rangers. He wasn't havin' no part of it."

"What direction did he go?"

"I didn't watch." The boy stuck out his chin in a challenging gesture. "For all I know, he went straight up."

Andy gave Rusty a quiet look that said it was no use. Corey Bascom was too cagey to tell his plans to a kid he had just met. Even if the boy knew more, which was unlikely, he had no intention of sharing it.

Rusty sent him back to his potato peeling. In a show of rebellion, Scooter cut the first skin even thicker than before and flipped it at the cook.

Bo said, "Youngun, I'd like to get a preacher ahold of you. A fire-and-brimstone Baptist."

Rusty and Andy looked at one another. Andy said, "Preacher Webb."

After reflection, Rusty rejected the idea. "Preacher's gettin' too old to take on a wildcat like this."

Andy said, "But you're not."

"Don't try to push that job off onto me. I've already been down that road once, with you."

"I turned out pretty good, didn't I?"

"This boy isn't you. Like as not he'd run off the first chance he got. And if he didn't, he'd make me wish he had."

"Think about it at least. Don't be quick to say no."

"I've already said it."

Andy accepted defeat, if only for the time being. He said, "I'd better go out and finish my turn on horse guard. See you about supper." He untied the sorrel horse.

Rusty said, "I see that Farley Brackett hasn't talked you out of Long Red."

Andy leaned forward and patted the sorrel on the shoulder. "He knows he'd be wastin' his breath."

Rusty watched Andy ride out to where the rangers' extra horses were loose-herded on grass.

The captain said, "I understand you raised Private Pickard."

"Mostly he raised himself, after the Comanches. I just tried to point him in the right direction from time to time and keep him from gettin' killed."

"Now he has a notion he can do the same for that vagabond kid. I'm afraid he is letting himself in for a terrible disappointment. A tree grows as the sapling is bent. This boy has been bent the wrong way too long."

"I guess Andy feels that he owes me, and the way to pay the debt is to do for somebody else what I did for him."

"That speaks well for his intentions, if not his judgment. You'll stay the night with us, won't you, Shannon?"

"So you can keep tryin' to recruit me?"

"You've already said no. I'll not make a nuisance of myself."

"Then I'll be glad to stay. Reminds me of old times."

The cook rang the supper bell. The rangers gathered around, filling their plates from pots and Dutch ovens. The captain glanced about, then asked, "Bo, where's your young helper?"

"He ain't no helper of mine. Sneaks off every chance he

gets. Didn't finish half the spuds I gave him to peel. You ever looked at his neck?"

The captain seemed puzzled. "Can't say that I have."

"He's got a ring around it. Born for a hangman's noose, if you ask me."

"That's just dirt."

After supper Len Tanner and two other rangers rode out to bring the horses up close to camp and relieve Andy of guard duty. The horses came in, and the rangers, but Rusty saw nothing of Andy. He walked up to Tanner.

"Where's Andy?"

"Didn't see him. The horses was scattered more than they ought to've been. It ain't like Andy to've rode off and left them."

Rusty felt stirrings of concern. "No, it's not. Wait 'til I get my horse. We'll go out and look for him."

Jim and Johnny Morris joined them without having to be asked. When they reached the area where the horses had grazed, Jim said, "Me and Johnny will split off and go around this way."

Rusty jerked his head at Tanner. "We'll take the other side."

He had ridden about two hundred yards when he saw Andy rise up out of the grass and stagger to his feet. Rusty whistled to Tanner, who had ridden a wider outside circle. Tanner came in a run.

Rusty saw a bloody streak down Andy's forehead, all the way to his jaw. Andy swayed as if about to fall. Rusty stepped down quickly from the saddle and caught him.

"Did Long Red fall with you?" he asked. So far as he had ever seen, the horse was surefooted.

Andy turned and caught hold of Rusty's saddle to steady himself. "Wasn't Long Red. It was Scooter."

"That kid?"

Tanner and the Morris brothers rode up. Tanner dismounted and took a critical look at Andy's head. "Looks like somebody gave him a six-shooter shampoo."

Andy started to nod but raised his hand to his head and grimaced. "Twice. You wouldn't think a boy that small could hit so hard."

Jim Morris said, "I been warnin' you about him. A little rattlesnake can bite you as bad as a big one."

Rusty said, "Let's get him back to camp. He can tell us about it there."

Jim pointed northward. "We found tracks of a horse headed off yonderway."

Andy said, "He took Long Red."

Tanner spat. "Thievin' little coyote." He mounted his horse, then freed his left foot from the stirrup. "You-all boost Andy up here."

Riding toward camp, Andy explained that Scooter had walked out around the horse herd. "Said the captain wanted to see me right away. He had stolen a pistol somewhere. Soon as I let him swing up behind me, he hit me over the head with it and shoved me out of the saddle. Then he hit me again for good measure. Next thing I remember was Rusty ridin' toward me."

"Ungrateful little whelp," Jim said. "He'd already be in jail if it wasn't for you."

Rusty said, "Not much chance of catchin' him now. It'll be dark pretty quick. By mornin' there's no tellin' how far he'll be gone."

"And on my horse," Andy lamented.

{ FOURTEEN }

Andy's head throbbed so painfully that there were moments when he thought he might die. There were other moments when he feared he might not. He expected the captain to lecture him on his misspent sympathy for a wayward boy, but evidently the officer decided the experience was lesson enough in itself. At daylight the captain detailed the Morris brothers and another ranger to find Long Red's tracks and determine if they could be followed. By late afternoon the men were back. They had lost the trail.

Andy had expected Rusty to start home, but instead he remained in camp. For the time being, at least, he was more concerned about Andy than about trying to find Corey Bascom.

Andy was sick at heart, partly from loss of the sorrel horse but more from the realization that his good intentions toward Scooter had gone for nothing. He felt betrayed. He kept wondering if he might have done more, or done better. In a way he could not analyze, he even felt that he had let Rusty down. Rusty had taken a chance on Andy against long odds a long time ago. What Andy had tried to do for Scooter had been meant as an oblique thank-you to Rusty.

Rusty seated himself on the ground near the spread-out blankets on which Andy lay, a wet cloth across his forehead. He said, "If it's any consolation to you, Farley Brackett is mad as hell. He says if anybody deserved to steal that sorrel horse, it was him."

Andy was too miserable to appreciate Rusty's dark

humor. He said, "Everybody kept tellin' me. I thought I could change Scooter the way you changed me."

"Maybe it was in his blood. More likely it's because he's been mistreated all his life. Beat a young horse every day and he'll outlaw on you. He'll reach a point where there's nothin' much you can do except shoot him. Else he's liable to kill you. That boy was ruined before you ever saw him."

"I guess. I just hoped for better."

"Look at the fugitive list the captain has. Most of the men on it had mothers and daddies who did the best they could to make somethin' out of them. Somewhere, every one of them came to a fork in the road and took the wrong direction. Most of them will never turn around. They'll stay on the devil's road 'til it leads them to the cemetery."

"You figure that's the case with Scooter?"

"He'll end up on the fugitive list, if he lives that long."

After two days Andy felt much better. He expected Rusty to start home, but Rusty showed no inclination to leave. He said he was hanging on a few days longer, hoping some word might come about Corey Bascom. Andy suspected one strong reason was that he enjoyed the rangers' company and the camp life that reminded him of other times.

Whatever the cause, Andy was comforted by Rusty's presence.

The third day after Scooter ran away, Andy saw a horse gallop into the edge of camp, lathered with sweat. The rider pulled up in front of the headquarters tent and dismounted, so exhausted he almost went to his knees. In a weak voice he called for the captain.

The officer came out before the rider could yell a second time.

The man struggled for breath. "Indians, Captain. We got Indian trouble."

Andy turned toward Rusty. He felt a cold dread. "I hoped I'd never have to face this."

Rusty said, "You had to know it was bound to come."

The captain called the company together. He asked Sergeant Holloway, "How many men could be ready to go right away?"

"We have four out on detail. Leaving a few to guard the camp, we have a dozen available men at best, sir, including ourselves."

"Very well, send a detail to bring up the horses."

Farley Brackett had not spoken directly to Andy since Scooter had absconded with the sorrel horse. Andy was conscious now of Farley watching him. He imagined the thought behind the critical eyes: that in a showdown Andy would not be able to go against his Comanche friends.

Rusty gave Andy a gentle nudge. "Somebody's got to help guard the camp. If you don't feel right about this, why don't you stay? Tell the captain you're still not up to a hard ride."

Andy wished he could. "I took an oath. Whatever the captain gives me to do, I'll do it."

"Would you feel better if I went along?"

Andy was not certain what his reaction should be. Rusty's presence always gave him a feeling of security. But in this case it might indicate doubt about Andy. "You're not a ranger anymore. It ain't your fight."

"If there's people bein' killed, it's everybody's fight."

Grim faced, the captain approached Rusty. "Shannon, we are shorthanded, as you can see. You have no obligation to us, and I would not be so bold as to ask you. But if you should decide to ride with us of your own free will, I would happily accept your company. I cannot promise that the state will pay you for your services."

"Half the time I *was* a ranger I didn't get paid for it. I'm not askin' for anything now."

"Spoken like a true Texan." The captain looked at Andy. "Perhaps you should remain here."

Andy said, "I heal fast. I'll go."

He knew the chances of Indians hitting this camp were remote. The report had them many miles to the north, where they had hit a group of cowboys on roundup and had driven off a substantial number of cattle as well as horses.

Farley said, "I can't figure what the Comanches would want with cattle. Their preference runs to buffalo."

Andy replied, "The cattle are for tradin', not eatin'. They drive them north to the canyon country and swap them to Comanchero traders for white-man goods. They don't know much about money, but they know how to trade. They've been doin' it a long time."

Farley grunted, malice in his eyes. "You'd be the one to know."

Andy clenched a fist. One of these days, he thought, me and you are going to knock heads. I'm betting that mine is harder.

The rangers pushed their horses as much as they dared, stopping to camp at dusk. Andy was tired, his head aching. Rusty, on the other hand, seemed rejuvenated. He said, "I feel like I never left the rangers. It's like I've stepped back into old days at Fort Belknap."

Andy said, "The captain would be tickled to have you sign on permanent."

"I might if it wasn't for Corey Bascom. And the farm."

"People like Bascom generally come to a bad end. Sooner or later he'll try to rob the wrong outfit and somebody'll blow his light out. It doesn't have to be you." He realized that what he said about Bascom sounded more than a little like Rusty's comment about Scooter.

Rusty frowned. "If it happens that way, well and good. But if it fell to me to be the one, well, . . . I owe him for Josie."

"Do you think you have to kill him before she can be at rest?"

"No. Before *I* can be at rest."

The ranch was little more than a rough cow camp, its few structures having picket walls and dirt-covered roofs. Its owners clearly intended it to be temporary. None of the cowboys had been killed, but the outfit had been shot up and had lost most of its horses, including several with saddles on.

The wagon boss walked out to meet the rangers. His left arm rested in a sling made of tarpaulin torn from a wagon sheet. His face reddened as he described the incident. "Caught us flat-footed, the boys all scattered around the herd. Took cattle, horses . . . even the camp dog followed and never came back."

The captain said, "I'm sorry we don't have a doctor."

"We taken care of ourselves." The boss raised his wounded arm a little and winced. "This don't hurt near as much as losin' the outfit. I am madder than hell. At them, at us. I'm even a little mad at you for not bein' here when it happened."

The captain nodded. "I suppose you're entitled. Would any of you like to ride with us?"

"We ain't got but two men still on horseback, but they're rarin' to go. It's been all I could do to keep them from chasin' off after the Indians alone." He cursed. "A cowboy with no horse is a sorry sight to behold."

The rangers tarried only long enough to water their mounts and for the two hands to saddle up and join them.

The wagon boss shouted as the riders moved away, "Give them hell, rangers."

The cowboys led the way to where the attack had taken place. "Lucky none of us got killed," one said. "They seemed more interested in gettin' away with the horses and cattle than in takin' scalps."

Holloway told the captain, "If they'd just taken horses they'd be hard to catch up with. But the cattle will slow them down a right smart."

The captain said, "That is our main hope. Otherwise they would probably be out of our reach already."

Andy knew from experience that the raiders would abandon stolen horses only under heavy pressure, for these quickly became regarded as personal property. They would more readily abandon the cattle if they discovered close pursuit. Those, after all, had value to them only for trading.

He hoped they would give up the cattle and push on at a fast enough pace that the rangers would not catch them. Long ago he had been forced to a reluctant choice between white people and red. But his stomach churned with a dread that he might have to fire upon those he had for years regarded as his own.

He felt Rusty's speculative gaze. Rusty, more than anyone here, should understand Andy's conflicting emotions. Farley Brackett studied him with open distrust.

Andy might stretch the facts about his age, but he had given a man's word. He would not back down from it.

A trail left by stolen horses could sometimes be difficult to follow, but to hide the tracks of a cattle herd was impossible. Andy could have followed it with one eye shut. The Indians must have been confident that the cowboys would not be able to follow and chastise them. It was possible they were unaware so far of the rangers' reinstatement. In the past they had feared rangers more than the army or civilian volunteers. They had regarded rangers as a warrior society of unyielding determination and fearsome power.

The trail became fresher, the tracks cleanly cut, the droppings soft and still warm enough that Andy could smell them. For a while now the rangers had been coming across young calves the Indians had left behind because they could not keep up the pace. Andy heard cows bawling. His nerves tightened. He saw Rusty quietly slip the rifle from beneath his leg and bring it up to the pommel of his saddle.

The captain gave an order for the men to stop and tighten their cinches. A slipping saddle could be fatal in a running fight. He said, "If anybody feels like communing with his maker, this would be the proper time."

Andy had a dark feeling it was too late to pray for what he had hoped most, that the Indians would slip away without confrontation.

Holloway asked, "Any orders, Captain?"

"Just one, Sergeant. When we see that they've spotted us, charge. Don't give them time to take count."

Rusty said, "Sounds like old Captain Whitfield. Bible in one saddlebag, whiskey in the other. He was hell on horseback."

The Comanches had three men trailing the herd as a rear guard. They appeared surprised by sight of the rangers riding up over a stretch of rising ground. They hesitated for a moment, seemingly undecided whether to stand and give fight or to run and give warning. One carried a rifle. He threw a quick shot in the rangers' direction and wheeled about, riding away at a high lope. His partners struggled not to be left behind.

The captain said, "We've caught them asleep. Let's wake them up." He motioned with his hand and spurred his horse into a run.

The rangers split around the herd. The cattle spooked at first, splitting off in various directions. Andy thought there might be a hundred or more. The animals stopped their forward movement once the rangers pulled back together beyond the herd.

Ahead, Andy saw dust kicked up by the remuda. The Indians were whipping them into a run. The two cowboys, eagerly responding to sight of their quarry, pulled ahead of the rangers. The captain tried to call them back, but they did not hear. Or perhaps they chose not to.

Rusty spurred his bay horse. He shouted at Andy, "Let's try and catch up to those cowboys. They're liable to get themselves into a fix."

Farley Brackett pushed his horse into a run that put him a little ahead of Andy and Rusty.

The Indians stopped running. Having stampeded the stolen horses, they pulled together into a defensive line. Rough-counting by twos, Andy guessed they numbered twenty or so. They looked like a solid wall.

The captain shouted, "Don't hit them head-on. Cut around the end."

The flanking maneuver momentarily confused the Comanches, but the surprise did not last long. They broke out of the line and made for a stand of timber. Several hung back, fighting a rear-guard action. Rifles and pistols cracked, raising clouds of white smoke. Arrows whispered like wind in a stovepipe. Andy saw a couple of warriors on the ground. He heard a ranger cry out as he was hit. The vanguard of the Indians reached the timber and turned to mount a defense.

The captain shouted, "Smite them hip and thigh."

The rangers lost any semblance of a line. They plunged into the timber by ones and twos. The combat was almost hand-to-hand. Gunfire racketed in Andy's ears. He saw several Comanches who offered good targets, but he could not bring his pistol to bear on them.

He became aware that Farley had gotten himself isolated out to one side and had the full attention of three warriors. His horse was down. The ranger dodged among the trees, afoot. Andy wanted to laugh over his antagonist's precarious situation, but he sobered quickly. Farley stood a strong chance of being killed. He forced down his resentment and spurred in that direction.

Andy wanted to give the Indians a chance to escape. In Comanche he shouted, "Get away! Run!"

One paused long enough to snap a shot at him with an old muzzle-loading rifle much too cumbersome to be effective from horseback. Two warriors disappeared into the heavier growth.

The third appeared determined to bring Farley down. Farley tripped over a deadfall limb. The Indian rushed his horse toward him, drawing back an arrow in his bow. Farley turned over onto his back, eyes desperate. His hands searched for a pistol that had fallen out of his reach.

Again Andy shouted in Comanche, "Get away!"

The Indian turned, swinging the point of the arrow toward Andy. Andy saw the face and recognized it. Holding his breath, his skin afire, he aimed his pistol, then let it drift to the warrior's left. His shot missed. So did the arrow. The Indian turned his horse away and followed the others into the trees.

Andy trembled. His pounding heart seemed about to burst. The man he had almost killed was a friend to Steals the Ponies.

Ashen faced, Farley struggled to his feet. He picked up the weapon he had dropped and quickly glanced around. "Let's get out of here before they decide to come back."

Andy extended his arm. Farley grabbed it and swung up

behind the saddle. He almost jerked Andy from the horse. Andy felt as if his arm had been wrenched from the shoulder.

Farley's voice trembled in the aftermath of fear. "Where's the rest of the rangers?"

Andy found it difficult to speak. "I lost sight of them in the trees. Whichever way we go, we're liable to run into Indians."

"Let's go someplace, even if it's wrong. I don't like it here atall."

Andy could understand that. "Which way?"

"Back out of this timber to where we can see somethin'."

Andy pointed his horse south, where open country showed through the trees.

Farley said, "I felt the devil's breath on my neck. It had the smell of brimstone."

Andy waited for Farley to thank him but soon concluded it was going to be a long wait. Instead Farley said, "You've got a reputation as a good shot. Wasn't no reason for you to've missed that Indian."

Andy would not admit that he had done so on purpose. He wondered if the Comanche might have missed for the same reason. "It's hard to hit a target when you're whippin' through the timber."

"Especially when it's a Comanche. Friend of yours?"

Andy did not reply. He reined up at the edge of the trees, hoping to see the other rangers. He heard continued firing at some distance and wondered how Rusty was doing. He wished they had not become separated in the excitement of the skirmish.

He heard a running horse and whirled around. A Comanche warrior was almost upon him, arrow drawn back. His mouth was open, making a war cry meant to chill the blood of an enemy. By instinct more than calculation,

Andy fired. The arrow drove into his shoulder, knocking him back against Farley. He would have fallen had Farley not held him. Shock was instant. Andy's head reeled. His stomach turned over.

He was aware that the Indian had fallen from his horse and lay in a twisted heap. His face was turned upward, his dying eyes open. Andy recognized him. He was from Steals the Ponies' band.

Andy's meager breakfast came up. He felt himself slipping from the saddle. Farley pulled him back. "Don't you fall, boy. You're liable to drive that arrow plumb through. I don't want two dead Indians on my hands."

Through a red haze Andy saw several rangers ride out of the timber, driving some of the reclaimed horses. Half a dozen Indians came out in an effort to head them off. They quickly spotted Andy and Farley and moved toward them. More Indians appeared behind, blocking escape.

Farley reloaded his pistol. "Hang on. We're fixin' to ride like hell." He put the horse into a hard run straight toward the half dozen warriors. He fired one shot after another, as rapidly as he could pull the trigger. He shouted at the top of his lungs.

"Out of the way, you dog-eatin' sons of bitches!"

Andy felt consciousness slipping away, yet he found enough resentment to murmur, "Comanches don't eat dog."

He was aware that the Indians were surprised by Farley's audacity. They pulled apart, letting him pass between them, then shooting at him in vain. Incongruously Farley laughed aloud. He fired once more and brought a man down.

Farley pulled up. The rangers circled protectively around him and Andy. Andy heard Rusty's worried voice. "Lift him down. We've got to get that arrow out."

Someone said, "The horses are gettin' away."

"To hell with the horses."

Several hands eased Andy from the saddle and lowered him onto his back in the grass. Andy could see swirling images of the men through a reddish haze. He felt his shirt being ripped open.

Rusty said, "A couple of you hold him down. I sure hope that arrowhead ain't barbed."

Andy felt a sharp pain as Rusty tested the shaft, trying to determine how deeply the arrow had penetrated. Rusty said, "Grit your teeth, Andy. This won't be any fun."

Andy started to say, "I'm grittin'," but the words never quite made their way out. Instead he gave a sharp cry as Rusty gripped the shaft and jerked it free. Andy felt as if he were spinning backward, sinking into a bottomless well that blazed with flame, then went dark. The hurting diminished, and he was briefly at peace.

Rusty examined the arrow. He said, "The point is broken off. I'm afraid it may still be in there, too deep to dig for."

Andy's sense of peace was shattered by searing pain as Rusty cauterized the wound with a red-hot knife blade. Andy was aware of a sharp smell of burning flesh. He knew it was his own.

Rusty said, "Sorry. I had it done to me once, and I know it hurts like hell. But out in the field there's no other choice."

Consciousness slipped away again. Andy could hear, but he was not sure what he heard was real. It might be a dream. He thought he heard someone say, "Maybe we can fix up some sort of drag, like the Indians do."

Rusty said, "Too bumpy a ride. Liable to kill him. Let's cut down a couple of those small trees. We'll make a stretcher."

Andy had a sense of floating on air. It took some time for him to realize that the rangers had rigged a makeshift stretcher with blankets and poles. He was being carried between two horses. The ends of the poles were tied into stirrups on each side.

He hoped the horses were gentle enough not to spill him. He had a feeling he would break like an eggshell. The wound in his shoulder felt as if a fire were burning in it. His mouth was so dry that when he ran his tongue over his lips he felt no moistening.

Rusty rode alongside him. Seeing that Andy had awakened he said, "Lay still. Else you're liable to get the blood started again. We like to've not got it stopped in the first place."

Andy had no intention of moving. It hurt too much. He was being jostled enough by the horses that carried him.

Andy found voice, though it was weak. He felt choked. "I killed a Comanche."

"You didn't have a choice. He was set on killin' you."

"But I knew him. He was one of my people."

"Maybe he knew you, too. That didn't stop him from comin' after you. Farley said—"

"Farley." Speaking the name came hard. "If I hadn't gone to pull him out of a tight spot I wouldn't have had to kill anybody."

"That's one way of lookin' at it. Another way is to realize that Farley saved your life, too. He held on to you and got you out of there."

"Where *is* Farley?"

"Helpin' drive the cattle. We got them back. Some of the horses, too."

"Anybody killed?"

"Not on our side. Couple of boys were wounded a little but not as bad as you. Can't say about the Indians."

Andy closed his eyes. He kept seeing the man he had killed. It was a face he knew. He did not want to remember the name, but it came nevertheless. The warrior had been known as Bugling Elk. He had had a piercing voice that could reach far across the prairie. Andy recalled hearing his war cry just before the warrior loosed the arrow. That cry would echo in his mind again and again, perhaps for the rest of his life.

He turned his head to one side.

Rusty said, "Hang on. I know it hurts."

It was not the wound that hurt most.

After long hesitation Rusty said, "There's somethin' else. It's good news in a way. It's also bad."

"How can it be both?"

"We found a sorrel horse amongst those we got back from the Indians. He's your Long Red."

It took a moment for Andy to grasp the ramifications. "What about Scooter?"

"We'd have to figure that the Indians got him."

Andy wanted to cry, but he was too old for it.

{ FIFTEEN }

Corey Bascom studied the cards he had dealt himself, then looked across the table into his adversary's eyes. He searched for a flicker of emotion that might betray the quality of the cowboy's poker hand. He saw a fleeting disappointment, quickly covered. He bet and the cowboy folded, as had two other players before him.

Corey had smiled little since learning of Alice's death. He did not smile now, smothering a momentary elation over winning. The penny-ante bank out at Brownwood had not been as flush as expected, and a four-way split had left him only a few days' traveling money. Since coming to Fort Worth he had more than doubled his stake, however. The lamp-lighted poker tables in Hell's Half Acre had been good to him. They usually were.

In recent years Fort Worth had become his favorite place to go for liquor, women, and some rewarding poker. Here trail outfits on their way to Kansas resupplied for the long trip that still faced them. Their cowboys grabbed a last chance to see the elephant and buck the tiger before beginning the last long leg of their trip north. They often stopped again on their way home.

For a man better than average at manipulating the pasteboards, it was a good place to pad out his roll so long as he did not pit himself against the real professionals from places like Chicago and Kansas City. The district's rowdy action had long offered temporary relief from his family's stifling influence. Though Bessie Bascom was his mother, and he had the affection for her a dutiful son should, she often rubbed him raw like burrs in his underwear. An occasional visit to Hell's Half Acre was akin to a safety valve on a steam boiler.

It had been several weeks since he had left the family, bitter that Lacey had shot Alice on his mother's orders. He had to leave, for had he stayed he might have killed Lacey. The temptation had been strong. His bitterness had only deepened since. For a time he had lost his grip to a point of feeling suicidal. He had provoked a fight with a gambler whose skill with a gun he knew was superior to his own. The son of a bitch had clubbed him to the floor with the heavy barrel of a Colt Navy revolver but had left him alive. Perhaps he had recognized Corey's brief madness for what it was and chose not to take advantage of it.

The close encounter with death had been shock enough to revive Corey's desire for life. He had wandered without purpose, always aware that local law enforcement might be on the lookout for him because of past offenses. Here in this raucous section of Fort Worth he felt relatively secure. Its peace officers were not inclined to be foolhardy. Some had a financial stake in the prosperity of Hell's Half Acre, exacting a percentage of the take as protection money. Several were known to own a substantial interest in some of the district's illicit enterprises. They were selective in their diligence as keepers of the law. Others who had no financial ax to grind were nevertheless aware of their own mortality and did not arbitrarily poke at hornets' nests.

Before he met Alice, Corey had invested enough in commercial female companionship to have bought a small ranch. Since her death the notion had repelled him. Odd, he thought. He had never expected one woman to take such a hold on him that he lost interest in all others. He had tried a couple of nights ago to break Alice's spell by going upstairs with a dark-eyed raven-haired beauty who affected a French accent and claimed to be from New Orleans. To his dismay he had not been able to get past her doorway.

He had never thought about ghosts enough to believe or disbelieve. Now he wondered if Alice's ghost might be riding on his shoulders.

Well, that New Orleans queen was probably just from Arkansas, anyway. Fort Smith, more than likely.

A rough voice demanded, "You goin' to play or just daydream about it?" The other players had shoved back from the table, but the cowboy evidently had not yet lost all of his money. Corey felt honor-bound to oblige him and see that he did not leave here overburdened. He ordered the cowboy a fresh drink and resumed the game.

As his pile grew and the cowboy's shrank, Corey became aware that a couple of men were watching him with more than casual interest. Their clothes were threadbare and dirty, as if they had been sleeping beneath a porch or in a haystack. He knew the breed on sight: two-bit footpads and pickpockets, feeding on the fringes of the real action like dogs prowling under a table in search of scraps fallen to the floor.

He sensed also that they had picked him as a target. Unless he stayed and played until dawn, he eventually had to leave the lamplight and venture out into the darkness. There they would pounce on him like coyotes on a rabbit.

Well, boys, he thought, you may be coyotes, but I ain't no rabbit.

The cowboy threw in his final hand with a gesture of disgust. "You just cleaned my plow."

Corey gave him back five dollars. "Never like to see a man leave the table dead broke." The cowboy hesitated. Pride told him to refuse. Practicality told him to take it. He took it.

Corey cast a quick glance at the two thugs. They were still watching him. He said, "Cowboy, step over to the bar and I'll buy you a drink."

Once there he said in little more than a whisper, "How would you like to earn some of your money back?"

"How? There ain't much I know to do except on horseback. I just proved I ain't no poker player."

"This won't take any skill. All you have to do is go out that door and start walkin'."

Suspicious, the cowboy said, "I was fixin' to do that, anyway. What's the catch?"

"Don't look behind you. Look in the mirror back of the bar. See those two ginks yonder in the corner? One's got a black wool hat. The other one's wearin' a cap he probably stole off of a railroad conductor."

"I see them."

"I think they've got it in mind to lift my roll. I'd like to see them disappointed."

"Then you'd ought to get you a policeman. I'm a trail hand, is all."

"Any policeman I'd find around here may be a friend of theirs. I want you to walk out ahead of me, then wait for me just out of the lamplight."

"You fixin' to use me for a decoy?"

"They won't hurt you. I won't give them the chance."

The cowboy thought it over for a minute. "I wouldn't do this if it wasn't for the money. If you let them kill me I'll be mad as hell."

"Don't worry. I'll be right behind you."

"So will they." The cowboy finished his drink. "Oh well, I'll probably get drowned anyway when we reach the Red River."

Corey watched the drover walk to the door, then pause to look back at the would-be robbers. He feared that might arouse their suspicion, but the thugs were paying no attention to the cowboy. Their gaze was fixed on Corey. He nodded a silent good night to the bartender, then strode at a leisurely pace across the room and out onto the wooden sidewalk.

The cowboy awaited him, just beyond the lamplight that fell upon the dirt street. Corey said, "Here, swap hats with me. Now start walkin' yonderway. Walk slow and stay out of the light."

He ducked into a dark passageway between the saloon and a mercantile store. In a moment he heard footsteps on the boards. A man's low voice said, "There he goes. Let's catch him before he gets to that next streetlamp."

The two footpads passed Corey's hiding place but did

not glance in his direction. He stepped out behind them. Without a word he swung his pistol and slammed it against the woolen hat. The thug went to his knees. His hat rolled across the boards and out into the dirt. Corey clubbed him again for good measure.

The second robber spun around, a small derringer in his hand. Corey struck the pistol barrel down across the man's hairy knuckles, causing him to drop the tiny weapon. He jammed the muzzle of his six-shooter into the man's wide-open mouth.

"If you don't want me to blow all your teeth out, you'll raise those hands," he declared.

The thug's hands shot into the air.

Corey called, "Cowboy, you can come back now."

The cowboy stopped but took a moment to size up the situation before he risked returning. He looked down at the robber crumpled on the sidewalk. "You must've scared him to death. I didn't hear you shoot."

"Just gave him a Sam Colt massage. He'll come around directly. Search this one. Be sure he doesn't have another gun on him."

The cowboy found no weapon. Corey poked the muzzle into the thug's stomach. "Are you a fast runner?"

The robber tried to answer but could not summon voice.

Corey said, "Let's find out. I'll let you start runnin'. I'll count to five, then shoot. Now go."

The cap fell off halfway across the street, but the thug did not stop to retrieve it. Corey counted to five, then put a bullet into a wall just behind the running man. It seemed to encourage him in his speed.

He knelt and went through the fallen robber's pockets. He found a watch and some folding money. He said, "I'll bet you don't even have a pocket watch, cowboy. Here, take this one." He picked up the derringer. It was an over-and-under model that allowed two shots. "How would you like an extra gun?"

"I wouldn't even shoot a rabbit with that little thing. It'd probably make him mad enough to come after me with his teeth bared."

"Well, I'll keep it. Never know when somethin' like this might come in handy." It was small enough that a lawman might overlook it. He stuck it in his pocket. Corey also kept the money. That seemed just inasmuch as the thug had intended to take *his*.

He was a little surprised that the shot did not attract curious onlookers. It took more than a single shot to excite the citizens of Hell's Half Acre. He counted off roughly half the money he had won from the drover. "Much obliged for the help, cowboy. Like a little advice?"

"As long as it don't cost me nothin'."

"Maybe it'll save you somethin'. Stick to playin' mumblety-peg. Poker ain't your game."

He was staying in a little ten-by-twelve room above a whiskey mill. He had used it several times during his visits here and knew he did not have to worry about the management giving him away to any policeman who had more curiosity than judgment. The room key had long since been lost, but a door key would only lead to overconfidence. Any burglar worth his salt could pick a lock as easily as he could pick his teeth. A pistol beneath the pillow was much more reliable for protection.

He climbed the outside stairs and started down the short hall toward his door. Instinct told him to pause. He had left the door closed, but now it was slightly ajar. A thin streak of lamplight showed around its edges. Holding his breath, he drew his pistol. He hit the door hard and rushed into the room, then jumped to one side in case someone was waiting for him with a gun.

He almost shot his brother Newley.

The surprise left him speechless, his heart pounding hard. "I like to've killed you," he said when his breath came back. "What the hell are you doin' here?"

Newley was his next to youngest brother and his favorite of the three. Lacey had always been an irritant to him, cruel and a little dangerous when left to his own devices. Little Anse had always been headstrong and impervious to advice from anyone except Ma and Lacey. Newley was his mother's obedient lackey to the best of his limited abilities, but he showed occasional signs of thinking for himself when he was not under her shadow.

Newley was in deeper shock than Corey had been. He was still looking down the muzzle of Corey's pistol. Shakily he said, "For God's sake put that six-shooter away."

Corey did. Newley swallowed hard. The color began coming back into his face. He said, "That's the second time lately I've come near gettin' shot on your account."

"You oughtn't to surprise me like this."

"I've been huntin' you from Fort Griffin to kingdom come. This is the third time I've been to Fort Worth. I figured you'd show up here sooner or later."

"What do you want with me? I told Ma when I left that I wasn't comin' back, after she had Lacey kill Alice."

"That's one thing I came to tell you. Alice ain't dead."

Corey went stiff, his body tingling. He stared at his brother, not sure he had heard correctly. "Not dead?"

"Lacey got the shakes and picked the wrong target. It was Alice's sister he shot, not Alice."

"Her sister?" Corey's head seemed to spin.

"The one called Josie. It was a natural mistake. Ma was

awful put out about it, though. She's still bound and determined to get Alice."

A chill passed through Corey. "Not if I can stop her, and I'll stop her if I have to kill her." He sat down heavily on the edge of the bed. Hell of a thing to say about one's own mother, he thought, but there weren't many mothers like Ma Bascom. "I'm glad you found me. That's good news about Alice."

"It ain't all good. You know Josie was fixin' to marry a farmer named Shannon."

"I remember some talk."

"Shannon thinks you're the one that shot Josie. He's huntin' for you with blood in his eyes. He mistook me for you. Came within an inch of killin' me." He explained about Shannon breaking into the room at Fat Beulah's.

Corey demanded, "Didn't you tell him it wasn't me that shot Josie?"

"I never got the chance."

"You were probably too scared to think about it."

This was a new experience for Corey, being sought for something he *didn't* do. Up to now he had always been guilty as charged. "If he finds me he'll wish he hadn't. There ain't no clodhopper goin' to get the best of me."

"This one might. He used to be a ranger. And he killed little Anse."

Corey was jarred again. "Little Anse?"

"You know he always thought he could do anything but walk on water. He thought he could draw and shoot faster than Shannon. But he couldn't." Newley explained that Ma had sent him and little Anse out to search for Shannon, to try to kill him before he could find Corey. Shannon had outsmarted them.

Corey's sense of loss over his youngest brother was tempered by his learning that Alice was still alive. He said, "I saw Shannon once at the Monahan place, so I'll know him on sight. But first I've got to think about Alice. If Ma has her mind set on seein' her dead, . . ."

"You know Ma. She says it has to be done. If Alice ever testified in court she could send us all to the penitentiary. Maybe worse."

"I'll worry about Shannon later. First thing I'll do is go to the Monahan place and steal Alice away. I'll take her so far that Ma and Lacey will never find her."

Newley seemed to approve. Like Corey, he had sometimes questioned Ma's opinions, though seldom to her face. That took more courage than he could usually muster. "I'll help you any way I can."

Corey was aware that Newley had had feelings for Alice. During the time she had been with the Bascom family he had seen Newley watching her with sad hound-dog eyes, wishing. Corey had no intention of sharing her, but he knew Newley would help him get her away. Once Corey and Alice were safe from Ma and Lacey he would cut Newley loose on his own. The boy was weak, but maybe he could find some backbone if he were free from Ma's poisonous influence.

"We'll leave come daylight," Corey said.

Ma always kept a dog or two. They were essentially worthless except that they alerted anybody within hearing when someone approached the cabin. Corey had heard her say she never expected much of a dog, so no dog had ever disappointed her. She had often been disappointed in her sons.

Corey remembered a number of occasions when she had also been disappointed in her husband, the late Ansel Bascom. She would chase him away with orders never to come back. He would return, however, and she would grudgingly accept him. After all, he usually brought money with him. She had carried on at the top of her lungs when the state police killed him, but Corey had suspected a lot of it was for show. At least she would never have to wonder anymore where he was.

Right now Ma was down to one dog. It barked long and loud until Corey dismounted and chunked a rock at it. It retreated behind the saddle shed and resumed the alarm. Ma stepped out of the picket house, a shotgun in her hands. She lowered it when she recognized the arrivals, but her stern face offered no warm greeting for the prodigal son.

She said, "I'd about decided you never was comin' back."

"I hadn't figured on it 'til Newley told me Alice is still alive."

Her face took on an ugly twist. "Only because Lacey ain't been able to get close enough to the Monahan house for a clean shot. She don't let herself be seen. I don't reckon you've worked up spine enough to do the job yourself?" She studied him a moment. "No, I didn't figure you would."

"I came here hopin' I might talk you into leavin' Alice alone. I'll take her far away, to where the law never heard of us."

"Sooner or later she'd get dissatisfied and want to come home. She's like a dagger hangin' over this family."

"Not if I take her plumb out of the country."

"You'll have to kill a bunch of Monahans to get her, and she wouldn't have anything to do with you after that. If she wanted you she'd have come back here already."

"Knowin' you intended to kill her? She's not a fool."

"Maybe not, but you are. If she ever got on a witness stand she'd talk like a revival preacher. Whatever me and Lacey done, we done to protect this family."

"Shootin' the wrong woman and settin' a ranger on my trail? The best protection I can think of is distance. Once I get Alice, you won't see any more of me or her."

"You ain't got her yet. We don't even know for sure if she's still at the Monahans'. Lacey thinks they might've spirited her away someplace."

"If so, they can't take her so far that I can't find her."

"Then you'd better be sure you find her before me and Lacey do. Otherwise . . ." She shook her head sadly. "I thought I'd raised you better than to let a pretty face turn you against your own. Your poor old pa would be mightily ashamed."

"My poor old pa never felt ashamed for anything in his life except gettin' caught. Where *is* Lacey, anyway?"

Ma jerked her head toward the cabin. "Catchin' him some rest. He's laid up many a night watchin' the Monahan place, hopin' for another chance at Alice."

"You tell him that if he tries again I'll kill him."

"You'd kill your own brother?"

"Dead as a gut-shot mule." Corey could not remember a completely happy day he and Lacey had ever spent together. He glanced at Newley. "You comin' or stayin' here?"

Newley shrugged as if neither choice offered any pleasure. "I reckon I'll go along with you."

Newley showed him where they had buried little Anse beneath a tree a couple of hundred yards from the house. The marker was a cross made from two pieces of pine lumber. Painted on it in crude letters was *Ansl Bascom.*

Couldn't even spell his name right, Corey thought. It didn't matter much. Nobody was likely to see it except family. The paint would weather away, the cross would fall over and rot, and the grave would be forgotten. It would be as if little Anse had never lived. Other than immediate family and the Bascoms' victims, no one had ever cared.

Poor kid never had much chance. He let Ma run his life, and obeying her had caused his death. Corey felt more resentment toward his mother than toward the man who had shot little Anse.

He asked Newley, "Are you' set for a few more days' ride? I figure on goin' to the Monahan farm."

"Why not? All I've done lately is travel."

Corey and Newley sat on their horses in the edge of the timber and studied the Monahan farm three hundred yards away. It looked no different than the last time Corey had seen it. He knew things had changed drastically within the family, however. He could only imagine what a shock Josie's death must have been, coming on top of Clemmie's illness. He had developed a grudging liking for the Monahan family, though he knew his elopement with Alice had created a hostility he would never be able to overcome. It would be useless to ride in boldly and assert his claim to his wife, even if he argued that it was the only way to save her. James Monahan would probably shoot him on sight. If he didn't, and Clemmie had recovered enough to hold a gun, she would probably do it.

No, the only way would be to slip in there in the dark hours of early morning and rush her away before the family could react. That would be no easy matter. If it were, Lacey would already have sneaked in and killed her. Lacey had a streak of cowardice that limited the risk he was willing to take. Corey told himself he had no such shortcoming. Being brave did not have to include being foolish, however. He would study the situation and plan his move carefully.

The time he had worked for the Monahans had made Corey familiar with the layout of the farm, where its buildings stood in relation to one another, where he could hide horses as near as possible and the route he could take to get into the main house. He remembered the configuration of the rooms and where Alice would be sleeping. This was knowledge Lacey did not have.

It was almost certain that someone would stand watch at night. Corey was confident he could find and take care of the guard. He felt he could get into the house and into Alice's room. The real trick would be getting her out and to the horses, especially if she resisted and put up a holler. The quickest way would be out the window. The Monahans probably would not risk shooting at him for fear of hitting her in the dark.

Newley asked, "What if she ain't there? What if they've snuck her away like Ma said? You might get in the house, but you're liable to have hell gettin' out."

That question had nagged Corey, too. "I wish there was some way to be sure she's there before I go dancin' around a bear trap."

"It's a cinch you can't just ride in there and ask them."

A horse left the barn and moved in their general direction. A small boy sat on its back.

Corey motioned for Newley to pull a little farther into the trees. "Yonder may be the answer. That's Clemmie's grandson Billy. I used to saddle his pony for him so he could ride. Him and me got along real good."

"Things may be different with him now. He's old enough to know that they don't speak your name anymore without addin' a cussword to it. And if he tells his folks he saw you, they'll figure out what you've got in mind."

"We'll keep him with us a while. When he doesn't come in for supper the menfolks'll start out huntin' for him. That'll make it easier for me to grab Alice and go."

Newley shrugged. "We've been charged with everything else. Kidnappin' a kid will be somethin' new."

"Not kidnappin'. Just borrowin' for a little while."

He waited until the boy had skirted around the edge of the timber and was out of sight should anybody be looking in his direction from the houses or barn. "You stay back," he told Newley. "He doesn't know you. You might scare him."

Corey rode out to intercept the youngster. Billy reined up, surprised.

"Howdy, Billy. How's my boy?"

Billy said nothing. He lifted the reins as if he were about to turn and run away.

Corey said, "Don't be scared. I'm not fixin' to hurt you. Just want to talk. What're you doin' out here by yourself?"

Billy swallowed hard. "Lookin' for a milk cow. She ain't come in for a couple of days. Daddy says she's probably had her calf and she's hidin' it out."

"Cows do that."

"Everybody's mad at you. They wouldn't want me talkin' to you."

"I know. They think I killed your Aunt Josie, but I didn't. I wasn't even here."

Billy seemed to want to believe. "You wasn't?"

"No. If I'd known it was goin' to happen I'd have stopped it. How's your Aunt Alice?"

"I don't know."

"But she's livin' right there in your grandmother's house. How come you don't know?"

"Because she's not there. Rusty Shannon took her away, him and Andy."

Somehow Corey was not especially surprised. They had smuggled Alice out under his brother Lacey's nose. He even began to see a little humor in it. "Where did they take her, Billy?"

"Down to Rusty's farm, I guess."

"Where is his farm?"

"I've never been there. They say it's a long ways. I've heard them talk about the Colorado River."

That did not tell him much. The Colorado River cut across most of Texas, starting somewhere up in Comanche country and flowing generally southeastward all the way down to the Gulf of Mexico. During the time Corey had worked for the Monahans he had heard them mention Shannon's farm a few times. He reasoned that it must be somewhere downriver, probably around Austin or farther east, where the settlements were no longer new.

He asked, "Are you sure they haven't mentioned the name of a town?"

Billy thought a moment. "Alice has written Granny a couple of letters. Postmark had the name of a place called Columbus."

Corey knew in a general way where Columbus was. He also knew that the letter had probably been posted miles from where Alice was staying. That was a logical precaution in case the wrong people saw it.

But Columbus was a starting place. It narrowed the search.

"Billy, it might be a good idea if you don't tell your folks you talked to me. I wouldn't want you to get a spankin' on my account."

"I wouldn't want one, either."

"And believe me, I didn't kill your aunt." He had developed a soft spot for the boy while he had lived here. Billy's approval meant something to him.

Billy said, "You were always nice to me. I never wanted to think you done what they said."

"You're a good boy. You'll be a good man someday. Now, you go find your cow. And remember, don't tell anybody about me."

The boy went on. Corey watched him a while, glad there was no reason to hold him, after all.

Newley rode closer. "You just lettin' him ride off?"

"There's no point in keepin' him. Alice is gone."

"I heard some of what he said. Where is this Columbus town?"

"Down on the Colorado River."

"What'll I tell Ma?"

"Don't tell her a damned thing. I'm goin' down there and hunt 'til I find Alice."

"And then what?"

"I'll cross that river when I get there."

{ SIXTEEN }

Bessie Bascom was churning butter when she heard the dog start to bark. She muttered under her breath, for she hated to be interrupted in her work. She picked up her shotgun and checked to be sure shells were in the chambers, then she stepped outside. She could not remember the last time a stranger had brought good tidings to her door. Her tensed-up shoulders relaxed when she saw that the incoming rider was her son Newley. He was alone.

"Where's your brother Corey?" she demanded as soon as Newley came within hearing distance.

"Gone."

Drawing a reluctant answer out of her sons could be almost as difficult as pulling their teeth. It always irritated her. When the boys became evasive it was a sign things were not going just right. In trying to avoid touching off her volatile temper they often carried her to the brink of violence and sometimes pushed her over. Every one of them bore marks left by her quirt, testimony to past outbursts.

"I ain't blind," she replied, "but where did he go?"

"Off huntin' for Alice. She's not at the Monahan place."

She had suspected that. "Has he got any notion where she's gone to?"

Her son's hangdog manner told her he was holding back. Dismounting, he did not look directly into her eyes. "Didn't tell me nothin'. Just rode off."

"Whichaway?"

"South."

"He must've had some notion, then. You sure you're tellin' me all of it?"

"As much as I can."

Now she was certain he knew more than he was admitting. She heard footsteps and saw her son Lacey walking up from the barn. She said, "Lacey, you've always had a knack for keepin' your younger brothers in line." He was half a head taller and thirty pounds heavier than Newley. "Corey has gone off after that Monahan wench. I think Newley knows where, but he ain't tellin'. See if you can persuade him."

Newley backed away. "I've done told you all that Corey told me. Ain't no use in us fightin'."

There was not much fight to it. Lacey got an arm under Newley's and around the back of his neck. He applied pressure until Newley cried out, "Enough."

Ma asked, "How's your memory now?"

She thought for a moment Newley was going to cry. Damned poor conduct for a grown man, in her opinion. He took after his old pa in some ways she could not abide. Ansel Bascom had always had more mouth than guts despite the glowing image of him she held up to her sons. She had wanted to make them better than their father had been, but she was often disappointed.

Newley regained his composure, to a degree. "He's just tryin' to save Alice. He knows you and Lacey want to kill her."

"Damned right we do. She's bad medicine for all of us, you included, if you had the sense to see it. Now, where's he gone?"

"He didn't tell me hisself, but I heard that little boy of the Monahans's say somethin' about a town called Columbus. It's way down on the Colorado River, the other side of Austin. Seems like that ranger Shannon has got a farm down there someplace."

"The one that killed little Anse?"

"That's him."

"So Corey figures if he can find Shannon he can find Alice."

Newley's voice took on a pleading tone. "He still loves her, Ma. Says if he finds her he'll take her a long ways off. She won't be talkin' to no court, nor testifyin' to nothin'."

"She sure won't if we can find her. And if Corey can, we can, too. You boys catch us some fresh horses to ride. And a pack horse. I'll go rustle up grub for the trip."

Newley protested, "I don't want no part of this."

"You'll go if I have to whip you like a chicken-stealin' hound. I swear I don't know what it'll take to put some manhood into you."

Lacey grabbed Newley by the collar and pushed him toward his horse. "Get goin'. I expect Corey has got a good start on us. We have a lot of country to cover."

* * *

Rusty and Tanner lifted Andy from the improvised stretcher and placed him upon a blanket on the ground. Fully conscious, Andy was aware that they had reached the cow camp. His shoulder burned all the way through. He imagined he could still feel the searing of the cauterizing blade.

Rusty asked, "You feelin' all right?"

Damn fool question, Andy thought, but he chose not to be sarcastic. He lied, "I'm makin' it fine."

The wagon boss was exuberant over recovery of the cattle. He counted the horses and accepted the losses with good grace. "You got back more than half of them," he said. "I'd already said good-bye to the whole bunch."

Though Andy knew the feeling was disloyal, he was glad the Comanches had held onto some of the horses. They had paid a considerable price. At least they would not have to return to their encampment empty-handed.

He was gratified to have Long Red again, but he grieved over the cost. He could only guess what had happened. He did not want to think about it, but the image refused to leave him. The kid probably had but one thought, to get away, and had ridden blindly into the Indian raiding party. Had he been only five or six years old they might have kept him as they had once kept Andy. But he was old enough that they would regard him as a man, a potential warrior against them. They would have made short and bloody work of him.

Perhaps everybody had been right, that Scooter was fated to a violent end, if not this way, some other. But Andy thought he had deserved at least one more chance to compensate for suffering through a life of abuse and deprivation.

Rusty had tried to ease Andy's distress. "Been many a

boy even younger killed for no fault of his own. He brought this on himself."

The wagon boss gave Andy a minute's brief sympathy for his wound before turning to other matters. He told the captain, "The least I can do is make you the loan of a wagon so you can carry your wounded back to camp. And we'll whup you-all up some dinner so nobody goes away from here hungry. I hope you like beans."

The captain said, "When men are hungry, a pot of red beans is like ambrosia."

The thought of food made Andy nauseous. He knew he was running some fever.

Farley had given Andy little attention since the skirmish. Now he walked up to the blanket where Andy lay and stared down at him with accusing eyes. He said, "We're even now. You ran off the Comanche that wanted my scalp. I toted you out of there before some other heathen could snuff you out. We don't owe one another nothin', do we?"

His tone of voice rubbed Andy like coarse sand. He muttered, "Not a damned thing."

"Good, because the captain needs to know what happened out there."

Rusty butted in. "And what *did* happen?"

"This boy had a clean shot at that first Comanche. Wasn't no way he could've missed unless he wanted to. I'm thinkin' he wanted to. If that Indian hadn't got scared off he'd have killed me deader than hell."

"But he shot the next one."

"It was *his* life on the line that time. If he hadn't fired, that arrow might've gone into his heart."

"You're makin' a serious charge. You'd better think about it twice before you talk to the captain."

"I'm tellin' it the way I saw it."

"You saw it the way you wanted to see it. You've carried

a grudge against Andy for a long time. Now, if you're lookin' for a fight, . . ."

Andy raised his good hand. "Rusty, don't. There's no use you and him bloodyin' one another. The truth is, he's right."

Rusty did not show as much surprise as Andy would have expected. He had probably sensed it all along but was willing to fight for Andy's sake.

Andy said, "I recognized the one that was after Farley. He used to teach me how to track game. I hoped I could scare him off without killin' him."

Farley said, "So you left him alive to raid again."

Rusty retorted, "Killin' or not killin' one Indian ain't goin' to make much difference. There's still aplenty more."

Farley said, "The point is that when it came to makin' a choice, he chose the Comanches over his friends."

Rusty argued, "You never was his friend. A friend wouldn't carry a story like this to the captain."

Their voices were becoming strident. Andy tried to shout to get their attention, but he could not muster the strength. He waved his hand. "You-all back off. I'll tell the captain myself."

Farley continued to glare at Rusty. "All right, but I want to be there to see that you tell it straight."

Rusty said, "Andy doesn't lie."

The captain came around when one of the cowboys brought up a wagon. "Pickard, you and Private Mitchell will ride in this the rest of the way back to camp. It should be more comfortable than that makeshift stretcher."

Andy said, "Captain, you may want to leave me behind after you hear what I have to say."

"That you hesitated about shooting an Indian?"

Andy had not anticipated that the captain might already know. "Somebody told you?"

"No, I guessed. I halfway expected it, under the circumstances."

"And you still let me come along?"

"I doubted it would make a life-or-death difference."

"It almost did. Maybe I'd have made the second shot good if Farley's life had depended on it. Maybe not. I can't be sure."

The captain frowned. "You're hurting, and you look feverish. This discussion can wait until we get back to camp and you are better fixed to know your mind." He motioned for a couple of rangers to lift Andy into the waiting wagon. They stretched him out on a folded blanket.

Rusty leaned worriedly over the sideboard. "If the ride gets too rough, be sure to holler. The point of that arrowhead may start workin' around in your shoulder."

Andy felt it would be fitting if a little of the arrow *was* still imbedded. It would afford a punishment of sorts for his having killed one of those he had considered his own people. It would be his penance.

Andy caught the welcome smell of wood smoke and knew the trip was almost over. By any standard the ranger camp was Spartan, but the line of tents looked like home. Reaching it meant an end to the wagon's jolting and jerking. The black cook came out to meet the arriving rangers. Andy saw him pointing with his forefinger, silently counting them one by one, smiling when he saw that none were missing. He turned his attention to Andy and Private Mitchell, the only two other than the wagon driver who did not come in on horseback. Mitchell had taken a bullet in his thigh, but it had passed through without striking a bone.

Bo clucked in sympathy. "Looks like you-all found the Indians you was lookin' for."

Tanner rode up and said, "We whupped up on them

pretty good." He described the fight in more detail than the cook probably wanted to hear. Andy cringed, especially at the account of his killing an Indian.

Rusty noticed his discomfort. He said, "Len, I think I heard the captain call your name."

Tanner left. He was back in a while. "All that shootin' must've done somethin' to your hearin', Rusty. Captain wasn't lookin' for me, after all."

By then the cook was busy in the mess tent, preparing supper. Tanner went in to finish his story, but Andy did not have to listen to it.

The captain came around to check on his wounded.

Andy said, "Captain . . ."

The captain waved him off. "Get some rest, Pickard. We'll talk about it tomorrow. Or maybe the next day."

Rusty waited until the captain was out of earshot. He said, "Leave well enough alone. The captain isn't blamin' you for anything, and you shouldn't be blamin' yourself."

"I can't help it. I didn't do right by the rangers when I pulled my aim off of that first warrior. And I didn't do right by the People when I shot the other one."

"You did right by yourself. If you hadn't you'd be dead and I wouldn't be standin' here tryin' to pound some sense into you."

"When do you figure on goin' home, Rusty?"

"I haven't decided. I was kind of enjoyin' the camp. Took me back to the old days. For a little while it even made me think maybe I'd like to join up. But that skirmish took me back to a part I never did like. The farm gets to lookin' pretty good."

"Will you take me with you when you go?"

"Thought you was tired of the farm."

"Like you said, that fight has made the farm look pretty good."

"You ain't been a ranger long enough to draw your first pay, hardly."

"It'd be blood money if I did."

"That's the fever talkin'. Wait a couple of days before you jump off into a ditch you might not be able to climb out of."

The next day Andy felt like leaving the blanket and walking around the camp a little. The cook waylaid him at the mess tent. "What you need for healin' is lots of meat, wild meat. Ain't nothin' better for you than venison. Come, let me fry you up a piece of backstrap."

"You gave me more at breakfast than I could eat."

"That was a while ago. This'll put strength in your legs, let you run like a deer."

"I don't care about runnin'. I just want to get to where I can ride so I can go home."

"What's this about goin' home? Mr. Tanner been tellin' me what you done out there. You're too good a ranger to be quittin' on us now."

"Don't take what Len tells you as gospel. If hell has a place for liars, he's due a good scorchin'."

"Just don't be in no hurry. My old master was bad to make fast judgments. Most generally they was wrong, like the time he seen somethin' in the brush, movin' toward his hog pen. Figured it was a mongrel dog. He went chargin' in there throwin' rocks. Turned out it was a bear. You never seen a fat old man run so fast."

The next day Andy asked Rusty to saddle Long Red for him. He rode him around the outside of the camp. His shoulder ached a bit but not as much as he expected. Rusty waited for him at the corral, silently asking with his eyes.

Andy said, "It's not so bad."

"You just made a little circle. It's several days' ride back to the farm."

"Give me a couple more days. I can do it."

"That Indian still weighs heavy on your mind. Do you think a couple hundred miles will make him go away?"

"It'll put me where I'll never have to do that again."

By the third day Andy was convinced he was ready. Rusty followed him to the captain's tent but remained outside. Andy asked, "You got time to talk to me, Captain?"

The captain studied him, then shrugged in resignation. "Your face betrays your decision. You are not a good poker player."

"I've decided to resign. I'm goin' home with Rusty."

"I believe you have it in you to become an exceptional ranger. Perhaps even an officer someday. May I suggest an alternative course?"

"Won't hurt to listen to it."

"In view of your wound and the healing time it will require, you are due a leave of absence. Without pay, of course. At the end of that time, if you are still of the same mind, I will accept your resignation with regret."

Andy considered. This was a way of leaving the door ajar without firmly committing himself. "Sounds fair to me, sir. I'll write you if I decide not to come back."

The captain extended his hand. "Don't push yourself too hard. You may be hurt more than you realize."

More than *you* realize, Andy thought. The pain was not all physical.

Andy hesitated at the front opening. He turned back. "If you ever find out just what happened to Scooter, . . ." Someone, sometime, might come across the boy's body.

"It's not likely we'll ever know."

Rusty frowned. "Looks to me like you're carryin' a double load, that boy and that Indian. You couldn't help either one of them."

Like you couldn't help Josie, Andy thought. Me and you are both saddled with ghosts.

They prepared to leave the ranger camp after breakfast. Rusty made one last attempt to postpone the trip. "A couple more days would make you stronger."

"In a couple of days we'll be closer to home."

Rusty took the pack mule's lead rope. After a mile or so he could turn the mule loose and trust it to follow the horses. "If that shoulder really gets to hurtin', let me know. We'll stop and rest."

"I'll holler." Andy had no thought of doing so unless the hurting became more than he could handle. He had made strong talk and intended to back it up. By mid-afternoon he was gritting his teeth in an effort not to give in to the pain. Rusty must have sensed it. He dismounted beside a narrow creek.

"We've come twenty-five miles or so. My bay is commencin' to slow down."

Andy was grateful but felt obliged to put up a good front. "Me and Long Red are doin' fine."

"We've got to consider the stock." Rusty unsaddled and caught the mule. He lifted the pack of provisions from its back. "Bo gave us enough vittles to get us to Friedrichsburg or maybe Austin. We can swing around and miss the troubles in Mason town."

"You know about them?"

"I didn't get a very warm welcome there. It's a local feud. No point in us gettin' mixed up in it."

"The rangers *are* mixed up in it, a little. The captain's been sendin' men over to try and hold the lid down."

"It's a good thing Texas has rangers again."

"It is. But there's no law says I have to be one of them."

They reached Friedrichsburg on the third day of a slow trip. Rusty said, "Bo was right good for a camp cook, but you're fixin' to get one of the best meals this side of Clemmie Monahan's table." He took Andy into the Nimitz Hotel for supper. Andy felt out of place with the white tablecloths and fine tableware.

Rusty said, "I could get spoiled in a hurry with fixin's like this."

Andy realized Rusty was trying to lift his spirits, to relieve for even a while the darkness that had come over him since the fight. He made up his mind to smile and enjoy it whether he wanted to or not.

At the easy pace Rusty set, they were more than a week in getting back to the farm. At a glance Andy knew someone had been taking care of the place in Rusty's absence. Tom Blessing and his sons, he guessed, and perhaps old Shanty. The corn was near shoulder-high. In the garden, cut and shriveled weeds showed the mark of a hoe.

Rusty said, "Maybe your shoulder will be a lot better by the time the garden needs much work again."

"It feels better this mornin' just by us gettin' here. I don't aim to lay around doin' nothin'."

"I don't want you takin' on very much for a while. You might ruin that shoulder. I'd have a cripple on my hands from now on."

"The place won't be the same without Len Tanner comin' around every so often."

"Ranger or not, he'll find a way. You go in and get a fire started so we can fix dinner. I'll unsaddle the horses and unpack the mule."

Tom Blessing came by in the early afternoon. He

shouted, "Hello the house" before riding all the way in. Rusty and Andy walked out on the dog run to meet him. Tom dismounted and led his horse up to the hitching post.

"Saw smoke from your chimney, but I couldn't be sure if it was you or some passin' stranger stopped to fix him a meal. Glad to see you home." He looked at Andy. "Thought you joined the rangers." He noticed Andy's bandaged shoulder. "What did you get in the way of?"

Rusty answered for Andy. "A Comanche arrow. Andy hasn't made up his mind if he wants to be a ranger anymore. How's Mrs. Blessing?"

"That Alice girl has been like a tonic to her. She's startin' to act like she's thirty again. Forty, anyway." Tom's smile gave way to an expression of concern. "I'm glad you've made it home. We've got to do somethin' about Alice."

Rusty turned apprehensive. "Somethin' happened to her?"

"Not yet, but she's awful homesick. Wants to go see her mother. Every time I leave the house, I worry that she may not be there when I get back."

"You think she'd go all by herself?"

Tom nodded. "I wouldn't be surprised. She's got nerve."

"Nerve runs in the Monahan family. But she can't take care of herself against the likes of Corey Bascom. He already tried once to kill her. He might get it done the next time."

"I wish you'd go talk to her. My wife tends to take Alice's side. Neither one of them seems to realize the danger she'd put herself in, strikin' out alone."

Rusty did not study long. He said, "I'll ride over there with you."

"You'll have to go by yourself. I'm on my way to town. Got to be in court for a couple of days."

"I'll try to talk her into stayin' a while longer."

"Stayin' may not be a good idea, either. I heard a feller was in town askin' how to find your farm."

"Corey Bascom?"

"Might be. The description fits what you've told me."

Rusty smiled coldly. "Maybe I won't have to hunt him anymore. Maybe he'll come huntin' me."

Tom said, "The only reason he'd be lookin' for you would be to locate Alice. If he can find out where you are, it's only a matter of time 'til he learns where Alice is. We need to move that girl to a safer place."

"I could bring her here. And when he comes for her, I'll have him."

Tom gave him a look of disbelief. "Use that girl for bait? It's not like you, Rusty. What if somethin' went wrong?"

Rusty reconsidered. "You're right. It was a fool notion that just popped into my head."

"The reason you brought her to my place was so her husband couldn't find her. Now I'm afraid he's fixin' to. She's been wantin' to go home, and I'd say that's the best place for her, amongst her own folks. They can protect her better than I can."

Andy had listened without saying anything. Now he told Rusty, "You snuck her away from home in the dead of night. You could do the same thing again."

Rusty nodded. "Looks like that's what I've got to do. Think you can take care of yourself 'til I get back?"

"You're talkin' to a ranger. Used-to-be ranger, anyway. Go and do what has to be done."

{ SEVENTEEN }

Rusty had just finished unpacking the mule. Now he packed again with provisions for the several days' ride to the Monahan farm. Andy helped where he could, though he had but one hand to work with. He said, "There's liable to be gossip, you and Alice goin' all the way up there by yourselves. It'll take several days . . . and nights."

"I've got no interest in Alice, not in that way. I'm just tryin' to save her life."

"And maybe playin' hell with her reputation."

"Reputation doesn't plow a field or put money in the bank, and gossip doesn't draw blood. Everybody knows it was Josie I wanted. Alice is too young for me."

"Not that much younger than Josie was. Looks a lot like her, too. All three of them Monahan girls favored one another."

Rusty felt a rising irritation. In an oblique way Andy was reminding him that he had lost Geneva, then had first been attracted to Josie because she resembled her older sister. True, Alice looked a bit like Josie, but that was different. Besides, she was married, or would be until justice overtook Corey Bascom. It wasn't in Rusty to trifle with a married woman even if she did remind him a little of Josie and Geneva.

Riding toward Tom's place, he considered the long trip ahead. He did not expect pursuit if they got away in the dark of the moon. They would strike out across country instead of following the usual trails, so interception would be unlikely even if Corey outguessed them.

He had an uneasy feeling that he was being followed. Looking back, he saw no one.

Getting Indian notions like Andy, he thought.

After a time he came to a dry creekbed and took advantage of its cover to double back on his trail. Still he saw no one. He decided Tom's report had cut the reins on his imagination.

Alice stood on the dog run, watching his approach. For a moment the sight of her was unnerving. He could easily have mistaken her for Josie. Andy's words came back to him. By the time Rusty reached the double cabin, Mrs. Blessing stood at Alice's side. She looked stronger than he had seen her in the past year.

Rusty took off his hat and spoke first to Mrs. Blessing because she was the oldest and due the deference. Then he told Alice, "I was talkin' to Tom. He said you're itchin' to go home."

"Don't try to talk me out of it. I've been away too long."

"Hear anything from your mother?"

"Her letters say she's a lot better. Walkin' on her own, doin' most of the things she wants to. But she still needs my help."

She sounds like Josie, too, he thought.

Mrs. Blessing said, "I hate to lose Alice, but she's right. It's time you took her home. She'll be a godsend to her mother like she's been to me."

Rusty had argued with himself on the way over here. Should he tell Alice that Corey might be about to track her down? He had decided she was entitled to know about the danger she faced. He said, "Somebody's been askin' questions about my farm. Tom thinks it was probably Corey. Once he finds me it won't take him long to find you."

The news did not disturb her as much as he had thought it might. "All the more reason I ought to go home."

"That's what I brought the pack mule for. Soon as it's good and dark we'll leave. You'd best pack whatever you want to take."

Alice smiled the way Josie used to smile, and Geneva. "*Home*. The prettiest word I know."

Mrs. Blessing said, "I'll miss you, but it's for the best if you're in danger here."

Rusty led the bay horse and the mule down to the barn. He took off the saddle and pack and poured some dry oats into a wooden trough. "Eat good, boys. You've come a long ways, and you've hardly got started yet."

The two women cooked supper, the best meal Rusty had eaten since the hotel in Friedrichsburg. Afterward he stood on the dog run or walked around the outside of the cabin, looking for anyone who might be out there watching. Dusk seemed to last for hours. He tingled with anxiety to be on his way.

At last, when he thought it was dark enough, he went out to the barn and packed the mule, then saddled the two horses. He was about to lead them from the corral when the mule snorted and poked its long ears forward. Rusty turned quickly, but not quickly enough. He caught a glimpse of a dark figure just before a gun barrel came down on his head. It knocked him to his knees and elbows.

A rough voice said, "I always found that the best way to win a fight is to get in the first lick. That one was for little Anse. Try to get up and I'll hit you again. That one will be for me."

Rusty felt paralyzed, unable to move. He knew this was Corey Bascom. He wanted to shout to Alice to stay away, but he could not summon voice.

He sensed that she was on her way to the barn. He could

hear her footsteps. She opened the gate and said, "I'm ready, Rusty."

Corey said, "Rusty ain't ready, but I am."

She made a sharp, involuntary cry before he grabbed her and clapped a hand over her mouth. "Don't holler. I wouldn't want somebody else to come out here and get hurt."

He removed the hand from her face. She gasped. "Corey! What're you fixin' to do?"

"Same as he was, gettin' you away from here before Ma and Lacey find you. I know they're lookin' because I've felt their breath on the back of my neck."

"What makes you think I'd go with you?"

"Because I ain't givin' you any choice. Listen, woman, I'm tryin' to keep you from bein' killed."

"Like you killed Josie?"

"I didn't kill Josie. That's the God's truth. Lacey done it. He thought she was you. Next time he may not miss."

She took a moment to consider that. "I'm inclined to believe you. But Rusty was fixin' to take me back to my people."

"That's too close to *my* people. I'm takin' you someplace where they'll never find you."

Rusty reached for the corral fence, trying to pull himself up. Corey raised the pistol. Alice caught his arm. "Don't, Corey, please. He was just tryin' to help me."

"From now on that's my job. You're still my wife. What's this man to you, anyway?"

"A family friend, that's all. Josie and him was plannin' on gettin' married."

"There ain't nothin' goin' on between the two of you?"

"Of course not. But please don't hurt him any more. He's already been hurt a way too much."

"I won't hurt him if you'll get on that horse and behave

yourself. We're leavin' here." He threw Rusty's pistol over the fence. He unsaddled Rusty's horse and ran it out of the corral. He remounted his own and grabbed the reins of Alice's horse. He said, "I don't know what all is packed on that mule, but it'll come in handy on the trip. Let's go."

As the two rode by the cabin, Mrs. Blessing stood on the dog run, a silhouette against lamplight from the kitchen. She shouted, "Alice, I thought you-all were headed north."

Corey said, "Don't answer her."

Alice shouted back anyway. "Rusty's hurt. Out at the barn. Go help him."

"Then who's that you're with?"

Alice tried to answer, but Corey gave her horse's reins a rough jerk. She swallowed the words.

Though the rising moon was little more than a sliver and yielded faint light, she knew they were traveling south. She kept looking back in the darkness, half hoping Rusty was coming, yet afraid of what might happen if he was. She believed what Corey had said about Lacey having killed Josie. Though Corey was capable of violence, she had found it difficult to believe he could have shot her sister. Lacey, on the other hand, . . .

They rode in frosty silence a long time. Finally he demanded, "Ain't you goin' to say somethin'?"

"There's nothin' to say. You've said it all."

"You might cry a little then, so I'll know you're still breathin'."

"I got over cryin' a long time ago, after Josie died."

"I told you I had nothin' to do with that. I came near killin' Lacey for what he done. I never intended for you to be hurt, nor none of your family. Damn it, Alice, I love you."

"Is this the way you show it, by kidnappin' me?"

"I'm not kidnappin' you. You're my wife. I'm takin' you where you'll be safe."

"And where is that?"

"Mexico. I figure we can lose ourselves down there. Nobody'll find us."

"What can we do in Mexico? I'd never feel at home there. I don't even speak any Spanish. Do you?"

"A few cusswords is all."

"I don't want to go to Mexico. I want to go home. I want to see my mother walkin' again. I want to see her movin' and talkin' natural."

Corey rode a while before he spoke again. "What happened to Josie was awful. I don't want it happenin' to you."

"It won't. My family would see to that."

"What about me? Chances are your brother James would kill me, or try to. Maybe you'd like to see me dead."

"No, I wouldn't. But I believe I could handle James."

"Think you could handle your mother, too? Clemmie's cut from pure rawhide."

"I'd tell them you're still my husband, that I still love you."

"Do you, or are you just sayin' that to get what you want?"

Alice fumbled for an answer that wouldn't come. "I did love you once. Lord knows I don't want to, but maybe I still do, a little. I don't know."

"There's a way to find out." He reined his horse in beside hers. He drew her up against him and kissed her. She pulled back in surprise, unsure how to react. He kissed her again, longer and harder. She felt an unexpected flush of warmth. She found herself responding with an eagerness for which she had not been prepared.

"See?" he said. "It's still there."

She tingled, not yet quite accepting what had happened to her. "Maybe a little bit."

"I never got over you, Alice. Seems like you never got over me, either, even if you thought so. We'll make us a good life together. You'll see."

"But I still want to go home, at least long enough to see for myself that Mama is all right. Take me there, and then I'll go with you wherever you want. Colorado, California. Any place."

"Is that a promise? You're not just sayin' it to stall for time 'til you can get away from me?"

"Us Monahans were taught never to lie."

He reined up. "All right. You know the risk. But if you're willin' to take it, so am I."

"I don't understand why your mother is so bent on seein' me dead. If I intended to tell what I know about the Bascoms I'd have done it a long time ago."

"That's what she was fearful of at first. I have a feelin' it's gone way past that now. Us three sons are all she's got left in the world. She sees you takin' me away from her. She's jealous, and she's afraid."

"And maybe a little bit crazy."

"Maybe. Anyway, Oregon is way out of her reach, and they tell me it's a pretty country."

"Just one more thing. I don't want to spend the rest of my life dodgin' the law with you. Are you through with robbin' stores and banks and such?"

"Never was very good at it in the first place. There's other things I can do. I'm a pretty good carpenter and a damned good blacksmith. I could even farm if I had to. I'll make us a livin' and do it honest. I swear."

She turned her horse around and pointed toward the north star. "Home is that way."

Reluctantly he reined up beside her, pulling the pack

mule after him. "You know what we might run into." He reached into his pocket and withdrew a small derringer. "Picked this up in Fort Worth a while back. Worst come to worst, you might need it."

She had been taught the use of guns ever since she was old enough to hold one. She had never handled one this small. "Looks like a toy."

"It's not. It can kill if you put the bullet in the right place."

She had never been far south of Rusty's farm. The darkness offered no landmarks, anyway. She trusted that if they rode north long enough they would come upon familiar ground. As she rode she puzzled over her contradictory emotions. She had believed any affection she once felt for Corey was gone, killed by his mother's cruelty and his own rough nature. But at least a remnant of it had survived, rekindled now by his presence. She found herself wanting him to take her in his arms and kiss her again. The thought made her ashamed, yet she took a guilty pleasure in it.

How could she hope to understand people like Corey and the whole haywire Bascom family if she did not even understand herself?

A glow in the east told her it would soon be daylight. Maybe now she could see a farmhouse and get some idea of where she was. She watched for chimney smoke. It was time for farmers and their families to be up and making breakfast. But she saw no smoke.

As the sun broke over the horizon and spilled early light across the land, she saw two horsemen.

Corey saw them, too. He said, "Damn. I hope that ain't Ma and Lacey." He drew his pistol. "Keep behind me."

The riders' faces were in shadow so that she did not recognize Rusty and Andy until they were within fifty yards. Rusty was hatless, a white bandage around his head.

She moved a little past Corey, trying to block him. "Don't shoot. They're friends."

"Not of mine." Corey brought the weapon up and drew back the hammer.

Rusty was quick to recognize Alice and Corey. He drew his pistol before he reached them.

Andy warned, "Careful. He's packin' as much artillery as you are."

Anger boiled up and strained Rusty's voice. "Move aside, Alice." He motioned with the weapon. "It's time for Corey to pay the preacher."

Her eyes pleaded as strongly as her voice. "You're wrong about him. He didn't kill Josie."

Rusty barely heard her. His hands shook with pent-up fury. "You don't owe him nothin'. I said move aside."

Andy had watched and listened, his mouth wide open. Now he pulled in front of Rusty and grabbed the hand that held the pistol.

"Hold on, Rusty. Hear her out."

"What's there to hear? He's lied to her and got her to believe it."

Alice said, "It wasn't Corey. He wasn't even there. It was his brother Lacey. He thought Josie was me."

Rusty did not want to believe. He had carried his hatred for Corey too long to turn loose of it easily. He jerked his hand free of Andy's grip and fired past Alice. Corey dropped his pistol and grabbed his right arm. He made a cry of surprise and pain.

Rusty saw that in his haste he had hardly more than scratched Corey. He leveled the pistol again. Andy grabbed

Rusty's hand and gave it a twist. The muzzle pointed downward. Andy shouted, "Pull that trigger and you'll kill your horse."

"Turn me loose. Corey's got it comin'."

"By law I'm still a ranger, Rusty. I didn't resign. I just took a leave. I'm arrestin' Corey, and if you don't cool down I'll have to arrest you, too."

Rusty glared at him but found that Andy stared back with eyes that reminded him of a Comanche about to kill. Andy said firmly, "Corey's my prisoner. He's got my protection."

Slowly Rusty relaxed his grip on the pistol. Andy wrested it from his fingers and stuck it in his waistband. He said, "Maybe she's right, Rusty. Maybe Corey didn't kill Josie. And again, maybe he did, but it's up to the law to sort it all out. You were a ranger long enough to know that."

Rusty was confused, a hot streak of anger still burning. "First time you ever laid a hand on me, Andy."

"I oughtn't to've had to. You just lost your head for a minute. Once you've cooled off you'll see that I'm right."

Alice broke in, "Corey's bleedin'."

Rusty's bullet had cut a gash along Corey's forearm.

Andy said, "See what you can do for him." He stepped down to retrieve Corey's fallen pistol. He stuck it into his waistband along with Rusty's.

Alice ripped off Corey's sleeve, already torn by the bullet. She wrapped it around the wound. "That'll hold 'til we get to Rusty's cabin. Then we can fix it proper."

Rusty wrestled with his emotions. He looked in Alice's anxious face and saw Josie. He had faced the man he had searched for, then he had missed a chance to kill him. He felt uncertain and deeply frustrated. "I've ridden a thousand miles tryin' to find him. Now you're tellin' me I ought to've been huntin' for somebody else all the time." His hands trembled.

"I'm sorry, Rusty. We were all wrong about Corey. He's been tryin' to help me in his own left-handed way."

Rusty turned aside. He did not want her to see the turmoil he was going through.

Andy broke his silence. "Alice, how come you-all to be headin' back this way? Rusty came by and asked me to help him cut your trail. He figured Corey was takin' you to Mexico."

"That was his intention. I talked him out of it. I told him if he'd take me home first I'd go with him anywhere he wanted."

Rusty regained some of his composure. "You'd go with him willingly? Surely you don't still love him?"

"I didn't think so. I thought I was over him. I guess I didn't know my own feelin's."

"They're wasted on him. Even if he didn't kill Josie, they could put him away for life for what he *has* done. He's wanted for robbin' a bank over at Brownwood. Lord knows what else."

Corey complained, "I'm leakin' my life's blood. If you-all stay here talkin' all day I won't live long enough to see the jailhouse."

Rusty said, "It'd serve him right to just leave him afoot and let him die in his own slow time."

Andy said, "You know we can't do that. Even an outlaw has got certain rights."

Rusty shrugged, still conflicted. "Just so he doesn't get away. If he does, I'll kill him for sure the next time."

{ EIGHTEEN }

Rusty rode in silence, nursing his doubts, fighting confusion. His stomach was uneasy. His head still ached from the blow Corey had struck last night. He only half listened to Andy throwing questions at Alice.

"What you goin' to do about bein' married to Corey? The preachers say 'for better or worse, richer or poorer,' but they don't say what you do if your man goes to jail."

"I guess that's part of the 'worse.'"

"A lawyer could get you a divorce."

"I don't think a Monahan has ever been divorced, not as far back as anybody knows. It'd raise a scandal from here to Georgia."

Rusty saw his farm looming up ahead. He glanced at Corey, who had both hands clasped around the horn. He had paled from shock and loss of blood.

Alice said, "We're almost there, Corey."

Rusty said, "*He* wouldn't be if I was a better shot."

They stopped in front of the cabin. Andy dismounted and moved to help Alice down from her saddle, then Corey. Rusty took his time. He did not offer assistance.

Andy said, "We'll find some clean cloth and bandage him right."

Rusty grunted. "Do what you want to. He's your prisoner." He had rather have left Corey out there alone and let nature take its course.

Alice took Corey's left arm. "I'll help you with him, Andy." She started to move, then halted abruptly. Rusty saw shock in her face.

Two men and a woman stepped out of the kitchen and

blocked the way onto the dog run. Bessie Bascom held her double-barreled shotgun. Lacey and Newley stood on either side of her. The old woman said, "Well, look who showed up. You people are the devil to find. Now you-all drop your guns on the ground."

Rusty had no weapon to drop. Facing the business end of those two barrels, Andy reluctantly placed his own pistol on the ground along with those belonging to Rusty and Corey.

Bessie's malevolent gaze fastened on Alice, then shifted to Corey's crudely bandaged arm. "What's the matter with my boy?"

Alice said, "He's been shot."

Bessie shifted the shotgun's muzzle toward Rusty. "Who done it? Him?"

Rusty swallowed, expecting her to shoot him.

The old woman stepped toward her son and reached out to touch the bandage. Most of the blood had dried, but a little was fresh enough to shine in the early morning sun. It stuck to her palm and fingers. She looked at her hand with revulsion and shifted her gaze back to Alice. "That comes from havin' truck with such as you. I told him you were a Jonah from the start." She swung the shotgun up into Alice's face. "You ain't puttin' a spell on any more sons of mine."

Corey stepped in front of Alice. He swayed a little but remained on his feet. "No, Ma, I ain't lettin' you."

"Get out of the way, boy."

"Before you can kill her you'll have to kill me."

The woman's eyes bulged with rage. "I'd kill anybody to protect what's left of this family."

"Not your own son."

"You've betrayed the family, just like your pa done. I killed him. I can kill you."

"It was the state police that killed Pa."

"They shot him, but I was the one told them where he'd be."

"You? Why?"

"I always kept this from you boys. He was fixin' to desert the family and run off with a saloon trollop. Now you're tryin' to run off with this piece of baggage."

Corey seemed shaken by the revelation. "She's my wife, and I love her. Killin' Alice will just make bad things worse. There's witnesses here, and one of them is a ranger."

"There won't be no witnesses when we leave." She laid the shotgun barrel against Corey's good arm and attempted to shove him aside with it. "Damn you, boy, I said move out of the way."

Corey tried to wrest the weapon from her but lacked the strength. He gave it a hard push instead, striking her chin with the barrel. She staggered. In attempting to regain her balance she let the shotgun tip down. One barrel fired.

Corey took the load in his chest and hurtled backward.

The old woman screamed. "Corey!"

She froze for a moment, choking down a rush of grief. Then she turned her fury back upon Alice. "You miserable Jezebel!" She brought the shotgun up again.

The tiny derringer flashed in Alice's hand. The shotgun tilted toward the ground and discharged its second barrel. It raised a small eruption of dust. Bessie shivered, her confused eyes fixed on Alice. She protested, "I kept tellin' him . . ."

Blood trickled from the corner of her mouth. She leaned forward, then struck the ground like a felled oak.

Rusty grabbed up his pistol from the ground. Lacey shouted, "Ma!" He reached for the weapon at his hip. It had just cleared the holster when Rusty's bullet struck him. He teetered, trying to level his pistol. Rusty fired again, twice. Lacey crumpled.

Rusty muttered, "That's for Josie."

Newley went to his knees, sobbing as Rusty and Andy swung smoking pistols in his direction. "Don't kill me. Please don't."

Alice found her voice. "Don't shoot him. He's harmless."

Rusty felt his finger tightening again on the trigger. He had to stop himself from following through as Andy moved in front of him.

Andy said, "Maybe you know him, Alice, but we don't." He took Newley's pistol. "I hope you ain't goin' to give us any trouble, Bascom. Been killin' enough already."

Newley shook. He tried to speak but brought forth only a little jibberish.

Andy surveyed the carnage. "Lord, what a mess."

Wearily Rusty seated himself on the ground. He extended his arms across his knees and rested his aching head on them. He felt his stomach churning. He had hoped avenging Josie would give him satisfaction. It had not. "I thought I'd shoot Corey and that'd be the end of it. I didn't figure it would come to all this."

Alice knelt beside Corey. She could do nothing for him. She lowered her head and wept.

Andy said, "Looks like he did love you, after all."

She was slow to answer, her voice subdued. "In his way . . . I guess he did."

Andy turned to Rusty. "At least it was the old lady that killed him, not you. You don't have to carry Corey on your conscience."

Rusty looked at the still form of Bessie Bascom. He felt

he should have some regret about the old woman, but he did not. His only sympathy went to Alice. "You don't have to report that Alice shot her. Tell them I did it. It'll save her some trouble and grief."

Andy nodded. "Trouble maybe, but not grief."

Alice held Corey's limp hand. A tear rolled down her cheek. In a thin voice she said, "I never saw anybody so poisoned with hate as she was. She always talked about protectin' her family, but she destroyed it herself."

"All but one." Andy nodded toward Newley, who was still on his knees, trembling.

She said, "He never was quite like the others. They always drug him along against his will."

Andy asked Rusty, "What do you think we ought to do with him?"

Rusty felt empty. At this point he did not care. "You're the law. You call it."

"I don't have a fugitive list with me. If he's wanted for anything I don't know about it." He approached Newley. "Stand up."

Newley arose on wobbly legs.

Andy said, "Get on your horse and see how far you can go before dark. Don't let your shadow fall on this side of the Colorado River ever again."

After a silent final look at his mother and brothers, Newley hurried to the barn where the Bascoms had hidden their horses. Shortly he rode out of the corral and put his mount into a lope, heading northward.

Andy returned to Alice. "Does that suit you?"

She nodded. "He's got the Bascom taint in his blood. It'll probably get him killed, but it won't be our doin'."

Andy said, "I'll have to go tell Tom Blessing about this. I'm still a ranger, but he's the local law."

Rusty raised his head and gave Andy a long study. He did not look like a boy anymore. He said, "You did good today. It's a pity you've decided to resign."

"I never said that. I said I was comin' home to heal up and to think about it. I'm still thinkin' about it."

Rusty arose, his legs weak. He walked into the cabin's kitchen and slumped into a chair. He felt wrung out, exhausted.

Alice followed him worriedly. "Are you all right?"

Rusty shook his head. "No. Maybe next week I'll be all right again, or next month. Right now I just feel used up."

Alice looked at him with sad eyes. It struck him again how much she resembled her older sisters. But she was not them, not Geneva and not Josie. She was Alice, just as Josie had been Josie and not Geneva.

Well, at least Josie could rest easy now, he thought. He wondered when *he* would.

Several days' ride brought a nagging ache back into Andy's shoulder, but he had no intention of telling anybody about it. He followed the San Saba River, hoping the cook had been out there with his pole and line. A mess of fresh-fried catfish would make for a tasty supper after all the fat bacon he had eaten on the trail.

He saw the tents ahead and was pleased that the ranger camp had not been moved in his absence. If he ever decided to get a place of his own and settle down he might very well choose such a pleasant spot on this river where tall pecan trees spread their heavy shade along the banks and the water ran clear and cool. It carried him back in memory to some of the better times he had spent with the Comanches.

The Comanches. Reports lately from the high plains had left him with mixed feelings. It was said the army had defeated them after an almost bloodless encounter in a faraway canyon and had run off their horses. They had no choice but to give up and start a long, sad walk to the reservation. That meant he would probably never be called upon to fight them again. The rangers could shift their main attention to lawless white men instead of Indians. Yet his sympathy went to the People, like his foster brother Steals the Ponies, afoot, confined, forced to accept the dubious charity of the federal government. It was too much for a proud race to have to bear. He grieved for them.

Len Tanner was on horse guard. He hollered and put his mount into a long trot to overtake Andy. "Hey, button, how's the shoulder?"

"What shoulder?"

"You back to stay?"

"If the captain will have me."

"He's been hopin' you'd show up. Where'd you leave Rusty?"

"At home. He's decided bein' a farmer is more restful than bein' a ranger."

"Rusty ain't gettin' no younger. The ranger life is for young men like me and you."

Tanner had some gray streaks in his hair, but Andy knew that to mention it would set him off into a longer speech than Andy wanted to hear. "Where are the Morris brothers?"

"On patrol. We been havin' a lot of fun chasin' after outlaws over in Kimble County. You'll enjoy it." He turned serious. "Did Rusty ever find that feller he was huntin' for?"

"Corey Bascom? Yes, that's over and done with."

"And Alice?"

"Rusty took her back to her folks. She's safe now."

"I sort of hoped her and Rusty . . . well, it would kind of make up to him for losin' Josie like he did."

"Who knows? Rusty took a mighty deep wound, a lot worse than what I got in my shoulder. Such things take a long time to heal." Andy looked toward the row of tents. "I'd better report to the captain. Let him know I'm ready for whatever he wants me to do."

A broad grin creased Tanner's freckled face. "He'll be tickled to see you."

The captain stood in front of the headquarters tent, watching Andy approach. Andy dismounted and gave him what passed for a salute in ranger circles.

The captain returned the salute in a manner even less military than Andy's. "I've been wondering about you, Pickard. Have you healed up?"

"Enough, sir. Reportin' for duty."

"Glad to have you. I'll put you back on the pay roster. And Mr. Shannon?"

Andy shook his head. "He won't be comin'."

"A pity. But we must all make choices in this life. If you're hungry, go ask Bo to fix something for you."

Andy saw a boy sitting at the mess tent, peeling potatoes while the black cook watched. He asked, "Is that . . . ?"

The captain nodded. "It's Scooter."

"I thought the Indians got him."

"So did we all. But when the boy saw they were about to overtake him he ran into a cedarbrake and hid. The Comanches hunted for him. They came so close that he said he could hear them breathing. He laid in the cedar all night, scared to death. But at daylight they were gone. He wandered around afoot for several days, hungry, dodging rattlesnakes. Finally some cowboys found him, fed him, and brought him to us."

"Maybe he learned somethin'."

"That he did. This experience took him to the edge of hell and showed him what death looked like, face-to-face. It turned him completely around. He even says 'sir' now."

"I guess I ought to go speak to him, tell him I've still got my horse."

"Good idea." The captain smiled. "Welcome back, ranger."

TEXAS VENDETTA

{ ONE }

For the last twelve or fifteen miles Andy Pickard and Farley Brackett had ridden in almost total silence. One ignored his partner, and the other tried to. They talked no more than the surefooted little Mexican pack mule that followed them across the Texas hill country's rocky ground. That suited Andy fine, for Farley was unlikely to say anything he wanted to listen to.

Andy speculated that the Ranger captain might have been sore at him for some reason, detailing him with dour Farley Brackett on this locate-and-arrest mission. The captain had said, "Brackett's a man I'd like to have beside me in a fight, but be damned if I'd want him for company before and after."

Farley usually looked as if he had just come back from a funeral. The captain had probably been glad to get him out of camp for two or three days and let the sunshine in.

Andy had to squint, riding directly into the setting sun. "Fixin' to be sundown pretty quick."

Farley grunted as if to say he could see that for himself and he resented the break in silence.

Night was going to catch them before they reached the Leach place. That was all right with Andy. He liked a little low-level excitement, but he had no interest in getting killed. He said, "We'd make too good a target ridin' up in broad daylight anyway. Captain told us those folks are apt to put up a fight if we don't catch them off guard."

Farley's eyes were as grim as the muzzle of a shotgun. "Anybody is liable to put up a fight when they're lookin' at a stretch in the penitentiary. These people ain't bright, but even a fool can sight down a gun barrel and kill you."

Andy and Farley carried a warrant for the arrest of one Joseph Bransford on a charge of robbery and attempted murder. He had ambushed a stock farmer back in Colorado County, leaving him for dead after taking money the farmer had collected for selling a team of mules. The captain had received a tip that Bransford was hiding out north of the Llano River on a hardscrabble homestead operated by his sister and her husband, Abner Leach. Leach claimed to be a farmer, but he was suspected of operating a way station for stolen livestock. No one had been able to prove it to the satisfaction of a jury.

So far as the captain could determine, Leach was not currently wanted by the law despite his shady reputation. However, it was probably only a matter of time before he was caught knee-deep in some ill-conceived activity that would put his name on the Rangers' fugitive list.

Farley said, "If we was to shoot them both, the taxpayers wouldn't have to foot the cost of a trial."

Coming from some people, that would be considered idle talk. In Farley's case, Andy doubted it was idle. "There's no charges out against Leach."

"There will be sooner or later. Shoot him now and we'll save some squatter from gettin' his livestock stolen."

Andy could see a certain twisted logic in Farley's view of summary justice, but it went against many stern lectures peace officers like Rusty Shannon had preached to him about the importance of law, about the presumption of innocence until guilt was proven. He wished he had Rusty with him now instead of Farley. "Rangers don't go around shootin' prisoners."

"Wake up and look around you, boy. Sometimes justice gets served out in the brush, where there's no witnesses. No petty-foggin' lawyers, no bought-off jury. Time you get a few more years on you, you'll know what I mean."

Farley had touched a sore spot. Andy was evidently the youngest man in the company, though nobody knew his age. The best guess was twenty years or a little more. Indians had killed his father and mother when he was small and had carried him off to raise as their own. Circumstances had thrust him back into Texan hands about the time his voice began to change. He had had to learn English all over again and stumble along on the white man's road, learning the hard way by trial and error—lots of error. Even with Rusty Shannon's guidance, it had been a rough road to follow after knowing only the ways of the Comanche.

He was keenly aware that he still looked young to be riding with the Rangers. He had recently tried growing a mustache in an effort to appear older. He had shaved it off after three weeks because it looked pathetically thin and weak.

Farley had remarked, "Old men try to look young, and young men try to look like their daddies. They're all lyin' to theirselves."

Andy was aware that an element of truth existed behind Farley's talk about shooting prisoners. He had heard whispered stories about outlaws shot "trying to escape." If a man was considered dangerous, it was safer to carry him in dead. And a quick burial was cheaper on the county. No criminal ever climbed out of the grave to file an appeal.

Many people were afraid of Farley Brackett, with cause. He had come home from the Yankee war with a long scar on his face and a deeper one etched into his soul. During Reconstruction years he had become a scourge to the federally backed authorities. The unionist state police had chased him often but had learned from bitter experience not to get close enough to catch him.

Once the old-time Texans regained political control of their state, transgressions against the former government had been forgiven, even applauded. The reorganized Rangers had been glad to have Farley join their ranks. He knew how men on the dodge thought and acted because he had been one. Andy thought he still had the shifty wolf eyes of a fugitive.

In the fading light of dusk Andy could make out a dim wagon trail. "You sure these tracks lead to the Leach place?"

Farley grumped, "Of course I'm sure. I'm always sure. I came this way before, huntin' a pal of Leach's that stuck up a Dutchman over in Friedrichsburg. Leach tried to point me onto the wrong trail. I ought to've shot him when I had the chance. We wouldn't have anybody to worry about now but Bransford."

They followed the wagon tracks until Andy saw lamplight ahead. "Looks like we've found the cabin."

"It never was lost. I knew where it was at."

"I guess we'll wait till they're asleep, then bust in?"

Farley assumed command by right of seniority and age. He looked at Andy as if the suggestion were the dumbest thing he had ever heard. "No, we'll make a dry camp and wait for mornin'. Bust in now and we'd have Bransford and Leach both to fight. That ain't countin' the woman, but I expect she'll just scream, faint, and fall down."

Andy argued, "In the mornin' they'll all be awake."

"We'll wait till the men are separated so we can handle them one at a time. Last time I was here, Leach came out about daylight to milk. We'll surprise him at the cow lot."

"And Bransford?"

"He'll give up when he sees we're fixin' to burn the cabin down around him."

"Or he'll come out shootin'."

"Good. We can finish him off legal and proper."

Andy protested, "We can't burn a cabin with a woman in it."

"She'll come out soon as her skirts start smokin'. With people like them, you don't ask permission or beg their pardon."

"I doubt the adjutant general would approve of it."

"The adjutant general!" Farley snorted. "Sittin' comfortable at a desk in Austin, writin' rules like he was dealin' with law-abidin' citizens. Out here the owl hoots in the daytime same as at night, and things look a lot different."

They moved back to the far side of a cedar-crowned hill where they could build a small fire without its being seen from the cabin. Farley commanded, "Cook us somethin' fit to eat."

Andy started to say, *You're a private same as me,* but changed his mind. The day might come when he had a showdown with Farley, but it would have to be over something more important than this. He took a pack from the back of the mule while Farley coaxed a small pile of dead wood into a blaze. Andy wished he had some of the dried buffalo meat that Comanches carried on long rides or the pemmican they made by pounding dried meat, berries, and nuts together. He preferred it over fatback broiled on the end of a stick. But he would settle for fatback because that was what he and Farley had brought, that and cold biscuits dried hard enough to drive a nail.

He knew no fat Rangers.

Water from their canteens yielded a cup of coffee apiece. Farley sat back, stretching his long legs, and slowly sipped his coffee as he might nurse a shot of whiskey. He seemed to withdraw into some private part of his mind, as distant as if he were back in the company headquarters camp on the San Saba River.

Andy broke a long silence. "I wish Rusty was with us." Rusty Shannon had taken charge of Andy when he was separated from the Comanches. He had become like an older brother.

"What's the matter, Badger Boy? You need a nursemaid?"

Farley took perverse pleasure in using the English version of the name by which the Comanches had known Andy. He was like some malevolent shaman who could summon up a dark and rumbling cloud from a bright and sunny sky.

Andy said, "Rusty always knows what to do."

"He's not a Ranger anymore, and it's probably a good thing. He always allowed the other feller too much of an edge. Sooner or later he'd get himself killed takin' pity on people that have got no pity comin' to them."

That was one thing Farley could never be accused of, Andy thought. "Rusty had pity on *me* when I needed help. And God knows I caused him trouble enough for a while."

Rusty had taken Andy into his log-cabin home on the Colorado River. He had managed to maintain his patience while Andy made the slow and painful transition from Comanche life. Andy had run away more than once, trying to return to his adoptive Indian family. He had fistfought boys for miles around when they ridiculed him for the Indian braids he refused to cut and the moccasins he wore instead of shoes.

The braids were gone now, and so were the moccasins. He wanted to fit in, to be the kind of Ranger Rusty had been. But he retained a remnant of Indian upbringing. It would probably always be there.

Drinking his bitter coffee, he lapsed into silence, pondering tomorrow and wishing he were as sure of himself as Farley seemed to be.

Morning was a long time in coming. Andy lay awake most of the night, visualizing the expected confrontation, imagining the worst that might happen. He pictured Leach's woman lying dead after the smoke cleared, much as he had seen his white mother dead years ago. It was one of his earliest memories, long suppressed because it was so terrible. The image still returned from time to time like a nightmare that would not wait for the night.

Farley seemed to harbor no misgivings. Andy listened to him snoring peacefully.

The stars still glittered when Farley came out from beneath his blanket. He looked up at them to get a rough notion of time. "We'd better be gettin' ourselves in position before daylight. Leach wakes up the rooster."

Andy was hungry. "Hadn't we ought to fix some breakfast first?"

"When we're done we'll make Leach's woman cook us a proper meal."

"Thought you were goin' to burn her cabin down."

"They raise pigs. We'll catch us a juicy shoat and have her roast it over the coals."

Andy started to pack the mule. Farley stopped him. "Don't you know a stupid mule is liable to smell feed and go in there brayin' his head off? We'll leave him here and pick him up when the job is done."

Chastened, Andy tied the mule.

The cabin was still dark as the two Rangers circled around to come in behind the milk shed. They left their horses in a clump of trees. The cow stood outside the gate, waiting in bovine patience for the grain that awaited her in the stanchion. She turned her head to watch the men approach on foot. She seemed to know they were strangers and drew away. She did not go far because she had not yet nursed her calf or had her morning feed. Hogs in a nearby pen grunted but quickly settled back down. Andy's nose pinched. He never had gotten used to the smell of pigs. Horses disliked them, and so did Comanches.

Presently he saw lamplight in the cabin window. A man came out carrying a bucket.

Farley said, "That's Leach. He's meaner than a boar hog with the hives. Be ready for real trouble."

"You don't figure on shootin' him, do you?"

"Not without he gives me cause. But if he gives me cause I sure won't take a chance with him."

Andy's hands were tense on his rifle. He could handle a pistol, but a rifle felt steadier and seemed to carry more authority. He could not see if Leach was armed. The man's face was featureless in the dim light of early dawn, but Andy could see that his body was broad and muscular. He looked as if he would be hard to handle in a fight.

Farley whispered, "He's got a six-shooter in his boot. Get set. It's liable to be a hell of a scrap."

Farley waited until Leach opened the gate for the cow to enter the lot. He stepped out into the open and said, "Hands up. We're Rangers." He shoved a pistol forward, almost in Leach's face.

Leach wilted and raised trembling hands. "Don't shoot. For God's sake, Ranger, don't shoot."

Farley seemed let down by the lack of resistance. "You're harborin' a fugitive. We got a warrant for Joseph Bransford's arrest."

"Go help yourself," Leach said in a quavering voice.

"He's in the cabin. Only please don't shoot. I'm a married man. My wife depends on me."

Disgusted, Farley told Andy, "Cuff this cowardly son of a bitch to the fence post." He turned back to Leach, waving the pistol in his face. "If you holler I'll blow a hole in your brisket."

Fear gave Leach's voice a high pitch. "I won't make a peep."

Andy said, "That was easy."

Farley did not hide his disappointment. "Bransford is apt to come at us like a mad bull. Be ready to shoot him."

"What about the woman?"

"Don't worry none about her. She'll wilt like bluebonnets in June."

A wagon stood in front of the cabin. Farley placed himself behind it. He motioned for Andy to take cover behind a dug well ringed by a circular rock structure about three feet high, with windlass and wooden bucket on top.

Andy thought it would be more effective to burst into the cabin and take Bransford by surprise, giving him no time to put up resistance. But Farley preferred confrontation in broad daylight, where he could see his target and have plenty of room to move around.

Farley shouted, "Joseph Bransford, listen to me. We're the Rangers. There's ten of us, and we've got this cabin surrounded. Come out with your hands up or we'll burn the place and roast you like a pig."

Andy heard a woman's angry shout from inside.

For emphasis Farley fired a shot that showered splinters from the upper part of the door. He called, "Let the woman come out first. We got no paper on her."

The woman came out waving a heavy chunk of firewood. She made straight for Farley, cursing him for twelve kinds of egg-sucking dog. She was tall and broad and looked as if she could wrestle a mule to its knees. As Farley raised his arms for defense, she struck him twice. Startled, then stunned, Farley almost went to his knees. He raised his arms, trying to fend off her blows.

"Damn you, Badger Boy, do somethin'."

Farley's hat rolled on the ground. His head was bleeding.

Andy twisted the firewood from her hand and cast it away, but she closed in enough to leave deep tracks of her fingernails upon Farley's whiskered cheek.

"Get this civit cat off of me."

Andy got an arm around the woman's wide waist and dragged her away from Farley, only to have her turn on him instead. He managed to grab her strong hands and pull them behind her back. He handcuffed her to one of the posts that supported the windlass. She cursed until her voice went hoarse.

Both men struggled for breath. Farley raised a hand to his head and then looked at it. He saw blood. "Damn you, boy, how come it took you so long?"

"I thought you said she was goin' to scream, faint, and fall down."

Farley gave him a look that would wither weeds. He dragged a sleeve across his sweating face and fired a shot through the open door. "You comin' out, Bransford, or do you want to fry like a slab of bacon?"

A shaken man appeared in the doorway, hands above his head. "I give up. You don't need to shoot no more."

The woman turned her fury on him. "You ain't no brother of mine, you snivelin' coward. There ain't but two of them. You could've got them both." She looked around with wide eyes. "Where's my husband? What you done with my man?"

Farley was too choked with anger and embarrassment to answer. Andy said, "He's down at the shed, holdin' on to a fence post. Ain't done his milkin' yet."

The Rangers had just one set of handcuffs apiece, and those were both in use. Andy tied Bransford's hands with a leather string cut from his saddle. He drew the binding down tightly enough that Bransford complained about the circulation being cut off.

Farley said, "Ain't near as tight as a noose around your neck. You're lucky that farmer didn't die. Now, where's the money you took off of him?"

The woman said, "Don't you tell them nothin', Joseph. That money's ours if you'll just keep your damn-fool mouth shut."

Farley tapped the muzzle of his pistol smartly against Bransford's upper teeth. "Bad advice can get a man killed. Tell me where that money's at or I'll scatter your brains for the chickens to peck on."

Andy hoped the prisoner would see that Farley was not bluffing.

Bransford was eager to tell. "It's in there," he said, pointing to the cabin. "Come and I'll show you." Andy followed him while Farley remained outside, wiping blood from his forehead. Bransford pointed his chin toward a wooden box beside the iron stove. "It's at the bottom."

Andy said, "Stand back yonder and keep your hands high in the air." He dug the stove wood out of the box until he found a canvas sack. He could tell by the feel that it was full of paper. Coins clinked together in the bottom when he shook it.

He demanded, "Is it all there?"

Bransford was trying not to cry. All that effort and nothing left to show for it. "Just spent a little on whiskey. And I left a few dollars with a woman over to Fort McKavett." He was trembling with fright. "What you Rangers goin' to do with me?"

Andy said, "Farley is plumb sore that you didn't put up a fight. But if I can keep him from killin' you, we'll take you to camp. Then I expect they'll send you to Colorado County to stand trial."

"What you reckon they'll give me?"

"Ten to twenty years, the captain said."

Bransford mumbled, "Ten to twenty years. Seems like an awful long time for no more money than I got."

"You shot the man you took it off of."

"I wouldn't have if he'd given it to me right off like I told him to."

Andy motioned for Bransford to walk outside ahead of him. The prisoner avoided his sister's smoldering eyes. He stared at the sack, his expression solemn. "Looks like by rights that money ought to be mine, seein' as I'm goin' to give up ten to twenty years payin' for it."

Farley shook his bleeding head in disbelief. "We sure got a sorry class of criminals these days. At least the Indians gave us an honest fight."

Andy said, "I'm takin' that as a compliment."

It was as much of one as he expected to receive from Farley.

A couple of horses grazed a few hundred yards away. Andy rode out and brought back the better of the two, a grulla gelding, for Bransford to ride. The woman fought the cuffs that held her against the well. "That's my husband's horse." She resumed cursing as the three men went down to the shed.

Bransford pointed out his saddle, and Andy put it on the horse for him. "Mount up." When Bransford was in the saddle, Andy fetched up his own and Farley's horses. He unlocked Leach's cuffs and transferred them to Bransford.

Leach rubbed his raw wrists, his face twisting. "You damned Rangers think you run the world."

Farley said, "We do, and we'll be back to get you the first time you let your foot slip."

"That's my horse you put Joseph on. His is that jug-headed bay out yonder."

Farley had no sympathy. "You just traded. They're probably all stolen anyway." He mounted his horse and poked the muzzle of the pistol in Leach's direction. "Come on back up to the cabin. We ain't plumb finished with you."

When they reached the dwelling Andy leaned down from the saddle and handed Leach the key to the handcuffs that restrained his wife. "Turn her a-loose, then give me the cuffs and the key."

Farley argued, "We ought to just leave her thataway. While her man filed those cuffs off of her, she'd have time to study on a woman's proper place."

"You want to pay the captain for the cuffs?"

"I reckon not. But watch her close when you turn her loose."

Fortunately the woman seemed to have used up most of her fight as well as all the profanity she knew. She stood in fuming silence, trying to kill Andy and Farley with the hatred in her eyes. Leach handed Andy the cuffs and key.

As the three rode away the woman shouted, "Our old daddy's turnin' over in his grave, Joseph, you givin' up so easy. You better ride way around this place when you come back."

Farley turned in the saddle. "Lady, he ain't comin' back."

Andy said, "Some lady."

Farley took a final glance at the cabin. "That place would look a hell of a lot better if we'd left it in ashes."

Bransford said, "You'd really burn it down with me in it?"

"I had the matches in my hand."

Andy remarked, "Thought we were goin' to have her fix us some breakfast."

Farley shook his head. "She'd poison us."

They fixed their own when they got back to where they had left the pack mule tied.

Andy asked Farley, "How's your head?"

"If she didn't break my skull, she bent the hell out of it. And you just stood there watchin'."

"I jumped in as fast as I could." Andy saw that Farley had no interest in his side of the story. "First water we come to, we'd better wash the blood off of your face. I've seen butchered hogs that bled less."

Farley gingerly felt of his head. "Look, it's enough that we bring the prisoner in like the captain told us to. There's no reason we've got to tell him about that woman."

{ TWO }

Nearing camp, the three riders came upon the company horses scattered to graze on an open flat. They were watched over by two Rangers taking refuge from the sun's heat by shading up under a live-oak tree. The end of the long ride lifted Andy's spirits. Fatigue seemed to slip from his shoulders. The prisoner had been sullen and quiet, slouching in the saddle. Andy could understand, given the likelihood that he faced a long prison sentence. Farley had spoken little. He carried his hat on his saddlehorn, for it had been painful to wear over the knot swollen on his head.

The sound of gunshots made Bransford sit up in alarm.

Andy tried to calm him. "Just some of the boys at target practice." The captain provided an ample supply of cartridges, encouraging his men to sharpen their marksmanship. Cartridges were one of the few things besides food that the Rangers were not obliged to furnish for themselves. Even food was supplemented by whatever game they could shoot or fish they could catch.

The company camp had been established on the bank of the wide, clear San Saba River. Tall pecan trees sent roots deep into the mud and cast a cool shade over a row of canvas tents. To this company of Rangers it was home. It was an easily movable home, its location subject to the region's changeable law enforcement needs.

Earlier, the frontier batallion had busied itself primarily with keeping hostile Indians out of the settlements or chasing those who managed to get in despite the long picket line of Ranger outposts. Now that task had been largely eliminated by a relentless army push against the warring Plains tribes. A concentrated military offensive, moving in from three directions, had forced most of the Indians to give up the fight and repair to the questionable mercies of the reservation. Except for occasional limited outbreaks, the Comanches, Kiowas, and Cheyennes had been put out of action.

Apaches still roamed the far western part of the state and prowled rough hills down along the Rio Frio and upper Nueces, but the most destructive of the Indian raids were over. Of late the Rangers had turned their attention to the criminals who infested the state, especially its less settled portions, where escape was often fast and easy. Nowhere were they worse than in the limestone hills west of San Antonio, where dense cedar brakes and deep, rugged canyons offered sanctuary, where water and game were plentiful and a man could live off the land if the climate elsewhere became too hot.

Thus the principal Ranger mission had shifted from Indian fighting to domestic law enforcement, to chasing murderers and thieves and border-jumping bandits, to breaking up feuds that broke out occasionally among a prideful, independent people hardened to violence and easily stirred to deadly force.

Protocol demanded that Andy and Farley deliver their report and their prisoner to the captain before they did anything else. Bransford cast anxious eyes at the camp as if he expected someone to step out of a tent and gun him down. He sweated more than the summer heat called for.

Several Rangers emerged from the tents or from under the shady trees to observe the three men coming in. Bransford's expression became even bleaker.

Andy said, "They won't shoot you in the middle of camp, not without you give them reason to."

Farley had transferred to Bransford most of the blame for his injury. "Even if they did, who's to tell? One Ranger ain't goin' to call down the law on another. We're decent people."

Bransford cast a fearful glance at him. He had probably expected a bullet in the back all the way from the Leach farm. Andy had said nothing to disabuse him of the notion, hoping fear would have a positive effect on his behavior.

Len Tanner's clothes were always too large for him except for the trouser legs. They were a little short. The lanky Ranger walked up and stared at the prisoner. "This the gink that goes around robbin' farmers?"

Andy said, "That's the charge, but he ain't been tried yet."

Farley studied Bransford like a hungry wolf eyeing an orphaned calf. "He's guilty, all right. You can tell by lookin' at him."

Andy said, "If that was the case, we wouldn't need judges and juries."

"Far as I'm concerned, we don't. If we shot them where we find them we'd save a lot of bother."

Sergeant Bill Holloway ducked to step out of the headquarters tent, then straightened his tall frame. He squinted against the sun. Deep turkey tracks pinched around bleached blue eyes. "I see you got your man."

Farley took offense. "We wasn't sent out there to *not* get him. We've come to turn him over to the captain."

"I'll take charge of him. Captain's busy right now."

Andy could hear the captain's angry voice through the canvas. Holloway jerked his head as a signal for the men to move away from the headquarters tent. He followed them far enough that they could no longer hear the voice.

He said, "Captain doesn't like to be disturbed when he's bawlin' a man out. Dick Landon put away too much bad whiskey last night over at Fort McKavett. Got into a cuss fight and tried to bend the barrel of his six-shooter over a citizen's skull. Lucky it was one of them hardheaded Dutchmen."

It was a seldom-discussed fact of Ranger life that isolation, boredom, and frustration led some men to drink heavily when off duty, and occasionally even on duty. This could result in unjustified confrontations with civilians unlucky enough to get crossways with them. Those men who became a frequent problem to their commanders were likely to be discharged quietly and encouraged to move on lest they taint the reputation of the service.

Landon had caused disturbances before. The captain had kept him on because he was a good Ranger when sober, bold when the occasion called for it, a crack shot with pistol or rifle. Drunk, he tended to create trouble where there had been none. It was said he came from a fighting family.

Farley grumbled, "Dick ought to never drink. Whiskey makes him mean."

Andy said, "Some people don't need whiskey for that."

Farley gave him a cold stare. "If you mean me, I don't go huntin' trouble. But if it comes, I don't run."

Farley had gone out of his way during Reconstruction times to antagonize the state police, who were easily aroused. But Andy saw no point in pressing the issue. Farley would never concede defeat.

Farley said, "I never shot a man that didn't need killin'. The only regrets I've got are over some I ought've shot but didn't."

Holloway said, "I reckon Dick had reason enough to get drunk. He helped bring his own brother in yesterday on a murder charge."

Puzzled, Andy asked, "How could he do that?"

"He's a Ranger. Dick joined to get away from a feud back in his home county. Seems like his brother Jayce killed a man on the other side and came out hopin' for Dick to give him protection."

"Instead, he brought him in?"

"Rangers do their duty or they quit."

"I don't know if I could do what Dick did."

"I think you would if the chips were down." Holloway led them around the cook tent and pointed. "We'll take your man down there."

The camp had no jail. For temporary confinement, prisoners were handcuffed to a chain locked around the thick trunk of a pecan tree a few steps up from the river. Most were removed to a regular jail as soon as possible.

Holloway said, "We'll throw your man in with Jayce Landon."

Landon sat on the ground, one arm locked to a sturdy chain. A big man, he stared resentfully at the officers and did not attempt to stand up. Andy untied a leather thong that had secured Bransford's handcuffs to the horn of his saddle. "Get down."

Bransford's legs were wobbly. Andy unlocked one side of the cuffs. He was aware that Farley watched closely, a hand on the butt of his pistol in case Bransford decided to make a break. Andy relocked the open cuff around the chain. This allowed movement up and down the chain but not away from it. Bransford tugged at the chain and found it heavy. "I've seen dogs treated better than this."

Farley said, "Dogs don't go around shootin' the taxpayers."

Holloway intervened. "There's no need to taunt the prisoner. Farley, you and Private Pickard go get yourselves some grub. I can hear your bellies growlin' all the way over here."

Bransford asked, "What about me? I'm starved half to death."

Holloway had no patience for complaining prisoners. "You'll eat when we're good and ready to feed you. Till then an empty belly will help you contemplate your sins." He walked off with Farley toward the mess tent. Andy remained a minute, studying Jayce Landon. His face bore a striking resemblance to that of his Ranger brother. At a little distance he might mistake Jayce for Dick.

Andy had been trying to discern if there was any way to recognize a criminal on sight. So far he had not come upon any common denominator. Bransford looked the part, at least as Andy visualized the outlaw type. He would have taken Landon for a preacher. Or perhaps a Ranger.

Bransford looked up at the open sky. "What if it comes a rain? We'll drown out here."

Andy had not observed a decent cloud in two weeks. "You can climb the tree and drag the chain with you."

Bransford groused until his fellow prisoner turned on him irritably. "Don't go rilin' them up or we won't get any supper. Some of these Rangers would throw their own brother in jail and lose the key."

Bransford shivered involuntarily. "That Farley Brackett kept starin' at me like I had a target painted on my back."

Landon showed no sympathy. "You're lucky if jail is all you're facin'. I'm lookin' at a rope. Gettin' shot might be the better way out." The prisoner rubbed his raw knuckles. Evidently his capture had not been without incident.

The black cook grinned at the Rangers as they approached. Andy grinned back in anticipation. He had rather eat Bo's high-rising sourdough biscuits than cobbler pie. Bo could make sowbelly seem like beefsteak. Somebody had been out hunting, so Bo was able to fry up some venison backstrap to go with Andy's and Farley's red beans. Andy believed in the Comanche adage that one should eat all he could hold when he could get it because it might be a while before he had it again.

Farley, for all his complaining nature, was normally a hearty eater. Today he nibbled tentatively at what Bo offered. By that, Andy knew he still had a considerable headache.

Bransford *was* lucky he had not been shot.

A towheaded boy brought a blackened coffeepot. He gave a glad shout at the sight of Andy sitting there. "Hey, Andy, did you get your man?"

"We always get our man." That was a shameful stretch of the truth, but the boy had begun taking pride in his loose association with the Ranger company. Andy wanted to encourage that feeling, for Scooter Tennyson had been headed down the slippery road to an outlaw life when the Rangers took him in.

Andy held out his empty tin cup. "You been stayin' out of trouble?"

The boy glanced at the black cook. "I ain't been allowed time enough to get in trouble. Give a darky a chance to give orders to a white man and he'll work him to death." He smiled at the cook to indicate he did not really mean it.

The cook smiled back, but his dark eyes showed he knew Scooter *did* mean it. "You finish washin' them dishes, boy, then fetch me up some firewood. After that you can go fishin' if you're of a mind to."

Scooter's mother was dead. His father was in the penitentiary. The boy had been riding with some of his father's outlaw friends until the Rangers captured him. Finding no relatives, they had more or less adopted him to steer him away from a pathway already blazed for him by his father. Andy had taken a special interest because of parallels with his own boyhood experience.

Scooter had been skinny and hungry-eyed when the Rangers first found him. He was filling out now, putting on weight. Andy said, "Looks like Bo's cookin' is good for you."

"I just wisht he didn't make me work so hard for it."

The boy was earning his keep by doing light chores around the kitchen tent and fetching wood, nothing that would cause him undue strain.

In a severe voice Farley said, "Work'll make a better man of you. Maybe you won't follow your daddy into the pen."

Stung, the boy took the coffeepot back to the fire.

Andy frowned. "You didn't have to say that."

"It's the truth. That kid was far gone before you got ahold of him. It'll be a wonder on earth if he doesn't wind up lookin' out through the bars just like his daddy."

"It doesn't have to happen that way if we give him a chance."

"*You* give him a chance. I ain't got the time or the patience."

The captain came along soon after Andy and Farley finished eating. Andy wanted to ask if he had discharged Dick Landon, but he knew it was not his business. He would know in due time.

The captain had regained his composure after dressing down the wayward Ranger. He said, "You-all did a good job."

Farley shrugged, then paid for it as pain stabbed him. "It's what we get paid so high for."

"Did you have much trouble?"

Farley did not answer, so Andy put in, "Not with the prisoner." He was tempted to tell about Leach's woman but chose not to rub salt into Farley's wound.

The captain bent to look at Farley's face. "You look like you tangled with a wildcat."

Farley looked into Andy's eyes with a silent warning. "Horse fell with me."

The captain studied him thoughtfully. "At least it didn't cripple you. I have another job for you and Private Pickard."

Farley went defensive. "To do what?"

"You two will deliver the prisoners back east to where they're wanted."

Farley was not pleased. "Handlin' two prisoners is a big responsibility. I'd rather take somebody older. This young'un is green as grass."

"Pickard is young, but he's not inexperienced. You were with him when he took an arrow wound."

"Delivered by one of his redskinned cousins. Gettin' wounded ain't no accomplishment. Anybody can do it."

"You two are the only men I can spare. If you don't feel that you can go, I will regretfully accept your resignation."

Farley glared at Andy. "I can put up with him if I have to."

Andy asked, "Where are we takin' the prisoners?"

"Southeast Texas. You'll deliver Bransford to the sheriff of Colorado County. Jayce Landon is wanted over the other side of Columbus. It seems an old feud has fired up again." The captain looked back to see if anyone could hear. "Dick helped bring his brother in, then went off on a drinking binge."

Andy said, "I can see why he would."

"Discipline has to be maintained or everything comes apart."

Andy studied the chained prisoners. "It's hard to figure people. Bransford looks like a hard case, but Landon looks like he ought to be preachin' Sunday services."

The captain shook his head. "You can't judge by appearances. Sometimes the men who seem the meekest and mildest have the bloodiest hands. And I've seen some ugly-looking preachers."

Andy saw a bright spot in the assignment. "If we take Bransford to Colorado County, I'll have a chance to stop by Rusty Shannon's farm." He looked at Farley. "And you could visit your mother and sister."

Farley grunted. "They don't want to see me. I brought too much grief down on them."

Andy was strongly conscious of family ties, having none of his own. He could not understand anyone rejecting family or being rejected by them. "That was a long time ago."

"Not long enough." Farley turned away. "If you're done with us, Captain, I'll go see after my horse."

"You're dismissed." Watching Farley retreat, the captain said, "He ought to be a sergeant by now, but he has a dark streak in him that confounds me. What's this about his mother and sister not wanting to see him?"

The memory still made anger rise in Andy. "It was back in the time of the state police. They mistook his daddy for Farley and killed him. Wounded his mother so bad she almost died. Farley figures his family blames him for all the trouble they had."

"Do they?"

"I doubt they do anymore. They know the war twisted him up inside."

"He's unpredictable, even a little dangerous. In some ways that makes him an effective Ranger. It also makes him risky to be around."

"He's like a bear I saw on a chain. Even when he acts quiet, he's liable to turn on you and bite your arm off."

"It's obvious I can't send Dick Landon on this mission. It would put him in an impossible situation. So it's up to you and Farley."

Andy shrugged. "At least I'll have a chance to see Rusty."

The captain nodded. "Tell Shannon that anytime he wants to be a Ranger again, he just needs to let me know. He's welcome in this company."

"I'll tell him, but he's had more than his share of trouble. I think now he just wants to be a farmer."

Scooter was carrying wood and dropping it into a pile near the cook's fire pit. Andy pitched in to help him. Scooter did not thank him verbally, but his eyes showed he was pleased. He said, "Soon as I get done fetchin' wood, I'm goin' fishin'. I never got to do no fishin' till I come to this camp."

"You like fishin', do you?"

"It's about the most fun thing I ever done." The boy had never been given much chance for fun, riding with a criminal father and his father's lawless companions. When he tried to read he followed the lines with his finger, mouthed the words slowly, and often gave up in frustration. What little writing he could do was in block letters, the words so badly misspelled that it was a struggle to decipher their meaning.

Andy said, "I never did any fishin' either before I went to live with Rusty Shannon. The Comanches leaned to buffalo meat."

"Somethin' else I'd like to do someday is hunt buffalo. I'll bet that'd be fun."

"I was too young to ride with the hunters. They made me stay with the women and children. We skinned out the meat after the hunters got through. That was the work part, not the fun part."

"I ever get the chance, I'm goin' to kill me a buffalo."

Andy shook his head. "You may never get the chance. They say hunters have scattered all over the Plains, killin' for nothin' but the hides. Pretty soon there won't be any buffalo left."

"How come the Indians don't stop them?"

"They've tried, but there's too many hunters. The army has driven most of the Indians to reservations. Tryin' to teach them to farm and eat beef." Sadness fell over him. "The ones I knew are too proud to take to the plow. I don't know what'll become of them."

"You ever think about goin' up yonder to see them?"

Andy dropped an armful of wood and looked northward past the river. "Sometimes. I've got lots of friends there. But I've got a few enemies, too."

"Take me with you. I'll help you fight your enemies."

"Maybe someday." Andy dusted himself off. "I'd best go see after my horse."

Scooter grinned. "I'll catch a fish for your supper."

Andy tousled the boy's unkempt hair. "Just what I've been hopin' for."

Farley was brushing his horse's back. He frowned as Andy approached. "You're wastin' your time tryin' to reform that dogie kid. He's got a taint in his blood. It's waitin' for a chance to bust out like a boil on the butt."

"It doesn't have to. If we treat him right . . ."

"I knew some folks who tried to make a pet out of a coyote pup. The wild blood always showed through. They finally had to shoot it."

"People told Rusty the same thing about me."

Escorting prisoners carried a degree of risk. The more severe the crime and the probable punishment, the more the risk. Andy had little concern over Bransford, who had shown his fearsome reputation to be all smoke and no fire. However, he had misgivings about Landon. The captain's information was that Landon and his kin were carrying on a blood feud with a family named Hopper. Family feuds in Texas could be long-lasting, and deadly as a den of snakes. Landon had waited for and shot one Ned Hopper on a lonely country road. Cornered by the Hopper-controlled law, he had wounded a deputy sheriff and made his escape, traveling west to seek help from his brother Dick. He had not considered that the telegraph was faster than the horse.

"You-all watch him," the captain warned as they prepared to leave early the next morning. "Don't give him any slack just because he's Dick Landon's brother."

Farley showed no concern. "If he makes a false move, it'll be his last one."

"Don't shoot him unless you absolutely have to. They want him alive back there."

Farley checked to be sure the two prisoners' hands were securely cuffed and the cuffs tied to their saddles. "Either of you makes a break, you're dead," he warned.

Ranger Dick Landon had watched from the front of the tent in which he slept. He came forward, his eyes full of pain.

His face and his halting walk showed the lingering effects of his drinking spree. He said, "Jayce, I'd give all I've got if I could've kept it from comin' to this. I came out here to get away from the feud. I wish to hell you'd brought Flora and done the same."

Jayce Landon turned his head away, not looking at his brother. He stared into the distance. His voice stung. "You went off and left the family. I done what needed doin'."

"When's it goin' to stop?"

"When we've filled up the graveyard with Hoppers."

Ranger Landon turned toward Andy and Farley. "I know he's wanted for murder, but he's still my brother. Don't mistreat him."

Farley said, "If anything happens to him it'll be of his own doin'." He jerked his head as a signal to start. Bransford led off. Farley followed closely behind the prisoners. Andy brought up the rear, leading a little pack mule.

Looking back, he saw Ranger Landon hunched in an attitude of misery. Andy told Farley, "I feel real bad about Dick."

"I've got my own worries. I ain't takin' on none of his. Dick had best watch out for himself and let the rest of his family go to hell."

"That's a cold way of lookin' at it."

Farley turned on him. "Don't be botherin' me with other people's troubles. Or yours either. Else I'm liable to leave you afoot and take the prisoners by myself."

Anger warmed Andy's face. "Looks like we understand one another."

"The important thing is that you understand *me*."

People who had known Farley as a boy said he had been a kindly youngster who enjoyed hunting and fishing and had sung in church. The war and the angry years that followed seemed to have burned all kindness out of him.

Once clear of camp, Andy turned the mule loose. It followed without having to be led. The morning sun was in their faces. The captain had suggested that they push hard to reach Friedrichsburg before dark so they could lodge the prisoners in a secure jail. That way both Rangers could get a good night's sleep without having to stand guard.

The day passed without notable incident, though Andy sensed that Landon was on edge, watching, wishing for a chance to escape. No such chance presented itself. Farley was always close by, a dark and brooding presence. They occasionally met travelers on the trail. Farley scrutinized them suspiciously and kept his hand on the butt of his pistol while they were within range.

"Landon was mixed up in a feud," he told Andy, "so we've got to watch out for both sides. His own people will look for a chance to free him and the other bunch will be lookin' to kill him. Both sides see me and you as enemies. Us bein' Rangers won't make a particle of difference."

Andy began to fear that night would catch them before they reached Friedrichsburg. Darkness would increase the danger in traveling with prisoners. He was relieved when they came into a wide valley and saw the German settlement. Though the town was relatively young, as were most along the western fringes of the state, its broad dirt streets were already lined with sturdy stone and brick structures built in a style brought from the Old World. They were a sign that its citizens were not transient. They had established deep roots and intended to stay.

A deputy received the Rangers at the jail. His English was heavily accented, his manner efficiently professional. He locked the prisoners in separate cells and suggested that the Rangers would be comfortable in the Nimitz Hotel.

Farley demurred. "I'm never comfortable spendin' my money foolishly. I'll sleep in the wagon yard."

Andy suspected the captain would have chosen the hotel, but the captain was better paid. Privates rode for thirty dollars a month. At least nowadays they actually received it. Rusty had told him that in earlier times they often went unpaid for long stretches while the state struggled with a thin and leaky treasury.

Andy followed Farley from the jail to the wagon yard, each carrying his rolled blankets. Farley turned on him and pointed up the street. "You don't have to copy after me. Go to the hotel if you're of a mind to."

"They don't pay me any more than they pay you." He knew it would look awkward if he, the junior of the two, took better accommodations. Farley was sure to let the other Rangers know. Some would take it as a sign that Andy was being uppity. Among proud Texans, that was a cardinal sin.

Andy let Farley stay a few steps ahead, befitting Farley's seniority. Anyway, he could do without Farley's company.

He thought about how pleasant it would be to order supper in the hotel, where they served meals on a white tablecloth. Maybe someday, when he had more money in his pocket. A working cowboy earned as much as a Ranger and seldom if ever had to face somebody with a gun and criminal intentions.

He bought a loaf of freshly baked bread and a spicy sausage to share with Farley. Farley bought a bottle but did not offer to share it. Nor did he bother to thank Andy for the supper. The man and his contradictions intrigued Andy as much as they offended him.

The darkness was compromised only slightly by a lighted lantern at the open front doors of the stable. Andy sat on a wooden bench, watching Farley tip the bottle. He broke a long silence. "I heard you say some people oughtn't to ever drink."

"I don't drink enough to let it get in my way."

Andy watched a match flare after Farley rolled a cigarette. He said, "Not that I give a damn, but I wonder what makes you itch so bad. You've never liked me from the time we first met."

The observation caught Farley off guard. "I never thought much about it. Didn't seem important. But now that you mention it, I *don't* like you. You stole a horse from me once."

"He never was yours in the first place." On the run from the state police, Farley had abandoned a worn-out horse and had taken one from Rusty. Farley's father gave Rusty a sorrel in return. Rusty turned the animal over to Andy, who named him Long Red.

Farley said, "I'd told my daddy I wanted that horse. Figured I'd earned him for all the work I did for nothin' on that man-killin' old farm."

"Guess he didn't see it like you did."

"Lots of things he didn't see like I did. Got to where I couldn't stay around him anymore. But those damned state police had no call to kill him." Farley's voice was bitter.

"You gave the carpetbaggers a lot of trouble. Don't you think you came out about even?"

"I tried to give them back as good as what they gave me."

"Why, then, did you wind up joinin' the Rangers?"

"The state police was mostly scallywags. The Rangers are *us,* the old-timey Texans. You think after all I went through in the war and with the carpetbaggers that I could ever settle down on the farm again? You think *you* could, after livin' with the Comanches?"

"If I set my mind to it. I just got a little restless, so

I joined the Rangers. Wanted to see if I could ever be as good as Rusty Shannon."

On that question he was still undecided. He knew he was not yet. He wondered if he ever would be.

Farley asked, "What do you think of the service, now that you've been in it awhile?"

"I didn't look for it to be fun. Mostly it's been long days in camp standin' horse guard or out followin' long trails that fade away before we find anybody. I can see why men like Dick Landon slip off and get drunk."

"Excitement is considerable overrated. Now you'd better go to sleep. We'll try and make Austin by tomorrow night if the horses hold up."

Farley had put his finger on one problem Andy saw with the Rangers. Not much consideration was given to how well the men held up. They were expected to perform regardless of circumstances. But allowances had to be made for the horses. A horse couldn't tell an outlaw from a Baptist preacher.

On reflection, Andy realized that he couldn't either.

They got an early start on what was going to be a long day's ride. Bransford griped about being rousted out before sunup. Landon said nothing, but his eyes were constantly at work, searching for a chance to get away. The same deputy who had checked the prisoners in checked them out and had Farley sign a release absolving Gillespie County of any blame should either prisoner make a break after leaving the jail.

"You watch that man," he warned, pointing at Landon. "All night his eyes are open. Look away from him this long"—he snapped his fingers—"and he will be gone from you."

As a precaution the deputy had put a set of leg irons on Landon. Fumbling with the key, Andy bent to unlock them so Landon could mount his horse. Landon brought his handcuffs and his fists down on the back of Andy's head, knocking him to his knees. Landon grabbed at the pistol on Andy's hip. Andy twisted away, falling on his side so Landon could not reach the weapon.

Farley shouted a curse and slammed the butt of his rifle against Landon's head. Landon staggered. Farley grabbed the back of the prisoner's collar and shoved him up against his fidgeting horse. "I've made allowances for you because you're a Ranger's brother. Next time I'll bust your head like a watermelon."

Andy pushed to his feet, his head aching.

Farley said, "See what comes of bein' reckless? Didn't the Comanches teach you to watch out for yourself?"

"My hat took the worst of it."

The deputy had observed the incident but had not been close enough to help. He told Farley, "Like I said, better you watch that man. The devil looks from his eyes out."

"I've got three men to watch after, and one of them is a careless kid who's supposed to be helpin' me. You want a Ranger job?"

The man smiled thinly. "I am better paid being a deputy only."

They rode out of town, the prisoners securely handcuffed to their saddles. Bransford glared at Farley. "You could've broke that man's head like an egg."

"He had it comin', and so will you if you keep exercisin' that jaw."

Andy's head drummed with pain. That was Landon's fault, but he could not condemn the prisoner for it. In Landon's position, standing in the shadow of the gallows, he thought he too would probably grab at any straw, no matter how flimsy.

By pushing hard they reached Austin at sundown. Andy

worried about the horses' ability to stand the pace. Farley assured him, "They'll make it. The tireder we keep the prisoners, the less trouble they're apt to give us."

Once Bransford and Landon were secured in jail, Farley and Andy reported to Ranger headquarters at the state capitol. It was a matter of form. Farley said he hoped local Rangers would be assigned to finish delivering the prisoners, but the officer in charge simply wished him an uneventful trip.

Andy was pleased, for he had counted on a visit to Rusty's farm. "Like it or not, Farley, you ought to see your mother and sister. They'll be disappointed if they find out you got so close and didn't stop."

"Mind your own business."

They left town on borrowed horses, for two hard days' travel had exhausted their own. Toward the end of the second day out of Austin they turned Bransford over to Sheriff Tom Blessing as ordered. Blessing, a large, blocky man built like a blacksmith, had known Andy since he had returned from his life with the Comanches. Andy asked him about Rusty and black Shanty York and others he knew around the county.

"Rusty's got thin enough to hide behind a fence post. He don't sleep enough and don't eat right. Still grievin' over that girl he lost. He's got a good crop in the field, though. As for Shanty, you know how it is with them darkies: you can't tell their age by lookin'. That black skin hides the lines."

Andy said, "I'll be goin' by to see Rusty once we've delivered this other prisoner."

Blessing frowned. "The word's already out that you're on the way with Jayce Landon. There's liable to be people waitin' for you. If I was you I'd deliver him in the dark of the night."

Farley had been listening to the conversation. "And act like we're afraid of his friends?"

"He's got more enemies than friends. If I was you, I'd be afraid of them all."

{ THREE }

Rusty Shannon leaned on his hoe and looked beyond the waving green corn toward a dark cloud boiling on the horizon. One more soaking rain should finish bringing the corn and his other crops to maturity.

I wish Josie could have been here to see this, he thought. But the prospect of rain brought no real pleasure. Very little did anymore, not since Josie had died.

A rider approached him, mounted on a mule. Rusty recognized Old Shanty's slight, bent form and walked out to the edge of the field to meet him. He removed his hat to wipe sweat from his brow and the reddish hair that had given him his nickname. Sprinkled with gray, it was uncut and shaggy because he'd lost interest in his appearance. He had not shaved in a week.

He lifted his hand in what he meant to be a welcoming wave, though it fell short. "Get down, neighbor, and give that old mule a rest."

Many white men would not shake hands with a black. Rusty did so without thought. Shanty had been a friend too long for racial proprieties to stand in the way.

"How do, Mr. Rusty. Kind of hot. Buildin' up to a summertime shower, looks like."

Shanty always addressed him as *Mister.* He had spent a

major part of his seventy or so years as a slave, and old habits died hard, if at all. He had inherited a small farm from his former owner. For a time he had had to struggle to hold it in the face of opposition from some in the community who resented his being an owner of property. That battle had been fought to a standstill with help from Rusty, Andy, and others like Sheriff Tom Blessing who had kindly feelings toward him.

Since losing Josie, Rusty had found it difficult to arouse much interest in his own farm. He frequently rode over to Shanty's place to help him with heavy work that had become too much for the old man to handle alone. In return Shanty felt obliged to repay in kind, whether Rusty needed his help or not. He had spent more time in Rusty's garden than Rusty had.

Rusty said, "I judge by the direction that you're not comin' from your own place."

"I been over to Mr. Fowler Gaskin's, helpin' him work his vegetable patch. Hoed his weeds. Picked him some squash and beans and tomatoes so he's got somethin' to eat. He's a sick man, Mr. Gaskin is."

Rusty snorted. "Sick of work, mostly. That old reprobate has enjoyed bad health ever since I can remember."

Gaskin was notorious for sloth, feigning illness and using his age as a crutch. He had made an art of chiseling others into doing for him the work he did not want to do for himself. His neighbors had long since learned to watch their property when he came around because he was likely to leave with some of it.

Rusty said, "You've done a lot of work for him, and I'll bet he hasn't paid you a dollar."

Shanty shrugged. "Mr. Gaskin's a poor man. Besides, the Book says I am my neighbor's keeper."

"He never was *your* keeper. He did his damndest to run you out of this country. He was one of them that burned your cabin down."

"We never did know that for certain sure. We just supposed. Anyway, I can't be grudgin' agin a sick old man. He says it won't be long till he's knockin' on them Pearly Gates."

Rusty could think of few things that would improve the community more than a funeral service for Fowler Gaskin. People would come from miles around to attend, just to be sure he was gone. No hog pen or chicken house was safe so long as he drew breath.

Shanty said, "He's been speakin' remorseful about all the wrong things he's done. Cries when he talks about his two boys that was killed in the war."

For years Gaskin had been using his sons' death in an effort to arouse sympathy. Most people around here had learned the truth long ago, that his sons had not died in battle. They had been killed in a New Orleans bawdyhouse brawl.

"That's just to get you to do his work for him, and do it for nothin'. He still hates you, but that doesn't mean he won't use you."

Shanty shrugged. "I'm just tryin' to serve the Lord any which way I can. Someday I may be old and sick myself. Maybe Mr. Gaskin will come and help *me*."

Perhaps, when cows fly over the moon, Rusty thought. It was pointless to continue the argument. Shanty was of a trusting nature. Freedom had not come to him until well into his middle age. Up to then it would have been considered presumptuous of him, even dangerous, to pass judgment on anyone white. Now he did not know how.

Rusty made up his mind to ride over to Fowler Gaskin's soon and read the gospel to him.

Shanty gave Rusty a quiet appraisal. "You're lookin' kind of lank, Mr. Rusty. Ain't you been eatin'?"

"It's been too hot to eat."

"It don't ever get *that* hot. That girl's still heavy on your mind, ain't she?"

"Some things ain't easy forgot."

"You don't have to forget. Just take the things that trouble you and set them on a high shelf where you won't be lookin' at them all the time."

"I've tried, but life has sort of lost its flavor around here."

"Maybe supper would taste better to you if somebody else cooked it. I could stay and fix you somethin'."

"Thanks, but by the looks of that cloud, you'd better be goin' home before you get soaked. I'll fix for myself if I get hungry."

Shanty soon left. Rusty knew it was too late to visit Gaskin. Tomorrow would be soon enough, or the next day. The extra time would allow him to think of more shortcomings to call to Gaskin's attention.

He was about ready to quit the field and do the evening milking when another visitor appeared. Rusty had counted Tom Blessing as a friend as far back as he could remember. Tom was a contemporary of Daddy Mike Shannon, who had been a foster father to Rusty. As a small boy more than thirty years ago, Rusty had been carried away by Indians after they killed his parents. Unlike Andy Pickard, he had been rescued a few days later. Because of Daddy Mike and Tom Blessing and several others, he had not spent years among the Comanches as Andy had.

After howdying and shaking, Rusty said, "Follow me up to the cabin, Tom. I'll fix us some coffee and warm up the beans."

"Beans." Tom gave Rusty the same critical study that

Shanty had. "You don't look like you've been eatin' regular, not beans or anything else."

"It don't taste all that good when you're by yourself."

"You oughtn't to be by yourself."

Tom had been arguing that Rusty needed a wife. He even had one picked for him. But the suggestion stirred up painful memories Rusty was still struggling to cope with. He sidestepped the subject. "I could fry up some bacon."

"Sorry, but I ain't got time. Need to get home and do the chores before it rains." Tom pointed with his chin. "I happened into Shanty on the road. Said he'd been by here."

"He was over at Gaskin's, doin' work Fowler ought to do for himself. Fowler needs a load of fire and brimstone dropped on him."

Blessing smiled. "If you do it, just don't kill him. The court docket's already full enough." He looked toward the building cloud. "I'd best get into a high lope."

The cloud had grown considerably since Rusty had last paid attention to it. "And I'd better get the cow milked. Need to carry some dry wood into the house too."

The cow was waiting at the milk-pen gate. Her calf was penned inside so that the two were separated all day. Rusty allowed the calf to nurse long enough that the cow let down her milk, then penned the cow and took the milk he needed for his own use. Done, he let the calf in again to finish what remained.

The cloud was coming up rapidly. Rusty hurried to the cabin with the bucket of milk, set it on the kitchen table, and went outside to fetch in a couple of days' supply of dry wood for the fireplace. He had barely finished when the rain started. The drops were large and in the first moments struck the ground with force enough that they raised dust.

He became aware of a roaring noise, rapidly growing louder. He knew immediately that it was hail.

"Oh damn," he said under his breath.

The air, so warm earlier, quickly chilled. The initial stones were no larger than the first joint of his little finger. Quickly, however, they became much larger, hammering the ground. Though he stood in the shelter of the open dog run, some of the hailstones bounced up and rolled against his feet. He stepped back into the kitchen door. The impact of ice pellets against the roof was loud as thunder. Soon the ground was white as if a heavy snow had fallen.

He shivered, but some of the cold came from within. An hour ago he had every prospect of a good crop. Now he wondered if a stalk remained standing.

As quickly as it had come, the hailstorm was gone. A slow, steady rain followed, the kind of rain he had needed in the first place. Water dripped down into the cabin from holes in the roof. He would have to replace a lot of shingles, perhaps all of them.

He pulled a slicker over his shoulders and stepped out to survey the damage. He did not have to walk all the way to the field. He could see it through the rain. Everything in it was beaten to the ground.

He had known people who worked off their frustrations with a burst of profanity. He stood in stony silence, shivering from the cold wind that had come with the hail. Rain rolled off the brim of his hat and spilled down his shoulders.

He saw a couple of dead chickens on their backs, their legs in the air. They had not made it to the shelter of the crude henhouse. Hailstones floated in the spreading puddles of rainwater.

Feeling as if a horse had kicked him in the belly, he

trudged back to the cabin, mud clinging to his boots. He had to move the bucket of milk because water was dripping into it. He brewed a pot of coffee and slumped into a chair, holding a framed photograph from the mantel over the fireplace. His throat tightened as he studied the face that smiled at him from the picture.

His shoulders were strong. They could bear this new burden; they had to. But they would bear it better if Josie could have been here.

He imagined what old Preacher Webb would say: *The Lord giveth, and the Lord taketh away.*

Rusty bowed his head. He sure as hell took it all, he thought.

The light of day brought no comfort. The rain was gone, and the morning sun was bright through breaking clouds. He walked first to the garden, where his tomato and okra vines looked as if a herd of cattle had trampled them. He had not removed the two dead hens. The other chickens pecked around them, oblivious to their sisters' fate. Some were half-naked, feathers stripped away.

His field was a muddy ruin. The only salvage he could see was to turn cattle in on it when the ground dried enough. They might find a few days' forage. But he would have nothing to put in his corncrib, much less to haul to town and sell.

He was well aware that a farmer's life was a constant gamble. Each year he bet his land, labor, and personal welfare against the threats of drought, excessive rainfall, heat, and untimely cold as well as insects and various orders of blight. Every so often the farmer would lose his bet, and the best he could hope for was a better next year.

Next year seemed a long way off, for this was still summer.

Rusty returned to the cabin and fixed breakfast, though he could bring himself to eat but little.

Tom Blessing rode up and hollered. His eyes were sympathetic as Rusty walked out to meet him. "Just ridin' around checkin' on my neighbors," Tom said. "Looks like that hail knocked the whey out of you."

Rusty could only shrug. "What about your place?"

"Not enough to break an egg, hardly. Looks like there was just one strip of heavy stuff, and it hit you the hardest of anybody. Missed Shanty's place altogether."

Rusty was gratified to hear that. "I may have to move in with Shanty this winter. What about Fowler Gaskin?"

Blessing shook his head. "I haven't been over there yet, but it doesn't look like the hail went that far."

Rusty felt regret. If Providence was even half-fair, Fowler's place should have been beaten into nothing but a puddle of mud.

Blessing said, "Preacher Webb always claimed everything happens for a reason. Said no matter how cold and cloudy the day, the sun is still shinin' someplace. Maybe you can replant."

"Garden stuff, maybe, but it's too late for corn. I won't be puttin' away any fresh money for a while."

Blessing faced the cabin. "Looks like your roofs got beat real bad. Want me to have a load of shingles sent out from town?"

"Can't afford to buy what I can make for myself. I've got plenty of timber down on the river. Tell you what you *can* do, though: see if you can find me a job."

"I'll try, but I'm afraid there's not much to choose from around here. Times are slow."

Rusty had not inventoried his toolshed in a while. He found his saw was missing. So were the froe and mallet he used to split shingles the time he had helped rebuild Shanty's burned cabin. He was certain he had brought them home after that job was done.

He knew where he was most likely to find them, at Fowler Gaskin's. That scoundrel had a habit of borrowing without asking. Stealing, most people would call it, for he brought nothing back except under duress. Rusty had never liked going to Gaskin's place, but he had already decided to raise Cain with the old heathen over his abuse of Shanty. He hitched his team to the wagon. The tools would be unhandy to carry home on horseback. He had no way of knowing what-all of his property he might find, things he had not yet missed.

For years Gaskin's cabin had leaned to one side, away from the prevailing winds. Logs had been propped at an angle against it to keep it from falling over. Trash and debris littered the premises around it. Gaskin sat on a bench in the shade at the front of the cabin, a jug within easy reach on the ground. He was rail-thin, his skin sallow. His ragged beard was mostly gray, laced with rusty streaks left by tobacco juice dribbling down his chin. He squinted bleary eyes in an effort to bring Rusty into focus.

"What the hell you doin' here?" he demanded. "I ran you off of this place, didn't I?"

Rusty climbed down from the wagon. "You've never run me anyplace that I didn't want to go. I believe you've got some tools that belong to me."

"No such of a thing. Ain't nothin' of yours here." Gaskin arose on wobbly legs, then dropped back onto the bench. "You've got no cause to come accusin' me. I'll sic my dogs on you."

Gaskin's two dogs had barked once, then had slunk away

at the wagon's approach. They had much in common with their master.

Rusty did not wait to hear any more of Gaskin's protests. He walked out to a half-collapsed shed and began to dig through tools and implements piled there in a heap. He found his froe and mallet. They bore the initials *RS*, which he had burned onto the wooden handles with a steel rod heated to a red glow. He also found his timber saw and a sledgehammer that belonged to him. He carried them back and placed them in the bed of the wagon.

Gaskin protested, "You got no right to carry a man's tools away. I'm liable to need them."

"Not unless you can get somebody else to use them for you. It's too bad you don't have four hands, Fowler. You could steal twice as much."

Gaskin stood up again, bracing one hand against his cabin. Rusty thought it was a toss-up as to which might fall first. Gaskin said, "You come on my land, you steal my tools, then you insult me to my face. If I wasn't old and sick I'd whup you good and proper."

"Speakin' of bein' old, you've been playin' on Shanty's sympathy when the truth is that you're younger and stronger than he is. I'm tellin' you to stop it or else."

"Or else what? You goin' to hit a poor old man?"

Rusty clenched his fists. "I might. I sure as hell might."

He climbed into the wagon and clucked the team into motion. Gaskin followed in short, shaky steps, shouting his opinion of Rusty and all his ancestors. The dogs came out from hiding and barked from a safe distance.

Gaskin had only a small field, for planting required work. But his corn stood tall, the stalks rustling in the wind. The hail did not seem to have touched him.

Rusty looked up and said, "Lord, next time You send us a storm, I hope You have a better sense of direction."

Reaching home, he carried the tools down to the river. With an ax he cut a deep notch in a tree in the direction he wanted it to fall, then used the saw. When the tree was down, he sawed it into shingle lengths. He dropped several trees before he thought he had enough. Then he began splitting off shingles.

In a couple of days he had a supply of them piled behind the cabin. He was on the roof, removing damaged ones when he saw a wagon and several riders approaching on horseback. He recognized Shanty on his mule. Tom Blessing loped ahead, one of his brothers spurring along behind.

Blessing shouted, "Got a bunch of your neighbors here. We can't do anything about the crop you lost, but we've come to help you put your roofs back on."

Rusty's dark mood lifted. It was a custom in rural Texas communities that neighbors work together. If a man was sick or hurt, his friends came to do whatever work was necessary. If hard luck befell him, the neighbors pitched in to set things as nearly right as possible. No one could guess when his own time might come.

Rusty climbed down the ladder and walked out to greet the visitors, shaking hands with each in his turn.

Blessing smiled broadly. "You need some good news after all that's happened to you. I saw Andy. He'll be by to visit you in a few days."

Rusty grinned. That *was* good news. "His arm wasn't broke, was it? He's written me just one letter since he's been in the Rangers, and it took up only half a page."

"He looked healthy to me. Him and Farley Brackett delivered a prisoner to me and had another they were fixin' to take a little farther. Said he'd see you before he heads back to the Ranger camp."

Rusty's grin faded. "He was with Farley Brackett?"

"I know him and Farley don't gee-haw too good, but

I suppose he had no choice. A young man needs to learn how to take orders so he'll know how to give them when his time comes."

Rusty said, "Farley wakes up every mornin' with a dark cloud over his head. And he's got a wild hair in him that pops out every now and then."

"Andy can think for himself. It's good for him to learn how to get along with all kinds of people. Even somebody like Farley."

Two women rode on the wagon seat, the younger one driving. The older of the pair was Tom Blessing's wife. Rusty had to look a second time before he realized the other was Bethel Brackett, Farley Brackett's sister.

Mrs. Blessing said, "Bethel and me are goin' to fix dinner for the workin' crew. Mind helpin' us carry some vittles into your kitchen? Looks to me like you need a good square meal."

"Been livin' on my own cookin', such as it is."

"What you need here is a woman." Mrs. Blessing quickly had second thoughts about what she had said. "I'm sorry. I wasn't thinkin'."

Rusty's momentary cheer left him. He forced a thin smile, though he did not feel it. "Been a while since I lost Josie. I think I've pretty well got over it."

He had not. He did not know if he ever would.

He turned toward Bethel. He remembered that Andy had shown a considerable interest in her once. Rusty had long wondered how a girl so pleasant-looking could have a brother like Farley. If he did not know her mother to be a woman of stern moral standards, he might wonder if the two had the same father.

He said, "Welcome, Bethel. Been a long time since that day you came here with your daddy, bringin' me a sorrel horse."

"The horse you gave to Andy." She smiled. "Have you heard anything from Andy lately?"

"Andy's not much for writin' letters."

"So I've noticed."

He suspected the sheriff had not told her Andy was due soon for a short visit. That meant she probably did not know Farley was with him. Perhaps Blessing had a good reason for not telling her. It might be that Farley had said he did not plan to visit his mother and sister. In that case it was just as well they did not know. Farley had caused them pain enough over the years.

Mrs. Blessing followed Rusty into the kitchen with a sack of flour. She looked back to be sure the girl was not within hearing. "Bethel has turned into a right pretty young lady, don't you think?"

Rusty sensed where she was heading. "But too young for me, and I'm sure I'm too old to interest her. She's more Andy's age."

"But Andy's not here. You are."

"I'm just not ready to be thinkin' in that direction."

"If not Bethel, then how about Alice Monahan? Alice is a sweet girl. She was a godsend to me when I was sick for so long. And she *is* a sister to Josie, or was."

Rusty had been in love with two of the Monahan sisters, Geneva and Josie. He had lost them both. He would not allow himself to consider another. "Looks like the Lord intends for me to be an old bachelor."

"It's not for us to say what the Lord intends, but I can't believe He wants you to spend your life alone."

Rusty was grateful for an interruption by Tom Blessing. "Rusty, let's get started on that roof."

Tearing out old shingles, placing new ones where they had been, Rusty told Blessing, "Thanks. You came in at just the right time."

"I know. When my wife takes a notion about somethin', she's like a cold-jawed horse. There's no turnin' her back. I just let her play it out to the end of the string." He frowned. "But you know, she's right. That hail didn't leave you much reason to stay around here till plantin' time comes again. If I was you I'd take a ride up to the Monahan farm. Alice might surprise you."

"I'm not lookin' for surprises. Unless you can surprise me with a good job."

"I've asked around. Haven't found anything."

Rusty felt the bleak mood settling over him again. "It's liable to be a long fall and winter."

{ FOUR }

The trip had not made Jayce Landon any less of a puzzle to Andy. In comparison to Bransford, who had been left in Tom Blessing's custody, Landon still looked as if he might be a preacher, or at least a law-abiding storekeeper. But Andy had a sore place on the back of his head from Landon's attack. And Landon had laid in wait to shoot a man. Bransford had never done that so far as Andy knew.

Farley Brackett said, "Don't waste sympathy on him. He's got blood on his hands."

"How about the state policemen *you* killed?"

Farley said, "They was lookin' at me. They could've shot me as easy as I shot them."

"Do they ever keep you awake at night?"

"Dead is dead. They don't come back."

Andy did not like the look of five horsemen riding to meet

them from the direction of Hopper's Crossing. He tensed, and again he wished Rusty Shannon were there. "What do you think, Farley?"

"I think *damn it.* I hoped this wouldn't happen." Farley reached across to recheck Landon's handcuffs and the rawhide strip that bound them to the saddlehorn. "Take a good look at them, Jayce. Are they friends of yours, or enemies?"

For the first time since the trip began, a smile creased Landon's face. "Some of my kin and a couple of my neighbors. They won't like it, seein' me shackled like a runaway slave."

"They'll like it even less if they try and turn you loose because I'll shoot you dead. Badger Boy, you better draw your weapon."

Andy already had. He was not surprised about being met on the road. Tom Blessing had warned that the word had gone out ahead and that it was wise to be prepared for anything.

Thirty feet from the approaching horsemen, Farley stopped. He placed the muzzle of his pistol behind Landon's ear. "You men had better put aside any foolish notions. The only way you'll get this prisoner away from us is if he's dead. And some of you will ride to perdition with him."

Andy's mouth went dry as he tried to read the men's intentions.

One rider pushed his horse a little past the others. His facial features resembled Jayce's so much that Andy guessed they might be brothers. Dick Landon must have come from a large family. "Now, Ranger, we just come to make sure he gets to town alive. The Hoppers would like to see that he don't."

Farley said, "And they'll have their way if you make a

move to help him. I want all of you to turn around and ride out ahead of us. Way ahead of us."

The men argued among themselves. Farley brought the conversation to a close by cocking back the hammer. Jayce gasped. Andy held his breath.

Jayce said, "You-all better do what he says, Walter. This Ranger is one mean son of a bitch."

The man called Walter jerked his head as a signal for the rest to comply. He said, "Don't you let your finger get nervous, Ranger. If somethin' happens to Jayce, you'll be dead two seconds after he is."

Andy sensed that whatever intentions the five might have had, had been thwarted by Farley's unyielding stand. They were not likely to try anything unless circumstances changed drastically in their favor.

Farley said, "Take a lesson from this, Badger Boy. Never give an inch or they'll run over you."

"You'd really have shot him, wouldn't you?"

"If it was the last thing I ever did."

Sweat rolled down Jayce's face. He trembled in fear's aftermath. "God, Ranger, but you're cold-blooded."

"I am, and don't you forget it."

"You don't know what kind of a man I shot."

"Makes no difference. Me and Badger Boy are paid to deliver you to the local sheriff. The rest is up to the jury that tries you."

"The judge is old Judd Hopper. He's a direct grandson of the devil himself. Him and the rest of them Hoppers'll do all they can to see me hung."

"You've got a brother who's a Ranger. Have you got one who's a lawyer?"

Landon looked behind him as if expecting pursuit. "This fight goes way back. Why can't the law stand aside and let the families work it out for theirselves?"

"I know how crazy-mean these feuds can get. You kill an enemy, then one of his family has got to kill one of you. It goes on and on till just about everybody is dead. Better for the law to hang you instead of one of your enemies shootin' you. Maybe that'd put an end to it."

"It won't end till that Hopper bunch is all dead and gone."

Andy shook his head. "I'll bet you don't even remember what started it."

"It commenced over an election for the county seat, but that don't matter anymore. It's a blood thing now."

Farley looked at Andy and shrugged. "No use arguin' with him. You can't talk sense to people like that."

Andy said, "It's a good thing for Dick Landon that he joined the Rangers and got away from the trouble."

Farley grunted. "Even Dick'll bear watchin'. He's got bad blood in him."

Andy could count on one hand the times he had heard Farley speak well of somebody, and he could give back a couple of fingers.

Jayce said, "If you think the Landon blood is bad, wait till you meet the Hoppers."

Hearing hoofbeats behind him, Andy turned in the saddle. He counted six riders. Farley demanded, "Who are they, Jayce?"

Jayce looked back in dismay. "They're Hoppers . . . Hoppers and their kin."

Andy said, "Five Landons in front, six Hoppers behind, and us in the middle."

Farley growled, "Best thing would be for us to pull out of the way and let them settle their stupid feud for good."

Andy considered the situation, then moved his horse toward the six men.

Farley shouted, "What do you think you're doin'?"

Andy did not answer. He drew his rifle from its scabbard, laid it across his lap, and rode almost within touching distance of the horsemen. "Which one of you is in charge of this bunch?"

A big bear of a man with a short, curly beard said, "Ain't nobody in charge. We're workin' together to see justice done."

"And your name?"

"I'm James Hopper. Big'un, they call me." He looked strong enough to wrestle a bull to the ground from a standing start. He was half a head taller and fifty pounds heavier than any of the men who rode with him.

Andy swung the rifle muzzle around to point at the man's belly. He jerked his head. "Come on, Big'un. You're ridin' up there with us. The rest of you stay back. If one of you makes a move against us and our prisoner, I'll blow this gentleman's lights out."

The bearded man protested, "I'll have you know that I'm a deputy sheriff. Appointed by the county judge hisself. What gives you the right to tell me what to do?"

"This rifle does. Are you comin' or do I shoot you right here?"

Hopper did not consider long. "I'm comin'. The rest of you better do like he says."

One of the riders was a smaller man but had the same facial features as Big'un. He said, "He's bluffin'. Say the word and we'll take him."

Big'un declared, "Shut up, Harp. We don't need no blood spilled here. Not mine anyway."

Andy started Big'un moving toward Farley and Jayce. Big'un said, "You look kind of young to pack so much authority."

"A gun makes everybody the same size."

Farley looked the deputy over, then turned critical eyes on Andy. "What did you bring him for?"

"For insurance."

"You think you could really kill him if you had to?"

"You said to never give them an inch."

Farley almost nodded in approval but caught himself. "Lookin' at you right now I'd swear you're a Comanche after all."

Andy took that as a left-handed compliment, the only kind Farley Brackett gave.

Jayce's face hardened, displaying his hatred of the bearded man. "Well, Big'un, looks like they've got you the same as they've got me."

Hopper's eyes burned with malice. "Not quite the same. They'll turn me loose when we get to town. They're already stackin' lumber over by the jailhouse to build your scaffold."

Farley broke in. "I've got half a mind to cut you two coyotes loose and let you go at one another, but there's probably some fool law against it. So both of you shut the hell up."

A mile from town they were met by the county sheriff. Jayce's supporters pulled to one side but did not leave. The Hoppers started to move up, but Andy made a show of pressing the rifle's muzzle against Big'un's midsection. That stopped them.

Big'un complained, "Damn it, Ranger, you got to bruise my ribs?"

A middle-aged man with gray hair and a slight paunch, the sheriff reacted sharply at the sight of Big'un being held at gunpoint. "What do you think you're doin' with my deputy?"

Andy said, "He was fixin' to get himself in trouble. We're protectin' him."

The sheriff turned his anger on Big'un. "Damn it, I told you to stay home, and keep all the Hoppers there too."

Big'un bristled. "We just come to make sure none of Jayce's kinfolks let him loose."

"That's my job." The lawman turned back to the Rangers, making no secret of his antagonism toward Jayce Landon. "Thank you, Rangers, for deliverin' this murderer. I'll take over from here."

Farley gave Andy a severe look that warned him to be alert. "Our orders are to deliver him safe to your jailhouse. Till then, he's still ours."

Andy watched the Ranger and the sheriff glare at each other. He knew Farley would stand his ground if it took all afternoon. The sheriff evidently came to the same conclusion. He said reluctantly, "All right. Another mile won't make much difference."

Big'un looked back for support. "A trial is goin' to cost us taxpayers money. There's a good, stout tree yonder. I say we drag Jayce over there and hoist him like a fresh beef."

The sheriff's voice crackled, "Shut up, Big'un. The judge crowded me into takin' you and Harp as deputies, but I don't have to listen to you talk like a damn fool." He pointed his thumb toward town. "All right, Rangers, Jayce is still yours till we get him to jail. Let's go before some idiot takes a notion to show how stupid he is." He looked at Big'un again.

A crowd had gathered to watch Jayce being brought to town. Andy had never seen so many angry people. Some supported Jayce, but it appeared that the majority were hostile to him. A couple of fistfights broke out as the horsemen approached the jailhouse door.

Farley muttered, "Keep a close watch. There's no tellin' what some hothead might do." He cut the leather thong that bound Jayce's hands to the saddlehorn, but the cuffs remained on the prisoner's wrists.

Andy stayed in the saddle, holding the rifle in a firm grip. Big'un slipped away from him and rejoined the five who had ridden behind. The sheriff opened the front door of the jailhouse but stood in the middle, blocking it for what seemed to be several minutes.

Giving somebody a good chance to shoot Jayce, Andy thought. He studied the people with anxious eyes.

The long road to justice had many a shortcut.

Farley took a firm grip on Jayce's arm and led him through the doorway, past the sheriff. This time Jayce showed no resistance. Instead, he seemed in a hurry to get inside away from the crowd. Andy dismounted and followed, walking backward, the rifle ready.

Farley said, "Badger Boy, would you mind fetchin' my saddlebags?"

Andy could not remember that Farley had ever asked him to do anything. He had always just told him.

A woman burst through the door and ran to the prisoner, her arms outstretched. "Jayce," she shouted. "Jayce!"

The sheriff tried to restrain her, but she was strong enough to break free. She embraced Jayce, sobbing loudly. Too loudly, Andy thought. He sensed that she was making a show of it. After letting her cry for a bit, Jayce's brother Walter pulled her away. "Come on, Flora, you oughtn't to act like that in front of these Hoppers. They've had too much satisfaction already, just seein' him brought in."

She launched a tearful tirade at the sheriff. "My Jayce is a better man than you, Oscar Truscott." She turned on the crowd. "He's better than the lot of you. All he done was kill a man that needed killin'. There's a whole bunch of you Hoppers needs killin'." She seemed to concentrate particularly on Big'un.

Andy thought he saw a look of satisfaction in her

eyes as Walter Landon led her outside. He wondered about it.

Farley withdrew some papers from the saddlebags Andy had brought. He handed them to Sheriff Truscott. "Me and Pickard have done what the captain ordered. Jayce belongs to you, but you'll need to sign this release."

Truscott signed with a flourish, smudging a little ink. "It'll be like havin' a box of dynamite in here, but I'm glad to have him. I hope the trial don't take long."

Big'un grinned. "It won't, not with Uncle Judd on the bench."

The wooden floor trembled as an iron door slammed heavily. The sound made Andy feel cold even though he was not the one being locked away.

Farley told the sheriff, "There's lots of people out yonder that would like to do the prisoner harm."

"You don't have to tell me my business. You Rangers have done your job. I expect you'll want to head west and put some miles behind you before dark." His voice was hopeful.

"Our horses need a rest. We'll bed down at the wagon yard and make a fresh start in the mornin'."

The sheriff shrugged. "Suit yourselves. There's a fair-to-middlin' eatin' joint down the street yonder, run by one of my wife's nephews. Nothin' fancy, but it's cheap."

"Sounds fine to me." Farley beckoned to Andy. "Let's go see to our horses."

Walking outside, Andy sensed the tension. His scalp tingled as if an electrical storm were building. It would take but little to set off a riot. The fight would be one-sided, for the Hopper crowd appeared to outnumber the Landons by a considerable margin.

Farley growled, "Don't look to the left nor the right. Just walk straight ahead. This don't concern us anymore."

"Jayce won't get a fair trial in this town."

"Don't matter. Even a fair trial would end up hangin' him. He's as guilty as sin."

Andy rubbed his throat. The thought of a rope around it gave him a chill.

Farley said, "It would've been better for him if he'd made a break along the way. We would've shot him, and it would already be over with. Now he'll sit in that jail cell broodin' about it. He'll die a thousand times before he ever feels the rope."

They ate a mediocre supper. A good one would have had no more appeal to Andy under the circumstances. He asked, "Doesn't it bother you that we brought Dick Landon's brother here to die?"

"Jayce put the rope around his own neck when he took aim on Ned Hopper. He tripped the trapdoor when he walked up and shot him a second time. It wasn't none of my doin', nor yours."

The stable keeper was a small man with a flushed face that indicated he was a favored customer at some bar up the street. He seemed to fancy the sound of his own voice. "You-all are the Rangers that brought Jayce in, ain't you? Bet you didn't know what a hornet's nest you was fixin' to stir up. Soon as it gets dark and some of the Hoppers get enough liquor in them, you'll see the biggest fireworks we've had around here since the Yankee war."

Farley said, "It's nothin' to us. We just want to get some sleep and head out in the mornin'."

"May not be much sleepin' done in this town tonight. Me, I ain't takin' sides. Their money all looks the same to me. I'll still be here when it's over."

Farley scowled. "It's a smart man who knows how to mind his own business."

"But ain't you Rangers supposed to keep the peace? Looks to me like you'd be out there amongst them, holdin' the lid down."

"Our orders were to deliver Jayce to the sheriff. From now on it's up to him and the court."

"The sheriff's married to a Hopper. He's got some in-laws he ain't real fond of, like Big'un and the judge, but they come with the deal."

Andy said, "It's a cinch there won't be anything fair about Jayce's trial."

The stableman looked around to see if anyone else could hear. "Ain't goin' to be no trial. Talk is that they're goin' to stage a fight and draw the sheriff away after dark. The jailer is a Hopper cousin. When his kinfolks come callin' they won't have to tell him twice to raise his hands."

Andy's jaw dropped. "They're goin' to take Jayce out and hang him?"

"No, they'll shoot him right there in his cell and scatter before the sheriff or the Landons have time to do anything about it."

Farley frowned. "Are you sure about this?"

"I got it from one of the Hopper boys. He was already tanked up on Kentucky courage."

Andy told Farley, "We've got to do somethin'."

Farley shook his head. "What's the use? They'll just keep tryin' till they get him. Feuds are nasty business."

He forked dry hay onto the ground and spread it evenly, then unrolled his blankets on it. "Best thing is to let the damn fools fight it out. Then we can hang the winners or send them to the penitentiary."

"I'll bet that's not in the captain's rule book."

"The book has got blank pages in it so we can write our own rules when we have to."

Andy did not consider long. "I didn't make this ride just to stand back and watch them lynch our prisoner." He drew his rifle from its scabbard on his saddle and dug into his saddlebag for extra cartridges.

Farley arose from his blankets. He gripped Andy's shoulder tightly enough to hurt. "They'll cut you to ribbons, and for what? Jayce is goin' to die anyway. If he doesn't do it tonight, he'll do it when the trial is over. Leave it alone."

"I can't."

"Listen to me, Badger Boy. Even if you *are* half Indian, you're worth more than Jayce Landon."

Andy thought that was an amazing admission for Farley. He could not think of an adequate response. "Like the man said, we're supposed to keep the peace."

"Ain't goin' to be peace in this town till they've killed enough of one another that they gag on the blood. You'd best look out for your own skin."

"What'll the captain say if we tell him we delivered Jayce and then stood by while a mob shot him to pieces?" Andy cradled the rifle across his left arm and walked out of the stable into the darkness.

The jail was a little more than a block away. He had a strong feeling of being watched, but he could see no one. He heard a horse somewhere behind the buildings, moving into a slow lope.

He pondered whether he should go inside the jail or wait for the Hoppers in front of it. He had heard of mobs burning a jail to get a prisoner. In such an event he could do little from inside. Besides, the jailer was in on the deal. He would probably do whatever he could to put Andy out of the way. He decided to take a stand outside, blocking the door.

The street remained quiet for a while. Andy began to wonder if the hostler's information was overblown. People sometimes made bold talk but did not have the stomach to follow through. Then he saw several men moving up the street toward him. He tightened his grip on the rifle. Though he could not distinguish the faces, he sensed that these were of the Hopper clan.

Sternly he said, "That's close enough."

A gruff voice shouted, "Step out of the way, Ranger."

Andy thought the voice sounded like Big'un's. He said, "I'm tellin' you to disperse."

The men moved closer but stopped when Andy leveled his rifle on them. Big'un declared, "You've got no jurisdiction here. You finished your job when you brought Jayce in."

Andy's throat was too tight for a reply. He hoped silence was more threatening than anything he might say. The men huddled, murmuring among themselves. Several more came up the street, joining them. By Andy's rough count there were fifteen, perhaps more.

One man edged beyond Big'un and the others. He said, "You're just a shirttail kid. You won't really shoot us." He paused a moment, gauging Andy's reaction, then moved forward again with confidence in his step.

Andy aimed the rifle, but he could not bring himself to squeeze the trigger. The blood rose warm in his face.

He sensed a movement on the street. A pistol blazed, and the man went down. He gripped his leg and squalled in pain.

Farley's voice was deadly. "Next shot goes in somebody's gullet." He fired again, kicking up dust in front of the mob.

Andy expelled a pent-up breath. Farley walked up and joined him in front of the door. His stern gaze never left the Hoppers as he muttered, "The graveyards are full of people who wouldn't pull the trigger."

"I tried. I just couldn't."

The wounded man lay on his back, gripping his bleeding leg. He kept hollering.

Farley said with contempt, "Listen to that brave son of a bitch, squealin' like a pig stuck under a gate."

Members of the mob conferred among themselves. Big'un shouted, "You're protectin' a murderer."

Farley said, "He ain't been tried yet."

"We come here to give him all the trial he needs."

Farley muttered, "If they rush us, shoot the foremost. That'd be the one called Big'un. If that doesn't stop them, shoot another."

"You'd do that for Jayce Landon?"

"No, for us. Right this minute we're in worse danger than he is."

Big'un shouted, "You Rangers can't stay here forever. We can wait."

Farley pointed the pistol at him. "You'll have to. Now you-all had better scatter because in one minute I'm goin' to shoot every man I can see." He held up his watch so he could read it in the moonlight.

The men lingered a little, then began to peel away. Some, like Big'un, shouted threats back over their shoulders, but soon all had retreated beyond sight, carrying their wounded man with them.

Farley said, "You have to talk to people in a way they understand, then be ready to back up what you tell them. Remember that and you'll live longer."

Andy shuddered. "You were really set to kill somebody."

"I would, if there'd been a brave man amongst them. But after one shot everybody started thinkin' about home and mother. That's generally the way."

"You told me at the stable that you wasn't comin'."

"I didn't intend to. I don't give a damn about Jayce Landon, but I didn't want to have to tell the captain I stood back and let a mob kill a Ranger. Even an ignorant Comanche Indian."

A stubborn streak would not allow Andy to show his pleasure. He had taken too much abuse from Farley to grant him the satisfaction. He looked down the dark, empty street. "I don't understand why none of the Landon bunch was here. Looks like they'd have turned out to protect Jayce."

"That does strike me a little peculiar. It goes to show that both sides are crazy."

After they had watched for ten or fifteen minutes Farley said, "I don't think they'll be comin' back for a while. I want to do some Dutch talkin' to that jailer."

Andy was not surprised to find that the front door had been left unlocked. He said, "I guess the jailer wanted to make it easy for them. All they had to do was walk in."

Inside, he locked and barred the door in case some of the Hopper people drank enough courage to come back. He did not see the jailer. Farley walked through the door that led back to the cells. He called, "Come here, Badger Boy. This is a sight to tell your children about if you live long enough to have any."

The jailer was handcuffed to the bars of a cell. The cell door was open. Jayce was gone.

Farley snickered at the jailer. "Now ain't you a pretty sight? How did you get yourself into this fix?"

The man's eyes were downcast. "Jayce has escaped."

"I figured that out for myself. What did you do, go to sleep on the job?"

"No such of a thing. The sheriff went to see about a fight. Soon as he was gone, Jayce pulled a gun on me. Just a little derringer, but it could kill a man."

Farley gave Andy a speculative glance. Jayce hadn't had a gun on him when the Rangers brought him into town.

Andy did not have to think about it long. He remembered

how Jayce's wife rushed up and hugged him. He would wager a month's pay that she stuck it inside his shirt during the moment of confusion.

He chose not to mention it. The woman had misfortune enough just by being Jayce's wife.

The jailer wailed, "Are you-all goin' to get me out of this mess?"

Farley came dangerously near smiling. "We ain't got the key."

"Look in the top desk drawer out yonder."

Andy rummaged around and found it. Freed, the jailer rubbed his wrist, raw from straining against the handcuff. "I think Jayce went out the back door. I heard a horse lope away. Some of his kin must've been waitin' out there."

Farley grunted. "So now he's took to the tulies."

The jailer wailed, "If the sheriff doesn't murder me, my kinfolks will."

"I've got half a mind to do it myself. On account of you, me and Pickard made a long ride for nothin'. And that mob out yonder could've killed us."

"You got to tell them it wasn't my fault."

Andy suggested, "Might be a good idea if we left town. They're liable to think we had a hand in this."

"Run away?" Farley took offense at the suggestion. "Last time I ran from anybody it was the state police. I swore I'd never run again. No, we'll stay and tell them how it was. Next time maybe they'll hire better help."

Someone began beating against the front door and shouting for the jailer to open it. The jailer appeared about to wilt. "Oh God, that's the judge."

Andy assumed that thwarted mob members had carried their frustration to the Hopper family leader.

Farley said, "Just as well let him in. But nobody else. This place could get crowded in a hurry."

Reluctantly Andy slid back the bar and opened the door just enough for Judge Hopper to enter. Several men were with him, but Andy pushed the door shut and barred it before any of them could bully their way in. Big'un shouted threats from outside.

Judd Hopper was a tall, angular man with gray chin whiskers and angry eyes that cut to the quick. "What are you Rangers doing here? Protecting the prisoner is the sheriff's responsibility."

Farley did not waver under the tirade. "I'm glad you said that. I think your jailkeeper has got a little news for you."

The jailer hung his head. His voice was little more than a thin squeak. "Jayce is gone."

"Gone?" The judge took long strides into the back room. His face reddened as he saw the open cell door and absorbed the full import of Landon's escape. He whirled around, jabbing an arthritic finger at Andy and Farley. "You-all turned him loose. I'll send you both to the pen."

Farley gripped the jailer's wrist so hard that the man cried out. "Tell him the rest before I twist your arm off and beat you to death with it."

Defensively the jailer explained that Landon had produced a pistol and forced him to unlock the cell. "Next thing I knowed he had me handcuffed to the bars. I hollered, but nobody heard me. Wasn't nothin' I could do."

The judge fumed. "I wish he'd killed you. I guess you know you're fired. You'll be lucky if some of my nephews don't flay the hide off of you. How did he get ahold of a pistol?"

Andy and Farley stood silent. The jailer spoke in a subdued voice. "We didn't make him take his boots off. Maybe he had it in one of them."

The judge slammed the cell door shut and then shook it in rage, gripping the bars tightly enough to turn his knuckles white. "I'll make somebody wish he was in the fires of hell instead of in Hopper's Crossing."

Farley beckoned to Andy. "I don't see nothin' more for us to do here."

Hopper demanded, "You're goin' to help us hunt him down, aren't you?"

Farley showed his disdain. "Ain't our fault you-all couldn't hold him. Our assignment was to deliver him to the sheriff. We done that, so now we're leavin'."

Andy slid back the bar and opened the door. As he and Farley left, a dozen Hopper partisans rushed in, bumping one another against the door in their haste.

Andy said, "The judge is liable to tell them it was our fault. Anything to shift the blame. We better get away from here."

"We ain't runnin'. We're walkin'. We'll show this bunch we ain't afraid of nobody."

"Maybe you're not, but I am."

Farley set a slow and deliberate pace toward the wagon yard. They had not gone far before Andy heard someone shout a curse. The voice sounded like Big'un's. A shot was fired. Farley spun half-around, grabbing his right side.

A man stood in lamplight that spilled through the open jailhouse door. He held a pistol. Andy raised his rifle and made a quick shot. The man went down, twisting in the dirt.

Farley swore under his breath. Andy asked, "How bad are you hit?"

"I don't know. It hurts like almighty hell."

"We'd better keep movin'. They didn't get to kill Jayce Landon, and they're fired up to kill *somebody*."

Andy took Farley's left arm to give him support. At the wagon yard he found the stableman standing in the open front doors, staring into the dark street. "Heard some shootin'. What . . ." He seemed to lose his voice when Andy and Farley came into the lantern's light and he saw Farley's bloody shirt.

Andy said, "Saddle our horses for us and throw our pack on that mule. Be quick." He helped Farley to a straight wooden chair and brought the lantern up for a close look. The bullet had struck high up and from behind. "Can you move your arm?"

Farley raised it a little.

Andy said, "Could've busted some of your ribs. You're bleedin' like a stuck hog."

Andy took out his handkerchief and pressed it against the wound. "Feel like you can sit in the saddle?"

"I don't see I've got much choice. Them crazy Hoppers'll be lookin' to finish the job."

The stableman brought their horses and the mule. "If I was you-all—"

Andy interrupted. "Is there a doctor in this town?"

"There is, but you'll be needin' an undertaker instead if you've got yourselves in Dutch with them Hoppers."

The stableman reluctantly gave directions, then helped Andy boost Farley into the saddle. Andy found the doctor's house, but he saw that several of the Hopper people were already there. The doctor would be treating the man Farley had shot. The one Andy had shot would probably be brought along shortly.

He said, "We'd better not stop here."

Farley nodded in painful agreement. "Doctor may be one of them Hoppers anyway. Whole town seems to be infested with them."

"I'm afraid you'll have to tough it out for a while."

Farley grumbled under his breath, "Badger Boy, you're a damned Jonah. You'll get me killed yet."

{ FIVE }

Andy feared he might have to hold Farley in the saddle, but Farley hunched over the horn and stubbornly refused help. The horse's every step hurt him.

They rode back down the road they had come on for what Andy thought must have been two or three miles. He saw lamplight in a window. "Farmhouse," he said. "Maybe they'll help us."

Farley's voice choked with pain. "If they ain't Hoppers."

"Even if they are, maybe they don't know what happened in town. No need in us tellin' them."

Andy strode up onto a wooden porch and knocked on the door. He heard a floor squeak as someone walked across it. The door opened, and a woman stood there, a shotgun in her hand. A cold feeling came to Andy's stomach. He recognized Jayce Landon's wife.

Her voice was like ice. "You're one of them Rangers. What do you want here?"

"I've got a hurt man outside. He needs help."

She looked at Farley but offered no sympathy. "You-all brought my husband back and turned him over to them Hoppers. Now you've got the nerve to ask for my help?"

An old man's voice came from a back room. "Who is it, Flora?" He came out carrying a pistol and squinted at Andy in the dim lamplight.

She said, "It's them Rangers, Papa. By rights we ought to shoot the both of them."

The bewhiskered old man poked the muzzle of his pistol toward Andy. "What you got to say for yourself?"

"I need help for my partner. He's been shot."

"By who?"

"By one of the Hoppers."

The pair's hostility began to fade. The old man said, "Thought you was in league with them, fetchin' Jayce in like you done."

"That was our job. But afterwards we stood guard on the jail to keep a mob from bustin' in. We didn't know Jayce had already broke out." He allowed a hint of accusation into his voice. "But I'll bet *you* knew it."

A satisfied look passed between the pair. The woman spoke first. "We ain't ownin' up to nothin'. But if you're lookin' to catch Jayce, you'd better have some damned fast horses. He left town on the best runner in the county."

"Right now I'm just interested in gettin' help for Farley Brackett."

The old man's attitude quickly mellowed. "Brackett, you say? Is he the one that gave them state police so much hell durin' the Yankee occupation?"

"He's the one."

"Lord amighty. Bring him on in here, boy. We'll see what we can do for him."

The woman still seemed reluctant, but she deferred to her father's judgment. Andy helped Farley out of the saddle and up the step.

The old man said, "Any enemy of the Hoppers is a friend of ours."

Farley growled, "I ain't their enemy, and I ain't your friend."

The old man appeared to take no offense. "He's probably half out of his head. Set him in that chair. Let's see how bad he's hurt."

They took off Farley's blood-soaked shirt, then peeled his long underwear down to his waist. Flora Landon held a lamp close and examined the wound, probing with her fingers while Farley ground his teeth. Andy got his first good look at her face. He thought her handsome, at least for a middle-aged woman. He figured her to be about thirty.

She said, "Looks to me like the bullet glanced off of the ribs. Gouged a pretty good hole comin' and goin', but it's a long ways from the heart. If he's got one."

Farley winced against the pain. His face was pale. "Ain't the first hole I ever had shot in me."

She frowned. "If you get blood poisonin' it may be your last. Grit your teeth, because this is fixin' to burn like the hinges of hell's front door." She washed the wound with whiskey. Andy thought for a moment that Farley might faint. She said, "We'll bind them ribs good and tight."

The old man said, "A broken rib is liable to punch a hole in his lung and kill him deader than a skint mule. Be better if he didn't ride horseback for a while."

The woman studied Farley with her first hint of sympathy. "I don't see where he's got a choice. Right now them Hoppers are probably searchin' all over Jayce's and my farm. When they get through there they'll be comin' here. I don't think you Rangers'll want to be around."

Andy said, "I was wonderin' if you folks have got a wagon I could borrow."

Flora looked questioningly at her father. He said, "This man faced up to the Hoppers and led them scallywag state police on a merry chase. You bet he can have my wagon." He jerked his head at Andy. "Come on, boy. Help me catch up my team."

He walked out onto the porch and stopped abruptly. "Daughter, you'd better come and look."

Andy saw flames in the distance. He could not guess how far away they were.

Flora gasped. "They're burnin' down our house, mine and Jayce's."

The old man nodded. "This place'll be next."

Andy heard horses coming. "Sounds like they're already here."

Flora declared, "Be damned if they're goin' to burn my papa's house." She reached inside the door and grabbed her shotgun.

The old man's bony hand pushed the shotgun muzzle down. "This house ain't nothin' but lumber and nails. I can build a new one. But the Lord Hisself can't build a new me or you."

Andy said, "It's too late to run. You-all get back inside and blow out the lamp. I'll talk to them."

Flora said, "I doubt as they're in a listenin' frame of mind."

"They'll listen to me or they'll answer to the state of Texas." He made his voice sound more confident than he felt. He stepped out to where he had tied his and Farley's horses. He lifted his rifle from its scabbard and got Farley's as an afterthought. He stood in the moonlight on the edge of the porch, his own rifle in his hand and Farley's leaning where he could reach it without much of a stretch.

He counted seven horsemen. An eighth followed behind. The deputy Big'un was in front as the riders came to a stop. He recognized Andy. "You Rangers again. Seems like you're everywhere."

"We try to be where we're needed."

"You know who we're after."

"Jayce Landon isn't here. I can vouch for that." He really couldn't. He had not seen anything here except the front room of the house. But the imperious lawman did not need to know that.

Big'un declared, "You Rangers have stepped way over the line. You helped a fugitive get away."

"He didn't escape from *us*. We delivered him like we were ordered to. He was the sheriff's prisoner. It was the sheriff's responsibility to see that he didn't bust out."

"I expect that woman of his knows where he's at. This is her daddy's house, and I'm bettin' she's in there."

Flora came out onto the porch, shotgun in hand. Andy started to tell her to go back inside, but he knew she would not heed him. She looked like a woman who would charge a bear with a willow switch.

She said, "I'm here, Big'un Hopper, and here I'm stayin'. It don't take much of a man to burn my house down, but it'll take a better man than you to run me out of this country. You or any of your other line-bred Tennessee ridge-runner kin."

The deputy moved his horse up closer to the porch. "If we ever find out you helped Jayce get away, you wouldn't be the first woman ever hung in Texas."

Andy shifted his rifle to point at Big'un. "There'll be no more talk about hangin', especially of a woman. You'd better back away if you don't want the whole Ranger force swarmin' this county like a nest of hornets."

"It ain't the Rangers' business to take sides in a local affair."

"It is when it comes to killin'."

Hopper seemed not to hear. "Flora Landon, I'm placin' you under arrest for aidin' and abettin'. You come down here."

She did not move. "You come up here and get me if you don't mind a load of buckshot in your belly."

For a minute Andy was not sure which way the pendulum would swing. Big'un seemed to weigh his chances, and anger appeared stronger than caution.

Farley Brackett walked out to join Andy and the woman on the porch. He held his arm tightly against his ribs, but in his hand was a pistol. He said nothing. He let his eyes deliver his threat.

Looking at Farley, the deputy took fresh stock of his situation. "Somethin' about you seems familiar to me. But I don't recollect that I heard your name."

"I'm Farley Brackett."

The name jarred Big'un. "From down in Colorado County? Somebody told me you was dead."

"I ain't heard about it."

Andy said, "And I am Andy Pickard." That name carried no weight with the deputy, but Farley's had drawn his full attention. Andy thought it was time to try to close the conversation. "You've got no grounds to arrest Mrs. Landon. You're trespassin' here on her daddy's place. You'd best be movin' on, or you're biddin' fair to see inside one of your own cells."

Big'un reluctantly began to cave. "You Rangers won't be stayin'. We can wait till you're gone." He pulled his horse around and started back in the direction of town. The other men followed, some grumbling about not finishing their job.

Flora looked at Farley. "Big'un almost lost his breath when he heard your name. You must've left some deep tracks."

Farley started a shrug but pain stopped it. His face pinched. "Would you have shot him in the belly?"

She replied, "I don't say anything I don't mean."

She went back into the house. Farley was ordinarily sparing with admiration, but he said, "There, Badger Boy, is what I call a woman!"

In the house, Andy said, "That was brave talk outside, but the Hopper bunch has got killin' on their minds. It would be smart if you folks left here for a while."

The old man told his daughter, "Get your stuff together and we'll go with these Rangers."

She resisted until her father said, "There ain't no shame in runnin' when it's the only way out. Jayce has done it. At least we'll live to hit them Hoppers another day."

Andy asked, "Where's Jayce runnin' *to*?"

The old man shook his head. "If I was to tell you that, you'd go after him."

"We would if it was our orders."

"Jayce ain't an easy man to warm up to, but he's the only son-in-law I've got. That's why I ain't tellin' you. Let's get that team hitched up. I don't fancy bein' around to entertain that bunch when they swaller a little more panther juice and come back."

Andy did not ask at first where Flora Landon and her father wanted to go. He simply turned the team away from the direction of town and the fire still burning in the distance. He and Flora sat on the wagonseat. Farley lay on blankets in the bed of the wagon. Flora's father rode Andy's horse. Farley's was tied on behind, trailed by the little pack mule. They traveled a couple of miles in silence, though Andy stopped the wagon several times to listen for sounds of pursuit.

He saw a new fire and knew the house they had left was burning. The old man cursed under his breath. "I'll build it back, and I'll bury a couple of Hoppers in the backyard for good luck."

Flora said, "I'll help you dig the hole."

Andy asked, "You-all got kinfolks you'd like to go to?"

Flora said, "Not till things die down some. We'd bring more trouble on them, and they've got trouble enough just bein' Landons and kin. Where are you headin'?"

"To Colorado County, to some folks that will take care of Farley."

"Mind takin' us with you? Papa and me need to be scarce for a while."

"What about your husband? He won't know where you're at."

"We'll come back when the Hoppers ain't lookin'. They'll find out that their houses can burn just as easy as ours did."

The bitterness in her voice reminded Andy of what Farley had said about feuds. Often starting over some trivial incident, they tended to grow out of all proportion into a senseless succession of brutal killings. Andy had heard of one bloody vendetta that began over nothing more than mistaken accusations about a few missing hogs.

He doubted that Flora knew the origin of the Landon-Hopper feud, but he asked anyway. That started a mild argument between her and her father.

She said, "It was when Old Man Hopper shot at Jayce's daddy and took a chunk out of his shoulder."

"No," the old man countered, "that come later, after one of them Hopper boys and his cousin tried to beat up on Jayce's granddaddy. That old man whipped the britches off of them all by hisself, then whittled a swallow fork in the Hopper boy's ear."

The talk left Andy with a feeling of futility. Families killed one another though they could not agree on what had started the fight. It was a process with no foreseeable end.

Farley became feverish, drifting in and out of reality. From time to time he mumbled incoherently. At other times he was lucid enough to ask, "Where we goin'?"

Andy would tell him, "You'll see." He feared that a better answer would touch off an argument.

Flora occasionally checked the bandage while Andy stopped the wagon. She asked, "How'd he get that scar on his face?"

Andy told her he had brought that home from the war.

She said, "I have a feelin' he's got other scars on him that don't show. He must be a hell-bender in a fight."

Andy admitted, "He takes care of himself."

"Didn't do so good this time, did he?"

"Somebody shot him from out of the dark. He didn't have a chance."

Seeing the Brackett farm took Andy back to a terrible night when Reconstruction state police had shot up the house in the mistaken belief that Farley was there. They killed Farley's father, Jeremiah, and wounded his mother. Ironically, Farley was miles away at the time.

Lying in the wagon, Farley was unaware of Andy's destination until they were within a hundred yards of the house. He pulled himself up to look over the sideboards. Sight of the place jarred him out of his dreamy state. "Damn you, Badger Boy, I didn't want to come here."

"You need lookin' after. Who'll do it better than your mother and your sister?"

"They won't want to see me." Farley made a feeble try at getting up, but he hurt too much to do it on his own. He managed to say, "I'll whup you, boy, soon as I get my strength back."

"You can try. Right now you couldn't whip a sick kitten."

Andy shouted as soon as he thought he was within earshot. "Hello, the house."

A young woman stepped out onto the porch, shading her eyes with her hand. "Andy?"

"I've got Farley here, Bethel. He's hurt."

She hurried toward the wagon. Her flaring skirts startled

the team, and Andy had to draw hard on the reins. Bethel gave Flora and the old man only a glance. She looked anxiously over the wagon's sideboards. "What happened to him?"

Andy said, "He's been shot."

Flora said, "He lost a right smart of blood."

Elnora Brackett and a black woman came onto the porch. Farley's mother watched anxiously as Andy and Flora helped Farley climb the steps. Color drained from her face. She said, "Bring him in. We'll put him in his own bed."

This was a large house in comparison to most Andy knew. Jeremiah Brackett had been a prosperous farmer before the war and before confiscatory Reconstruction taxes had stolen much of his property.

The black woman led the way down the hall and into a spartan room devoid of furniture except for a bed and a chair. Farley had not spent much time in this house after going off to war and later coming home to the desperate life of a fugitive, defying the occupation authorities.

His mother said, "That bandage is soaked. It needs changing." She held her son's hand as Andy cut through the bloodied cloth. "Is Farley in trouble again?"

She had reason to ask, for her son had led a reckless life after returning from the war. Andy told her, "No, he got this in the line of duty." He explained about delivering Jayce Landon, about standing off a mob, and about shots fired on a dark street. He said, "I brought Farley here because I thought his family would take better care of him than anybody."

Bethel touched Andy's arm. "You did the right thing."

"He didn't want to come. He thinks you-all still hold it against him for his daddy gettin' killed."

Bethel seemed surprised. "We got over that a long time ago."

Mrs. Brackett had lost two sons in the war and her husband in its aftermath. She said, "He's the only son I have left. He should know we'd stand by him."

"That's what I told him. Maybe he'll believe it, comin' from you." Andy doubted Farley was in any condition to follow the conversation. His eyes were vacant, staring at nothing.

The wound looked angry around the edges. Elnora fretted about the possibility of blood poisoning. She cleansed the opening and replaced the bandage with help from Bethel and the black woman.

Only then was there time for Andy to introduce Flora and her father and explain why they were with him.

Bethel said, "Thank you-all for your help. You're welcome to stay here as long as you want to."

Flora said, "It won't be long. Soon as I think them Hoppers are lookin' the other way . . ."

Andy said, "I'll go over to town and fetch the doctor. We don't want to take any chances with Farley."

Bethel asked, "Have you had anything to eat?"

"I guess I did, but I don't remember when it was."

"I'll fix you something before you go. Maybe we can get Farley to take some broth."

In the interest of time Andy settled for warming up some beans and smearing a heavy load of butter on cold biscuits. He was aware of Bethel's eyes. She stared at him while he ate.

She said, "You quit coming around to see me."

"I've been tied up with the Rangers."

"Before that, though. I hope I didn't say or do anything . . ."

"You didn't. I just got real busy. Anyway, it seemed to me like you were havin' company enough without me. And

I had a notion that I reminded you of the night the state police came."

The memory darkened her expression. "I would remember that anyway, with or without you. I kept hoping you'd come around. You will come back, won't you, with the doctor?"

"Yes, I'll want to see what he thinks about Farley and how long he'll be laid up. Then I'll visit with Rusty before I report back to the captain."

She touched his hand. "If what happened to my brother is any measure of life with the Rangers, I don't want to see either one of you go back."

He did not pull his hand away. In the past he had wondered how a girl like her could have a brother like Farley. He stared at her, trying to find any facial resemblance. He said, "It's a pretty good life most of the time. There's more boredom than excitement. The food's good when we're not out on patrol."

"The pay isn't much, is it?"

"I don't need much. They feed me. Rusty Shannon never let me pick up any wasteful habits."

"Maybe you could use some. Maybe you could come and see a girl once in a while."

"You mean that?"

"If I say it, I mean it."

He had heard that statement from Farley several times. Farley and his sister might not look alike, but they thought alike in some ways.

Bethel came outside to watch Andy get on his horse. He said, "Looks like you-all have had a good rain." The ground was muddy, and water stood in the fields.

"A storm passed through here a few days ago. All we got was rain, but your friend Rusty caught a terrible hail. It just about wiped him out."

"Sorry to hear that." Andy paused a moment, feeling a rush of sympathy for Rusty. "I'll be back with the doctor soon as I can."

{ SIX }

Andy was not prepared for the ruin that had been Rusty's field. A maturing crop of corn had been battered into nothing more than stalks, standing bare and broken. Leaves and half-developed ears were pounded into the muddy ground. The devastation was complete.

Approaching the cabin, he saw that its roof was newly shingled, as was the roof of a smaller cabin Rusty had built for Andy when he had expected to bring Josie Monahan home as a bride. Several chickens pecked about the yard. Some had lost many of their feathers. Patches of bare skin showed through.

Andy called out. He heard an answer and reined his horse toward the shed where Rusty kept his farming implements and tools. Rusty stepped out into the open, leather harness in his hand. Recognizing Andy, he forced a smile, though Andy knew smiling must come hard to him these days.

"Hey, Andy, I'll put this stuff away, then we'll go up to the house." Rusty went into the shed, emerging without the harness. The smile was gone. He looked haggard. "Tom Blessing told me you'd be comin'. I suppose you got your prisoner delivered."

Andy dismounted to shake Rusty's hand. "For what it was worth." Andy would tell him about it later. Right now he was having difficulty absorbing the damage he saw around him. "Looks like you had a buffalo stampede."

Rusty had always stood tall and straight. Now his shoulders sagged. His voice was weary. "You can put up a fight against most things that come at you. You can whip down a fire or dam up against a flood. But a storm like this, all you can do is hunker down and watch it happen."

"I see you got new roofs."

"Neighbors." Rusty led Andy into the kitchen. "Had anything to eat?"

"Ate dinner with the Bracketts."

For a moment Rusty's eyes seemed to light up. "I'm glad you went by to see that Bethel girl. She's been askin' about you."

"It wasn't on account of her." Andy explained about the Jayce Landon affair and Farley's being wounded.

Rusty frowned. "Farley always did draw lightnin'." He and Farley had had their differences. "Lots of young men around here think Bethel Brackett is the best-lookin' thing in a hundred miles."

"She looks all right."

"Just all right?"

Andy was aware that Rusty had been trying a long time to promote a romance between Andy and Bethel. "Why don't you pay court to her yourself?"

Pain came into Rusty's eyes. "You know the luck I've had when it comes to women."

Andy wished he could take back what he had said. It had slipped out. "I'm sorry."

"No matter. I've halfway come to accept things like they are. I didn't need that hailstorm, though."

Rusty turned away, but not before Andy saw grief rekindled in his eyes. On the mantel stood a tintype of Josie

Monahan. Andy could only imagine how many times a day Rusty must look at that picture.

He asked, "Ever hear anything from Alice?" Alice was Josie's younger sister.

"Not directly. Got a letter from her mother. Clemmie said the boy Billy keeps askin' about you."

"Nothin' from Alice herself?"

"I've got no reason to expect anything. There's nothin' between us. Never was."

Andy had hoped there might be.

Rusty poked at coals banked in the fireplace until they glowed red. "I'll boil us some coffee. It'll tide us over till suppertime."

Andy placed small sticks of dry wood atop the coals. "What're you goin' to do, Rusty? You've lost the year's work. It's too late in the summer to replant your field."

"I've got meat in the smokehouse and hogs runnin' loose on the river. I won't starve."

"You're not one for sittin' around idle."

"There's always work to do if I feel like lookin' for it. But lately I've been askin' myself what's the use?"

Rusty's dark mood made Andy uneasy. He said, "How about gettin' away from this place for a while? Come back to camp with me. You could sign up with the Rangers for three months or six months, however long you want to. The captain said he'd be tickled to have you."

Rusty toyed with the idea but resisted at first. "Rangerin' is for young men like you."

"There's older men than you in the force. Len Tanner is about your age. The Morris boys ain't far behind."

"I'll admit it'd be good to ride with them again." Rusty walked to the door. He looked out past the dog run to his ruined field. "The thing is, I'm gettin' to where when night comes I want a real bed, not a blanket on the hard ground."

Rusty was thin and drawn. Andy wondered how many meals he had cooked, then not eaten. "I always thought you enjoyed your time with the Rangers."

Rusty nodded. "I did, even with the long trips and the days I didn't eat. There's a lot of satisfaction in ridin' with a bunch of men you like and respect."

"Then come along with me. I guarantee that the captain will be pleased to see you."

"I'll admit I'm a little tempted."

"It might do you good to see some fresh country. This farm could pretty well take care of itself from now till spring plantin'."

Rusty gradually warmed to the idea. "I could turn the milk cow and her calf out together. I could take the chickens over to Shanty so the coyotes don't get them."

Perhaps later, when more healing time had passed, Andy could talk Rusty into traveling up north to visit the Monahans. If he spent time close to Alice, he might finally see what everybody around him already knew.

Bethel Brackett stood on the porch watching as Andy and Rusty dismounted in front of her house. She spoke first to Rusty, then to Andy. "Going back to camp already? I hoped you might stay awhile longer."

Andy said, "It's time I reported for duty. Just came to see about Farley so I'll know what to tell the captain."

He caught a moment's disappointed look before she hid it. She said, "Farley's stubborn and hard to get along with, but he always was. He's raisin' a ruckus about wantin' to go back to camp."

"He can't be ready yet."

"No, but he thinks he is. Nothing counts with him except what he thinks."

"What about Flora Landon and her daddy?"

"They're still here. Farley actually smiles when Flora comes into his room. I think he's a little taken with her."

Guess he's got some human feelings after all, Andy thought. "Reckon they know where Jayce is at?"

"I make it a point not to ask questions. If anybody comes around hunting for information, I won't have to lie to them." She managed a weak smile. "You-all are not in too much of a hurry to stay and eat dinner with us, are you?"

Rusty took the decision out of Andy's hands. "We'd be much obliged."

That was how it had always been, Andy thought. He never got to make a decision of his own unless he was by himself. He was always in Rusty's shadow, or someone else's.

He remembered how to reach Farley's room, but he chose to follow Bethel anyway. He enjoyed looking at her, though he would not tell her so, or Rusty.

Farley lay on his bed, atop the covers. Pale, unshaven, he was fully dressed, even to his boots. His shirt was only partially buttoned because of a bulky bandage wrapped around his ribs. He grunted at the visitors, either a halfhearted greeting or a dismissal. He had always lacked confidence in Andy, and he had only a strained tolerance for Rusty. Both had gotten in his way more than once.

Farley said, "I hope you're ready to ride, because I sure am. I may just beat you back to camp."

Andy saw worry in Bethel's eyes. She said, "You wouldn't get ten miles from home before you fell off of your horse. You'd lie there and bleed to death."

Farley said, "I got hurt worse than this in a skirmish with the Yankees and still rode thirty miles before dark."

Bethel shrugged. "How can you talk sense to a man like that?"

Andy saw no reason to tell her it was useless to try. She knew it better than he did. But he sensed that Farley understood the truth. Despite his blustering, he was not ready to ride, nor would he be for a while.

Rusty said, “Farley, I hear you and Andy turned back a mob.”

Farley grunted. “It was a damn-fool thing to do, seein’ as the man they was after had already lit out.”

“You didn’t know that at the time.”

“This Badger Boy of yours was all set to try it by himself. When he takes it in his head to do somethin’, you couldn’t beat it out of him with a club.”

Rusty nodded. “I’ve got no quarrel with that.”

“Fool kid could’ve got us both killed.” Farley glowered at Andy. “Look what happened to me. I deserve it for takin’ pity on him.”

Rusty said, “You got it for doin’ the right thing.”

“That Jayce Landon is a knot-headed idiot. The only reason I’d give a damn what happens to him is that he’s got a wife who ought to’ve done better for herself. And a good-hearted daddy-in-law. Do you know he’s out in the field right now, workin’ like a hired hand? And her with him.”

Andy took that for a sign Farley might be mellowing. The Bracketts still had the help of a black woman who once had been their slave. She now worked for her keep and received a modest wage when Elnora and Bethel had any money to pay her. When they did not, she stayed anyway. She had nowhere else to go. Andy could hear her clanging pots and pans in the kitchen. It reminded him he was hungry.

Farley tried to get out of bed but gave up. “I’m damned tired of takin’ my meals in bed like a baby.”

The black woman brought him his meal, but he ate only

a little of it. He stared at the window and offered no more conversation.

Flora Landon and her father came in for dinner. Andy noticed that the first thing she did was go to Farley's room to see about him. She came back shortly, grinning. She said, "I thought Jayce knew every cuss word in the language, but I believe Farley could teach him some. When he finally gets up he's liable to drag that bed outside and burn it."

Her father asked Andy, "Seen any more of Sheriff Truscott or Big'un?"

"No, but I ain't been lookin' for them."

"Watch out. They're liable to come lookin' for *you.*"

The meal finished, Andy felt reluctant to leave. For one thing, visiting with Bethel and her mother seemed to have brought some life back into Rusty's eyes. But duty's call was loud. Andy jerked his head at Rusty. "It's a long way to the San Saba."

Farley shouted from his bedroom, "Saddle my horse for me. I'm goin' too."

Bethel cast a sad glance at Andy.

Rusty said, "Farley knows he can't. It just gets under his skin to have to depend on other people."

Andy and Rusty said their good-byes to Elnora and the Landons. Bethel followed them out onto the porch. She told Andy, "Write me a letter once in a while. Let a body know you're still among the living."

"I'm not much of a hand with pencil and paper. But I'll try."

Rusty said, "I'll see that he does."

Riding away, Andy looked back. Bethel remained on the porch, watching them.

Rusty said, "One word from you and she would follow you anywhere."

"To a Ranger camp? What could she do there?"

"You won't stay with the Rangers all your life. Nobody does."

They rode awhile before Andy said, "I'm tempted to go back up the river and see if there's any news about Jayce. Dick Landon would want to know about his brother."

Rusty threw cold water on the idea. "I've heard stories about the Hoppers and the Landons. Especially the Hoppers. I'd as soon see you stick your head into a rattlesnake den."

"I wish there was somethin' we could do about that double-dealin' Big'un."

"Time has a way of payin' off his kind of people. Chances are that some Landon will clean his plow or he'll get caught dippin' his hands into the county treasury."

"I hate to ride away and leave things hangin'."

"If trouble is lookin' for you it'll find you without you huntin' it. Let the Landons and the Hoppers fight it out amongst theirselves."

The next morning they rode for several miles in brooding silence. Andy was thinking about the unfinished business with Big'un Hopper and his kin. He suspected Rusty was thinking about his farm and Josie Monahan.

At length Andy said, "Folks holler about savage Indians, but I don't see that they're any more savage than people that go feudin' and killin' one another. Most of them don't even know anymore what the fightin' is about."

Rusty pointed out, "Comanches kill Apaches any time they can. And Apaches kill Comanches the same way."

"That's different. They're blood enemies."

"Why? What started it?"

Andy tried in vain to remember if anybody had ever told

him. "I'd guess it might've commenced over horses a long time ago. Somebody stole them and somebody else wanted them back. Or maybe somebody insulted somebody. With Apaches, who cares?"

"See, you ain't got past all of your Comanche raisin'. You hate Apaches without knowin' why. Comanche or Apache, they're all Indians. It's a family feud just like with the Landons and the Hoppers. And it doesn't make a lick of sense."

That stung, although Andy could not quite reconcile himself to Rusty's viewpoint. Every Comanche knew that Apaches were like rattlesnakes, to be killed wherever they were found. Children were taught that lesson as soon as they were able to learn. "It's the People's way," he said.

"Killin' one another is the Hoppers' and the Landons' way. The Lord never made any perfect humans, Indian or white."

West of Austin the rugged topography always lifted Andy's spirit. It seemed to lift Rusty's too, for his eyes brightened as he surveyed the rough terrain, the live-oak flats, the limestone layers that were like broken stair steps up the sides of the hills. He said, "I never spent much time out in this part of the country. I wish I had. It's pretty."

"Pretty wild."

"If I was just startin' out and didn't already have my farm, I think I'd find me a place out here. I'd set my roots deep and never leave it the rest of my life."

Andy was gratified to see Rusty beginning to come out of the darkness. "I've studied on it some myself."

He remembered older Comanches' accounts of long hunting trips down into this land rich in water and grass and game. By the time he was with them they never ventured this far south anymore except to raid. The Texans had made it too dangerous for them to stay. In Andy's view the hill country had not yet been spoiled by civilization. Most of it was too rough to be violated by the plow except for narrow valleys where soil had washed down from the steep hillsides to accumulate deep and rich. In springtime it was like a boundless garden exploding in color with bluebonnets and other wildflowers. Now in summer the season of blooming was gone and the maturing grass was more brown than green. Spring was short, but the memory was long.

It was a perfect haven for grazers and browsers, wild and domestic. Now and then Andy glimpsed white-tailed deer. Alert to danger, they bounded into the cedar thickets and live-oak mottes long before the horsemen reached them. A hunter needed stealth and steady nerves to stalk them with a rifle. How much harder it would be, he thought, to stalk them with a bow and arrow as the Indians traditionally did.

He saw wild turkeys too. He brought one down with a well-aimed shot to the head.

"What did you do that for?" Rusty asked. "It's hard to strip off the feathers without boilin' water to scald the bird."

"I'll skin him like a squirrel. He'll make a nice supper." Andy was proud of his shot. Bringing down a turkey with a rifle was a test of marksmanship. Rusty had taught him so well in the use of the rifle that Andy was now the better shot. In fact, when he gave it any thought he realized that Rusty had taught him most of what he knew about living in the white man's world.

Having finished all he wanted of the turkey, he sat on the ground a little way from the dwindling campfire. The night was warm enough that he did not need the heat. He said, "You're studyin' me awful hard."

Rusty said, "I was wonderin' with your Indian raisin' why you ever decided to be a Ranger. Rangers and Comanches have fought one another ever since Stephen F. Austin's time."

"It's more like the life I had with the Comanches than the life I had on your farm."

"But it's not a job you'd want to spend the rest of your years at. Even if you could depend on it, which you can't. The state is always runnin' out of money. You never know from one month to the next if you'll get paid."

"Money's not the main thing."

"It's easy to say money's not important when you've got a little in your pocket. It looks different when you don't have any. First time the state's money gets tight they'll cut the Rangers again. Folks back in East Texas will say the Indian fightin' is done so there's no use spendin' that tax money. But let a bank get robbed or somebody get killed and they'll holler, 'Where's the Rangers?' "

An owl hooted. Andy felt a chill. "Hear that?"

"It's just an owl in the tree yonder. He's probably lonesome for company."

"I don't like owls. They bring nothin' but bad luck."

"That's just an old Comanche notion."

"Some Comanche notions are real. Owls are bad medicine."

Andy lost himself awhile in memories of his Comanche life. He was shaken back to reality by the sound of a horse's hoofs striking against the limestone rocks. He reached for his rifle.

A voice called from the darkness, "Hello, the camp. All right if I come in?"

Rusty shouted, "Come ahead." He was watchful but did not seem worried. Andy's instincts told him to keep his hand on a gun.

The rider dismounted at the edge of the firelight and tied his horse where it would not kick dust into the cook fire. He appeared to be of middle age. He had several days' growth of whiskers, though his hair was cut short. If he carried a weapon it was hidden. "Glad I seen your fire. I was about to make a cold camp, and a hungry one."

Rusty said, "You're welcome to what's left of a skinny turkey. You've traveled a ways by the looks of you."

"Several days, but I think I'm gettin' close to what I'm lookin' for. You-all know anything about a Ranger camp out thisaway?"

Rusty said, "Reckon we do. You thinkin' about joinin' up?"

"Me join the Rangers? Not hardly." The visitor seemed to find dark humor in the thought. "But I've got business with them."

Andy was still tense, trying to gauge the stranger's tone of voice. "You got a quarrel with the Rangers?"

"No, I stay away from the law and hope it stays away from me. Took me a long time to learn that, and I've got the gray hair to show for it. You say you know where the camp is at?"

Rusty said, "We're headed that way ourselves."

The stranger stiffened. "You're Rangers?"

Andy did not like the reaction. "I am. Rusty's fixin' to be. Is there somethin' we can do for you?"

"The Rangers been keepin' somethin' of mine."

Andy burned to ask for more details, but he considered it ill manners to be inquisitive without a clear reason. The visitor attacked the remnant of turkey as if he had not eaten in two days. Andy boiled a can of fresh coffee. The stranger blew steam from a cupful and drank it without waiting for it to cool.

Rusty said, "It ain't much, but it's the best we can do travelin' across country."

The stranger made a gesture of approval. "It's mighty fine. Where I been they don't know nothin' about makin' coffee, or much of anything else."

Andy itched to ask him where that was, but if it was important he would know in time. If it wasn't, it made no difference.

The stranger rubbed his stomach with satisfaction. "Couldn't be no better if you'd served it on golden plates. I'm obliged." He poured the last of the coffee. "Be all right with you fellers if I spread my roll here tonight and ride along with you tomorrow?"

Andy had doubts. But Rusty said, "I don't see any reason not to."

"I ought to let you know right off. I just come from a stretch in the penitentiary. You might not be comfortable with the likes of me around."

Andy's suspicions were confirmed. "If you escaped, we'll be honor-bound to take you in."

"No, I served my time and got out legal. They gave me a few dollars and a suit of clothes. Said they didn't want to see my ugly face no more, and I promised them they wouldn't."

Rusty said, "As long as you've paid up fair and square, I don't see where we've got any kick comin'. I'm Rusty Shannon. This is Andy Pickard."

The stranger nodded but did not offer to shake hands. "My name's Tennyson. Lige Tennyson."

Tennyson. Andy's pulse quickened. "Have you got a boy that goes by the name of Scooter?"

The stranger spilled some of his coffee. "You know him?"

Andy stared into the fire, his stomach uneasy. "I know him."

He was sure now why Lige Tennyson had come looking for the Rangers.

{ SEVEN }

Tennyson walked off into the darkness to take care of necessities. Andy said, "We can't let him take Scooter away."

"He's the boy's daddy."

"But he's an outlaw. He's been in the pen."

"He's served his time."

"What if he goes back to his old ways and drags Scooter along with him? We can't let that happen."

Rusty was sympathetic but offered little comfort. "If his mind is set, the only thing apt to stop him would be the court. You know a good judge?"

"I don't even know a bad judge. Well, Judd Hopper. I just know that kid was on the road to hell before me and some of the others took him by the scruff of the neck. We may not be able to rescue him the next time."

"Maybe Tennyson has decided to walk a straight line. I've known men that slipped once but never did it again."

"An old horse doesn't change his color. I've got a bad feelin' way down in my gut."

Though he knew it was unlikely, Andy could not shake a suspicion that Tennyson might steal their horses and make off with them in the dark. He dozed fitfully, never falling into deep sleep.

Tennyson snored all night.

Frying bacon for breakfast, Rusty noticed the droop of Andy's shoulders. "It won't help for you to lay awake fret-tin'. If the boy's daddy wants him there's not much you can do."

"Maybe the captain can."

Andy studied Scooter's father as they rode. It had long seemed to him that there should be something in a criminal face that marked it as different. He could find nothing unusual in Tennyson's unless it was the restless eyes, constantly searching. He had seen the same characteristic in frontiersmen used to being in Indian country, ever on the lookout for danger. Watchfulness was not necessarily a sign of a criminal mind.

Tennyson asked many questions about his son. "I'll bet he's growed up to be a man, almost. It's hard to picture him that way. Last time I seen him he stood about waist-high to a tumbleweed."

Andy looked for any sign of hope. "You may not know him, and he may not know you. You might've grown too far apart to fit back together again."

"Give us a little time. Blood will always tell."

Blood. That was what Andy worried about. Lige Tennyson's blood ran in Scooter's veins. It was an outlaw strain.

Andy said, "Scooter's come a long way. Sergeant Holloway's been schoolin' him in readin' and writin' and figures. It'd be a shame to take him away from that."

"I studied a few books while I was boardin' with the state, and I was always pretty good at figurin' up sums. I'll teach him all I know."

That was the problem, Andy thought. Lige knew too many of the wrong things.

They rode into camp at midafternoon and reined up in front of the headquarters tent. Sergeant Holloway stepped out, his turkey-tracked eyes pinched against the sunshine. Holloway gave Tennyson a glance, then turned to Andy and Rusty. "Rusty Shannon! It's good to see you back. You figurin' to stay awhile?"

"If you-all will have me."

Holloway asked Andy, "Where's Farley? Don't tell me he decided to resign." He looked a bit hopeful.

"Farley got shot up a little. I left him with his family till he heals up enough to ride."

Andy was about to give Holloway the details when the captain emerged from his tent. He acknowledged Rusty and told him he would be glad to have him sign up for whatever period Rusty might choose. Then he diverted his attention to Andy. "I received a wire saying you and Brackett delivered your prisoners all right."

"Delivered and signed for. But Jayce Landon didn't stay a prisoner for long."

"So I understand."

Andy explained about Jayce's escape from jail. He omitted his belief that Jayce's wife had slipped him the derringer, for she was in enough trouble with the local law. She didn't need the Rangers hounding her as well.

Dick Landon came up in time to hear most of it. He smiled broadly as he listened to the account of his brother's flight. "I figured he'd get away if he had even a ghost of a chance."

"Got away slicker than wagon grease. My guess is that he put the county line behind him as fast as his horse could run. He left a bunch of disappointed Hoppers, not to mention the county judge."

"Judd Hopper!" Dick spat the name as if it were a wad of bitter tobacco. "The old son of a bitch has stolen half of the county."

Andy said, "Sheriff Truscott seemed like a decent sort, considerin' what-all he's got to deal with."

"But he's got Judd Hopper's leash around his neck."

Tennyson listened intently, saying nothing as his eyes cut from Andy to Dick to the captain.

The captain impatiently changed the subject. "Tell me again how Brackett got wounded. The wire was much too sketchy."

Andy repeated the account. The captain asked, "And you're sure you shot whoever did it?"

"I saw him fall and grab his leg."

The thought seemed to please the captain. "There's nothing so stupid as a feud, and Texas seems to be suffering an epidemic of them. The trouble isn't over just because you-all managed to ride away. It may follow you out here."

That thought was not new to Andy. "Any shots we fired were in self-defense, plain and simple."

The captain said, "From what I know of that county, the court belongs to the Hoppers. If they take a notion you've thrown in with the Landons, your testimony in court wouldn't be worth a Continental." His face indicated concern. "I'll need you to write a full report at your first convenience. Perhaps I can get it to Austin ahead of any protests from the judge or the sheriff."

The captain turned his attention to the visitor. "You say your name is Lige Tennyson? Somehow that has a familiar ring."

Tennyson shrugged apologetically. "I'm sorry to say that too many people used to know my name. Five years down at the state hotel has taught me that the outlaw road is all uphill, through flint rocks and cactus. But I've wrestled with the devil, and I've finally pinned him to the floor."

"Well and good, but what brings you to this camp?"

"I've come to claim my son. He's the boy called Scooter."

The captain's brow wrinkled. He gave Tennyson a more intense scrutiny. "I believe I see a family resemblance."

"The Tennyson blood has always showed out strong. Ain't goin' to be no trouble about me takin' my boy, is there?"

"I'll have to satisfy myself that it's the right thing to do. I'll want to see what the boy says."

"He's his daddy's son. He'll want to go."

"That I shall determine for myself. Follow me, Mr. Tennyson." The captain strode toward the cook tent. Tennyson took long steps to catch up with him. Andy trailed along. Rusty stayed behind, talking to Holloway.

The black cook looked up from his Dutch ovens, puzzled by the crowd converging on him. "Howdy, Captain. A little early for supper. Got coffee ready, though."

"We're looking for Scooter."

"He's out draggin' up firewood. Ought to be back right soon." Bo's forehead creased with worry. "He ain't got in no trouble, has he?"

"No trouble. His father has come to see him."

Bo seemed at a loss for words. He started to extend his hand but reconsidered and drew it back. He would not expect a white stranger to shake with him. "You're Scooter's daddy?" His voice hinted at the same misgivings Andy felt. "You and him been away from one another a long time."

"Too long, but I'm fixin' to make it up."

Bo looked at the captain and at Andy, a silent pleading in his eyes. "I hope you ain't fixin' to take him away. That boy's been a right smart of help to me."

Instead of replying to Bo, Tennyson turned to the captain. "You got him takin' orders from a nigger?"

The captain stiffened. "He listens to all of us. That's how a boy learns."

"Not a boy of mine. I want him growin' up proud and strong. He's got no business playin' servant to anybody, least of all a nigger."

The captain's face flushed as he struggled for an answer. Andy knotted his fists.

They were distracted by a scraping sound. Scooter approached on horseback, dragging several long, dead tree branches at the end of a rawhide rope. He brought them up even with a remnant of woodpile and jumped to the ground. He retrieved the rope and coiled it. "That ought to last a couple of days, Bo. You want me to chop it up?"

Bo's eyes were troubled. He did not answer.

Tennyson said, "You're through doin' chores around here, son."

Scooter noticed the visitor for the first time. He blinked in confusion.

Tennyson bent down. "Don't you recognize your old daddy?"

Scooter appeared at first to disbelieve what his eyes told him. "Pa?"

"Son, I've come to fetch you away from this place. It's time me and you was partners again." He opened his arms.

Scooter hesitated another moment, then accepted his father's hug. "Pa, I didn't know who you was."

"Five years make a lot of changes in a man. But not as many as in a boy." He pushed his son off to arm's length and gave him a long study. "You've growed a sight bigger than I expected. You're might near a man."

"Might near."

"Have you missed me?"

"I didn't think I'd ever see you again."

"There was times I wondered too, but you'll see a lot of me from now on. We've got places to go and things to do."

"Where we goin'?"

"We'll talk about that. How long before you're ready?"

Scooter looked to the officer for an answer. "Is it all right with you, Captain?"

The captain was slow to answer. "Son, you're free to do whatever you want to. Just be sure you know your mind."

"This is my daddy." Scooter looked at Bo. "You're always talkin' about Scripture. Don't it say in the Book that I'm supposed to obey my daddy?"

The cook's words came reluctantly. "It ain't for me to tell you what you should do. All I know is that you've been a changed young'un since you've been with us."

Scooter turned back to his father. "These Rangers have treated me real good."

Tennyson said, "But they ain't your kin. Blood is what matters most in this world."

Scooter pondered his dilemma, his freckled face twisting. "I guess I belong with my daddy."

The captain nodded gravely. "If that's your choice."

Andy protested, "Scooter, you were ridin' with outlaws when we found you. You don't want to be doin' that again."

"I'll be ridin' with my daddy."

Andy wanted to grab the boy and shake him until he changed his mind, but he could not bring himself to lay a hand on Scooter. He said, "You're makin' a mistake."

The captain said, "Leave him alone, Pickard. I told him the choice was his."

"But he's makin' the wrong one."

Tennyson said, "Keepin' a boy away from his kin is like cuttin' off the roots to a tree. It ain't right. He needs to know who he is and who his people are."

Scooter asked, "We don't have to leave today, do we?"

Bo put in, "Stay a little longer and I'll fix this boy a supper like he ain't never had before."

Tennyson considered. "Supper? Sounds all right to me. My horse is about give out anyway."

Andy had found that tired horses were always a logical excuse for inaction.

Rusty had come up by then. Taking him aside Andy told him, "Maybe this'll give me time to talk Scooter out of the notion."

Rusty frowned. "Careful. If you push him into a decision he comes to regret, he'll resent you the rest of his life."

"If he makes the wrong decision, he'll resent me for not advisin' him better."

Rusty shrugged. "Looks like you're rimfired either way you go."

Bo joined them. He seemed unable to conceive of the boy going away. He said, "When he first come here I felt like skinnin' him alive. But us all workin' together, we've made a pretty good kid out of him. Maybe he'll still decide not to go with his daddy."

Andy said glumly, "Maybe. But if *my* real daddy was to show up, I guess I'd want to go with him. Kin is kin."

"There's a difference. Your real daddy was a peaceful farmer, so they say. He wasn't no outlaw."

Andy noticed that Tennyson sought out Dick Landon and talked with him at length. Later, when he had a chance, Andy asked Dick what Tennyson had been so interested in.

Dick said, "He asked a lot of questions. Told me he heard talk in the pen about the fight between the Landons and the Hoppers. I told him I've been tryin' to stay out of it, but it's hard when so many people are tryin' to hunt down my brother."

"Maybe Jayce has got to Mexico by now."

"I doubt he'd go there without Flora. No, he'll stay close enough to keep in touch with her and the rest of the family."

"Then he's always in danger of bein' found."

Dick's face darkened. "Them that find him, they'll wish they hadn't."

* * *

Andy had expected trouble to come sooner or later from Sheriff Oscar Truscott or at least his deputy, Big'un Hopper. He had not expected the county judge to show up at the Ranger camp in a buggy, sided by Big'un and another Hopper on horseback. Andy remembered Big'un calling this one Harp. The family resemblance was strong.

Judge Hopper looked to be in the final stages of dyspepsia. He stopped at the headquarters tent first, conferring awhile with the captain. The captain in turn sent for Andy.

The captain's face was sober, but Andy could sense anger simmering beneath the surface. "Private Pickard, Judge Hopper has made grave charges against you and Private Brackett."

Andy stood straight and defiant. "We expected somebody would." He wondered why Sheriff Truscott had not come instead of the judge. He had sensed almost from the first that friction existed between the sheriff and his in-laws.

Big'un poked a thick finger toward Andy's face. "This man and his partner contrived for a prisoner to escape."

The captain maintained a stern attitude. "And how did they do that? Private Pickard brought me a signed release certifying that the prisoner had been delivered into the sheriff's hands. All further responsibility was the sheriff's."

Big'un said, "They claimed they'd searched him, but he had a gun on him. He forced the jailer to turn him aloose."

Andy said, "Didn't you or the sheriff search him too before he went into the jail?"

"We took you-all's word."

"I distinctly remember seein' you feel of Jayce's pockets."

"He must've had it someplace else. In his boot, maybe.

We trusted you Rangers to be sure he didn't carry any weapon when you turned him over to us."

"He didn't." Andy was gratified that the Hoppers evidently had not figured out something that seemed obvious to him: Flora Landon had slipped her husband the derringer. He did not want to make their job easier or the woman's life harder than it already was.

Big'un declared, "One of them Rangers wounded a cousin of mine. Took a chunk out of his leg. He'll never walk straight again."

Andy retorted, "The way most of them were liquored up that night, he wasn't walkin' very straight before."

The captain frowned at Andy, a quiet signal for him to tread lightly.

The judge looked up the row of tents. "Where is that other Ranger, the one named Brackett? Why is he not out here?"

Andy did not answer. He decided that was for the captain to do if he so chose.

The captain said, "He is recuperating from a wound some of your people inflicted upon him."

"I asked you where he is."

"And I have chosen not to say. Any business you have with him, you can take up with me." The captain's firm stance made it plain that he did not intend to tell more than he already had.

Big'un broke in, "We understand you've got a man here by the name of Landon."

The captain said, "Yes. Private Dick Landon."

"Do you know he's a brother to the fugitive?"

"I do, but I've kept Private Landon here in camp or on assignment nearby. You cannot implicate him in this fiasco."

"He didn't have to be there. I'm bettin' that him and

Pickard and Brackett were in cahoots. And I'm bettin' he knows where his brother is at. He may even be hidin' him somewhere close to this camp." Big'un's voice rose as he spoke.

The judge said, "I have sworn out a warrant for the arrest of Pickard and Brackett and your Ranger Landon. I intend to bring them before the grand jury." He removed some papers from his vest pocket.

The captain planted his feet a little farther apart. "You are out of your jurisdiction." Nevertheless, he gave the documents a cursory inspection. His voice edged toward the sarcastic. "Signed by Judge Judd Hopper. I wonder why the Hopper name does not surprise me."

"I was duly elected by the voters of the county. Those papers are as legal as if they were signed by Sam Houston himself."

The captain handed back the documents. "I cannot accept these. I do not know if the signature is genuine."

"I just told you."

"I do not know if *you* are genuine. You have shown me no documentation to prove you are who you say you are."

Big'un said, "You can see my badge."

"Any half-sober silversmith can counterfeit a badge. The men you seek are Rangers under my command, duly sworn. You will not have them unless I receive direct orders from the adjutant general."

Big'un said, "He's way to hell over in Austin."

"Probably, if he is not away on an inspection tour somewhere across the state. I suggest you go to Austin and wait for him."

Big'un started to turn his horse away but paused to curse the captain. "We ain't done yet. You'll be wishin' you'd never heard of us Hoppers."

The captain said, "I already do. Leave this camp, or I

shall place you under arrest for disturbing the peace. I may come up with another charge or two if I set my mind to it."

Andy watched the judge's face flush a deep red. He thought Hopper might be in some danger of bursting a blood vessel. Big'un gave the judge a cautionary look. "Better ease off, Uncle. You know what the doctor told you about them conniption fits." He turned his eyes to the captain. "Looks to me like he needs a drink."

"We don't keep liquor in camp."

"Some water, then."

The captain offered no sympathy. "There's a whole riverful of it down yonder."

Big'un and the judge rode down toward the river. Harp followed a length behind. He had never spoken. Andy surmised that he simply rode in his kinsmen's shadow.

Sweating heavily, Andy said, "Thanks, Captain. I was afraid you might give them what they asked for."

"The Rangers stand by their own."

"Those Hoppers are a hard bunch. From what I heard, so are the Landons. Dick is an exception."

"Perhaps. Given sufficient provocation, there is no telling what any man might do, including yourself. I gather you have had no experience with a real Texas family feud."

"Not like this one."

"They can be vicious. They can draw in an entire community, including people who are no blood kin. Back in the time of the republic, two groups known as the Regulators and the Moderators went to war against one another. It took Sam Houston and the Texas army to stop the bloodshed."

"I've heard about that one."

"Sometimes it's hard to stay neutral, but we have to. It's our job to keep the peace, even if we have to kill some people to do it."

"Big'un Hopper is a determined man, and so is the judge. Do you think they'll just turn around and go back?"

"I'll see that they do. I'll send Len Tanner as an escort to see the three of them safe from Indian attack the first forty or fifty miles."

"There hasn't been an Indian attack around here in years."

The captain smiled thinly. "And we want to keep it that way."

Andy thought by the time the Hoppers listened to a one-sided conversation from Len for fifty miles, they would not want to come back. He could talk the ears off a dead mule.

{ EIGHT }

The Ranger company had given Scooter an unclaimed fourteen-year-old horse recovered from a thief, along with an old saddle and a bridle acquired the same way. He had been as proud as if the rig were brand-new and the horse a three-year-old. He rode beside his father, who had not told him their destination but had set out after breakfast in an eastward direction.

A squirrel chattered at them from the limb of a pecan tree. Lige said, "There's supper." He drew his pistol and fired. The squirrel toppled, its head gone.

Scooter whistled. "Man! I never even seen a Ranger shoot like that."

"It ain't nothin' you can't learn to do. Just got to set your mind to it. I'll learn you."

Lige motioned, and Scooter dismounted to retrieve the squirrel. Lige said, "Keep watchin' for another. We can have us a regular feast as good as what that darky's been fixin'."

"Ain't many can cook like Bo."

Lige frowned. "Them Rangers had no business lettin' you do chores for the likes of him. You're white, and don't you ever forget it."

"Bein' black ain't Bo's fault. He's good people."

"As long as he knows his place."

At dusk they sat before a campfire, watching two squirrels broiling on the ends of long sticks. Scooter said, "Been a long time since we camped together. So long I can barely remember it."

"We'll do it a lot more. We're partners, me and you." Lige leaned forward for a look at the squirrels. "I done a lot of campin' when I was younger. Bet you didn't know I lived for a few years up in the Cherokee nation."

"With the Indians?"

"They was good Indians."

"I didn't know there *was* any good ones. Comanches come awful close to killin' me once. I hid out to where they couldn't find me, but they sure tried. They come so close I swear I could smell their breath."

"The Cherokees are a different breed. I had me some good friends amongst them, and we cut some real shines together. Of course I was a sight younger then." Lige mused for a while, staring into the fire. "I got it in mind to go back up to the nation and find me a Cherokee wife. They each got a head right to some land. Me and you could get us a good little farm that way."

"You'd marry an Indian just to get some land?"

"It ain't easy for a poor man to get ahold of good land these days. Besides, there's other advantages to bein' married. Me and your mama had a pretty good life together. I miss her."

"I don't know how I'd take to havin' an Indian mother. I'd keep thinkin' about them Comanches wantin' to scalp me. I'd wonder if she had the same notion."

"Them Cherokees live like white people. Got their own government. Even got their own newspaper."

"Still, I don't know as I'd like it. I might not go with you up there."

"You'll go where I say." Tennyson's face clouded with anger that came quickly and faded the same way. "The Good Book says to honor your father."

"You've read the Good Book?"

"Parts of it."

"You believe everything it says?"

"The parts I agree with. I heard a lot of preachin' while I was back yonder workin' for the governor. So we'll follow the Book, and you'll go where I go."

Scooter had forgotten how mercurial his father's moods could be. He remembered how hard his father could slap him with an open hand, then hug him tenderly. He decided to step with caution. "And where'll that be?"

"Back where that feud is goin' on. I talked to Dick Landon, and I watched that judge and the deputies. I figure a man good with a gun ought to be able to hire out to one side or the other for high dollars. That'd set us up fine for goin' to the Cherokee nation. But first we need us a little road stake."

"Road stake?"

"Travelin' money. There's a nice little bank over in Kerrville. I think I could talk them into makin' us a loan."

Scooter did not hide his misgivings. "When you say loan, you're really thinkin' robbery."

"Robbery is an ugly word. *Borrowin'* touches softer on the ear."

"I doubt as the Rangers would see the difference."

"You're not with the Rangers anymore. It's time you quit worryin' about what they think."

"I was with Arliss and Brewster and another feller when they held up the bank in Brownwood. Scared me near as bad as them Comanches did."

"There's nothin' to be scared of when you know what you're doin'. Watch me and learn. Every boy needs to master more than one trade."

The Rangers had told Scooter that Kerrville and several other towns in the hill country had a strong German influence. They explained that in the years before the war, many groups of Europeans—German, Polish, Alsatian, Irish—had immigrated into Texas, usually settling into enclaves among their own kind, where they felt comfortable.

All he knew about Germans was that they talked differently from most people though they looked like just about everybody else. He wondered if the men in the bank would understand Lige's words. But of course they would understand his meaning. Everybody knew what a gun meant when they looked at it from the front end.

He was sure Andy and Bo and everybody else back in camp would be furious at him and Lige both. But he knew he could not talk his father out of the notion. Lige was better at talking than at listening.

Lige gave the bank several minutes' scrutiny. "I was in there six or seven years ago. Doubt it's changed much."

"You've robbed it before?"

"I looked at it as a loan. Never intended to keep the money permanent. I always figured on payin' it back someday when I could. Just ain't been able to. Besides, it ain't right, some people havin' so much money and some not havin' none. What the government ought to do is take up all the money in the country and divide it equal. When you look at it that way, all I'm doin' is seein' that we get our share. That's what democracy is all about."

Scooter saw three horses tied in front of the bank. He wondered if their riders would stand idle while Lige single-handedly robbed the place. "Hadn't you better go in and look things over first, Pa?"

"They might recognize me from last time. Best thing is to get straight to business. Now you stay in the saddle and hold my horse. I'm liable to be in kind of a hurry when I come out."

Hands shaking, Scooter took the reins his father handed him. "What if things go wrong and you don't come out?"

"Then run like hell. The penitentiary ain't no place for a growin' boy." Lige turned away, carrying his saddlebags over one arm.

Scooter's stomach churned. He tried to ease the tension by pretending that his father was only teasing him, that he actually intended to negotiate a legitimate loan. The fantasy faded like a wisp of smoke. The truth was as solid and forbidding as that stone bank building.

A friendly voice called, causing him to freeze. "Howdy, Scooter. What you doin' so far from camp?"

He turned, trembling. Ranger Johnny Morris walked toward him. Scooter stammered, trying for some kind of answer. He remembered that the captain had sent Johnny on a mission of some kind a few days ago.

"I'm with my pa," Scooter managed. "He came and got me."

"Your pa? I thought he was in . . ." Johnny broke off. "Where's your pa now?"

"He went in the bank."

"The bank!" Johnny turned on his heel, drawing his pistol as he ran. He barely had time to enter the front door before Scooter heard a shot from inside.

Lige rushed out, a smoking pistol in one hand, the saddlebags slung over the other arm. He tossed the bags to Scooter and grabbed the reins from Scooter's hand. "Hang on to them bags. Hold them tight."

He swung into the saddle and fired a shot through the open bank door. Someone stepped quickly back out of sight.

Lige shouted, "Let's go. This town ain't got no friendlier."

Scooter was too frightened to talk until they had cleared the outskirts of town. They galloped eastward alongside the rock-strewn Guadalupe River and its tall cypress trees. Looking back, he could see no one in pursuit, but he reasoned that they would soon be coming. "I hope you didn't kill somebody."

Lige cursed. "Everything was goin' just dandy till some feller come stormin' in with a six-shooter. Wasn't nothin' I could do but shoot him before he could shoot me."

"That was a Ranger. He was a friend of mine."

"When it comes to the law, us Tennysons ain't got no friends."

Scooter wanted to cry but couldn't. "Did you kill him?"

"Things went too fast. I just know I hit him. He ought to've minded his own business. I was mindin' mine."

Scooter felt a measure of relief, but not enough. "That *is* his business, chasin' robbers."

"Don't call me a robber again or I'll take my belt to you. I swear, young'uns these days have got no respect."

Scooter's anger flared, the aftermath to his earlier fear. "If you ain't a robber, what are you?"

"A rebel. They got too many laws in this country, and

I've fought against damn near all of them. I was born free. I intend to stay that way."

Scooter thought that might not be easy. "The Rangers will all be after us now, and they don't stop at no county lines."

The news from Kerrville brought all the off-duty Rangers to the headquarters tent. The report was that a bank robber had badly wounded Johnny Morris. A boy had been with him. The message did not offer any names, but Andy was sure Lige Tennyson was the culprit. Scooter was a witness at the least, perhaps even an unwilling accomplice.

Andy told the captain, "I had a bad feelin' about Tennyson from the start. I want to go over there."

"I don't think I should let you. You're too close a friend to the boy."

"Everybody in camp was friends with Scooter. He's liable to end up killed if we don't get him away from that outlaw daddy."

The captain's face indicated that he was going to turn Andy down, but he said, "All right. I'm sending Sergeant Holloway and Rusty Shannon. You can accompany them. Saddle up. You'll leave in twenty minutes."

Rusty and Andy were sitting on their horses in front of the headquarters tent when Sergeant Holloway came out carrying his rifle. They had blanket rolls tied to their saddles, grub from Bo's kitchen hanging in cloth sacks. The sergeant walked to where a Ranger had Holloway's horse saddled and waiting. He said nothing. Conversation tended to be sparse on a serious Ranger mission.

The three Rangers rode far into the night, following a wagon road that wound through the valleys and between the hills. Andy judged that it was past midnight when they rode up to the jail in Kerrville. For the last couple of hours he had felt the horse gradually tiring beneath him. He doubted the animal had another hour of travel left.

The sergeant knocked on the door several times before a sleepy-headed deputy sheriff answered, holding a lamp so he could see the faces before he opened the door all the way. He recognized Holloway on sight. "I was sort of expectin' you Rangers, but not at this hour of the night."

Holloway said, "Rangers don't get much sleep when outlaws are on the prowl. How's Johnny Morris?"

"He'll live, but he was hard hit. Goin' to be a long time before he does any Rangerin' again."

Rusty asked, "Where's he at?" He and the two Morris brothers had been friends for years.

"Over at the doctor's house. I wouldn't go beatin' on the door now, though. Him and the doctor both need sleep. You can bunk down here till daylight. I got some empty cells."

Holloway thanked him for his thoughtfulness. "We'll need to put our horses away first. I'll want to talk to witnesses as soon as we can. We're pretty sure we know who the culprit is."

The deputy nodded. "Your Ranger told us the boy's name is Scooter Tennyson. The robber was the boy's daddy."

Andy asked, "Did Scooter help with the robbery?"

"The Ranger said it looked to him like the kid was holdin' the horses. Said he hoped the young'un didn't realize what was goin' on."

The sergeant frowned at Andy. "For the time bein' we'll give Scooter the benefit of the doubt. But if he knew what his daddy was doin', and he helped, we'll have to consider him an accessory."

"He's just a kid."

"A kid can pull a trigger."

Andy found a jail cell a poor place to sleep. The bunk was rock-hard. He had never given much consideration to the comfort of people he helped to arrest. He thought perhaps in the future he might be more conscious of prisoners' rights.

Holloway had little use for a bed after sunup nor was he sympathetic with others who would rather sleep than meet the new day. He hollered, "Daylight!" at the top of his voice. He was not accustomed to saying it twice. Andy had slept in his clothes, all but boots and hat. He donned the hat first, then pulled on his boots.

The deputy soon emerged from his living quarters. "Got water and a wash pan out by the back door. I'll see if I can scramble up some breakfast."

Andy appreciated the fresh eggs, though the deputy cooked them too long and gave them a scorched flavor. The biscuits were soft and warm. He smeared them liberally with fresh butter and dipped them in blackstrap molasses. Good biscuits could make up for a lot.

His thoughts ran to Scooter. He wondered where the boy was now. Camped out along a trail somewhere, more than likely, possibly hungry and frightened. He thought of Johnny Morris lying in the doctor's house, in pain from a bullet wound that could easily have killed him.

Damn Lige Tennyson. Andy wished there were a dozen of Tennyson, and every one of them was locked up in the Kerrville jail. Or better, buried at the back side of the Kerrville cemetery.

Andy kept glancing at the sergeant, wanting him to hurry his meal. Holloway took note of his impatience. "In due time. Johnny may still be sleeping."

The deputy said, "The robbers headed east along the river road. We trailed them a ways, but we lost their tracks because they was mixed with so many others. There's no tellin' which way they went once they got plumb clear of the town."

Johnny Morris was awake and propped up in bed. His face was pale, his cheeks drawn in, but his eyes lit up when he saw his fellow Rangers. He said in a thin voice, "I thought for a while I was fixin' to go absent without leave."

The sergeant smiled. "That'd be desertion. You're too good a Ranger for that." He quickly got down to business. "We figure the robber was Lige Tennyson. Are you sure it was Scooter you saw?"

Johnny said, "It was him, all right. I was surprised to see him sittin' there holdin' a second horse. When I asked what he was doin', he said he was waitin' for his daddy. I remembered that his daddy was supposed to be in the pen, so I figured he didn't go in the bank to make a deposit."

"And you set out to stop him?"

"The bank was dark. Comin' in from the daylight, I couldn't see much. The robber shot me before I got a good look at him."

Andy said, "Reckon Scooter knew what his daddy was up to?"

"Maybe there wasn't nothin' he could do about it."

The sergeant said, "He could have ridden away and left his father."

Andy argued, "You couldn't expect him to do that. He hadn't seen his daddy in five years. He wouldn't leave him so soon."

"In the eyes of the law he's old enough to make choices, even the hard ones."

A visit to the bank filled in some extra details but did not change the cardinal fact that the holdup man was almost certainly Lige Tennyson. A quick-thinking teller had filled the saddlebags with low-denomination bills and a stack of blank counter checks so that the bank's loss was minimal.

Tennyson must have been sorely disappointed when he stopped to count the fruits of his labor.

Holloway said, "Comin' up short, he'll likely pull another robbery before long. I'll wire Austin a description, and the adjutant general's office will send it across the state. I doubt that Tennyson has any idea how the telegraph lines have spread durin' the time he was in the pen."

Impatience stung Andy like a case of hives. "Every time he does it he puts Scooter in danger. Sooner or later they'll run into somebody who's a good shot."

"We'll try to pick up his trail. Maybe we'll have better luck than the townfolks did."

Andy burned inside. He wished he had Lige Tennyson in front of him right now. He would gladly shoot him, even if Scooter hated him for it afterward.

Lige Tennyson had been in a dark mood since he had stopped to open the saddlebags and find out how rich he was. Scooter watched him uneasily, fearful that he might become the whipping boy for his father's frustrations. So far he had not, but Scooter remembered harsh punishment inflicted long ago for minor infractions.

Lige had turned the air blue. "Damned teller with his clean white shirt and necktie. A dirty crook is what he is, cheatin' me thisaway. I wouldn't put it past him to've stuck the real money in his pockets and then claim I got it all."

Scooter considered the implications. "That'd be double robbery, wouldn't it, robbin' you and the bank both? He could go to jail twice."

Lige rumbled on, "I'd go back and blow his lamp out, but the town'll be swarmin' with Rangers by now. We got to keep movin'."

Scooter figured his father was probably right about the

Rangers. He wondered if Andy and the others were on the trail right now. Lige had been careful to stay on the river road at first so their tracks would be difficult to separate from the others. They had turned off at a place where the road crossed a field of gravel deposited by some long-ago flood. They had not left a track that he could see.

He was torn between a wish that the Rangers would catch up with them and a fear that if they did, they might shoot first and discuss consequences later. He had heard enough talk in camp to know that at times it was considered good judgment to bring a prisoner in dead rather than alive. Under stressful circumstances the Rangers were prone to be both judge and jury.

Lige muttered, "We ain't got near as much money as I figured. We're goin' to have to find us another loan."

Scooter said, "We don't have to *borrow* money that way. We could find work and earn it fair and square."

"Doin' what? I never was no good at a town job. Tried clerkin' in a store once. Pretty soon I was talkin' to myself. I done a little work as a ranch hand, but I never saw an outfit that didn't have a bunch of rank horses they expected you to ride. I'm gettin' too old for that. Banks, now, that's somethin' I know a right smart about. You just walk in, get their attention in the right way, and they'll generally loan you anything you ask for."

"Sometimes they've got guards with guns."

"If you want money, you've got to go where the money is at."

They came in sight of a modest frame farmhouse. Lige signaled for Scooter to stop. He studied the place awhile, then observed, "Crops ain't well tended. Weeds look to be doin' better than the corn."

Scooter smelled wood smoke and saw that it was coming from the backyard. A skinny middle-aged woman carried water from a steaming wash pot to a wooden tub, her thin back bending under the strain. She began scrubbing clothes.

Lige speculated, "Widder woman maybe. If she had a man the weeds wouldn't be takin' the field that way."

Scooter worried, "We ain't fixin' to rob her, are we?"

Lige seemed scandalized that his son would think such a thing. "There's no gain in holdin' up poor folks. They've got nothin' to give you anyway. But maybe we can get us a woman-cooked meal. You're lookin' a little drawed."

Scooter had not had much to eat except for squirrel and somebody's young shoat they had caught rooting for acorns. "Whatever you say, Pa."

The woman raised up from her scrub board as they approached the rear of her house. She seemed unconcerned. Scooter supposed she reasoned that a man traveling with a boy at his side presented no threat.

Lige touched fingers to the brim of his misshapen hat. "How do, ma'am. Me and my son are just passin' through. We noticed that your garden stands in need of weedin'. We wondered if we might trade a little service for a good meal. The boy ain't et proper in a while."

Scooter thought the woman looked a little like his mother when she gave them a weary but grateful smile. She said, "That'd be a mighty welcome trade. My husband's laid up with a broke leg, and things around here have got away from me some. Soon as I get these clothes on the line I'll see what I can cook up for you."

Lige nodded. "If you'll kindly direct us to where your husband keeps his workin' tools, me and the boy'll get busy."

She accompanied them to a small frame barn where a hoe, a rake, and smaller tools were neatly arrayed. She said, "You wouldn't see things in this shape if my husband was able to work. Neighbors come now and again to help, but they got needs of their own to see after."

Lige said, "We'll do the best we can."

There was only one hoe. Lige told Scooter, "I'll pull up the big ones by hand. You foller along and cut down the littler ones."

Lige worked faster with his bare hands than Scooter could with the hoe. "Pa, you act like you've done this before."

"I got lots of practice while I was studyin' at the state school. They expect you to earn your keep. When we get that farm of our own up in the territory, we'll be doin' a lot of this. Watch out you don't cut them tater vines instead of the weeds."

Scooter soon worked up a sweat. He was not sure he looked forward to that farm of their own, but maybe it would keep Pa happy enough to give up his forays into the banking business.

Between them they finished most of the garden before the woman called them to supper. The food made up in quantity what it lacked in variety. She said apologetically, "It ain't fancy, but there's nourishment in it for a growin' boy. Lucky we still got ham and fatback and such in the smokehouse from last winter."

Lige said, "It's mighty fine."

The woman's husband had limped to the table, aided by crutches. One leg was immobilized by splints bound securely with strips of cotton cloth. He said, "I'm much obliged to you fellers. As you can see, I been about as much use around here lately as teats on a boar hog."

It was obvious to Scooter that the place had been a long way from prosperity even when the farmer had full use of both legs. The little furniture he saw looked as if its best service would be as kindling to start a blaze in the fireplace. Newspapers had been pasted to the wall in lieu of wallpaper. They might block the wind that pushed between the siding's raw pine boards, but they would do little to shut out summer heat or winter cold.

The woman noticed Scooter's silent appraisal of the room. She said, "It ain't much, but it's ours. We done it all ourselves. Grubbed it out of the ground, me and my husband, with the Lord's help."

Lige said, "Glory be to the Lord."

That startled Scooter. He doubted that his father had given the Lord much thought when he robbed the bank in Kerrville.

The farmer said, "If you-all ain't in too much of a hurry, you're welcome to stay all night. Eat breakfast before you go on your way in the mornin'."

Lige said, "That's kind of you. We couldn't go much farther before dark."

Scooter observed that his father enjoyed other people's cooking far more than his own. That was probably one reason he was eager to find himself a Cherokee woman, beyond the possibility of profiting from her head right to land in the territory. Scooter worried that somebody might have picked up their trail and be following it even as they idled at this farmer's table, but Lige seemed not to share his concern. With a warm and solid meal in his belly, he appeared content to accept the world on its own terms.

There being no sign of rain, Lige elected to spread a little hay on the ground and unroll his blanket on top of it. "Ain't nothin' healthier than the clean outdoors with the stars for your ceilin'," he said. "For five years the only stars I seen was through a high window with bars in it."

"Pa, are you sure a farm is what you want? These folks have got one, and they're as poor as church mice."

"Because they ain't got enough land. Me and you, we

ain't goin' to settle for nothin' small like this. We're goin' to have a big farm with a big house and lots of stock. We'll have cornfields stretchin' as far as the eye can see. I've had lots of time to plan it all out. I know just where everything is goin' to be—the house, the barns, the fields."

"All that is goin' to take lots of money."

"The reason most people don't have enough money is that they don't have the guts to go where it's at and get their fair share."

As they finished breakfast Scooter saw his father stick a roll of bills into the sugar bowl when the farmer and his wife were looking away. He said nothing about it until they had put the little farm behind them.

"You said we ain't got much money, but I seen you leave a wad of it for them folks."

"Do good where you see the need and the Lord will reward you. Next time maybe He'll lead us to a bank where the teller ain't a crook like that last one was."

{ NINE }

Sergeant Holloway held out little hope of finding Lige's and Scooter's tracks. Too many others had been made along the river road that led eastward from Kerrville, including those of the earlier posse. The sergeant was about ready to give up.

He said, "Anywhere there's a telegraph, the local authorities will be on the lookout for Tennyson and the boy. These modern communications are the wonder of the world. Did you know a man can board a train in New York and get to

San Francisco in less time than it takes to ride horseback from Fort Worth to San Antonio?"

Andy argued, "But we're not goin' to San Francisco, and most of Texas doesn't have a railroad yet. Lots of places ain't even got a telegraph."

He chafed with impatience, but he was just a private. It was the sergeant's place to make decisions.

Rusty recognized Andy's anxiety. "We've come this far, Bill. Won't hurt us to try a little longer."

Holloway reconsidered, respecting Rusty's long experience. "Wouldn't want the captain sayin' we quit too quick. Andy, how's your trackin' eye?"

Andy feared his reputation was better than his ability, for most people assumed his Indian background gave him an advantage in following trails. But a show of confidence might keep Holloway from abandoning the search. "Nothin' wrong with my eyes."

He had found long ago that he had better hunches than most people. He wondered if it might come from his association with the Comanches, who put a lot of faith in intuition, visions, and dreams. When the three riders reached a place where a flood had deposited a large bed of gravel at a bend in the river, he had one of those hunches. He said, "If I was wantin' to cover my trail, right here is where I'd quit the road. A buffalo herd wouldn't leave tracks in that gravel."

Holloway said, "It's your hand. Play it."

Andy moved forward while Rusty and the sergeant waited so they would not add their horses' tracks to any already there. He rode along the leading edge of the gravel deposit until he found the trail of two horses. A light shower had created a thin skim of mud. The tracks had dried hard enough to preserve them from the wind's destructive touch.

His hunch told him these marked the passage of Lige and the boy. He waved his arm.

"We're on the money," he shouted.

Rusty dismounted and studied the tracks. "One horse's forefoot turns out a little, like he might've been crippled at some time."

Andy said, "That'd be Scooter's. I remember the old brown they gave him had a funny way of walkin'. Kind of paddle-footed." He felt a rising excitement. "What about it, Sergeant?"

Holloway pointed his chin eastward. "We came to catch a bank robber. We're not doin' it sittin' here."

It occurred to Andy after a while that Lige had evidently not put much effort into hiding his trail. He probably thought he had followed the well-traveled road far enough to throw off a posse. Now and then the trail would disappear on hard ground or in thick grass, but Andy would manage to pick it up again a little farther on. Lige's direction seemed well set.

Holloway said, "Looks like he's headed almost due east. We can afford to lope up some. Even if we lose the trail awhile, we ought to be able to cut it again. Maybe we can gain on him."

The second day they had not seen the trail in a while but were traveling on faith and hope. Spotting a small frame house, they stopped to water their horses. A gaunt, hard-used farm woman came out to greet them. The sergeant introduced himself. "We're obliged for the water. We'd be glad to pay for it."

She demurred. "I don't see how I can charge you for water. It's a gift from the Lord."

The sergeant smiled. "The Lord didn't dig that well for you, did He?"

"No, sir, me and my husband done that. But the Lord was lookin' on and made sure we found water."

Holloway handed her a silver dollar. "I'll pay the Lord His share next time I get to church. Been any strangers pass this way the last day or two?"

"The only people been by here lately was a man and a boy. Fine folks. They taken time to hoe the garden for me. My husband is laid up and can't work."

Andy stiffened. "Did you hear any names?"

"I don't recall that he ever introduced himself, exactly. And the boy just called him Pa." She frowned, trying to remember. "Seems to me I heard him call the boy by name, but I can't remember what it was."

"Could it have been Scooter?"

Her face brightened. "I believe it was. You know them?"

Holloway said, "We do. Were they still travelin' east when they left here?"

"They was. But I can't imagine what interest you Rangers would have in God-lovin' folks like them. Even after workin' for their keep, they left some money for us."

Kerrville bank money, Andy guessed. Tennyson could afford to be generous with it. It wasn't his.

The sergeant said, "May I be so bold as to ask how much?"

"Close to fifty dollars. I wanted to give it back, but they was gone by the time I found it."

Andy said, "It doesn't make sense, him *givin'* somebody money."

The sergeant said, "It's a waste of time to try and figure out people like Tennyson. They serve the Lord one minute and the devil the next. Tryin' to stay in good with both sides, I guess."

Riding away, Holloway seemed cheered. "He gave those folks most of the little bit he got in Kerrville. He'll be needin' more. We already wired Austin to send a warnin' to all the banks. Next time Tennyson tries to make a withdrawal, he may find himself lookin' down a dozen gun barrels."

Andy felt a dark foreboding. "What about Scooter?"

"Let's hope his daddy thinks enough of him to leave him out of harm's way."

Rusty brooded. "I can't figure Lige. If it was me and I was on the dodge, I'd go west to where law is scarce. I wouldn't go back where there's a badge on every section corner."

Holloway said, "Where law is scarce, there aren't many banks either. A workin' man goes where the work is. Or in Tennyson's case, where the money is."

Rusty said, "If I didn't know better I'd say he's headed almost directly toward my farm."

Andy said, "He'd have no reason to be goin' there."

Holloway said, "You can bet Tennyson knows what he's doin', or thinks he does. He wouldn't be travelin' this direction without he had cause. I'd give a month's pay to know what it is."

The third day Andy lost the trail and could not find it although he crisscrossed several times, returning always to a generally eastward direction. Toward dark the three Rangers came upon a family of movers camping with a tarp-covered wagon and a trail wagon hitched behind. The wagon tongue was pointed west. A young boy herded half a dozen cows and a bull. Andy could only guess at the disappointments that had put these people on the road to new country and a fresh start.

Holloway hailed them in an easy, smiling manner. "How far you-all headed?"

The man was straightening harness. "Pecos River or bust. We hear there's cheap land out there."

Cheap for a good reason, Andy thought. Charles Goodnight had called the Pecos River "the grave of a cowman's hopes." But settlers were starting to drift out that way regardless. So long as there was new land, there was always a chance, or at least the illusion of one, even where it didn't rain enough to grow much more than greasewood and prickly pear.

The Indians were not alone in following dreams.

As he had with everyone else they met, Holloway asked if they had seen a man and a boy traveling east.

The mover said, "We did. They rode into camp just as we was fixin' to have supper last night. Ate with us and rode on. Nice-actin' folks, they was."

The woman said, "Shy kind of a boy, though. Acted like he was scared to talk. I reckon he hasn't been out among strangers much."

Rusty asked, "Did they give any names?"

The man thought about it. "Not that I remember, and we didn't ask. I always figure if a man wants you to know what his name is, he'll tell you. If he doesn't want to, he's probably got a good reason."

Holloway politely turned down an invitation to stay for supper, explaining afterward that the people didn't look as if they had enough that they could afford to share. He said, "At least we're travelin' in the right direction. If we can find where those folks camped last night, maybe we can pick up Lige's tracks again."

The effort proved fruitless. They came across evidence of several campsites where fire pits had been dug and wood burned for cooking. Some were fresh enough to have been used within the last night or two. But Andy found no tracks he could identify as the paddle-footed brown's.

Holloway looked discouraged. Andy feared he might decide to quit. He had another hunch, that they were closer than they had been since they started, even if he could find no trail. But hunches would not carry a lot of weight with the sergeant. He was inclined to believe only what he could see, hear, or feel.

The land became increasingly familiar. Andy realized he had ridden over it with Rusty, looking for strayed cattle. Rusty acknowledged that they were not far from his farm.

Holloway asked, "Do you want to go by and see if everything is all right?"

Rusty said, "I haven't been gone long enough for much to've gone wrong. Unless Fowler Gaskin has come over and carried everything away." He had to explain about Gaskin.

Holloway understood. "I used to have a neighbor like that. He finally threw a conniption fit and died. You never saw so many people smilin' at a funeral."

"I doubt the Lord is anxious for Fowler to show up. He'll probably outlive us all."

Rusty's horse stumbled over a rough spot on the trail. "He's tirin' out. I expect they all are. How about we ride over to Sheriff Tom Blessing's and see if he can get us a change of horses?"

Holloway frowned. "We've already stretched pretty far past our district."

The Rangers did not have to stop at county lines. They were free to operate anywhere in the state. However, efficiency required that they remain within their own appointed areas of responsibility unless in pursuit or on a specific assignment.

They stopped at Rusty's farm. Nobody was there, a relief to Rusty. "I was half-afraid we'd find Fowler takin' up residence while I was gone. He did it once before when I was off chasin' after Indians."

The fields were as desolate as when Andy had last seen them in the wake of the hailstorm. Some plants were making a feeble try at regrowth, nature's eternal effort at survival, but they were stunted and doomed to be killed by frost before they could mature. In contrast to the fields, the garden showed signs of fresh work, freshly risen greenery.

Rusty said, "Shanty's been over here."

They went into the cabin and cooked a meager dinner. Andy noticed that Josie's photograph was missing from the mantel. Rusty must have carried it with him, though Andy had not seen him looking at it. He probably did that in private. Grief was taking a long time to heal.

Done with the meal, Rusty said, "Let's get on to town. Stoppin' here is like visitin' a graveyard."

They came upon Shanty's cabin. At Rusty's call, Shanty came out grinning. "Mr. Rusty, Andy. You-all ain't already quit bein' Rangers, have you?"

Rusty introduced him to Sergeant Holloway. "We've been trailin' a bank robber. He's got a boy travelin' with him. Anybody like that passed this way the last day or two?"

"Not as I noticed. I see most folks that come along this road. Anyway, what would a bank robber want with me? I don't have nothin' anybody'd want to steal."

"This one might've *given* you money."

"Then he sure ain't been by, because there ain't nobody given me nothin'."

Holloway grimaced. "I'm afraid we've played out our string. Tennyson may not stop till he gets halfway across Louisiana."

Andy clenched a fist in frustration. "You mean we're turnin' back?"

"I'll wire the captain and ask him what he wants us to do."

Andy said, "As long as we're this close, don't you think we ought to go by the Brackett place and see about Farley? He may be healed up enough to go back to camp."

"You and Rusty can do that while I stay in town and wait for the captain's answer."

Andy had a bitter taste in his mouth. He had far rather be taking Scooter back to camp, but he might have to settle for Farley Brackett.

At least he would see Bethel for a little while.

Scooter sat nervously on his horse half a length behind his father's while Lige quietly studied the town that lay before them. He had seen Lige count his money last night and frown.

Lige said, "Can't tell from here if this place is big enough to have a bank. Only way to know is to ride in and see."

Scooter asked, "How many times we got to do this, Pa?"

Lige turned to study him. "You're shakin', boy. Ain't nothin' to be scared of. Your old daddy knows what he's doin'."

"So do the Rangers. How do you know there ain't a bunch of them waitin' for us?"

Lige's eyes narrowed. "I can tell you ain't cut out for this business. That's why we need to travel on up to the territory and get us that farm as soon as we can. But we got to have money first, don't you see?"

"Most people don't get it this way."

"Everybody has got to find out what he's good at. I'm good at the bankin' business. Now come on, let's see what this place has to offer." His spurs jingled against his horse's sides. Scooter hesitated, then followed, his eyes searching for something to be afraid of. There was plenty, most of it imaginary.

They rode down the length of the short street. Lige slumped in disappointment. "This burg ain't big enough to support a bank. I'd settle for a good general store, but the only one I see don't look very prosperous. I wonder when the hard times are goin' to be over with."

"Seems like it's been hard times ever since I can remember."

"That's on account of the war. It's been more than ten years, but Texas ain't got over it. Times was flush before the Yankees started all that trouble. There was money enough for anybody who had the nerve to go and get what was due him. I can remember when I had so much gold that I had to have a packhorse to carry it."

"What went with it, Pa?"

"Money's like water. It dribbles out between your fingers no matter how hard you try to hold on to it. And who knew those good times were fixin' to end? We thought they'd go on and on."

They turned and rode back up the street the way they had come. Lige's attention was fixed on the general store. It was a square-fronted frame building innocent of paint. Farming tools and wooden barrels were displayed on the plank sidewalk, against the wall. A sign in the window advertised chewing tobacco and prickly bitters. Lige said, "I wonder what day it is. Used to be that Saturday was when all the farmers came to town. A good general store would have a lot of cash on hand."

"I think it's Wednesday, Pa. Or Tuesday."

"We can't wait around for Saturday. When you can't have all you want, you settle for what you can get." He dismounted in front of the store, stretching his arms and back. Scooter had heard him complain about rheumatism.

Lige handed over his reins. "Hold them. I'll go see to business. Stay awake, because when I come out I'll be lookin' to travel."

Scooter accepted reluctantly. "I'll be right here."

Lige patted him on the leg. "You're a good boy. You've got the makin's of a good man."

If you don't get me killed, Scooter thought.

A large man with a black mustache and a dark expression blocked Lige's entry into the store. He held up a hand that looked as big as a hindquarter of beef. The other hand rested upon the butt of a pistol high on his hip. "Just a minute, stranger. I need to know your name."

Scooter saw a small silver badge on the man's vest. A chill went all the way to his toes.

"My name?" Lige seemed momentarily taken aback. "What for?"

"I'm a deputy sheriff. We got a wire tellin' us to look out for a man and a boy that robbed a bank out west someplace. You've got a boy with you."

"My son," Lige said. "What do you mean, you got a wire?"

"Ain't you heard about the telegraph?"

"I've heard tell, but I never knew it'd come to a little place like this."

"They're gettin' it just about everywhere. There ain't a horse alive that can outrun it. Now what's your name and what you doin' here?"

Scooter searched Lige's face for a clue about what his father might do. He wondered if he might shoot this deputy the way he had shot Johnny Morris at the bank in Kerrville. He froze in dread.

Lige tried running a bluff. "My name's Simon Good. That's my boy Willy. We're just poor farmers passin' through on our way to help my baby sister over in Colorado County.

Her husband is laid up with a broken leg and can't work his field."

Scooter realized his father was drawing on the experience of the farm couple with whom they had spent a night.

The deputy demanded, "You got any papers to prove you're who you say you are?"

"What would I carry papers for? Ain't got but little money, either. If we'd robbed a bank, don't you think we'd be carryin' a lot of money? You can search us. If you find more than twenty dollars you can keep it."

The deputy had developed a deep and doubting frown. He approached Scooter. "Is that right, kid? Is your name Willy Good?"

Scooter could not bring himself to speak. He could only nod.

The deputy asked, "Is the boy slow-minded that he can't talk?"

Lige said, "He's hardly ever got off of the farm. Ain't used to town. It's natural that he'd get a little scared when a sheriff starts askin' him questions. It never happened to him before."

The deputy softened. "Didn't mean to upset you, son. Just doin' my duty, is all. You and your daddy have got honest faces. It's plain to see that you ain't the bank robbers they're lookin' for. Besides, their name is Tennyson, not Good."

Lige blinked at the sound of his name, then shook his head. "What would bank robbers come into a little town like this for?"

"Right enough. We ain't even got a bank."

"This town'd probably starve a banker to death. All right if we go on about our business?"

"As long as it ain't bank robbery." The deputy laughed at his own joke. No one else did.

The lawman walked on, ambling toward an ugly stone courthouse that stood two stories tall at the end of the street. It had a cupola with a clock that either was not running or was off by several hours. It was a poor town, Scooter thought, that couldn't afford to fix a clock.

Lige watched the deputy. "Damn. They already know my name. Makes me want to cut down every telegraph line I come across."

"Maybe we ought to forget that road stake and go straight to the Cherokee nation."

"We can't go there broke." Lige considered for a minute before going into the store. To Scooter's surprise he was not in a hurry when he came out. Lige bit a chaw from a plug of tobacco he had just bought.

Scooter said, "You didn't do any business?"

"One look and I could tell there wouldn't be enough money in the till to make it worth the risk. We'd have that deputy on our tail before we could clear town. Probably the sheriff too, and no tellin' how many townfolk. We'll have to give up the luxuries and get by on what we've got till we get to where they're havin' that feud. Our luck will change there, you just wait."

Scooter tried to recall what luxuries they had had. Offhand, he could not remember any.

When they reached the edge of town he said, "I'm a Jonah to you, Pa."

"How do you figure that?"

"You heard him. They're lookin' for a man and a boy travelin' together. If you was by yourself, they wouldn't look at you twice. The next place we come to, they might not be as easy to fool as that deputy was."

"We ain't splittin' up, if that's what you're gettin' at. We already been apart way too long. Anyhow, where would you go?"

"Back to the Ranger camp. They're good to me there."

"They wouldn't be good to you no more. They know you was with me in Kerrville. Like as not they'd send you to one of them reformatories and keep you there till you're old enough to shave. I've heard stories. They'd feed you bread and water and put the whip to you every day."

Scooter shuddered.

Lige said, "We'll take roundance on the towns from now on till we get to where we're goin'. Me and you are stickin' together. Father and son, like it was before I went off to work for the governor."

{ TEN }

One of the Bracketts' black field hands sighted the two Rangers' approach and went running to the main house ahead of them. His frantic manner said he was on his way to give warning.

Rusty took that as a sign of trouble. "He acts like he's afraid of somethin'."

"Probably didn't recognize us."

The sight of strangers would not ordinarily arouse fear on the Brackett farm, though memories lingered of times during Reconstruction when Farley was having difficulties with carpetbag authorities. Seeing the visitors before the visitors saw him had been the difference between life and death.

"Got any hunches, Andy?" Though Rusty on occasion had played down Andy's hunches, he was aware that they proved correct often enough to be disturbing. It was as if Andy had some supernatural power, though Rusty had not brought himself to accept that premise.

Andy said, "Maybe Farley has threatened to peel the hide off of him if he lets somebody come without lettin' him know."

"That sounds like Farley."

Bethel stood on the porch, arms folded in an attitude of defiance until she recognized Andy and Rusty. She hurried down to meet them, her eyes anxious. "Lord, I've prayed for you-all to come."

Andy's pulse quickened. "Trouble?"

"Two days ago. A deputy sheriff showed up looking for Flora Landon."

"Did he find her?"

"Yes. He dragged her away, him and five others. He took Farley too. Wouldn't listen to us trying to tell him he was still too hurt to ride."

A large bruise darkened her cheekbone. Andy demanded, "Who did that to you?"

"The deputy, when I tried to hold on to Farley. He was a big fellow. Pushed Mother off of the porch too. She's stove up so badly she can barely walk."

Andy's face heated. "That'd be Big'un Hopper. What about the old man, Flora's daddy?"

"He was out in the field. They missed him. He slipped away as soon as the posse was gone. Probably went to tell Jayce Landon."

Andy dismounted for a closer look at Bethel. He touched her cheek. "Are you sure you're all right? Nothin' worse than that bruise?"

She reached up and pressed her hand against his. "Nothing that won't heal. Except I'm still mad enough to chop that big deputy into little chunks and feed him to the hogs. I'm worried about what they might be doing to my brother. They accused him of helping with the jailbreak."

"Big'un has accused me too, but he's a liar. He knows me and Farley had nothin' to do with that."

"Just the same, I'm afraid. They treated Farley rough. They knew he was wounded, but they didn't care. That deputy seemed to take pleasure in hurtin' him."

Andy's antipathy for Farley Brackett mattered little now. Farley was a fellow Ranger. "What're we goin' to do about it, Rusty?"

"By rights that's a decision the captain ought to make, or at least the sergeant."

"They're not here. So what would you do if you had to make the decision?"

Rusty said, "The Rangers have always taken care of their own."

"The longer we wait, the more time they've got to torment Farley. And Flora Landon."

Rusty had one reservation. "Don't forget that the law over there would like to jail you too."

"Just let Big'un try. He'll see hell from the bottom side."

Bethel agreed to send a field hand to town to find the sergeant and advise him that Andy and Rusty had proceeded on their own volition. She asked, "Do you know how you're going to handle this?"

Rusty said, "Like Rangers always handle things: straight-ahead on."

Andy had no quarrel with that.

Andy pointed down the street toward the courthouse. "The jail is on the other side. Hard to see it from here." He drew his pistol to be certain it was fully loaded.

Rusty said, "I'd leave that thing in the holster, was I you.

It's always better to try and talk your way through. There's time enough later to shoot your way out."

Andy holstered the weapon, but only after inserting a cartridge in the chamber he customarily left empty for safety.

Rusty warned, "Remember, we're here on our own. We don't have authorization from the captain, or even Sergeant Holloway."

"Any reason we have to tell anybody that?"

"None at all. We might even lie a little if it helps."

Andy could not see that they were attracting any particular attention as they rode down the hoof-scuffed street, stirring a little dust with their passage. The few people they encountered had no reason to know they were Rangers. Neither wore a badge, for the state had not yet adopted an official design. Some Rangers fashioned their own, most often from Mexican silver pesos. Neither Andy nor Rusty had chosen to do so. Silver was hard to come by.

The stable keeper stood outside the big doors of the livery barn. Recognition made his jaw sag. He started to raise his hand in greeting but withdrew the gesture before it was completed.

Rusty asked, "Friend of yours?"

Andy explained that the hostler seemed to be neutral in the Hopper-Landon feud, accepting business from both sides. "He was some help to me and Farley, but nobody saw it except us. I suspect he'd duck in his hole like a prairie dog if things started to pop around him."

"I notice a lot of the store signs have got the name Hopper on them. I haven't seen a one that said Landon."

"There's considerable more Hoppers than Landons. That's why the Hoppers have control of the county. Dick Landon was right to join the Rangers and get away from here. If I was a Landon I'd leave too."

"There's not much logical about a feud. Family pride gets tangled up in it, and hate twists people to where they can't see straight."

"I don't understand that. I guess it's because I don't belong to a family. Not a white family, anyway."

Rusty's face pinched with a momentary sadness. "Neither do I. But maybe that helps me understand it better. I'd give all I've got to be part of a family."

Andy knew Rusty was thinking of the Monahans, especially the lost Josie. He said, "We've got one another."

Rusty nodded. "Two orphans thrown together by the luck of the draw. That's not quite the same." He forced a half smile. "But it's the best we've got."

Andy tensed as the jail came into view. "How about we barge in there like we had the whole Ranger force behind us? Catch them standin' on their left foot."

Rusty made no argument. "You've been here before and know the layout. You do the talkin' and I'll follow your lead."

Andy had long been used to following Rusty. It struck him as strange now for Rusty to be the follower.

I can't keep leaning on Rusty all of my life, he thought. But there was still much he did not know. It would be easy to make a costly mistake. He had made several in the course of growing up, mistakes that had brought trouble to others as well as to himself.

Well, if I make a mistake again, it won't be for standing back.

He did not knock on the jail door. Finding it unlocked, he pushed it open and stepped inside. Sheriff Truscott sat at a desk. Startled, he dropped papers he had been reading and jumped to his feet. Andy made several strides, stopping so close that he could have reached across the desk and grabbed the sheriff by his shirt. Truscott was not wearing his pistol. It and its belt and holster lay at the edge of the desk. He made no move to reach them.

Andy summoned the strongest voice he had. "You don't need that gun. We're Rangers, and we're here on official business."

The lawman seemed slow to gather his wits. "I know you. You and your partner Brackett was the ones helped my prisoner get aloose."

"We had nothin' to do with that. I think you know it. Now you've got Farley Brackett locked up here on false charges. This is Rusty Shannon. Him and me, we've come to get Farley."

"That's easy said."

"Either we leave here with him or you'll have the state adjutant general and his headquarters Rangers down here. You'll feel like you been tromped by a buffalo herd."

Truscott's face reddened as he struggled for a reply. "Everybody and his damned dog has been tryin' to tell me what to do lately."

Andy had bitten off a big chunk with his bluff, but there was no backing down now. "What do you say, Sheriff? Do you turn him loose or do we go in and take him?"

Big'un Hopper walked in from the back room where the cells were. "What in the hell's goin' on out here?"

Truscott pointed his chin at Andy and Rusty. "These men are Rangers."

Big'un grunted. "I know them. That young one anyway." He pointed at Andy. "I can spot a Ranger half a mile away. Further sometimes."

Truscott said, "They've come for Brackett."

Big'un's jaw dropped. "You better not let them have him. Uncle Judd would bellow like a bull."

Judd. Andy remembered that was the judge's given name.

Judd Hopper had survived the hazards of the vendetta to become patriarch of the clan.

Truscott turned on Big'un with sarcasm. "Maybe your Uncle Judd would like to come talk to these Rangers. They claim to have the state law behind them."

"Us Hoppers are the law here."

"Here, maybe, but nowheres else. You want Austin sendin' a force down here to poke around? Me and you and your uncle Judd would likely wind up in the penitentiary. And some of your other kin, besides."

"I say we ought to secede from the state of Texas like Texas done from the Union."

Truscott shook his head impatiently. "Big'un, I wish you was twice as smart and half as loud."

Rusty spoke for the first time. "You remember what happened to that other secession. Texas lost."

The deputy seemed to swell up to a couple of sizes larger. "I don't see but two of you."

Rusty said, "We're Rangers. Two is enough."

Truscott looked away from the big deputy. "I guess we can give up the Ranger. We still got Jayce's woman."

Big'un said, "And givin' her three meals a day at county expense. You know what I favor givin' her." He turned into the light. Andy noticed a ragged cut and discoloration around his right eye.

The sheriff snapped, "I told you to stay out of her cell. She gave you just what you had comin'."

"Yeah, but I'd have given her somethin' too if you hadn't come in there raisin' hell. I'd show her again why they call me Big'un."

Truscott's eyes betrayed concern as he glanced at Andy and Rusty. "Damn you, Big'un, keep talkin' and some folks in this town will peel your hide with a horsewhip. Won't matter if you *are* a Hopper."

Andy had an ugly mental image of Big'un forcing himself on Flora Landon, or trying to. Fighting down his anger, he demanded, "Now, what about Farley Brackett?"

The sheriff gave Hopper a go-to-hell look. "Go on, tattle to Uncle Judd, but I don't care to have the Texas Rangers on my neck. I'm givin' them Brackett."

Big'un scowled. "You'd better hold on to that woman. We ain't done with her."

"Don't you be tryin' to tell me what to do, even if you are the judge's pet nephew. Yes, we'll keep her for now. I'm spreadin' the word that I'm willin' to trade. If Jayce Landon will come and surrender himself, I'll let his wife go."

Big'un's square jaw dropped. "You wouldn't do that."

"Damn right I'd do it. We ain't all lost our sense of decency."

Big'un glared. "You're a poor excuse for a Hopper."

"I ain't a Hopper at all. I made the mistake of marryin' one, but my name is still Truscott. And I'm still the sheriff of this county."

"We'll fix that, come next election."

Andy told the sheriff, "Looks like you need to move to some county where there ain't any Hoppers."

"I've thought about it. A lot." Truscott jerked his head as a signal to Andy and Rusty. "Come on back."

A set of keys lay on top of the desk. Big'un grabbed them to keep them from Truscott. "If I was runnin' this office, a lot of things would be different."

Truscott jerked the keys from Big'un's hand. "You ain't, no matter how many times you kiss Uncle Judd's ass." He unlocked the door to the cell block. "Brackett, you got company."

A blanket hung in front of one cell. Andy realized it was a concession to Flora Landon's privacy. The builders of the jail had not considered female prisoners. From behind the blanket came a woman's angry voice. "Oscar Truscott, if you let Big'un in this cell again I swear I'll kill him. Even if you hang me for it."

Truscott said, "I've told you I'm sorry, Flora. If he ever tries it again I'm liable to kill him myself."

Rusty vented his anger. "A man who would abuse a helpless woman ought to be shot. Or at least tarred, feathered, and run out of the county on a rail."

Andy suspected Rusty was thinking about Josie Monahan.

The sheriff said, "Whatever else you might say about Flora, you can't call her helpless. She fights like a cornered wildcat."

Rusty added, "Big'un ought to be *in* jail instead of helpin' run it. I don't see how you can keep him as a deputy."

"The judge don't give me no choice. I have to try and keep peace in the family. Most of the Hoppers think Flora deserves anything that happens to her. I've thought about shuckin' the whole business and leavin' here for good."

From inside another cell came Farley's grumpy voice: "I'd be willin' to pay for your train ticket."

Farley stood hunched, one hand gripping a bar to steady himself. He seemed not to see well. "Who's that out yonder? If it's Big'un come to beat on me again . . ."

Truscott said, "It's a couple of Rangers, fixin' to take you out of jail. And out of the county, I hope."

Farley squinted to recognize Andy and Rusty. "Badger Boy, you took your sweet time gettin' here."

Farley's face was bruised and skinned, one eye swollen almost shut. Andy turned angrily on the sheriff. "How could you let somebody do that to him?"

"Like I said, I don't call all the shots. I can't be here all the time."

Farley's good eye seemed afire. "You don't try any too

hard. When that good woman was hollerin' her head off, you was awful slow in comin'."

"She took pretty good care of herself."

"But if she'd been a weaker woman, Big'un would've got what he went in there for."

Truscott unlocked Farley's cell and pulled the iron door open. Its hinges squealed. "Come on out. You're leavin'."

Farley was unsteady but waved off Andy's instinctive move to help him. "They ain't managed to cripple me yet." He held one hand to his ribs, where he had taken the bullet.

Andy demanded of Truscott, "Have you had a doctor come and look at him?"

"Once, when we first got him here. He gave old Doc such a cussin' that he won't come back."

Farley muttered, "Damned quack done me more harm than good. Like to've killed me, pokin' with his fingers. Then Big'un come and tried to finish the job."

In the outer office, Big'un watched darkly as the sheriff took Farley's belongings from a desk drawer. They amounted to little: a pocketknife, a few coins, a leather wallet. Farley looked in the wallet and grunted, "Empty."

Truscott shrugged. "There's people in and out of here all the time. I can't watch everybody."

Farley turned to Andy and Rusty. "Oscar stays out of the office a right smart, like he don't want to know everything that's goin' on. And what does go on around here would gag a buzzard." He gave Big'un a blistering look.

Big'un declared, "If it was up to me you'd stay in yonder and rot."

Farley pointedly ignored him. "I had a six-shooter. I ain't leavin' this place without it."

Reluctantly Truscott opened another drawer and withdrew a pistol, belt, and holster. "It's empty. Leave it that way as long as you're in this county."

Farley strapped the belt around his waist. He checked the pistol and found it empty of cartridges as the sheriff had said. He took a step toward Big'un. "If this was loaded I'd shoot you right now."

"You might try. Once."

"Even unloaded, it's heavy enough to make a hell of a weapon. If I wasn't inclined to be peaceful I'd hit you up beside the head with it, like this." He swung the pistol so quickly that Big'un had no time to dodge. The heavy barrel struck just behind the deputy's temple. Big'un went to his knees.

Farley said, "It's a good thing I'm of a forgivin' nature. If I wasn't, I'd hit you again, like this." He swung the pistol and knocked Big'un to the floor. He gave the sheriff a challenging look. "Any charges?"

Truscott made a poor effort to hide a smile. "I reckon not. But get out of here before he comes around."

Andy and Rusty hustled Farley outside. Rusty said, "If you'd hit him one more time you'd probably be up for murder."

"He deserved it. What a roastin' he's got comin' when the devil gets ahold of him. And the sooner the better."

Andy asked, "Do you think you're strong enough to ride?"

"I'm strong enough, but I ain't goin' nowhere. I'm stayin' right here till I see that poor woman set loose."

Andy said, "That 'poor woman' sounded pretty strong to me."

"Not strong enough to keep beatin' off the likes of Big'un. She took him by surprise the first time. Next time won't be as easy."

"I heard the sheriff tell him not to try it again."

"Oscar and Big'un hate one another's guts, but Oscar ain't goin' to stay and face him in a showdown. He'd leave town before he'd stand up to Judge Hopper and the rest of his kinfolks."

Andy said, "This Uncle Judd must be a ring-tailed panther."

Farley said, "He came into the jail once and looked me over like I was a beef bein' dragged to the slaughter. I could see why folks are scared of him. Even Big'un."

"But they're kin."

"Big'un has got plenty to be scared of besides Judd Hopper. When the Landons hear what he tried to do to Flora, he'll be lucky to see another sunrise. I'm stayin' here and make sure the word gets out."

Rusty said, "The Rangers aren't supposed to get tangled up in personal feuds unless there's a killin'."

Farley's lips pinched together. "There'll *be* a killin'. It'll be Big'un's."

They took their horses to the livery barn. The hostler seemed hesitant at first to accept them but softened when Rusty offered him money. "Havin' you-all in my wagon yard is like standin' in a storm with a lightnin' rod in my hand." He focused his interest on Farley. "I figured if you ever came out of that jail it'd be feet first. Big'un was braggin' that he'd see to it."

Farley said, "Big'un ain't seein' anything real clear right now."

The hostler seemed to pick up on Farley's implication. "The Landons would give you a medal if you was to put Big'un's lights out. Even a Hopper or two might chip in."

"I didn't put his lights out. I just turned the wick down a ways."

"That'll tickle a lot of people who ain't even kin to the Landons." The man paused, reflecting. "It ain't fair to put all the blame on Big'un, though. Jayce shot his brother Ned. You wouldn't believe it, lookin' at Big'un now, but as a young'un he was the runt of the litter. Other boys picked on him all the time. It's no wonder he got mean. Once he started comin' into his growth, he got over bein' a runt but he never got over bein' mean."

Andy said, "I suppose he paid back the boys that had picked on him?"

"He's still doin' it. One of them was Oscar Truscott."

Farley gave the hostler a minute's speculative study. "I don't suppose you're the type that spreads gossip."

"Not me. Gossip is a sin."

"If the Landons was to hear what I'm about to tell you, there's no tellin' what they might do." He proceeded to describe Big'un's attempted assault on Flora Landon.

The stableman listened with rapt interest, his eyes wide. He shook his head and clucked in sympathy for the woman. "Nobody likes Big'un very much, not even some of his kin. This would sure rip his britches if it was to get out."

"I'm tellin' you in strict confidence."

"It won't go no further."

The stableman led the horses away to turn them loose in a corral. Farley made a grim smile. "By sundown the story will be all over town and halfway across the county."

Andy said, "It's like you painted a target on Big'un."

"Right between his eyes."

{ ELEVEN }

Lige Tennyson surveyed the small town from a bend in the road a quarter mile away. He looked as if he had ordered whiskey and been given milk. "I'm disappointed.

I thought Hopper's Crossing would be a lot bigger than this."

Scooter echoed his misgivings. "Don't look like enough of a place for people to fight a feud over."

"They ain't fightin' it over just the town. Once there's been blood spilt, a feud don't have to be over anything else in particular, just blood. Other reasons don't count anymore."

"You really think they'll pay you to fight for one side or the other?"

"It's been nothin' but amateurs so far. I figured somebody'd be willin' to hire a professional. At least I thought so till I saw how puny a town they've got. Well, I'll ride on in and look things over. Worst come to worst, I can always visit the bank, if they've got one. But there may not be twenty dollars of real money in the whole shebang."

"Want me to come with you, Pa?"

"No, you shade up in them trees yonder and wait for me. The laws are still lookin' for a man and a boy travelin' together. It's better if you stay out here where it's safe and don't cause no notice."

Scooter accepted without argument. His father had demonstrated early on this trip how suddenly he could explode into a rage, though his temper usually cooled as rapidly as it flared.

Lige removed his feet from the stirrups and stretched his legs without dismounting. The long ride had stiffened him. "Be a good boy and maybe I can bring you some candy."

"I'd be tickled, Pa."

Lige looked back once and was pleased to see that Scooter had ridden that paddle-footed old horse into the shade and had dismounted to rest and wait, as he had been told. He smiled and thought how lucky he was to have such a good and obedient son. During his years of incarceration he had worried a lot about what would become of the motherless boy. He had not left him in the best of hands, letting him fall in with the no-accounts Arliss and Brewster, but he had had little choice. He had feared that the authorities would put Scooter into some bleak orphan's home if he stayed around where they would notice him.

That was the way with government, always messing in where nobody had invited it, he thought. Life would be a lot less complicated if there wasn't some law to get in a man's way every time he tried to turn a dollar or do something that pleasured him.

A good boy deserved a better horse. Lige had it in mind that when they left here and started up toward Indian territory he would watch for a better mount and do a little quiet trading. It was a father's duty to provide for his son. Nobody was apt to think enough of one horse to trail them all the way to Red River and beyond.

The town was as inconsequential close up as it had appeared from a distance. The residential area consisted of no more than a dozen houses, most built of rough-sawed pine lumber. The main street, actually only a wide wagon road, had a handful of business buildings: a general store, a cotton gin, a blacksmith shop, a church, a livery barn with several log corrals behind it. He noticed right away that there was no bank.

Scooter had been right. It was not worth fighting over.

He stopped in front of the general store and tied his horse to a hitching rail strung between two posts, its rawhide strips almost rotted through. A mongrel dog lying in the shade of the storefront made a halfhearted effort to get up and move out of the way, then settled back down. Lige had to step over him.

A couple of elderly loafers sat on a bench, watching him

with a curiosity that told him the town did not have so many visitors that they went unnoticed.

He remarked, "Not too busy around here today. I thought Hopper's Crossing would be a livelier place."

An elderly man with a long gray beard and a cane said, "Hopper's Crossing is. But this is Landon's Flat. Hopper's Crossing is about six miles further up the road."

Lige felt relieved. Maybe the trip hadn't been a waste after all. "My mistake. I didn't know this place was here."

"Neither do many other people. That's the trouble. Now, if we'd won that fight over the courthouse . . ."

The other man looked as if he had just bitten down on a sour persimmon. "Spilt milk, Homer. No use hashin' over somethin' that happened a long time ago."

The man named Homer reacted with impatience. "There's plenty others still hashin' it over. That's what the feud is supposed to be about, even if most folks have forgot."

Mention of the feud brought Lige to full attention. "What do you mean?"

The sour-faced one said, "Been thirty-forty years ago. There was an election to decide which place was goin' to be the county seat. See that big empty lot over yonder?" He pointed an arthritis-twisted finger. "That was goin' to be our courthouse square. But them crooks over in Hopper's Crossing voted more than once and throwed in their horses and dogs. Stole the courthouse from us, is what they did. Us Landons put up a squawk, and the shootin' started. There's more of them Hoppers than there is of us, and they own most of the money."

Lige saw his chance. "Maybe what you-all need is a real gunfighter, somebody who knows what needs doin' and how to do it."

"A man like that would cost a lot. Like I told you, most of the money is over in Hopper's Crossing with their names on it. Bein' the county seat, their town prospered while ours . . . well, you can see for yourself."

Lige's first reaction was sympathy, but his practical side did not tolerate it for long. He hadn't come all this way to donate his services. He had come for the best reason he knew of: money.

He asked, "If you was to want to shoot the top man of that Hopper bunch, who would it be?"

The two old men looked at each other. The sour one said, "Judge Judd Hopper is the head of the clan. But if it was me doin' it, I think I'd shoot Big'un Hopper first. The judge runs the family, but Big'un is the one he sends out to do the dirty work. He enjoys his job."

"Where would a man find Big'un Hopper, if he was of a mind to look?"

"He's a deputy under Sheriff Oscar Truscott. He fiddles to the judge's tune, though. He don't pay much attention to Oscar, nor anybody else besides old Judd. Come to a showdown, he might not listen to Judd either. He's built like a bull and got a head like one."

Lige said, "Sounds to me like he'd be the one to kill, all right." But he was thinking Big'un would be the one to see about a gun-toting job. It was evident if he was to make any real money out of this situation, it would have to come from the Hoppers. Teaming up with the Landons would be like fishing in a dry hole.

He was about out of tobacco, and he had promised Scooter some candy. He remembered how much he had liked candy when he was a boy and how seldom he ever had any. Life was going to be better for his son than it had been for him, no matter what Lige had to do to make it happen.

Always in the back of his mind when he entered a place like this general store was the feasibility of emptying its cash box. He dismissed the idea in this case. From the looks of things he wouldn't get much more than tobacco money. He would stir up all the John Laws within a hundred miles and almost certainly spoil his chance of profiting from the Hopper-Landon feud. If prison had taught him nothing else, it had taught him patience.

The clerk seemed grateful for even so small a sale. Lige thanked him and turned back toward the door, thinking that Scooter was the only one who profited much from this trip. At least he would be getting some candy. On reflection Lige realized the knowledge he had picked up was likely to be of good use. At least he knew not to waste his time with the Landons. He would try the Hoppers instead. Failing that, the Hoppers' town must have a bank to hold all that money.

The two loafers had not moved from their place on the bench. Homer said, "Didn't take you long to do business."

Lige said, "Ain't much business to be done around here. That dog looks about as busy as anybody in town."

Like the old loafers, the dog had not moved.

Scooter waited in the shade of the trees as he had been told. Lige handed him the sack of candy. "Don't eat all of that at once. It'll make you sick at your stomach. Good things need to be stretched out so you enjoy them longer."

"Thanks, Pa." Scooter took a piece of hard candy from the sack. He held it up and stared appreciatively at it for a minute before he put it in his mouth. He talked around the candy. "I don't reckon you saw a bank?"

"Takes money for a place to have a bank. This wasn't the town I thought it was. We'll do better in the next one."

"We goin' there today?"

Lige looked up at the sun. "We still got some daylight ahead of us. Ain't no use wastin' it."

He set his horse into an easy trot. Scooter followed,

crunching the candy with his teeth. The sound made Lige's skin tingle. His own tobacco-worn teeth would crumble if he put them through that torture.

He said, "I sure wish we could give these horses a good bait of oats. They've earned it, bringin' us this far."

The candy made Scooter's words sound garbled. "Oats cost money, don't they, Pa?"

"We'll have money when we get through with our business here. Them old fellers back yonder told me the Hoppers have done right good. I figure they'll be willin' to fork over for gettin' some of the Landons out of their way."

"You'd kill them people, Pa?"

"You've got to look at it from my side, son. Them people don't mean nothin' to us. They're goin' to kill one another anyway. I don't see nothin' wrong if I push things a little. I'm bettin' the Hoppers would be glad to keep their hands clean by turnin' their dirty washin' over to somebody else. Wouldn't be nothin' the law could do to them, and me and you would be long gone."

"Them Landons are liable to shoot back."

"The bigger the risk, the bigger the gain. Even marryin' an Indian woman and gettin' head-right land, we'll need some start-up money in the territory."

Scooter asked, "You reckon you'll make a good farmer, Pa? Been a long time since you done much of it."

"I growed up with my hands shaped like a plow handle. It's a good life."

He had not always thought so. Years ago he had decided that harvesting banks and prosperous storekeepers was better than picking cotton. Graying hair and arthritis now draped a nostalgic curtain over fading memories of a sore back and bleeding fingers.

They stopped in a stand of timber half a mile from

Hopper's Crossing. "We'll make camp here. We've got the river for water and plenty of deadfall wood for a cook fire. Ain't nobody liable to pay us much mind."

Scooter asked uneasily, "You goin' to visit the bank, Pa?"

"Maybe later, when I'm done with the other business. Right now I'm goin' in to stable my horse awhile and get myself a haircut. I want to find out what direction the wind blows."

Scooter did not understand about the wind. It was coming out of the south. He could tell that without having to ask anybody.

Lige said, "Ain't no place better than a barbershop or a livery stable to find out what's goin' on in a town. I want to learn more about that feud and be sure who to talk to about offerin' my services."

Scooter seemed resigned to being left alone. "I'll keep out of sight, like before."

"I'm sorry, son, but once we get up into the territory, there won't be no need for you to hide anymore. There won't be no Texas law up there. We'll ride together, proud as two peacocks in the sunshine."

Lige sought out the livery barn first. The stable hand met him at the open doors of the barn.

"Want to put your horse up for the night?"

"I won't be stayin' that long, but I'd like him to have a bucket of oats. He's been rode a long ways, and he's kind of drawed."

"So are you," the stable hand said. "If you're hungry there's a pretty good eatin' place up the street yonder, toward the courthouse. How far have you come? Where'd you start from?"

"Over east." That was the opposite of the truth, but somebody toting a badge might come along and ask questions of the liveryman.

Lige figured he had come to the right place. This man looked like a talker, and Lige had come to listen.

Lige was fairly sure he recognized Big'un Hopper as the deputy sheriff walked out of the jailhouse. He had the stableman's description and his own memory of the lawman who visited the Ranger camp on the San Saba. Hopper was one of the largest men Lige had ever seen. He had a bandage wrapped around his head, a present from an angry Ranger, the stableman had said. Lige approached him warily, for he could not be sure how seriously Hopper took his responsibilities as a lawman.

"I expect you'd be Big'un Hopper."

From Lige's viewpoint the deputy towered like the cupola atop the courthouse. He outweighed Lige by at least a hundred pounds. Big'un took a belligerent stance. "I don't know you. Give me a reason why I ought to even talk to you."

"I think I could be of service."

"I don't need no ditches dug nor fields plowed, and we generally got a prisoner or two to sweep out the jailhouse."

"Them things ain't my specialty anyway. I do most of my work with this." He dropped a hand to the butt of his pistol. "I hear you Hoppers have got enemies."

Hopper showed a flicker of cautious interest. "Even if we do, what business is it of yours?"

"I could handle them for you at so much per head. All you'd have to do would be to point them out. I'd lay them out. Wouldn't be nothin' the law could hang on your family because I ain't no kin to any of you."

Hopper's interest grew. "Let's go in the jailhouse yonder and talk about it."

The thought of entering a jail gave Lige a chill. "If it's all the same to you, I'd rather we went someplace else. Someplace where nobody would see or hear us."

Hopper pointed to a small frame building with peeling red paint. "The blacksmith is shoein' horses out of town. His shop is private enough if you don't mind a horse or two."

The place smelled of iron and burned coal. Lige walked through it, checking the horse stalls, then peering out the back door to be sure no one was near enough to overhear the conversation.

Hopper asked, "Sayin' I was to agree to somethin', how do I know you could do the job? You don't look like no notorious gunfighter to me. I don't even know your name."

"For now, just call me Bill Smith."

Hopper seemed amused. "Smith? We've entertained a lot of your kinfolks in that jail yonder, one time and another."

"If I was to tell you my real name you'd recognize it. But I don't think I ought to, seein' that badge you're wearin'."

"This badge ain't tattooed on my skin. I know when to look the other way." Hopper's face twisted in a minute's silent study. "I'll give you a chance, but I don't want you seen with me or any other Hoppers. I don't want folks to make any connection."

"I don't care to have too many people see me anyway. I expect there's a reward out. They might get notions."

"I know an old farmhouse nobody is livin' in. You can stay there. When I've got somethin' lined up, I'll come and talk to you."

"I'll be needin' some supplies for me and my boy."

"Boy?" Hopper's eyebrows went up.

"My son. He's travelin' with me."

For a moment Hopper seemed to reconsider. "That's an extra witness. It's a complication I hadn't figured for." A calculating light came into his eyes. "Travelin' with a boy.

Seems to me I've seen a flier." He snapped his fingers. "Timson. Wanted for bank robbery."

Lige corrected him. "Tennyson. At least you know a little about my reputation."

Hopper smiled as if he had just drawn four aces. "I believe you'll work out perfect." He drew some bills from his pocket. "This ought to tide you over for a week or two. Now here's how you get out to the place." He squatted on his heels and drew a map in the sandy floor.

Hopper left the shop first. Lige waited a bit so no casual observer was likely to realize they had been together. He moved to the shop door, then took two fast steps backward into the shadows. Surprise quickened his pulse. He could hardly believe what he saw: the two Rangers named Rusty and Andy and a third man who limped along, hunched over as if hurt.

Involuntarily he held his breath until the burning in his lungs forced him to expel it.

How in the hell could they have tracked us so far?

He felt trapped. He had been confident he had shaken off pursuit. Now here were these damned Rangers, so close he could hit them with a rock. He retreated to the back of the shop, where the shadows were darkest, and watched as the three passed the front door. He barely dared breathe. For a fleeting moment he entertained the notion of shooting them while they weren't looking. With a little luck he might get all three before they had time to realize what was happening.

But he dismissed the idea. Back-shooting had never been his style. Anyway, chances were that at least one would survive long enough to put a bullet in him. What would Scooter do then? The boy would be lost if his father failed to show up. Lige gradually calmed and tried to think rationally.

There was no question of staying in town to buy supplies. He had to get out of this place as quickly as he could without letting the Rangers see him. Perhaps they were not after him in the first place. Perhaps something else had brought them here, far from their camp on the San Saba. If that was the case, they would not be expecting to see him. He intended to make certain they did not.

He had tied his horse behind the bank. He did not know why he had chosen that spot except that something in his nature always seemed to draw him to banks. He eased back to the front door so he could watch the Rangers. He saw them enter the livery stable and disappear into its darkness. He went out through the back door of the blacksmith shop and hurried to his horse. He left town in a slow trot to avoid attracting attention. He looked over his shoulder until Hopper's Crossing was well behind him, then set his horse into a lope.

It was a point of pride for Lige that his son watched his surroundings closely. He seemed to see everything that went on around him. Scooter walked out a little way to meet his father.

"Thought you was fixin' to get a haircut."

"Changed my mind. Didn't get supplies, either. I saw a couple of your Ranger friends, Andy and Rusty."

Scooter's eyes opened wide. "They after us?"

"Could be, or maybe we've just fallen into a run of bad luck. I didn't stay around to ask them."

"What'll we do, Pa?"

"We'll ride back to that last town and buy what we need. Then we'll go to a farm a feller told me about. He said it's a good place to stay out of sight till I'm called on to do a job."

The farmhouse was about as Big'un had described it, no better and no worse. It appeared not to have had permanent tenants for several years. Broken shingles on the roof would let water leak into the house when rain fell. A front windowpane was broken.

Scooter eyed the place with misgivings. "It'll take a week to clean this place up."

"We may not be here a week. At least this place is mostly in the open. We can see anybody who comes this way."

"You lookin' for somebody to come after us?"

"With the Rangers, you never know."

But Lige was worried not only about the Rangers. He did not entirely trust Big'un Hopper. The odds were that the man had been on the level about hiring him for a job. But after all, he *was* a deputy sheriff. He had recognized Lige and remembered he was wanted for bank robbery. Perhaps he was simply setting Lige up so he could claim the reward, if any was offered.

Well, Lige Tennyson had not lived this long by trusting to luck. He had learned long ago that those who keep a hole card and watch out for themselves are usually the luckiest.

"We'll fool them. They'll expect us to be in the house. But we'll camp in the barn back yonder. If the wrong people come, we can ride out the back and be in the timber before they know what happened."

{ TWELVE }

Andy thought the doctor was going to slam the door in their faces when he saw Farley Brackett. He stood with hands pressed against the jamb on both sides, blocking the doorway. He was a little gray-bearded man with rolled-up sleeves and an apron stained by old blood specks that never washed out. He looked as if he had just smelled a skunk.

He said, "Last time I treated that man he cussed me like a mule skinner. If he's not dying, take him to somebody else."

Andy said, "His wound is tryin' to heal, but we don't like the color around the edges. We'd take it as a favor if you'd look at him."

Reluctantly the doctor drew back from the door. "First cussword I hear out of him, I'll put a twitch on his nose the way I'd do an unruly horse."

Farley growled, "I told you he's just a horse doctor."

Andy said, "Be watchful what you say. He might decide he needs to cut on you, and I'll bet he could make it hurt."

The doctor said, "Your damned right I can. How did this disagreeable son of a bitch ever get to be a Ranger?"

Andy decided it might be wise to let Farley answer that for himself, but Farley had nothing to say except, "Let's get on with it."

He took off his shirt and shed the long underwear from his arms and shoulders. The doctor peered closely at the healing wound, then poked it with the tip of his finger. Farley shouted, and the doctor grinned.

"A little angry around the edges," he said, "but it's coming along. I wouldn't worry about it."

Farley said, "Of course you wouldn't. It ain't yours."

Andy asked, "Do you think he can ride?"

"He can if he's willing to put up with a lot of hurt and the risk of bleeding again. If it was me I'd wait a few days before I started off on any long trip back to wherever it is you-all come from."

Farley pulled up his underwear and put on his shirt. He moved gingerly, trying to minimize the pain.

Andy asked, "What do we owe you, Doctor?"

"I've got a special deal for Rangers since it's their duty

to protect us even if they have to shoot us to do it. My services are free the first time. After that it's regular rates. A man dumb enough to get shot a second time doesn't deserve any favors from me."

"Thanks. Maybe we can send you some payin' customers."

"You already have, the night you two knuckleheads faced that mob in front of an empty jailhouse."

Andy tried to help Farley down the front step, but Farley motioned irritably for him to back off. "Don't treat me like I'm crippled. If whoever shot me is watchin', I want him to know that he didn't do but half a job."

"What if he tries to finish it?"

"I'm hopin' he does. I'd like to return the favor."

Rusty had not gone with them to the doctor's house. He had talked little during the time they had been in Hopper's Crossing. His gaze was often vacant, his thoughts seemingly far away. His concern over Farley's wound had been that of one Ranger for another, not one of personal friendship. His relationship with Farley had been uneasy since the time Farley's transgressions against Reconstruction authorities had brought trouble to Rusty's door.

He was brushing his horse when Andy and Farley entered the stable. He gave Farley only a fleeting glance, and he asked no questions. "I'm thinkin' about goin' on back to the San Saba," he said. "The captain's probably wonderin' what's become of us."

Andy said, "The doctor says it might be better if Farley doesn't ride just yet."

"He stands a good chance of gettin' shot again in this place. If he doesn't want to go stay with his mother and sister, he can batch at my farm till he's healed up better. I doubt that the Hoppers would want him bad enough to hunt him down over there."

Farley said, "I'm in no hurry to leave here. I want to see Big'un get what's comin' to him."

Rusty gave him a grim look. "Suit yourself, but it's time me and Andy was leavin'."

Farley lay down on a steel cot the liveryman had dragged out for him. "If the captain complains, tell him he can fire me."

Andy pointed out, "Without bein' a Ranger you'd have no authority to enforce the law."

"The law ain't enforced much here anyway."

Late in the afternoon the stableman came into the building and stopped to blink until his eyes adjusted to the dim light. He looked behind him before he approached the three Rangers. "I ain't gettin' myself mixed up in you-all's troubles, but I got a message for you."

Andy took the lead. "What about?"

The stableman looked back again. He lowered his voice. "Walter Landon came to my house. Said he was speakin' for his brother Jayce. He heard about the sheriff's promise to let Flora Landon go if Jayce would turn himself in."

Farley sat up on the edge of the cot. Pain from the quick movement made him wince. "Anything to get her out of that jail and away from Big'un."

Rusty asked, "What's this got to do with us?"

"You Rangers delivered Jayce here in the first place. He'd like you-all to be the ones to do it again."

Rusty said, "He wouldn't need us to deliver him. He could just deliver himself."

"He knows one or another of them Hoppers would kill him before he ever saw the inside of the jailhouse. But if you-all were guardin' him, they might not try."

Andy said, "Maybe they would and maybe they wouldn't. If they didn't, they'd just wait till he was in jail, then break in like they tried to do the last time."

"At least his wife would be free. If he got killed before he went into the jail, Oscar Truscott might not feel like he had to live up to his promise about Flora."

Andy frowned. "Jayce seems to've made up his mind he's goin' to get killed one way or another."

Rusty's eyes were cold. "After all, he committed murder." Since Josie's death he had lost sympathy for criminals who had blood on their hands. He had that much in common with Farley.

Andy argued, "In a way he's still our responsibility. It was Rangers who caught him and Rangers who brought him here."

Farley said, "He's set to hang anyway. A good, quick bullet would be better than chokin' at the end of a rope."

Andy turned back to the stableman. "How do we go about meetin' up with Jayce?"

"After dark a couple of his kinfolks will come in the back way lookin' for you. Be saddled and ready. They don't want you bringin' any guns."

Rusty said, "We're not goin' anyplace without guns."

"You'll have to talk that over with them, not me. I'm just deliverin' the message."

Andy looked at Rusty. "You and me. Farley's not in shape to be ridin' anywhere."

Farley said, "Like hell." He rose to his feet but sat down again, sucking in a sharp breath and bringing his hand up to the wound. "It's just as well. I don't want to look at Jayce, anyhow, after what he's put his good woman through."

Rusty asked, "Can we trust these Landons?"

The stableman considered. "Their word is good. Their only bad failin' is that they like to kill Hoppers. It's brought a right smart of grief down on them."

Rusty said, "It's our job to bring Jayce in, not make deals with him. But I suppose it won't do any harm to talk."

The stableman looked behind him. "If anybody asks, I had nothin' to do with this. Wouldn't be healthy for me to get on the Hoppers' bad side."

Andy and Rusty delayed saddling their horses until full dark in case some Hopper might be keeping an eye on them. They waited inside the barn's back door. After a time Andy heard a gate latch move. From outside, a voice spoke just above a whisper.

"Rangers? You-all in there?"

Andy looked to Rusty to answer, for he was senior. Rusty said, "We're here. Who are you?"

"Walter Landon, but that don't matter. Are you ready for a ride?"

"We've been waitin' for you." Rusty opened the back door and led his horse out. Andy followed. He saw two men, though in the darkness he could not make out their faces.

Rusty asked, "Where's Jayce Landon?"

Walter Landon's voice was young. "Not far. We'd rather you left those guns here."

"The guns go or we don't."

Landon yielded with a shrug. "Then give us your word you won't do anything against Jayce till he's had a chance to talk with you."

"That's fair enough. Lead out."

They rode about an hour. Andy realized the two men led them in a zigzag pattern to confuse them should they try to retrace their path in the daylight. But he had a good sense of direction. He knew they traveled generally northwestward.

A dark farmhouse loomed ahead. Landon hooted in the manner of an owl. From the house came an answer. No real owl would have been fooled, Andy thought. Nor would any Comanche, even given their dread of owls.

Landon warned, "Don't neither of you make any suspicious moves. Jayce is mighty edgy."

Andy did not doubt that Jayce had a rifle or six-shooter trained on them. It did not seem probable that he would have summoned Andy and Rusty out here only to kill them. Nevertheless, Andy felt cold.

He saw a movement on the dark porch and heard a voice he recognized as Jayce's. "Get down and tie your horses, Rangers. We'll parley out here. The house is hot and dark, and I don't favor lightin' no lamp. You sure none of the Hoppers followed you?"

Walter said, "We were careful."

Jayce asked Andy, "How's your head? Too bad I had to club you that time, but I needed to try and get away."

"The swellin's long gone."

"Where's the Ranger that gave me a beatin' for it?"

"Farley Brackett is laid up. Took a bullet tryin' to keep a mob from breakin' into jail and killin' you. We didn't know you'd already lit a shuck."

Jayce showed no sign that he felt any guilt, or any sympathy for Farley. He turned to Rusty. "Don't believe I know you. You *are* a Ranger, ain't you?"

Rusty made no effort at sounding friendly. "Name's Shannon. I've been a Ranger off and on since before the war. The *other* war."

"Damned poor way to make a livin', but I guess everybody has got to be somethin'."

"What do you consider yourself to be?"

"A Landon first, then a Texan. I shot Yankees durin' the war, but I was fightin' Hoppers when I was a kid."

"The last killin' you did wasn't any fair fight."

"We didn't always fight the Yankees fair, either. Main thing was to win. Polite gentlemen generally die first."

Andy could see the exchange drifting from the subject at

hand. He said, "We didn't come here to talk about who's to blame. We're supposed to talk about you tradin' places with your wife in jail."

Jayce's voice hardened. "I heard about Big'un and her. I've got to get her out of there, whatever it costs."

Walter argued, "Givin' yourself up is an awful price to pay, even for Flora. You know how long you'll last in that jail. And even if you lived till the trial, Judge Hopper would see you hang before the sun went down."

Jayce shook his head. "I don't see no other way."

Rusty said, "There might be one. What do you-all think of Sheriff Truscott?"

Jayce's voice was sharp. "He's a Hopper-in-law, but he's a cut above the others. He's about as fair as you'll find amongst that tribe."

Rusty nodded. "That's the impression I got. On the way out here I've been thinkin' about a deal we might put to him. We'd turn you in to the law but in another county."

"This county or some other, it ain't apt to make a lot of difference in the long run."

"If we can get you a change of venue, you'll at least have a fair trial in some court besides Judge Hopper's."

"A change of venue won't save my neck. Ned Hopper was a son of a bitch, and I killed him. I ain't denyin' it. I'd holler it from the roof of the courthouse." Jayce stared off into the darkness, weighing Rusty's proposition. "You got a place in mind?"

"Sheriff Tom Blessing is a good friend of mine. Whatever the outcome, he'll see to it that you're dealt a square hand."

Jayce stared into the darkness while he considered the proposition. "At least it'd be somebody besides a Hopper who put the rope around my neck." Jayce beckoned his kinsmen into the house. Andy could hear the low murmur of voices but could not make out what they were saying. When they returned to the porch Jayce said, "Go talk to Oscar Truscott. If he says yes, I'll surrender. Not to anybody else, just to you Rangers."

Rusty told Truscott they needed to talk to him in private. Truscott called to the jailer. He was not the same man who had been on duty the night of Jayce's escape. That unfortunate had prudently left town before daylight and had not been seen since. "Curly, go get yourself a drink. Maybe two of them. Don't be in a rush to come back."

The jailer gone, Truscott said, "I heard by the grapevine that you-all went out of town last night."

Rusty replied, "You must have eyes everywhere."

"I don't miss a lot."

"We had an interestin' visit with an acquaintance of yours."

"Jayce Landon? You didn't bring him in, though."

"No, but we worked out a deal for you." Rusty explained his idea about delivering Jayce to a more secure jail and seeking a change of venue.

Truscott frowned at first but gradually softened. "I know Tom Blessing. If he said it was fixin' to freeze on the Fourth of July, I'd carry my coat with me to the celebration."

"He'd take good care of your prisoner."

"I'm just wonderin' who'd take care of *me*. Things'd get ugly around here when Judge Hopper and Big'un and the rest got wind of what I'd done."

"If we handle it right, it'll be over with before they know."

"But I'd still be here afterward." Truscott mulled it over. His mustache began turning up in a tentative smile. "It'd probably lose me a wife, but she's took to sleepin' in another room anyhow, and her cookin' wouldn't tempt a hog." The smile broke into full bloom. "I'd love to see what it feels like to look the judge in the eye and tell him I'm through shinin' his boots. And I've wanted for a long time to poke Big'un in the eye with a sharp stick."

"When're you goin' to release Jayce's wife?"

"Right now, into your custody. She's been an albatross around my neck." Truscott reached into a drawer and withdrew a printed form. He dipped a pen into an inkwell and scribbled some lines. "Bring this back to me with Tom Blessing's signature on it, swearin' that he's got Jayce Landon locked up."

Rusty took the paper. "When it's all over you can catch up on your sleep."

"Not after the word gets out." Truscott led Rusty and Andy back to the cells. He said, "Gather your things, Flora. You're leavin'."

She remained hidden by the blanket that covered the front of her cell. Her voice was anxious. "What've you done to Jayce?"

"Ain't even seen him, but he's agreed to give himself up to these Rangers if I let you go."

She pulled the blanket aside, her eyes fearful. "You know he's got no chance if he comes back in here. I ain't lettin' you trade me for him."

Truscott told her that Jayce would be jailed in another county. She chewed her lip. "I'd rather see him run off to Mexico or someplace."

Rusty said, "He wouldn't do that, not and leave you in here. He's that much of a man, at least."

She declared, "He's a better man than any I see here."

Truscott said, "You better git while the gittin's good, Flora."

"I'll go, but if I get a chance to help Jayce get away I'll damned sure take it."

The sheriff grunted. "I don't doubt that." He unlocked the door. "I'll leave the blanket up. Likely nobody'll miss you before mornin'."

Flora came out carrying a small canvas bag. Her hair was disheveled, her dress wrinkled from sleeping in it. Truscott walked ahead of her and blew out the lamp in the front office. "You-all better go out the back door." He opened it cautiously and peered out into the night. "Looks clear."

Flora paused. "Oscar, for a Hopper-in-law, you're a better man than I thought." Then she was out the door.

The sheriff warned Rusty and Andy, "You-all better keep a close eye on her. She meant what she said about helpin' Jayce get away."

Rusty said, "You've got to respect a loyal wife."

"Jayce never deserved her. I can't see why she chose him over his brother Dick. There's no figurin' women."

Andy had not expected Truscott to release Flora so quickly, so they had not brought an extra horse for her. Andy put her up into his saddle. "I'll go back to the stable and get Farley's horse. He won't be needin' it for a while."

Rusty said, "While you do that I'll get her out of town, to where Walter Landon said he'd be waitin'."

"I'll find you."

In the stable, Farley arose stiffly and sat on the edge of his cot. He watched by lamplight while Andy saddled up. "You stealin' another horse from me, Badger Boy?"

Farley never would give up needling him about Long Red, Andy thought. "Call in the law if you want to."

Farley shook his head. "I can guess why you need him. Tell her not to use spurs. He's liable to throw her off."

* * *

At the edge of town Andy put Farley's horse into an easy lope. He caught up to Rusty and Flora before they reached the farmhouse where Jayce was supposed to be hiding.

Rusty asked, "Anybody see you?"

"Just Farley and the stable hand. They won't be talkin'."

Flora was still nervous about her husband. "This place where you're takin' Jayce, are you sure it's safe? Them Hoppers have got a long reach."

Rusty said, "If you're lookin' for an ironclad guarantee, there ain't any. But it'll be safer than that jail back yonder. There's not a better sheriff in Texas than Tom Blessing."

"From what I've seen of sheriffs, that ain't a strong recommendation."

"You've got to realize that savin' him from a lynchin' doesn't change things for him in the long run. He hasn't got much of a future either way."

She squared her shoulders. "Maybe. We'll see about that the first time somebody gets careless."

Walter and a couple of other men stepped down from the porch to meet them in the yard. The house was dark, but Andy could see a rifle in Walter's hands.

"That you, Flora?"

"It's me. Where's Jayce at?"

A figure stepped out from a black corner of the porch. "Right here, darlin' girl. Come see Papa."

Flora did not wait to be helped down from the horse. She slid out of the saddle and hurried to the porch as Jayce stepped to the ground. They embraced, then Jayce pushed her off to arm's length to look her over. "Are you all right?"

"Why wouldn't I be all right?"

"I heard about Big'un. I wanted to kill him."

"Him bein' bigger just makes it easier to hit him where it hurts the worst. I laid it on him good."

Andy grinned, remembering the bruises and cuts on Big'un's face. He was probably bruised in other places where it didn't show.

Rusty was impatient. "We better be movin'. No tellin' how soon before the Hoppers'll find out she's gone."

Jayce said, "I can't figure Oscar Truscott lettin' you go so easy."

"He trusted the Rangers. Bad as I hate to say it, you and me have got to do the same."

Jayce turned to Rusty. "You'll let her ride along with us, won't you?"

Rusty nodded. "It won't be safe for her here, at least till things cool off. Tom Blessing will see to it that nothin' happens to her."

Walter said, "Maybe some of us better ride along with you too."

Andy started to protest, but Rusty spoke up ahead of him. It seemed to Andy that he always did when something really important was at hand. "Andy and me are escort enough." Rusty's hand was on the butt of his six-shooter.

It would be easy for the Landons to overwhelm the two Rangers and set Jayce and Flora free. Andy suspected such a notion had prompted Landon's offer. Normal restrictions did not apply in family feuds. When survival was at stake, acts normally regarded as treachery were considered justified.

Flora told Walter, "I wish you'd let my daddy know that I've gone with Jayce."

"I'll see to it. We've got him hid. Big'un and his bunch might want to take it out on him when they see that they've lost you and Jayce both."

Andy saw no sign that any of the Landons followed as he and Rusty rode away with Jayce and Flora. But he slipped his pistol out of its holster and held it for the first couple of miles, just in case.

{ THIRTEEN }

The morning was far along when they rode up to the jail where Tom Blessing kept his office. Jayce surveyed the frame building with disapproval. "It don't look any stouter than the one over at Hopper's Crossing. At least that one's built of brick."

Rusty said, "They've talked for years about buildin' a better one, but the county's always short of money."

"Short or not, I'll bet the taxes ain't cheap."

"No, but there's still never enough money."

Andy looked toward the courthouse. It was his theory that the county's financial problems resulted mainly from leaky fingers. People normally tight with their own money were sometimes loose with other people's. In any case it made for interesting politics, each side promising to waste less than the other.

Tom looked up in surprise as Rusty and Andy ushered the Landons into his office. His expression showed that he recognized Jayce on sight.

Rusty said, "Brought you an early Christmas present. I know you didn't ask for it, but here it is."

Blessing studied Jayce with misgivings before looking back at Rusty. "You sure ain't Santy Claus. What do you want me to do with him?"

"Keep him away from the Hoppers till he can stand

trial. And we'll need to get him a change of venue out of old Judge Hopper's jurisdiction."

"I guess I can take care of the first part. You'll need to talk to a lawyer about the other." He looked at Flora, a question in his eyes.

Rusty said, "This is Jayce's wife. We need a safe place for her too."

"This jail ain't really fixed up for a woman. Any charges against her?"

"Not unless she tries to help Jayce get away. Again."

Tom thought about it. "She'd be good company for my wife out at the farm."

Flora objected. "I want to stay in town, where I can be close to Jayce."

Tom shrugged. "You can put up at Mrs. Smith's boardin'house. But if the Hoppers was to come lookin', it wouldn't be hard for them to find you there."

Flora's jaw set grimly. "It'll be their own fault if they do. They don't know how good a shot I am."

Andy wondered what she intended to shoot them with. She'd had no weapon when she left Truscott's custody, though one of the Landons could have slipped one to her later, in the darkness. Andy had checked Jayce to be sure he was unarmed, but he had not felt comfortable about putting hands on Flora. He did not intend to do it now. Some things had to be taken on faith, or at least on hope.

Tom said, "I'll need help guardin' Jayce. Can't be here twenty-four hours myself, and I've only got one deputy. If the Hoppers was to come down on us in force, one man couldn't stop them."

Rusty said, "Me and Andy. He's more our prisoner than he is yours anyway. I'll wire the captain for permission."

Tom nodded. "I'm obliged." He touched a finger to a

marked calendar behind his desk. "District judge is due to hold court here next week. I'd like to get Jayce on the docket as quick as I can. The sooner he's out of this jail, the better I'll feel."

Flora said, "If you-all would turn your backs for a minute or two, you wouldn't have to worry about guardin' Jayce. Him and me would be on our way to Mexico."

Rusty said, "I halfway wish we could, but that'd break our agreement with Sheriff Truscott."

Andy said, "And our oath as Rangers."

Jayce said, "Don't worry about it, darlin' girl. I ain't been hung yet. A lot can happen."

Tom frowned. "Don't be gettin' notions. It's been a long time since I shot a prisoner tryin' to escape. I didn't sleep for a week afterwards, but I done what I had to. I'd do it again."

Jayce's voice was full of irony. "I sure wouldn't want to cost you any sleep." He took Flora into his arms. "Us Landons have died of everything else, but there ain't none of us ever been hung. If things go my way, I'll send for you from Mexico. Or maybe South America. I hear it's mighty pretty down there. They pull fruit right off of the trees, and nobody has to work if they don't want to."

To Andy that sounded more like Preacher Webb's version of heaven. It seemed unlikely that Jayce Landon was going to end up in heaven, or anywhere close to it.

Tom got his keys and motioned toward the back room where the cells were. "Like I said, Rusty, you sure ain't no Santy Claus."

Sheriff Truscott glanced up from a paper he had just signed as Big'un Hopper entered the office. The sun was already two hours high. In the past Big'un's perpetual tardiness had irritated Truscott, but this morning it was welcome. He would have been even happier if Big'un had not shown up at all. The two men tolerated each other only because Judge Hopper forced them to.

Big'un snapped, "Is that all you got to do, sit there writin' letters?"

"Writin' reports is part of the job. Austin always wants to know what's goin' on here."

"When I get to be the sheriff I'll tell Austin to go to hell."

"What makes you think you'll ever be sheriff?"

Big'un headed toward the cells in back. Truscott said, "I've told you to stay away from Flora unless I'm with you."

Big'un snickered. "Afraid I'm goin' to give her what she's been needin'? If I get a notion to do that, it'll take more than you to stop me. Hell, I got the notion right now." He resumed his march toward the cells. Truscott reached into a drawer and withdrew a set of brass knuckles he had taken from a Dallas footpad who had not been half so tough as he thought he was.

Big'un came roaring back, face splotched with anger. "What've you done with her? Where's she at?"

Truscott almost smiled. "I ain't got the faintest notion. I traded her for Jayce, like I said I would."

"You're lyin'. Jayce ain't there either."

"I turned him back over to the Rangers. They've taken him out of the county to get a change of venue."

Not quite believing, Big'un said, "Uncle Judd wouldn't give you permission to do that."

"I know he wouldn't. So I didn't ask him."

Big'un made two long, angry steps toward the sheriff's desk. Truscott raised his hands defensively, showing the brass knuckles. Big'un saw them and stopped, but his face kept getting redder. A wail of rage rose in his throat.

Truscott said, "Careful, you're fixin' to bust a blood vessel. That seems to be a Hopper family trait."

"You had no right."

"I'm the sheriff."

"You won't be sheriff long, not when I tell Uncle Judd about this."

"I'm sheriff till the next election. After that, you and the judge can go to hell for all I care. The Hoppers and the Landons and the whole damned county too."

Big'un's eyes narrowed. "You may not live till election." He stamped out the door.

It would not be long before Judd Hopper came boiling into the office just as Big'un had. Truscott found it odd that he felt relief rather than dread. In the past he had never been able to face down the judge. The man's overpowering presence had always cowed him. But now that the fat was in the fire, he almost looked forward to the confrontation. This time he had nothing to lose. He had already resolved to give up his office when his term was finished. The judge could do nothing to hurt him.

As he expected, Judd Hopper flung the door open and strode in, Big'un just behind him. The judge demanded, "Is it true what my nephew's been tellin' me?"

Truscott was surprised by how calm he felt. "Big'un has got a reputation for abusin' the truth, but in this case I expect he told you the straight of it. I let the Rangers have Jayce."

The judge placed his palms flat on the desktop and leaned across toward Truscott. His breath was hot on the sheriff's face and reeked of chewing tobacco. "You know I wanted to try him in my own court."

"I doubt that it'll make much difference where he's tried. He's guilty, and he'll be sentenced to hang."

"But his crime was committed here."

"Against your kin. Any normal judge would recuse himself from the case if it involved his own family."

"I wanted to personally have the pleasure of tellin' him he's fixin' to hang by the neck until dead, dead, dead."

"Big'un and his cronies would see to it that he was shot or hung before he ever got to trial. They tried it the last time, only the bird had already flown."

The judge sputtered, struggling to raise more argument but seeing the futility of it. His face was crimson, and veins stood out on his temples. "You're through in this county, Oscar. I'll see to it."

"Ain't much you can do till election. After that you can have the whole shebang."

The judge gave Truscott a look that would wilt cactus, then spun on his heel, starting toward the door. Big'un protested, "Ain't you goin' to do somethin', Uncle Judd?"

His uncle gave him no answer. Big'un followed him outside. Catching up, he said, "Looks to me like there ought to be somethin' you can do."

The judge's voice dripped sarcasm. "You want me to shoot him?"

"That ain't a bad idea. I've got half a mind to do it myself."

"If you do, you've got no mind at all. No Hopper can afford to shoot him. The state would have a dozen Rangers down here before you could spit."

Big'un thought about it. "What if somebody else done it, somebody who has nothin' to do with any of us Hoppers?"

The judge took a few more steps, then stopped, suddenly intrigued. "What do you mean, somebody else?"

"There was an old man—"

The judge raised a hand to stop him. "Don't tell me. I've got to stay clean. I don't want to know anything about it."

"All right. I'll wait a day or two till Oscar figures he's got us up a stump. Then don't be surprised at anything that happens."

The judge stared at him, torn between doubt and hope. "Nephew, you're not the brightest lamp in the window, but occasionally you think with your head instead of your fists. I hope this is one of those times."

"It is. You'll see."

Two days later Big'un made a show of rifling through the recent fugitive notices in the sheriff's office. He and Truscott had barely spoken since the confrontation with Judge Hopper. Now Truscott glanced up irritably from a report he was writing. "What're you lookin' for?"

"A telegram that came in here a while back. Described a man who robbed a bank out west."

"You think you've got a line on him?"

"Maybe. Feller told me about somebody he seen at the old Yancey farmhouse." He found the telegram and ran a stubby finger along the lines. "Sure enough sounds like the man, all right."

His interest piqued, Truscott took the telegram from Big'un's hand. "You certain this is him?"

"Can't be certain of nothin', but the description fits. The telegram mentions a reward. I thought I would ride out and at least take a look. I could use the money."

"If this is the right man, you'd probably get your head shot off. I'd best go with you."

Big'un feigned a protest. "I can handle it."

"Don't worry about the reward. It's all yours. But if this is the real bank robber it's liable to take two of us to bring him in."

"Suit yourself."

"I'll saddle up and meet you here in ten minutes. This report can wait till I get back."

Big'un smiled grimly as the sheriff walked outside.

"Hell, Oscar, you ain't comin' back."

Scooter Tennyson sat in a rickety chair leaned back against the barn door, dozing in the warmth of the early-fall sun. He dreamed he was fishing in the San Saba River and Bo brought an ax from behind the kitchen tent, telling him to cut more wood.

He awakened with a start, remembering that he was supposed to keep watch while his father slept inside. Blinking the sleep from his eyes, he saw two horsemen approaching. He froze in panic for a moment, then rushed into the barn.

"Pa, wake up. Somebody's comin'."

Lige Tennyson was quickly on his feet, grabbing for his pistol. He hurried to the barn door. "They're almost on us. You was supposed to keep watch."

"I'm sorry, Pa."

"Sorry don't fix it." Lige squinted, then relaxed. "One of them is that deputy I told you about, Big'un Hopper. Reckon he's come to give me a job like he promised. But I didn't figure on him bringin' anybody else." He started to put away the pistol, then thought better of it. "You stay back out of sight just in case."

"All right, Pa."

Lige walked out into the open. He kept the pistol in his hand but lowered it so it would not appear to offer a threat.

Big'un eyed the pistol with suspicion, but his voice sounded jovial enough. "Howdy."

"How do, yourself."

The other man spoke. "Do you go by the name of Tennyson?"

"Sometimes. Depends on where I'm at and who I'm talkin' to. And who *am* I talkin' to?"

So quickly that Lige missed the move, Oscar Truscott drew a pistol and pointed it at Lige's belly. "I am the sheriff of this county. I am placin' you under arrest for bank robbery and attempted murder. Drop that pistol."

Lige let the weapon fall to his feet. Confused, he looked at Big'un. "What kind of a trick is this?"

"Not quite the kind it looks like." Big'un drew his own pistol. Lige saw murder in the man's eyes and braced himself for a bullet.

Instead of aiming at Lige, Big'un pointed the pistol toward Truscott. The sheriff blinked in confusion.

Big'un said, "Looks like election is comin' sooner than you thought, Oscar." He squeezed the trigger. Truscott jerked. His horse jumped as the sheriff slid down over its left side.

Truscott looked up in mortal pain. "For God's sake, Big'un."

"God ain't watchin', Oscar." Big'un leaned from the saddle and fired again.

Observing from the barn, Scooter froze in shock.

Lige said, "God amighty. What did you do that for?"

Big'un smiled grimly. "The county is fixin' to get a new sheriff. A bank-robbin' fugitive just killed this one."

Shaken, Lige said, "Me? I ain't fired a shot."

"Nobody'll believe that. He came to arrest you, and you shot him."

"You bottom-dealin' son of a bitch."

"I found out a long time ago that you do what you have to if you want to win." He raised the pistol to fire.

Scooter hurled a rock almost the size of his fist. It struck Big'un's horse on the chest. The animal reared and whirled away. Big'un involuntarily squeezed the trigger. The bullet smacked against the side of the barn.

Lige scooped up his own pistol and fired as Big'un struggled to regain control of his mount. Big'un got off one more shot, then spurred hard to move out of range. Lige steadied his pistol and fired once more. He thought he might have grazed Big'un, but he was not certain.

Scooter stepped hesitantly toward the fallen sheriff. He wanted to throw up. The man's eyes were open. "I think he's alive, Pa. He's lookin' at me."

"No, son, he's halfway to either heaven or hell." Lige bent to close the lawman's eyes. "Like as not he was a good sheriff, but he sure picked a coyote for a deputy."

"What'll we do now, Pa?"

"Only one thing *to* do. We'll run like a rabbit."

"Where to?"

"There ain't nothin' but Texas all around us. Soon as that deputy gets to town and tells his story, every badge toter in the state will be huntin' for us. They'll shoot us down like hydrophoby dogs." For a moment Lige drifted toward despair. He blinked away tears. "They won't stop to ask your age."

Scooter's alarm intensified. He remembered seeing his father cry only once, when Scooter's mother had died.

Lige said, "I done you a bad wrong, son, bringin' you into this kind of a mess. Best thing I can do now is to send you back to your Ranger friends, where I found you."

"I don't know if I could find my way. I'm stayin' with you, Pa."

Lige's eyes were bleak. "When bullets get to flyin' they don't care who they hit. Man or boy, a bullet can't tell the difference."

"How far do you reckon it is up to the Cherokee country?"

"A long ways. There's probably fifty sheriffs between here and the Red River. That don't even count Rangers and town constables."

"We can travel in the dark of the night and hide durin' the daytime."

"That's the only thing to do. We'd better saddle up and get gone before that four-flusher comes back with a posse fired up to kill us both."

From the corner of his eye Scooter sensed a movement. Turning, he shouted, "Look out, Pa. He's comin' back."

A bullet thumped against the barn. Big'un had reversed direction and spurred toward them, firing as he came.

Cursing, Lige leveled his pistol. "Down, boy. Flat on the ground." He took two shots at the deputy.

Dropping to his knees, Scooter felt something strike his hip. It burned like a hot poker.

One of Lige's bullets grazed Big'un's horse. The animal squealed and broke into pitching. Big'un grabbed the saddlehorn and held on with both hands. He dropped the pistol. The bridle reins went flopping.

Lige tried to get him in his sights, but the horse's frenzied bucking made it impossible. Big'un managed to get hold of the reins and bring his mount under a measure of control. He turned toward town. The animal alternated between running and pitching. Lige took one more shot, but it was an empty gesture.

He said, "Get up, son. We got to go."

Scooter moaned. "Somethin's wrong, Pa. I can't get up."

Lige dropped to one knee, eyes fearful. "My God, he hit you."

Scooter looked down at his hip. He saw the blood and felt nausea wash over him. Though Lige was skinny as a log rail, he picked up his son and carried him to the old house's back porch as though he weighed nothing at all. "Slip them britches down, son. Let me take a look."

Scooter's hands were trembling. He could barely manipulate his belt buckle.

Lige asked, "Does it hurt bad?"

"It's startin' to. Mostly it burns."

Lige felt around the wound, then wiped his bloody fingers on one leg of his trousers. "Looks like the bullet went plumb through. Might've nicked the bone, though. I need to take you to a doctor."

"You can't go to town. Folks there would kill you in a minute."

"At least I've got to stop the bleedin'. Then we have to make a lot of tracks. You think you can ride?"

"I don't know. Maybe you ought to leave me here."

"And have that deputy kill you to shut your mouth? That's the reason he turned around and came back, hopin' to finish us both so we couldn't tell what we seen here."

"Would anybody believe us?"

"Not likely, but he can't take the chance. He's got to kill us."

He fetched a half-empty whiskey bottle from his blanket roll in the barn. "This is goin' to burn like the fires of hell. Holler if it helps."

Scooter hollered, but it did not help.

Misery in his eyes, Lige said, "Somewhere we'll find somebody who can help you. Till then, you've got to hang on, boy."

Big'un had a dozen men with him, all Hoppers or Hopper kin. Approaching the farmhouse, Deputy Harp asked, "Hadn't we better go in slow and careful?"

Big'un kept his horse in a stiff trot. "That outlaw will be miles away from here by now. But we'll pick up his trail and ride him down like a lobo wolf, soon as we do right by poor old Oscar."

A wagon trailed a couple of hundred yards behind. It would take the sheriff's body back to town for proper services and burial.

Old Oscar ought to be grateful to me, Big'un thought, rubbing his sore arm where Lige's bullet had grazed it. I've made a hero out of him. Every Hopper woman in town will cry at his funeral, and some that aren't even kin.

Harp said, "Reckon why that robber picked this place to hide out?"

Big'un replied, "Like as not them Landons put him up to it. Probably had him hired to kill some of us and keep their own hands clean. But me and Oscar flushed him before he had time to do any such of a thing."

"Damned shame your horse went to pitchin' when you tried to protect Oscar. You could've finished that killer then and there."

Nobody had questioned Big'un's account about Tennyson shooting Truscott in cold blood and about Big'un's horse going into a panic at a critical moment. Horses were like that. "Don't worry, we'll get him sooner or later. But everybody better remember, we're up against a murderer who won't stop at nothin'. He won't give any mercy, and he's got no mercy comin' to him. Shoot to kill."

"What about the boy?"

"Just remember that he put a bullet in Oscar too. He's already ruined for life, travelin' with an outlaw daddy. He's probably carryin' the trace of a noose around his neck." He had heard it said that anyone destined to hang bore a faint birthmark that foretold his fate. Perhaps it was the mark of

Cain that Big'un had heard preachers talk about. He had looked for it on his own throat and had been relieved not to find it.

Truscott lay where Big'un had left him except that he had been rolled over onto his back, his arms folded across his chest and his hat covering his face.

Harp said, "Odd, ain't it, that an outlaw would do such a thing for a sheriff?" He lifted the hat to look at Truscott's face. "Looks natural, Oscar does, like he's just asleep. You reckon he felt any pain?"

Big'un remembered the pleading look in Truscott's eyes before the second shot. "I doubt he ever knew what hit him, it happened so fast." Nevertheless, the memory made him shiver. He turned in the saddle to hide the emotion from the posse members. "Where the hell is that wagon?"

Harp stepped up close to the house. He said, "Did Oscar ever reach the porch?"

Big'un replied, "No, he fell right where he is now."

"Then you must've hit somebody. There's blood up here."

The stain had soaked into the dry old wood. Big'un studied it and felt a quick uplift. Maybe he had shot the old reprobate after all. He hoped it was a fatal wound. The boy would soon be caught, wandering around by himself. Given any kind of chance, Big'un would see to it that he did not live long enough to testify about what had really happened.

One of the men had circled the house. He shouted, "I've found their trail."

Big'un rode out to look. The tracks headed north. "Funny they'd go that way. Was I them, I'd head for Mexico."

Harp suggested, "Maybe they figure on some of the

Landons helpin' them. We ought to wipe out the whole damned litter, or at least run them out of the county."

Big'un was surprised at how well this whole affair had played into his hands. "But the first thing we got to do is catch these killers. Afterward we can deal with Jayce Landon. We'll do what we had figured to do when we had him in our jail."

"We don't know where the Rangers took him."

"There's still one Ranger in town, the one called Brackett. He'll know."

"He won't tell."

"Yes, he will. One way or another, he will."

{ FOURTEEN }

Sergeant Holloway had returned to the San Saba River camp. Rusty sent the captain a brief wire explaining the situation and requesting permission for him and Andy to guard Jayce until the circuit judge reached town. The captain wired back advising that additional ranger help would be sent if requested. Tom Blessing decided not to ask for it.

"Got to save the taxpayers' money where we can," he said. "Lots of them think we're stealin' it or throwin' it away on luxuries."

Andy smiled. If the courthouse or jail contained any luxuries, he had failed to see them. The place begged for a coat of paint, and a piece of cardboard had been tacked up where a windowpane was missing.

Flora was on her long daily visit to her husband. She responded to Tom's comment. "Jayce'd feel better if you would ask the captain to send brother Dick."

Rusty frowned. "Dick would take it hard, watchin' Jayce tried for murder. We all know what the outcome'll be."

She said, "Havin' him here would be a comfort to Jayce. I'd feel better too."

Rusty gave in. "It's against my better judgment, but I'll wire the captain."

When Flora left, Andy told Rusty, "Somebody said Jayce and Dick both courted Flora."

"It's a shame she made the wrong choice."

"When Jayce is gone she'll have a second chance. Maybe she'll take it."

Rusty observed him quizzically. "I knew that Farley Brackett was some taken with her, but I didn't know you were too. She's ten years too old for you."

Andy's face warmed. "It's not that way at all. It's just that she's got a lot of gumption. You have to admire that."

"You'd better admire her from a distance. She'd shoot you in a minute if it would save her husband."

"I'd call that gumption."

So far as Andy could tell, Rusty had shown no interest in Flora as a woman. He saw her only as a complication in his effort to guard Jayce, to keep him from escaping and at the same time to protect him from his Hopper enemies. Rusty seemed too tied up in his grief over Josie Monahan to involve himself with another woman. Andy's subtle and sometimes not so subtle efforts to arouse his interest in Josie's sister Alice had bumped against a stone wall of resistance.

Every time Andy went to the cells he felt Jayce's eyes watching him, calculating, ready to seize any opportunity for a break. Tom Blessing did not allow Flora direct contact with her husband. She did her visiting from a cell ten feet away from Jayce's. She could not even hand him tobacco. Either Tom or Rusty would examine it first, then pass it to Jayce.

Anyone who took a meal tray to Jayce had to leave his pistol in the front office and slide the tray through a wide slot in the cell door. Before anyone entered the cell to empty the slop jar or sweep out, Jayce had first to shove his arms out with a bar between them and submit to being handcuffed.

Andy said, "Tom's carryin' things to an extreme."

Rusty replied, "By the time you put in as many years as he has, you'll know not to get careless with the likes of Jayce Landon. He'll grab any chance, and he'll be willin' to kill anybody who stands in his way. So would Flora, I'm thinkin'."

Andy found it hard to imagine Flora killing anyone, even to save Jayce. But he took care not to get close enough that she might grab his pistol.

Farley Brackett's arrival took Andy by surprise. His face was bruised and swollen, cut in half a dozen places. He attempted to dismount by himself but fell to hands and knees. His startled horse jerked free and ran several yards before turning to look back.

Andy rushed to help. Though he had never liked the dour Ranger, he felt outrage at seeing him so badly battered. He lifted Farley to his feet and held him to keep him from falling again. He said, "You look like you've been drug at the end of a rope."

Farley's lips were swollen and cut. His speech was distorted. "Where's Rusty? Got to see Rusty."

"He's inside. Hang on to me. I'll get you there."

Farley had difficulty in keeping his legs under him. With

Andy's support he labored up the step and through the door. Rusty sat at Tom's desk, writing a report for the captain. Tom lay napping on a cot, one arm over his face to shield his eyes from the light. He had stood watch for half the previous night. Awakening, he pushed up onto his elbow. "What in the world . . ."

Rusty strode across the room to help. Tom arose from the cot and motioned for them to place Farley on it.

Rusty demanded, "Who did this to you?"

Farley cursed under his breath as he stretched out on the cot. "Big'un. Who else? There's hell to pay over at Hopper's Crossing. The Hoppers are tied up in a manhunt. But when they get done with that they'll be comin' for Jayce."

Rusty said, "They know where we brought him?"

"They do now. Big'un had him a set of brass knuckles. I didn't have the strength to give him much of a fight."

"Nobody could blame you for tellin' him."

"I didn't tell him nothin', but the little feller that runs the livery stable spilled it all. He had heard you-all talk enough that he knew you brought Jayce over here."

"So you figure Big'un will be comin' after him?"

"As sure as New Year's follows Christmas. I ought to've killed him when I had the chance. I will yet."

"Better not. Remember, he's a deputy sheriff."

Farley cautiously ran his fingers over some of the angry cuts on his face. "Worse than that. He's the actin' sheriff now by order of Judge Hopper."

Farley explained about Truscott's murder. "Accordin' to Big'un, it was old man Tennyson and his boy that done it. He put out an order to kill them both on sight."

Andy felt his heart sink. "Scooter?"

"Big'un said him and the sheriff went out to make an arrest. The old man and his boy shot it out with them."

Andy declared, "Scooter wouldn't do such a thing."

"It don't matter whether he did or not. Big'un put out the word to take no chances, to shoot the both of them on sight."

Andy felt a chill. "He must be lyin'."

"Like as not, but most of Hopper's Crossing believes him. They're huntin' high and low, like a pack of coyotes. I wouldn't bet a Confederate dollar on the daddy or the boy either one livin' to get away."

Andy turned to Rusty in anguish. "We've got to do somethin'."

"Lige Tennyson picked his own road."

"I doubt that Scooter had any say in the matter."

"We wouldn't have any idea where to look for them. Anyway, it's our assignment to guard Jayce."

For the moment Andy hated Jayce Landon and Lige Tennyson both. Most of all he hated Big'un Hopper, responsible for their having to guard Jayce and for the shoot-to-kill admonition that put Scooter in jeopardy.

Flora called from the back room. "You-all come and let me out of this cell."

Farley pushed up onto his elbows. "You-all got that good woman under arrest?"

Rusty said, "We're tryin' to make sure she stays good." He explained the conditions under which she was allowed to visit her husband. "She passed a gun to him once. We don't want her doin' it again."

Farley eased. "I didn't know anybody figured that out besides me."

Andy said, "You think you're the only one around here that's got any brains?"

Tom released Flora from her cell and followed her out into the office. The sight of Farley's battered face stirred her to indignation. "I don't suppose he fell off of a horse."

Farley said, "It wasn't a horse that done this to me. It was a jackass."

"Turn Jayce loose for a few days, and I promise you Big'un won't trouble anybody again."

Rusty said, "I'm sore tempted, but how could we know Jayce wouldn't head south for Mexico?"

"You could hold me here in his place. He'd turn himself in again like he did before."

"Maybe. Maybe not. Jayce knows Tom Blessing wouldn't mistreat you like Big'un did. And Tom couldn't hold you for long since there's no charges against you."

She argued, "No tellin' who-all Big'un is liable to stomp on before he's through. What Hopper's Crossing needs is a few funerals, startin' with Big'un and his uncle Judd. Give Jayce a chance and he'll see to it."

Farley said, "Once I get my strength back, I'd be glad to see to it myself."

Scooter swayed from one side to the other in the saddle. Lige said, "Stay awake, son. You don't want to fall and start the bleedin' again. It's taken too long to get it stopped in the first place."

But he realized Scooter was not simply falling asleep. Fevering, he teetered along the brink of unconsciousness.

"I've got to find help for you, and damned soon."

Because the bullet had passed through, he had hoped his son would be able to keep riding until they put a lot more distance behind them. But instead of starting the healing process, the wound was getting uglier, and Scooter's fever was rising. Lige's hopes for escape had all but vanished. At first he had circled around a few farmhouses, fearing word had gone out that he had killed the sheriff. Now that he made up his mind to accept the risk, he had ridden for miles without seeing a house.

He had only a general idea where he and Scooter were. He hoped they had crossed into another county, where Big'un would have less influence. He had started north, hoping to throw off or at least delay pursuit, then had turned westward where there would be fewer settlements, fewer people to witness their flight. That, however, complicated his search for someone to help Scooter. He had given up the notion of riding only in the dark of night. He traveled boldly in the daylight.

At last he saw a small cabin. Smoke drifted from the chimney. "Hold on, son. Maybe these folks can help you."

He heard the sound of an ax, then saw an old black man chopping wood behind the cabin. Disappointment left a sour taste in his mouth. "Damned little help we'll get here."

The old man straightened and leaned on the ax while he rubbed his sleeve across his eyes in an effort to wipe away the sweat and sharpen his vision. Then he came limping out to meet Lige and the boy. "That young'un looks to be in a bad way."

"He's in need of help. Any white folks livin' close by?"

"Not close enough by the looks of him. There's the Shannon place over yonderway, but nobody's home. And there's Old Man Fowler Gaskin. You wouldn't take a stray dog to him."

"What about town?"

"It's a right smart of a ways. Too far for the boy to keep ridin' horseback, I'm afraid, and I ain't got a wagon. Bring him in the house. I'll see if there's somethin' I can do for him."

Lige had always considered it gospel truth that black folks were supposed to be subservient. He took the old man's blackness as an indication that the cabin was probably filthy and infested with vermin. The thought of taking Scooter in there repelled him. Yet he saw no choice.

He said, "I'm goin' to need hot water to clean him up."

"That won't take long. I got plenty of firewood, and there's water in the well."

The cabin's single room was bedroom and kitchen all together. Lige was pleasantly surprised to see that the place was clean. He asked, "You got a woman, I suppose?"

"Never had no chance to get married."

"The place looks too neat not to have a woman in it."

"I used to belong to Mr. Isaac York. When he was sober he was particular about keepin' the place up. He wasn't sober much, but I got in the habit of sweepin' and scrubbin' for the times when he was."

Lige gave the cot a doubting look. He distrusted it but was in no position to be choosy. He gently placed Scooter on the top blanket and pulled down the bloody trousers. Sight of the wound made him sick to his stomach. "How about that hot water?"

"It'll be comin' in a minute. What happened to this boy?"

"It's best you don't know. Then you can't tell them anything."

"He's been shot, that's plain to see. And I'm guessin' you're the ones the Rangers told me about."

Lige's nerves tightened. "The Rangers? What did they tell you?"

"Told me about a man and a boy that robbed a bank out west someplace. I got no money in a bank here or anywheres else, so it don't scrape no skin off of my nose."

Defensively Lige said, "The boy had nothin' to do with it."

"It don't seem likely he would, him bein' so young."

"How often do the Rangers come by here?"

"Ain't seen one in a while. Rusty Shannon was the last to come by."

The name jarred Lige. "Rusty?"

"He's the neighbor I was tellin' you about. A hailstorm beat down his crops, so he's gone back to Rangerin' 'til spring-plantin' time."

Lige thought of his ride with Shannon and Andy to the San Saba River camp, where he'd picked up Scooter. The Ranger had seemed to be a man of dark moods. "I've met Shannon. He didn't have a whole lot to say."

"Hard times been doggin' his steps like a hungry wolf. He was all set on marryin', but his woman got shot and killed. He's a booger against men that breaks the law."

"And boys too?"

"He's got a soft spot for hard-luck boys. I mind the time he caught a white boy ridin' with the Comanches. They had stole him when he was little. Rusty taken him in and treated him like a brother. First time I seen Andy he was about the size of your boy here. Turned into a fine young man."

"Andy? Would his last name be Pickard?"

"Sure would."

"He was kind to my boy, Scooter."

"I ain't surprised. It would be his way of payin' back for what-all Rusty done to help him."

Lige tried washing away the blood, but his stomach turned over. He had seen lots of bloodshed in his day, but this time was different. This was his son.

The black man offered, "I'll clean him up for you." He took the wet cloth, rinsed it, and began washing around the wound. "This looks bad. I wisht I had whiskey to pour in that bullet hole."

Lige thought he could use some whiskey himself. "We need to cauterize that wound. Else it's apt to go to gangrene."

The black man's face twisted. "Old Shanty couldn't do that to this boy. I know how much it hurts. One time Mr. Isaac got drunk and taken a notion that I ought to be branded like he branded his critters. It was a long time before I could sit in a chair."

"I'm his daddy. It's my place to do it. You got a butcher knife I can heat?"

Reluctantly Shanty fetched a knife from his crude cabinet. "I'll hold him for you, but I'm shuttin' my eyes."

Scooter had been unconscious. He awakened screaming at the touch of the hot blade. With tears in his eyes Lige kept pressing against the wound until the smell of burning flesh became too much for him. He rushed out of the cabin and threw up.

He reentered after a few minutes. Shanty said, "The boy's unconscious again. He ain't feelin' nothin'. I rubbed some hog lard over the burn."

"Is there a doctor in town that we can trust?"

"Folks around here swear by Dr. Parsons."

"I'd be obliged if you would fetch him."

"Like as not I'll run into Sheriff Tom Blessing. What will I say?"

"I don't see why you'd have to say anything."

Shanty considered. "I never was no great shakes at lyin'. Folks see through me in a minute. But maybe Mr. Tom won't ask me nothin'."

"I hope not. Folks have already accused me of shootin' one sheriff. No tellin' how high they'd hang me if it was two."

The doctor spent an hour with Scooter. Lige watched him intently, looking for some sign of what he was thinking, but Parsons had the blank expression of an expert poker player. When Lige could stand the strain no longer, he demanded, "What's his chances?"

The doctor's eyes made a silent accusation. "They'd be better if somebody competent had seen him sooner. He lost a lot of blood, and what he didn't lose is in some danger of blood poisoning."

Lige's eyes burned. "You sayin' I'm fixin' to lose him?"

"I'd be lying if I told you he's going to be fine. But he's young and generally healthy. He's got that much on his side. I would caution you against moving him for a few days."

"This ain't no place for him." Lige gave Shanty an apologetic look. "Sorry, but that's the way I see it."

The doctor beckoned Lige outside and said, "There's not a kinder-hearted man in this county than Shanty York. You're letting his color cancel out your better judgment."

"I can't overlook it, though. It's the way I was raised."

"It got a lot of good men killed during the big war. For this boy's sake I hope you'll put those notions aside. At least for a few days, until he's stronger and better able to move."

"Looks like I ain't got much choice."

Back inside, Lige found Scooter half-awake. He placed a gentle hand on the boy's shoulder. He told the doctor, "There's people lookin' for us. I'd rather we wasn't found."

"I knew who you were as soon as Shanty told me about you. Lawmen over half of the state are on the hunt. The claim is that you two shot the sheriff over at Hopper's Crossing."

"But it ain't true. It was the sheriff's own deputy done the shootin', and he shot my boy too."

Lige could not tell whether Parsons believed or disbelieved him. That poker face gave nothing away.

The doctor shrugged. "It's been a long time since anything good came out of that county. Almost any funeral over there could be considered community improvement. Do you know I am obliged by law to report any treatment I do on gunshot wounds?"

"I remember when private matters stayed private."

"It seems that the government pokes its nose into just about everything these days. But I might get so busy that I don't turn in my report for a while. People my age are apt to be forgetful at times."

"What do I owe you, Doctor?"

A knowing smile crossed Parsons's face. "Did you come by the money honestly?"

"Some folks might argue either way about that."

"Just drop a couple of dollars in the plate the next time you go to church."

"If Scooter comes out of this, I'll let him do it."

Lige and Shanty stood on the narrow front porch, watching the doctor's buggy raise dust on the town road. Lige asked, "You a Bible-readin' man?"

"I don't read it, exactly, but I listen to the Word anytime I get the chance."

"Do you reckon the Lord allows for a righteous killin'?"

"You thinkin' about that deputy sheriff?"

"He does lay heavy on my mind."

{ FIFTEEN }

An hour past dark Big'un Hopper reluctantly rode into town with a volunteer posse of six men. Horses and riders were so weary that they seemed barely able to hold their heads up. It had been another hard day's ride, and a futile one. Big'un had mistakenly thought it would be easy to track the fugitives and put so many holes in them that their bodies would not float.

His cousin Harp said, "It's like angels lifted them up and carried them away. Or maybe it was the devil. Don't seem like the angels would help them that killed Oscar Truscott."

They had certainly not done anything to help Big'un. He had wanted to continue the chase if it killed half the horses, but the exhausted posse members had threatened to rebel. Even Harp had argued their side. If they couldn't find the trail in the daylight, they sure as sin wouldn't find it in the dark, he said.

Big'un knew they were right, though he had verbally chastised them and even threatened to beat up Cousin Wilbur, who had been a chronic bellyacher all his life. He knew the longer the fugitives remained at large, the less likely he was to find them. He hoped that Lige Tennyson's wound was serious enough to make him go to ground somewhere. After that, the boy would be easy. Sure, some people would balk at shooting him, but Big'un had told everyone who would listen that the boy had participated in the killing of Oscar Truscott. Once a young wolf got the taste of blood, he argued, he was beyond taming. Best thing was to shoot him at the first opportunity.

So far as he could tell, no one had doubted his story. Not even a Landon had spoken out against him. But if Lige and his boy had a chance to tell their version often enough, doubts might begin to surface.

It must have been the devil's doing that he had not been able to kill them at the farmhouse the way he had intended.

As the posse began to break up, Big'un declared loudly, "I'll expect every one of you to be here and ready with fresh horses at first light. Bring enough grub to last you for three or four days."

He heard a lot of groaning and knew that half of them would not show up. Things had come to a pretty pass when a man could no longer count on loyalty from his kin.

After the others pulled away, Harp said, "You never did like Oscar in the first place. Looks like we ought to be takin' care of Jayce Landon instead of chasin' over hell and half of Texas lookin' for that old man and his boy. The truth be told, they done you a favor. They made you the sheriff."

"You gettin' cold feet, Harp?"

"No, but I'm gettin' an awful sore butt. You have any idea how far we've ridden?"

"We'll ride a thousand miles if we have to. Jayce ain't goin' nowhere. We'll get around to him, but we've got this other business to finish first."

Harp accepted, but not with any grace. "If you say so, but was I you, I'd be givin' that Tennyson a medal."

"You've got no sense of justice."

Harp started to turn away but stopped, considering. "You sure you ain't just makin' a show for Oscar's widow?"

Big'un exploded into rage. "What kind of a man do you think I am? She's blood kin."

"She's good-lookin'. I ain't seen nothin' yet that would make you back away from a good-lookin' woman."

Big'un was tempted to lay the barrel of his new pistol against the side of Harp's head. But Harp was a better tracker than Big'un. He needed him. Someday when all of this was over, he would teach Harp a whole new code of conduct.

As he rode by the darkened courthouse a familiar, gruff voice hailed him. Judge Hopper walked out and jerked his head in silent command. Big'un dismounted but had to hold on to his horse for a minute while his knees threatened to collapse from fatigue.

The judge's voice was impatient. "I gather that you had no luck."

"We had luck, all right. All bad."

"This is the third day you've been out on the chase. Don't you think that's enough?"

"It won't be enough till we get them."

"No tellin' how far they've traveled by now. Everybody in town knows you and Oscar didn't like one another. Some are beginnin' to ask why you've let yourself become obsessed with this hunt."

"I've got my reasons."

"And I can guess what they are. But if enough other people start to guess the same thing, you're liable to be in more trouble than you can handle."

"You sayin' I ought to quit the chase?"

"I'm sayin' they're probably in another jurisdiction by now. Let somebody else capture them."

"I can't. I've got to be the one that does it."

The judge stared solemnly at him. "I've seen some smart men convicted in my court, all because they got in too much of a hurry and were careless enough to leave witnesses behind. Good night, nephew."

Big'un watched his uncle walk away and become lost in the darkness. He gritted his teeth and slammed his palm against the seat of his saddle, startling the tired horse into jumping away from him.

At that moment he realized that his uncle had served notice in an oblique way. If Big'un got into trouble over Oscar Truscott, he was on his own. Judd Hopper's court would be of no help.

Damn you, Lige Tennyson, he thought. This is all your fault.

* * *

Lige stood in the middle of Shanty's garden, chopping weeds. He had been a little put off at first by the notion of doing chores for a black man, but it was better than sitting around fretting over Scooter's still-raw wound. That little cabin seemed to shrink a bit more every day.

Shanty rode up from the river on his mule. Lige straightened and wiped sweat from his face onto his sleeve. "Find your hogs all right?"

"Not all of them. I got a notion Mr. Fowler Gaskin has been over this way."

"Damn, but I hate a thief. Somebody ought to ride over to Mr. Gaskin's and plant a load of buckshot where it'll remind him what the Gospel says."

"It won't be me. Only reason I keep a shotgun is to kill varmints."

"From what you've told me, Gaskin is the biggest varmint around here."

"The Book says judge not if you don't want to be judged your own self. Now and then I get tempted, but I can't speak my mind free like if I was white."

Lige had never given thought to the fact that blacks had to be extra careful in expressing themselves lest they anger those whites who would not hesitate to inflict punishment. Lincoln's Emancipation Proclamation had granted them freedom on paper. It had not freed them from the invisible chains.

Shanty asked, "You looked in on the boy?"

"A while ago. He was asleep. That's what he needs the most, but I don't know how much more he can get."

"How come?"

"A couple of riders came by. I stayed in the cabin where they couldn't see me. I couldn't help thinkin' they're part of a posse, huntin' me and my boy. We need to be movin' along."

"Scooter's at a ticklish stage in his healin'. He oughtn't to be on his feet, much less in a saddle."

"If people keep comin' by, we may not have no choice."

"You're all right if you stay inside. Most white folks who pass by here wouldn't go in my cabin if you was to offer them twenty dollars."

"I expect the reward on me is a lot more than twenty dollars."

Shanty squinted against the sun, then lifted his hat to shade his eyes. "Looks to me like we're fixin' to have some more company, Mr. Lige."

Lige took only a fleeting look. "Good thing you seen him. I didn't." Bending over as if that would make him less visible, he retreated to the cabin. Shanty tied the mule, then picked up the hoe and continued the work Lige had begun.

Long before he could see the man's face, Shanty knew the visitor was Fowler Gaskin. Like Shanty, he rode a saddled mule, though a poor one that showed its ribs. Gaskin had a way of hunching over that identified him as far as a man could see him. Shanty forced a false smile. "How do, Mr. Gaskin."

Gaskin took a look around before he replied. "Anybody here besides you?"

"Ain't hardly anybody ever stops at my place."

"You heard what happened?"

"Ain't much to hear around this little old farm."

Fowler sat up straighter, enjoying the feeling of importance that came from being the bearer of news. "Been a killin' over yonder a ways. Seems like a man and a boy was wanted for robbin' a bank, and when the sheriff went to arrest them they shot him."

Shanty feigned surprise. "Wasn't Tom Blessing, was it? I sure would miss Mr. Tom."

"Naw, it was over the county line, by Hopper's Crossin'. Been a *re*ward posted. I wondered if you've seen anybody like that lately."

"Ain't seen hardly anybody at'all."

"I could sure use that *re*ward money." Gaskin looked hard at Shanty. "I seen a couple of strange horses grazin' out yonder a piece. Didn't know you had any horses."

Shanty began feeling nervous. He thought he saw suspicion in Gaskin's eyes. "Ain't mine. Strays followin' the river, I expect."

"If it was me, I wouldn't let nobody's strays be eatin' up my grass."

"Horses don't know nothin' about property lines. I figure somebody'll come along and claim them."

"Maybe so." Gaskin looked toward the cabin as if he expected to see someone. "Mind if I stop at your well and get a drink?" Normally he never asked; he just took.

"Help yourself." To refuse him would strengthen Gaskin's suspicion. Shanty had never refused him anything. He could only hope that Lige remained inside and kept quiet. He went on with his hoeing, but his worried gaze remained fixed on Gaskin.

Gaskin brought up a bucket of water on the windlass but took no more than a sip before dropping the bucket back into the well. He gave the cabin a long study. When he rode away he changed direction and kept looking back over his shoulder.

When he felt that Gaskin could no longer see him, Shanty laid down the hoe and went to the cabin, half trotting, half hopping on his arthritic legs. Lige came out onto the narrow porch to meet him. "Anybody we need to worry about?"

"It's past the worryin' part. That was Mr. Fowler Gaskin, and he looked like a dog that just found a bone."

Lige's eyes narrowed. "You didn't tell him nothin'?"

"Didn't have to. He seen your horses. I'm fair certain he figured it all out for hisself."

"That old mule of his don't look none too swift. I could catch up to him." Lige's eyes made Shanty feel cold.

Shanty said, "Ain't you already got trouble enough?"

Lige sobered. "Then me and my boy have got to get away from here before he comes back and brings some others with him."

"If you try to take Scooter very far, he ain't goin' to make it."

Lige's eyes showed fear. "I'm willin' to take my chances, but my boy . . ." The fear turned to anguish. "Ain't there no place safe for him?"

"The jail."

Lige stared as if he could not believe what he heard. "Jail?"

"Sheriff Tom Blessing's jail. Mr. Tom ain't goin' to let nobody touch Scooter or do him any hurt."

"My boy don't belong in jail. He ain't done nothin'. I'll admit I done the bank robbery like they said, but that was me, not him. He done his best to talk me out of it."

"I believe you, and I'll bet Mr. Tom will too. He'll see that Scooter gets the right doctorin'. He'll also see that nobody does him harm."

Lige wrestled with his doubts. "I've spent the biggest part of my life tryin' to stay out of jail. Puttin' that boy into one on purpose goes against everything I believe in."

"It'll be the savin' of him."

"You're probably right, bad as I hate to think so. But if I go with him I'll have gray whiskers down to my knees before I get out. If they don't hang me."

"I can take him. It'd be easier for you to keep hidin' out if you don't have the boy on your hands."

Lige nodded reluctantly. "I wouldn't go far. I'd want to be where I could sort of keep an eye on things."

Shanty considered. "Mr. Rusty's place. Him bein' a Ranger, I doubt as they'd do much lookin' around there. You could camp in the timber down on the river. If there was any news I could come and tell you."

Lige looked as if it would not take much to make him cry. "Ain't been but a little while since I got my boy back. It's a mean thing to think about us bein' apart again."

Shanty could only shrug. For this, he had no answer.

Scooter was too weak to get on his horse without help, and he bit his lip to keep from crying out in pain as his father lifted him into the saddle. Shanty said, "We'll stay in the timber as much as we can. It's a longer trip that way, but maybe we won't run into anybody."

Scooter's voice was almost too weak to be heard. "I'll be all right. Where are we goin'?"

Lige and Shanty had decided not to tell him until they had to. They knew he would resist the plan to separate him from his father. Shanty said, "To some good folks that'll take care of you."

It was dark by the time they reached the edge of town. Lige became agitated when he saw that a number of people were out on the street. "Why ain't they at home?" he demanded. "Even chickens know to go to roost come night."

Shanty said, "Maybe you better not go no further."

Lige turned to his son. "Shanty's takin' you on in. I'm goin' to have to quit you here."

Scooter was dismayed. "You're not stayin' with me?"

"It's for the best this way. But I ain't goin' far. Anything happens, I'll be here in a jiffy." He hugged his son, then looked away quickly, blinking. He cleared his throat and turned to Shanty. "I ain't never had much use for your people. Always thought they was shiftless and sticky-fingered. But you've done mighty fine by me and my boy. If there's ever anything you need . . ." He did not finish. He rode off into the darkness without looking back.

Scooter called after him, but his voice was soft and did not carry far.

Shanty said, "Hush, boy, you don't want the wrong people to hear you." He waited a minute, watching and listening. "Looks like there ain't nobody comin'. Let's go before somebody sees us."

"Where we goin'?"

"Told you while ago, to some good people who'll watch out for you."

As soon as he saw the jail, Scooter sensed the plan. He tried to turn his horse around, but Shanty caught the reins. "Hold on, boy. It's all right."

"You turnin' me in to the law?"

"Sheriff Tom Blessing ain't goin' to hurt you, and he ain't goin' to let nobody else do it. You can't keep runnin', the shape you're in."

"They'll try to make me tell where my daddy is at."

"You don't know, so you can't tell them much. Let me help you down. I'll take care of your horse later."

Though Scooter was not heavy, he was almost too much for Shanty. The old man sank halfway to his knees before setting the boy on the ground. "Hold on to me," he said. "I won't let you fall."

Shanty knocked on the door, then rubbed his knuckles, arthritis making them ache. In a minute someone opened the door slowly and cautiously. The muzzle of a pistol showed first. Then Andy Pickard poked a lamp out into the darkness.

"Shanty? What you doin' out this time of the night?"

"Brought you somebody."

Andy shouted, "Scooter!" He opened the door wide, looking past Shanty and the boy. "Got his daddy with you?"

"Just the boy. He's hurt."

Andy laid the lamp on the floor, then picked Scooter up and carried him inside. He laid him on a cot. "Better bar that door behind us, Shanty. Some folks from Hopper's Crossing have been hangin' around, lookin' for a chance to bust in."

"Nobody knew I was bringin' the boy here."

"It's not Scooter they've been after, not here at the jail." He explained that Jayce Landon was safely lodged in a cell.

Shanty said, "They're huntin' Scooter too. He witnessed a shootin'."

"So I've heard. They've got word out all over the country. They say his daddy murdered Sheriff Truscott."

"Scooter and his daddy tell it different. They say the sheriff's own deputy done it, then throwed the blame on Mr. Lige and the boy."

Andy absorbed that as he looked down at the youngster. "How'd Scooter get shot?"

"That deputy. He tried to kill the both of them so they couldn't tell what he'd done."

"Sounds like Big'un Hopper."

Scooter rasped, "That's him. That's what Pa called him."

Andy frowned. "If it was anybody else I'd find it hard to believe. But with Big'un, I'm not surprised at anything." He turned away. "I better go wake up Tom. He's been stayin' in the jail ever since we brought Jayce over here. Sleeps with one eye open."

Shanty said, "Come mornin' we better fetch the doctor. He treated the boy once, but he sure needs lookin' at again."

Andy blinked. "The doctor's already seen Scooter?"

"Once, out at my place."

"He didn't come and tell us about it."

Shanty headed off a smile. "I guess he ain't found the time. Doctors get awful busy."

"In some localities more than others."

Tom lay on a cot in an empty cell. He was already half awake when Andy went in to fetch him. He said, "I heard the door. I didn't hear any fight, so I supposed it wasn't any of the Hopper bunch bustin' in."

Andy explained about Scooter and his version of Truscott's death.

Tom said, "From what you-all have told me about this Big'un, maybe the boy's tellin' it straight. But we can't pass judgment. That's for a court to do."

"True enough, but we've got to give the boy protection."

"Sounds to me like he needed protection from his father."

"That's what I tried to tell the captain when he let Lige Tennyson take Scooter away with him."

"Where do you reckon the old man is now?"

"No tellin'."

"No matter. Our main job right now is to see that the Hoppers don't get to Jayce before he's had a chance to stand trial. If they want Lige Tennyson, they'll have to find him theirselves."

"From what Scooter and Shanty say, Big'un's liable to want Scooter as much as he wants Jayce."

"Let him come and try. Ain't nobody gettin' into my jail unless I put him there. Do you suppose anybody saw Shanty bring the boy in?"

"I think somebody is watchin' everything we do."

{ SIXTEEN }

Big'un Hopper was so tired that when he tried to pull the saddle and blanket from his horse's back he dropped them. He expelled a long breath and reached down, then straightened, pressing his hand against his back in a futile effort to ease the pain.

He muttered to himself, "The hell with it. Let them lay." He slipped the bridle over the horse's ears and watched the animal turn toward the water trough. He was eager for a drink himself. It would be a mix of coffee and whiskey, light on the coffee.

Carrying a lantern, Harp walked out to the corral. "It's been dark for two hours. I thought you never was goin' to give it up and come in."

The words were not exactly critical, but Big'un took them that way. Most of his kin had been walking the long way around him the last few days, afraid he might bite their heads off. Or worse, badger them into joining his posse to hunt for Lige Tennyson and his brat. He said, "If the rest of you won't go with me, I'll keep goin' by myself. I won't quit till I get them."

Harp hung the lantern on a nail. "You can quit huntin' for the boy, at least. We know where he's at."

Big'un stiffened. "Keep talkin'."

"He's over yonder in Tom Blessing's jailhouse."

Big'un swore. "How do you know?"

"You recollect that you put Cousin Bim to watchin' the jail so we'd know if they tried to smuggle Jayce out of there? He seen an old darky bring the boy in."

"How did he know it was the right boy?"

"He hung around close and listened to the talk. It was the Tennyson kid, all right, and he was wounded."

"Who would've wounded him?"

"I reckon you did. We found blood on the porch, remember? You thought you had shot the old man, but it looks like you hit the boy instead."

It took Big'un a minute to absorb that. He had aimed at Lige, but hitting a target from a running horse was always highly chancy. Until he saw the bloodstains he had not thought he'd hit anyone. "Anybody see anything of the boy's daddy?"

"No, but it ain't likely he'd go far without knowin' his son was goin' to be all right. I figure he's hidin' close by." Harp's voice dropped. "And he's apt to be killin' mad. Was I you I'd be keepin' four walls around me and no windows. That broad back of yours makes a good target."

Big'un shivered at the thought of a bullet smashing between his shoulder blades, severing his spine and setting him afire. It could happen if Tennyson was the crack shot he had claimed to be.

Harp said, "If we could just figure some way to smoke him out . . ."

Big'un said, "You told me an old darky brought the boy in. Know who he was?"

"Bim never heard his name, but I've been thinkin' about that old man Gaskin. He said he had a notion where Tennyson and the boy was at. Wondered how much we'd pay for the information and if we'd let him have some of it in advance."

"I remember. Everybody said he was just a lyin' old drunk always lookin' to get money without havin' to work for it. I gave him a cussin' and sent him on his way."

"Maybe you cussed him too soon. It just come to me that he said he thought they was hidin' out with a darky.

Could've been the same one that brought the boy to town."

Big'un felt as if Harp had struck him. "You knew that and still you stood by and let me run Gaskin off?"

"Thinkin' ain't exactly my long suit. I leave most of that to you."

"Reckon you could find out where Gaskin lives? I'd get him to take us to that darky."

"He oughtn't to be hard to find. He's got a reputation."

"Then get at it. And next time somebody offers information, don't be so quick to run him off."

Fowler Gaskin's place looked about as Big'un expected. "I never could understand how some people can live in a pig sty. He ain't crippled, is he?"

Harp said, "From what I heard, the only thing crippled about him is his ambition."

Gaskin's garden was badly in need of attention. Big'un indulged in a moment's revulsion at the many signs of neglect. Not seeing the old man, he hollered in the direction of the leaning cabin, "Gaskin, come out here." In a lower voice he added, "Before the whole thing falls down around you."

Gaskin ventured as far as the doorway, peering at the visitors through pinched eyes. "Who's that hollerin'?"

"Come out here. I want to talk to you."

Gaskin reached back inside the door and brought out a shotgun. Big'un tensed, wondering if the old reprobate had the guts to fire it. Gaskin said, "I remember you. You talked awful mean to me. I got no business with you now."

Big'un pushed his horse forward and wrested the shotgun from Gaskin's weak and trembling hands. "Yes, you do. You said you knew where we could find Lige Tennyson."

"I said I *thought* I knew, and you cussed me out like I was a nigger. I don't let nobody treat me thataway."

Big'un asked, "How much would it take to make you change your mind?"

Gaskin's anger subsided. "A sight more than I asked you the last time."

"How do we know Tennyson is still there?"

"You don't. But if he's gone, I'll cut the price to half."

Big'un reached down and grabbed a handful of Gaskin's shirt. He yanked the old man up against the horse. "You greedy old robber, I'll pay you what I figure the information is worth, and not a dollar more."

Gaskin cried, "You wouldn't treat me thisaway if my boys was still here. They died fightin' for the South."

"That war is over, old man. We've got a new one now." He gave Gaskin a push that almost made him fall backward. "Go saddle your horse. You're takin' us to that darky."

Gaskin whined, "I ain't got a horse. All I got is a pokey old mule."

"That'll do. Saddle him or ride bareback, I don't care which."

Looking back in anxiety, Gaskin trotted awkwardly toward the barn. Big'un tossed the shotgun through the cabin's open door and heard it clatter on the floor. He said, "I ought to shoot the old rascal on general principles."

Harp said, "I doubt that many folks would show up for the funeral."

Gaskin led the saddled mule from the corral. He had regained a little of his bluster, but not much. "I'll be tellin' Tom Blessing about this. He don't let people come into his county and mistreat the voters."

"Stop talkin'. Get on that mule and ride."

* * *

Big'un was a little surprised by the neatness of Shanty's little farm. The garden and the field had been hoed. The crops looked healthy, in contrast to Gaskin's. He said, "I thought this place belonged to a darky."

Gaskin said, "It does. Mine used to look like this before I got down in my back."

He must have been down in his back for a long time, Big'un thought. It took years for a place to get as run down as Gaskin's.

Shanty was standing in front of a small frame shed, brushing a mule's back. He tried for a smile but could not mask his uneasiness.

Big'un asked Gaskin, "Is this the man who harbored Tennyson and the boy?"

"I'd bet a thousand dollars."

"You never saw a thousand dollars." Big'un turned to Shanty. "We know you took the Tennyson boy to town. Where's his daddy?"

Shanty considered a minute before he offered any reply. "I ain't got no idee."

Big'un assumed the old man was lying. He swung his quirt, striking Shanty across the shoulder. "I ain't got the patience to play games with you, boy. Where's he at?"

Shanty rubbed the burning shoulder. "I swear, mister, I don't know."

Big'un lashed him again. "That ain't the answer I want to hear. Try again."

Shanty's body shook, but he stood his ground. "I can't tell you what I don't know."

"He was with you. He's bound to've told you somethin'."

"He didn't tell me nothin'. Said it was better for me not to know."

Gaskin's courage had improved. He said, "These old darkys will lie to you every time. Give me that quirt and I'll put the fear of God into him."

Big'un suspected Gaskin was afraid he might not get his money if Shanty did not tell his tormentors what they wanted to hear. "Back away, Gaskin, before I use the quirt on *you*." He struck Shanty across the back. The old man flinched and choked off a cry.

Big'un said, "I'll bet you got aplenty of whip scars on you, old man. You'll have a bunch more if you don't talk."

Shanty drew up into a knot. "I been tellin' you the truth. That's all I can do."

Big'un raised the quirt again. Harp caught his arm. "You're fixin' to kill him. You don't want another killin' on your conscience."

Big'un's chin dropped. "What do you mean, *another* killin'?"

Harp's eyes narrowed. "I expect you know what I mean."

"Who you been listenin' to? Somebody been makin' talk?"

Harp's face twisted. "There's several wonderin' why you want that old man and his boy so bad, seein' as they eliminated Oscar Truscott and got you the sheriff's job."

Big'un's eyes smoldered. "Is that them talkin', or is it just you?"

Harp raised both hands in a gesture of surrender. "I ain't doubtin' you a particle. I'm with you all the way. I'm just tellin' you what some folks are sayin'."

"Don't you be listenin' to people who make idle talk. You just listen to me."

"I am, Big'un, I am."

Gaskin understood none of the conversation. He watched, frustrated. "Are you quittin'? You just fixin' to ride away without him tellin' you what you came to find out?"

Harp glared at him. "Looks to me like he's told all he knows. There's no use beatin' a dead horse."

Gaskin got down from his mule. "He ain't dead yet. I'll make him talk." Shanty drew his arms in tightly as Gaskin moved toward him.

Big'un pushed his horse between the two men. "I told you, Gaskin. Get back on your mule." He raised the quirt for emphasis.

Gaskin backed away. "I done my part. You owe me."

Big'un felt like quirting Gaskin, but instead, he dug a silver dollar from his pocket. He tossed it to the ground in front of the man.

Gaskin picked up the coin and flushed in anger. "A dollar? Is this all, just one dollar?"

"It's a dollar more than you're worth. If you don't want it, I'll take it back."

Gaskin put the coin in his pocket.

Big'un shook the quirt at him. "Now get away from here before I give you what you really got comin'." To Harp he said, "I hate a man who would betray his neighbor for money. Even a nigger neighbor."

Hunched in pain, Shanty watched as Gaskin got a handhold on the mule's ragged mane and pulled himself up. He said, "Mr. Fowler, my old dog died, but I'm fixin' to get me another one."

Gaskin snarled, "Your old dog was worthless. What you want another one for?"

"So that if you ever come messin' around my place again, I can sic him on you."

Gaskin's face colored. He turned to Big'un and Harp. "You-all goin' to let a nigger talk to a white man that way?"

Big'un said in disgust, "I don't see no white man."

* * *

In the midst of Big'un's frustration an idea began struggling to break free. *Smoke him out,* Harp had suggested. Harp was about to speak, but Big'un raised a hand to stop him, to keep him from interrupting his thoughts before the idea was fully hatched. He asked, "They still got the same old jailhouse?"

"Not much ever changes over there."

"I spent a night in that place once, years ago. They said I was drunk and disorderly."

Harp grinned. "Was you?"

"I expect so. Ain't been back in that town since. I decided not to give them any more of my business."

"It's their loss, then."

Big'un cast a glance over his shoulder to be sure Gaskin wasn't following to plead for more money. The old reprobate had put the reluctant mule into a long trot toward home. "How many people they got standin' guard at the jail durin' the night?"

"Generally a night watchman patrollin' the street outside. Three Rangers and the sheriff sleep inside. A deputy usually goes home."

Big'un rubbed his chin while he let his imagination run free. "Ought not to be hard to take care of the watchman. A couple of guns at the front door and one or two at the back could keep anybody who's inside from comin' out."

"What good will it do you if they stay inside? You couldn't get at them."

"That old jail is mostly built out of lumber. Say a fire was to start along the outside wall. That thing would go up fast, and if them on the inside couldn't get out—well, wouldn't that be a shame?"

Harp stared slack-jawed, awed by Big'un's audacity.

Big'un said, "First I'd like to know just what's goin' on

in that place. I need a man to see inside. I want you to find me somebody who'll do anything for fifty dollars."

"There's aplenty of them around."

"This has to be somebody Jayce nor nobody else in that jail would recognize. Somebody who wouldn't mind gettin' a little drunk and disorderly and spendin' a night or two in the hoosegow. But somebody we can rely on."

"That's some combination."

"Find him."

"You're goin' to a lot of trouble just to get rid of Jayce Landon."

"That boy too. Let somethin' happen to him and like as not his old daddy would come runnin'. All I need is one clear shot. Now let's go where I can get me a bottle of whiskey. I got some thinkin' to do."

{ SEVENTEEN }

Used to being in Rusty Shannon's shadow, Andy was pleased at Rusty's attitude. He seemed to be leaning Andy's way in regard to Scooter.

Tom Blessing was still trying to make up his mind. He said, "The boy's fevered. Maybe he really saw what he says happened, or maybe it's the fever made him think he did. No jury is goin' to take his word against a lawman's."

Andy argued, "Even a *good* lawman goes bad once in a while, and Big'un's been a counterfeit from the start."

"I've known some lawmen who were bad to start with. Others learned it on their own. But I can't believe anything as cold-blooded as the boy tells about."

Rusty put in, "Whether it's real or he imagined it, Scooter's better off in here till everything settles into place. If Big'un did kill Truscott, he'll be lookin' to silence the boy. If it was Lige that did it, he'll probably stay around close so he can know what's happenin' to Scooter. That gives us a better chance to catch him."

Scooter lay on a steel cot in one of the cells. The iron-barred door was left open, for he was not technically a prisoner. Flora sat on the edge of the cot, keeping a damp cloth on the boy's head. She had all but adopted Scooter as soon as she first saw him. She had never had a child of her own. Andy doubted that this was for lack of trying on Jayce's part.

Jayce feigned jealousy. From his cell he shouted, "Darlin' girl, you're payin' more attention to that boy than to your poor old neglected husband."

Flora tried to sound sarcastic. "He's younger, he's better-lookin', and he's got nothin' on his conscience."

"He will have by the time he gets a little older. Show me somebody who's got nothin' on his conscience and I'll show you somebody who's spent his life asleep."

Listening, Andy conceded to himself that his own conscience sometimes troubled him when he had time to pay attention to it. In his first years back in the white man's world after his time among the Comanches, he had given those who befriended him plenty of reason to wonder if they should have left him where he was. He had caused anxiety for Rusty in particular. Looking back, he could well understand how Rusty might have given up on him, especially when he threatened to run away and rejoin the Comanches. Instead, Rusty had taken him back to the Indians at considerable danger to himself. Andy had found it impossible to remain in that other world, though even now he still grieved over having lost his place in it.

He sometimes questioned if he belonged in this one either.

The hard truth was that he did not fit comfortably in either world, white or red.

Jayce Landon had talked Tom into bringing a couple of forked tree branches to his cell so he could fashion a set of crutches for Scooter. He had promised, "I ain't fixin' to hit anybody over the head with them. The boy needs to be gettin' up and movin' around some. He'll need help with his walkin'."

Now he had a pile of wood shavings in the cell. He had trimmed away the bark and smoothed the surface with a pocketknife borrowed from Tom. He said, "These things'll need some cloth wrappin' to see that they don't rub sores under his arms. Otherwise, they're finished."

Tom said, "If they're finished, I'll thank you to give me back that knife." He extended his hand.

Jayce acted embarrassed. He handed the knife back through the bars. "Sorry. I almost forgot."

Andy knew Jayce had not forgotten anything, but he had hoped the sheriff would. Tom Blessing seldom forgot anything important.

Flora said, "I'll finish them up." She started back toward Jayce's cell, but Tom stopped her. He had never allowed her within reaching distance of her husband. He knew about her slipping a derringer to Jayce in the Hopper's Crossing jail.

He said, "I'll bring the crutches to you. Slide them out here, Jayce." Almost apologetically he added, "I appreciate what you two are doin' for the boy, but I can't afford much trust. Given the slightest chance I think you'd be out of here like a turpentined cat."

Jayce shrugged. "I told you that when I first came."

Flora wrapped cotton cloth around the top of the crutches as padding. "Feel like givin' them a try, Scooter?"

The boy turned himself around and cautiously put one foot on the floor. He had to use both hands to get the other leg into place. His face twisted with pain. Andy hurried to help him. "Does it hurt?"

Scooter grimaced. "Sure it hurts. But lift me up and see if I can fit them things under my arms." He was wobbly. Andy kept hold of him so he would not fall.

Scooter said, "I feel like I'm goin' down flat on my face. A little dizzy too."

"Don't be in a hurry. It'll take you a while to get the knack." He remembered a time long ago when a horse fall had left him with a broken leg. The crutches at first had seemed bent on bringing him down.

Tom asked, "Rusty, what did you find out about that bunch of riders who came to town this mornin'?"

Rusty said, "They were just Mexican traders bringin' a string of half-broke horses to sell to the farmers hereabouts. There wasn't a Hopper amongst them."

Tom said, "Strangers worry me, but the merchants wouldn't abide me turnin' them back at the edge of town. Visitors bring in money."

"It wouldn't be hard for a bunch of the Hoppers to slip into town at night. They'd love to get a clean shot at Jayce."

"That's why I put him in a cell that ain't got a window in it. As long as he stays there he's as safe as in church. Then after the judge gets here . . ." Tom did not finish. He did not have to.

Andy frowned. Flora did not deserve to be reminded constantly that her husband had an appointment with a rope. He said, "I need some fresh air. I think I'll go take me a little walk around town."

Rusty warned, "Keep watchin' over your shoulder. I wouldn't put it past the Hoppers to grab one of us and try to make a swap for Jayce."

Andy had not thought of that. He realized he should have. Rusty was usually a step ahead of him. Sometimes he despaired of ever catching up. He said, "If that happened, what would you do?"

Rusty said, "We're responsible for keepin' Jayce from harm till he's had his day in court. If it meant havin' to sacrifice one of us, that's what we're paid for. It's part of bein' a Ranger."

Tom nodded in silent agreement.

Their logic disturbed Andy. Jayce Landon was an admitted murderer. A death sentence was almost certain. To trade the life of a Ranger—any Ranger—to let Jayce live a couple of weeks longer seemed beyond reason. Andy deferred to the judgment of Rusty and Tom but retained his skepticism.

"I'll be careful," he promised.

Tom said, "Before you go, would you mind lettin' that drunk out of his cell? I expect two nights in there have sobered him up good."

The man had raised a ruckus in a saloon where things were usually so quiet the place could almost be taken for a Sunday school. Not wanting the burden of extra prisoners during this time of potential trouble, Tom had tried to let him off with a warning. At that point the drunk had thrown a chair through a glass window, and Tom no longer had a choice. Property must be respected, whether saloon or church house.

Andy unlocked the cell and beckoned with his thumb. "You've had enough free meals. Sheriff says he doesn't want to see anything but the backside of you leavin' town."

The man picked up his hat. He had brought nothing else in with him. He rubbed his chin. "I sure do need a shave."

"Go get it in some other town."

Andy followed him out into the sunshine. The former prisoner blinked against the brightness and looked up and down the street. "Where'd you-all put my horse?"

"In a corral at the wagon yard."

"Hope he got fed better than I did."

In a minute he was gone.

The weather was still warm, but with each passing day the sun edged a little farther to the south. The smell of fall was in the air for a while in early morning, though summer still ruled later in the day. Andy wondered how winter's cold would affect Scooter's healing.

Farley Brackett sat on the jail step, whittling a scrap piece of pine down to a pile of shavings that littered the ground at his feet. The cuts and bruises on his face were healing. "Where you headed, Badger Boy?"

"Just takin' a look around."

"What're you lookin' for?"

"I don't know, exactly."

"If you don't know what you're lookin' for, how you goin' to know it when you see it?"

Annoyed, Andy said, "Maybe you ought to go with me and help me look."

"Can't. I'm guardin' the front door. If you get yourself into any trouble, Badger Boy, you'll have to fight your own way out."

Andy could accept advice, even criticism, from Rusty or Tom, but he drew the line at Farley. "You just watch me."

"Oh, I'll be watchin' you, all right. But don't expect me to come runnin'. Last time I did that I got myself shot."

Andy never expected anything pleasant to come from Farley, and he was rarely disappointed. He wanted to think of a good retort, but none came, so he did not try for the last word. He walked through an open gate in the fence that surrounded the courthouse and jail. He stopped a minute to look up and down the dirt street. Before many more days it would be bustling as farmers in mule-drawn wagons began hauling the first of their cotton crop to town for ginning. Farm families with fresh money in their pockets would be crowding in to buy clothes and other necessities for the coming winter.

Right now the street was quiet. It looked about the same as he had known it during the years since his return from Comancheria except that the town had grown. He saw nothing to be concerned about.

He spotted a farmer he knew and walked over to talk with him. The farmer shook Andy's hand, then looked across toward the jail. He said, "I hear you-all have got a dangerous man locked up, and you're afraid somebody may come and try to bust him out."

"Some people would like to. We're prepared for them."

"Just the same, I ain't lettin' my family come to town till everything is over with. I wouldn't want them to get in the way of a shootin' scrape. Or maybe you can guarantee me that there won't be one."

"I can't even guarantee that the sun will rise and set tomorrow the same as it always has."

The farmer grunted. "I hope the judge shows up pretty soon and gets this mess over with. My wife is bustin' to come to town and see what's new over at the mercantile."

Andy admitted, "It won't be a bad idea to hold her at home a little while longer."

"Maybe you-all better send for some more Rangers."

"There's already three of us, and only one jailbreak to worry about. The head office in Austin figures three is probably two Rangers too many."

"You ought to take up farmin', Andy. All you got to worry about is drought, flood, hail, grasshoppers, and low prices."

Andy walked on down the street with no particular mission in mind except to look for something or somebody that seemed out of place. He peered into the mercantile store and saw no one except the storekeeper and a woman customer. He stepped through the door of a saloon and glanced over the half dozen men there. All the faces were familiar except one, and he looked like a drummer peddling his wares. The saloon was more than just a place for drinking. It was a public service of sorts, a social center where men could meet and swap news and views, a trading site for discussing deals and shaking hands on them. More horses and mules and cotton bales had been sold there than at the livery barn or the gin.

The barkeeper said, "Come on in. No use standin' there blockin' the door."

"Just lookin' for somebody." Andy went back outside, remembering what Farley had said. He did not know who he was looking for. How would he know him when he saw him?

Down at the livery stable, toward the end of the street, a man sat in a straight chair leaned back against the door. Andy at first took him to be the proprietor but after a closer look realized he did not know the man. Yet the face seemed vaguely familiar.

"Howdy," Andy said, trying to remember.

The man stared back, his eyes not friendly. He did not speak.

Andy said, "Seems like I ought to know you." He remembered now. "Your name would be Hopper, wouldn't it?"

"Might be."

"A while back me and Farley Brackett were on our way to deliver Jayce Landon to the sheriff at Hopper's Crossing. You were with a bunch that tried to stop us."

The man's tone was insolent. "That might be too."

"So what're you doin' here?"

"I've got to be somewhere."

"Not here unless you've got business. What's your business?"

"I've got a wife who bitches at me all the time. I come over here now and then to get drunk without her knowin' about it. Any law against that?"

He did not look drunk. Andy thought he could guess Hopper's real reason. He said, "I think you better move on out of town."

"Look, Ranger, I'm spendin' good money here, and I come by it honest. If I've broke any laws, tell me. If I ain't, then leave me the hell alone."

Andy was losing the argument and knew it. He had no grounds for running Hopper out of town. If he did so anyway, he might be subject to legal action. If he did not, and somebody got hurt, he would be blamed for not acting when he had the chance. It was enough to make him wonder why he had chosen to be a Ranger.

For a moment he considered going back to the jail and asking Rusty what he should do. But he had leaned on Rusty far too many times. Sooner or later he had to begin deciding such matters for himself.

He warned, "Watch yourself."

Hopper replied, "I always do. And them that's around me."

Andy returned to the jail. Farley still sat on the step. He had a new piece of wood to whittle on. The earlier one lay scattered in curled shavings on the ground.

Andy said, "I'll bet you didn't know we're bein' watched."

"I know. Bim Hopper's sittin' over yonder at the stable. He's spied on us for several days."

"You knew about him all that time?"

"Spotted him as soon as he showed up. I got to know Bim pretty good when Big'un and his bunch drug me away from my mother's place. He's got mean eyes, and fists hard as a pine knot."

"What are we goin' to do about him?" Andy instantly regretted asking advice, especially from Farley.

Farley said, "I'm waitin' for him to make a wrong move so I can shoot his ear off, or maybe his big toe. Somethin' he'll remember me by."

"He says he's in town to get drunk."

"He ain't been drunk since he came here. He's watchin' for us to let our guard down so him and his cousins can storm the jail and drag Jayce out."

Andy did not admit it, but his thinking ran the same as Farley's.

Farley said, "I hope they try. It'll be the best fight I've been in since I shot hell out of the state police."

Andy was disgusted. "This ain't some kind of entertainment show. There could be dead men layin' out in the street."

"The world could get along just fine without some of them Hoppers. They're a nest of vipers."

"They might not be the only ones killed."

"Have you taken a good look at that old jail? It ain't pretty, but it's bull stout. A whole regiment couldn't bust in without they had a cannon."

Andy was not pacified, but arguing with Farley was like trying to converse with a fence post. He went on up and entered the jail.

Rusty asked, "See anything?"

"There's a man watchin' us from over at the stable."

"Yeah, a cousin to Big'un Hopper. We've been keepin' an eye on him."

"How come you didn't tell me about it?"

Rusty smiled. "We thought we'd see how long it took you to spot him yourself."

Testing me, Andy thought, irritated. Like I was a new recruit.

After consideration he realized the description fit. He stood small against experienced lawmen like Rusty and Tom, even Farley. But he said, "Hadn't we ought to run him off?"

"It's better we leave him where we can watch what he's up to. The time to worry is when we *can't* see him."

Andy went to the window and looked up and down the street again. In a minute he said, "There's one thing you didn't know."

"What?" Rusty asked.

"That drunk we just let out of jail. He's over yonder talkin' to Bim Hopper."

Rusty and Tom both moved quickly to the window. Tom swore, "Well, I'll be damned. Looks like we've had a spy in our midst."

Rusty nodded. "Looks like."

{ EIGHTEEN }

Big'un Hopper looked back to be sure nobody had deserted him. He had twisted arms to the breaking point to get the six men who accompanied him on this punitive expedition. It would not take much of a scare to send most of them scurrying back to Hopper's Crossing. The only ones he felt he could depend upon were cousins Harp and Bim. Even those would bear some watching.

The wagon jolted along behind with several cans of coal oil he had brought. He could not afford to buy it locally because he would be remembered and the finger of blame would be pointed straight at him.

At dusk they were within half a mile of town. "Let's pull over into them trees yonder," he said. "We'll wait till the dark of the moon."

Cousin Wilbur pulled his horse in beside Big'un's. "The closer we get, the less I like this whole notion. I'm in favor of us gettin' Jayce, but there's other people in that jailhouse too. We could be charged with murderin' them all."

"Not unless we get caught. They can suspicion all they want, but suspicion don't hold no water in court. Anyway, I told all of you what we were goin' to do. I ain't lettin' you back out now."

"Accordin' to Bim there's a kid in that jail. What about him?"

"Remember, he's an outlaw's boy, and he was in on the killin' of Oscar Truscott. He's probably got the mark of a noose around his neck anyway."

"I still don't like it."

Big'un grabbed his cousin's shirt just below the throat and shook the man harshly. "Any more of that talk and I'll see that you walk all the way home."

He was much larger and stronger than his kinsmen. They might grumble, but when the voices quieted down Big'un was confident he would still prevail. He softened his tone. "Uncle Judd gave us a warrant for Jayce's arrest."

Harp asked, "Does Uncle Judd's jurisdiction reach over into another county's jailhouse?"

"He's a judge, ain't he?" Big'un trusted that none of them understood the limitations of Judd Hopper's jurisdiction. They knew all there was to know about mules and horses, cows and plows, but the intricacies of law were a mystery to them.

Wilbur frowned, considering the matter. "If Uncle Judd approves, I reckon it's all right."

Actually, Big'un had told his uncle only that they were going after Jayce. The judge had not let him explain. He had said, "I do not want to know anything about this. Then I can truthfully swear that I do not know what was done or who was responsible."

Big'un had thought it wise not to tell the judge that Jayce might be only one of the casualties, that others might include a couple or three Rangers and possibly even a sheriff. The old man could get downright unreasonable about anything that might bring state investigators in to snoop around. He had some skeletons of his own that were not buried deeply enough for comfort.

Big'un stretched out on the ground to rest while he waited for darkness. He tried not to sleep, fearing part of his crew might quietly slip away. He had some kinfolks who weren't worth killing, but now and then they were useful to him.

If all of the Confederate Army was like them, he thought, it's no wonder the damn Yankees whipped us.

He had not gone to war himself. The judge had pulled political strings to shield as many Hoppers as possible from conscription, arranging for Landon men to take up the slack. That served the demands of patriotism and reduced the enemy's numbers as well.

He waited until the stars were in full array, then prodded his kinsmen into reluctant motion. "The sooner we get the job done, the better chance we'll have to get out of this county before daylight. There won't be nobody able to identify us."

By the time they reached the first houses at the edge of town Big'un saw that he had lost two of his helpers in the darkness.

Harp said, "It's Wilbur and his no-account brother-in-law. We ought to've left them at home."

Big'un cursed. "When I get through with Wilbur . . ." He looked fiercely at those who remained. "If the rest of you have got any idea of quittin', put it out of your mind. I'll shoot the next man who turns back." He knew he would not, but it was important that they believed he would. When his temper was up, even the town dogs knew to slink away.

Only a few of the houses showed lamplight. Most folks had gone to bed. Things were working out according to plan. If he and his helpers got the job done quickly they should encounter little trouble from local citizens.

The courthouse and the adjoining old jail were like an island in the center of an open lot surrounded by a wooden fence that sagged in a couple of places. Big'un motioned for the driver to stop the wagon. They could carry the cans of coal oil from here. But first he had to locate and eliminate the watchman who patrolled the streets and periodically circled the courthouse. He waited a few minutes until he saw a man walking along the fronts of the buildings along the square, trying the doors to be certain they were locked.

Few people here were likely to recognize Big'un, but as a precaution he pulled his neckerchief up to cover his face. He stepped into the dark open space between two stores and flattened himself against a wall. He listened to the watchman's footsteps on the wooden sidewalk. As the shadowy figure crossed the opening, Big'un moved out behind him and clubbed him with the barrel of his six-shooter. He struck a second time to be sure the man remained out of action for a while. He dragged the limp body into the darkness between the buildings and left it.

He returned to where the others waited beside the wagon. "The watchman is out of the way. Now let's pull the wagon up to block the back door. Then their only way out is the front."

It took a little pushing and maneuvering to position the wagon over the single step so that the door could not be opened far enough for anyone to pass through.

A man stepped around the corner of the jail and stopped abruptly, drawing a pistol. "What're you-all up to?"

Before Big'un could think of a reply, a dark figure appeared behind the intruder and slugged him.

Big'un said, "Good work, Bim. He like to've caught us before we was ready." He unhitched the team and motioned for one of the others to lead the mules away. Big'un lifted a can from the bed of the wagon. "Let's give them walls a good dose of coal oil."

A cousin who went by the nickname Jaybo argued, "The thought of somebody burnin' up in a fire gives me the shakes. We could use a rail for a batterin' ram and bust the door down."

Big'un resisted an impulse to hit him in the mouth. "Would you want to be the first one to rush in there with three or four guns aimed straight at your gut?"

"If you look at it that way . . ."

Big'un assumed the argument was finished. "Bim, you watch the back door so no citizen comes and sets them free. The rest of us will take the front. If they try to bust out we'll shoot them. If they don't they'll know what hell is like before they get there."

Harp said, "Folks'll come runnin' to fight the fire."

"A shot or two in their direction will turn them back. This oughtn't to take long, dry as that lumber is."

Big'un tossed a match at the base of the jail's rear wall. The flames quickly licked their way up to consume the coal oil. He trotted around the side and lighted a couple of places. He motioned for his helpers to join him a few feet from the front door. He started a fire there, then drew his pistol and waited. "This'll be like pottin' fish in a water bucket."

Andy had turned in early, but he was not having a restful night. The folded quilt that served in lieu of a mattress did little to hide the fact that beneath it lay wooden slats that got no softer no matter how he turned. Farley Brackett occasionally broke into fits of loud snoring.

Rusty did not snore, but now and then he spoke a few words in his sleep. One word Andy recognized was "Josie." Though Rusty never spoke of her anymore, Andy sensed that she was still much on his mind. A couple of women here in town looked a little like her from across the street. Andy had noticed that Rusty seemed momentarily startled each time one of them appeared.

He managed to doze off and on, but the spells were short-lived. He worried about what was to become of Scooter. The boy was able to walk without the crutches Jayce had fashioned for him, though the effort was awkward and caused him considerable pain.

Scooter's father was hiding out there somewhere. Of that, Andy was sure. As soon as the boy healed enough to travel,

Lige Tennyson was likely to steal him away. And to what? An outlaw life, probably, and most likely a short one. Andy had been considering the possibility of beating Lige to the punch, of taking Scooter where his father would never find him. Andy would have to resign as a Ranger, but he would be willing to pay that price. He would never be able to compensate Rusty directly. If he could do for Scooter what Rusty had done for him, however, that would be repayment of a sort.

And where could he take the boy? The Ranger camp had served as a temporary shelter, but it could not offer what he needed over the long term. The Monahan family kept coming to mind. They were generous, open-handed people who once had all but adopted Andy as one of their own. Surely they would do the same for another boy badly in need of a stable home and a sense of direction. And they lived far to the northwest, up in the Fort Belknap country of west-central Texas. Lige would have no idea where to begin looking.

It had been Flora's habit to spend most of the day at the jail, caring for Scooter and talking to her husband through two sets of bars. She would retreat to the boardinghouse at suppertime, not returning until morning. Tonight, however, she knocked urgently on the front door shortly after dark. "It's Flora," she said. "I've got somethin' to tell you-all."

Andy waited to see if someone else would get up and find out what she wanted. Farley grumbled, "Badger Boy, go let her in."

Andy's cot was farthest from the door, but he knew he could not outwait Farley. He had gone to bed with his clothes on, all but his boots. He lifted the heavy crowbar that blocked the door. "Anybody out there besides you?" he asked Flora. He was mindful of the possibility that someone might use her to gain entry and free Jayce, or kill him.

"Nobody," she said. "But somebody may be comin'."

She stepped inside, and Andy closed and barred the door. She said, "Scooter's daddy just came to see me at the boardin'house."

"Old Lige? How did you come to know him?"

"He's never been far from town. He noticed me comin' and goin' from the jail, so he followed me to the boardin'house and introduced himself. Every day he comes and asks me about his boy. Tonight he saw somethin' he didn't like, and he asked me to give you-all a warnin'."

"About what?"

"He was camped in some timber just outside of town. A while before dark some men came with a wagon and stopped to rest awhile. Big'un Hopper was leadin' them. The old man doesn't know what they're up to, but it can't be anything good."

Rusty had left his cot and stood nearby, listening. "Where's Lige now?"

"Somewhere close, you can bet. He's worried on account of his boy."

One of Tom Blessing's temporary deputies had been sleeping in an open cell. He pulled on his boots and said, "I'll go take a look around."

Rusty said, "Much obliged. If you see or hear anything suspicious, give us a holler."

The deputy took a rifle from the office's gun rack. He said, "You-all want to bar the door behind me?"

Flora walked out with him. Andy set the crowbar in place.

Farley stretched out on his cot. "It'd take half the Yankee army to bust these heavy doors open. I'm goin' back to sleep."

Scooter had listened quietly. He said, "That's my daddy she was talkin' about. Did she say he's here?"

Andy said, "Somewhere around. He ain't forgot you."

He wished Lige would.

Andy had no intention of going back to sleep. Thinking he heard low voices outside, he left the cot and walked to the window. At first he saw nothing, for the night seemed pitch black. He stepped back and stumbled into a tin can filled with ashes, substituting for a cuspidor. It clattered and rolled across the floor.

Farley's gruff voice demanded, "Don't you know we're tryin' to sleep?"

"Sorry."

Farley recognized the voice. "I might've known it was you, Badger Boy. For God's sake, go back to bed."

Andy was about to when he saw a flickering light reflecting upon the ceiling. He swung back toward the window. "Fire!" he shouted. "There's a fire outside."

Farley said, "You're crazy." But he got up and looked for himself. "By God, Rusty, the place *is* on fire."

With that Rusty was on his feet too. He quickly pulled his boots on. Recognizing the possibility of trouble, he had been sleeping in his clothes, as had the others. Tom Blessing was also up from his cot.

Andy lifted the crowbar out of its brackets and dropped it to the floor. He pushed the front door partway open. Blistering flames leaped into his face, and he jerked back instinctively. A bullet struck the facing, followed by another, which thumped into the heaviest part of the door. He pulled the door shut.

Rusty said, "That Hopper bunch. They knew they couldn't break in. They're tryin' to burn us out."

Andy trotted to the back door. He could push it only a few inches before it bumped against something solid. The opening was too small to squeeze through. Someone outside fired a shot that splintered the frame. He said, "They got the back door blocked."

Farley strapped his gun belt around his waist. "Be damned if I'll stay here and burn."

Tom said, "The front door is the only way out, and they're waitin' for us there. But we've got no choice."

Rusty said, "Scooter can't make it on his own, and Jayce is locked in a cell. We can't leave him there to die."

Farley said, "They're goin' to hang him anyway."

Andy said, "I can carry Scooter."

Farley said, "If you let Jayce out he'll run like a scalded dog."

Rusty repeated, "We can't leave him to burn."

"He will anyway, soon as the devil gets ahold of him."

From behind his bars Jayce shouted, his voice on the edge of desperation, "Get me out of this trap."

Tom tossed his keys to Andy. "We'll take our chances on him. Turn him loose."

Eye-stinging smoke was already boiling up in the section that contained the cells. Jayce coughed heavily. Andy swung the cell door open and said, "You're on your honor."

Jayce made no response except to lower his head and cough into his hands. Once he was out of the cell area he said, "Let me defend myself. Give me a gun."

Tom Blessing said, "You know we can't do that."

"I ain't goin' out there empty-handed." Jayce stepped to Tom's desk and opened a drawer. He withdrew a pistol and spun the cylinder to see if it was loaded. "Now, are we goin' out there, or are we goin' to roast like a beef on a spit?"

Rusty accepted the situation without argument. "We'll go out shootin' and make them duck their heads. Andy, you follow close with Scooter. We'll be between you and them. Maybe they won't even see you."

Andy felt guilt about letting others stand the greater risk, but he knew if the boy tried to hobble out on his own, he would not get far past the door.

Farley gave a rebel yell and flung the door open. His pistol blazed. Tom and Rusty and Jayce burst out just behind him, firing at shadows. Andy crouched low, carrying Scooter in his arms.

Andy had heard Rusty say that rapid fire did not have to be accurate so long as it made the enemy keep their heads down. The Rangers and Jayce had cleared the door and were halfway to the fence before the Hoppers regained their wits enough to fire back.

An angry voice shouted, "Shoot, you cowardly sons of bitches. Shoot."

Andy would bet a month's pay the voice belonged to Big'un.

Someone in the Hopper line cried out like a hurt dog.

In the center of the yard was a well with a windlass and a circular stone wall three feet high. Andy dropped behind it. "Flatten out, Scooter, and pull your legs in."

He peered over the rim of the well, seeking a target. He fired once to no apparent effect.

He could hear excited shouts from over in town. Aroused citizens were beginning to respond to the fire and the shooting.

The Hoppers had lost their advantage. Now with the blazing building behind them, their silhouettes became targets. Rusty fired, and Andy saw a man fall. Then Rusty went down. Andy's heart jumped, and he fired at the spot where he had seen a pistol flash.

A rifle opened up from just beyond the perimeter fence. Someone had joined the Rangers in their fight.

Even with the light from the fire, Andy could see no faces he could swear to in court. A large figure arose from a squatting position and ran hard, disappearing around the corner while bullets whispered around him. Andy was almost certain he had seen Big'un Hopper.

A plaintive voice cried, "We give up. Don't shoot no more."

Andy sensed that Rusty was out of the fight. He took it upon himself to shout, "Everybody hold your fire. You Hoppers, raise your hands and stand up where we can see you."

The voice said, "I'm the only one still able to stand. Don't shoot."

The man who had fired from the other side of the fence climbed over, rifle in his hand. He had a shuffling gait. Andy recognized Lige Tennyson. Lige called anxiously, "Scooter! Where you at, boy?"

"Pa?" Scooter pushed to his feet and leaned against the well to steady himself. "Is that you, Pa?"

"It's me. Are you all right? They didn't hit you?"

"No, sir. Andy wouldn't let them." Scooter and his father hugged each other fiercely. Scooter cried, "What you doin' here, Pa? They'll put you in jail."

"I had to know if you're all right." A section of the jail wall fell inward. A shower of sparks lifted high into the air, then fell. "Don't look like they've got a jail to put me in."

Andy said, "You got here awful fast."

"I didn't have to come very far. Did Mrs. Landon deliver my message?"

"She did. But none of us expected fire."

The jail began caving in, sending waves of blistering

heat rolling across the yard. The townspeople set up a bucket brigade. It was too late to save the jail, but they worked to keep the adjacent courthouse from catching fire.

Farley limped badly. In the flickering light of the flames Andy saw that one trousers leg was bloody. "Looks like you didn't dodge quick enough," he said.

"Like I keep tellin' you, Badger Boy, you're a damned jinx. Every time you're around, somethin' happens to me. You better take a look at Rusty. I think he's harder hit."

Rusty lay twisted on the ground, his right hand gripping a bleeding left shoulder. He swore under his breath, fighting against the pain.

Andy dropped to his knees beside him. "How bad is it?"

"Busted the shoulder, I think. Big'un done it before he turned and ran."

In a flash of anger Andy said, "I'll catch him. I'll make him wish he never got out of bed this mornin'."

"What about the Hoppers? Big'un was the only one I saw leave."

Andy made a quick survey. One Hopper was dead and one dying. Another had an arm bloody and dangling uselessly. The only one on his feet identified himself as Jaybo. The one with the bad arm refused to answer any questions beyond admitting that he was called Harp. He said, "I want a lawyer. And if I don't get a doctor, I'll bleed to death."

Andy knew that under these circumstances some Rangers would simply put another bullet into him. He was tempted. "The doctor'll see to Rusty first. He can look at you later if you're still alive."

"You'd let me sit here and die?"

Farley said angrily, "Why not? You'd've let us burn to death."

Jaybo whined, "I didn't want to come here in the first place, but Big'un—"

Harp hissed, "Shut up. Don't tell them a damned thing."

Andy said, "You're lucky you're not facin' a murder charge." He looked around. "Where's Jayce?" His eyes widened. "Anybody seen Jayce?"

His gaze swept the yard. For a moment he thought Jayce might have fallen to the Hoppers' guns.

Farley put the obvious truth into words. "I told you. He's took to the tulies, just like I said he would."

A woman's voice cried, "Jayce!" Flora Landon held her long skirt up clear of the ground as she ran across the yard to the Rangers. "Did Jayce get out?"

Andy said, "He got out, and then he lit out."

It took her a moment to absorb what Andy said. She began laughing and crying at the same time. "He got away?"

Farley said, "Slicker than a greased pig."

Solemnly Andy told her, "You know we'll have to go after him again. He's still got a murder to answer for."

"A justified killin'."

"Murder is never justified."

"A good killin' isn't always murder." Flora looked around to see who might be able to overhear. She lowered her voice. "You know what Big'un tried to do to me in Oscar Truscott's jail?"

"I heard. They said he didn't get it done."

"But he *did* get it done once before. Him and his brother Ned caught me alone at home. I couldn't fight off two of them." She looked at the ground. "I was too ashamed to tell about it, but I was so bruised up that Jayce knew by lookin' at me. That's why he killed Ned. He'd've killed Big'un too, but you Rangers never gave him the chance."

Andy thought about it. "Then it's more than just the feud. Big'un has had an extra reason for wantin' to see Jayce dead."

Flora nodded. "As long as Jayce is alive, Big'un has to be afraid he'll get the same thing Ned got."

Andy mused, "I wonder if Big'un knows Jayce is on the loose again, and it's his own doin'."

Farley pulled his trousers leg up to examine his wound. "We ought to stand back and let Jayce have him. We could arrest Jayce later and charge him for two killin's instead of one."

Andy shook his head. "That wouldn't be accordin' to law."

"Law ain't always justice. There's some things they never wrote in that book."

Andy rarely found himself agreeing with Farley, but in this instance he thought Farley made sense. The Comanches would never fret over piddling technicalities.

The doctor had come and was examining Rusty's wounded shoulder. "How does it feel?"

Rusty sucked in a painful breath. "It hurts, damn it! How do you think it feels?"

The doctor shouted, "Somebody bring a wagon. We've got to get this man over to my house."

The wounded Harp Hopper whimpered, "I'm bleedin' to death."

The doctor said without sympathy, "I'll probably have to take your arm off. Don't be in such a hurry to part with it."

Rusty looked up at Andy. "We have to see if we can find Big'un before Jayce does."

The doctor said, "You're not going to do anything, not for a while. That shoulder looks bad."

Rusty told Andy, "Then it's up to you and Farley."

"Farley's wounded too. Not as bad as you, but he won't be ridin' for a while."

Rusty fretted, "It's too much for you to handle by yourself."

Andy put on an air of confidence to cover his doubts. "I can do it. One thing bothers me, though. I can't charge him with murderin' Sheriff Truscott. The only witnesses were Scooter and his daddy. You've already said no court would take their testimony."

"But you can charge him with attempted murder of peace officers and with malicious destruction of this jailhouse. That should put him away for a few years."

Farley grunted. "Bury him six feet under and he'll never be a bother to anybody again."

Tom Blessing had been busy with the bucket brigade. The jail finally collapsed into a blistering-hot pile of charred wood and glowing coals. Only its two stone chimneys remained, standing like markers in a graveyard. When the courthouse was out of danger Tom walked over to join the Rangers. He checked on Rusty and Farley, then said, "Your prisoner sure made a mess out of my jail."

Rusty tried to smile but could not quite bring it off. "You've been wantin' a new one for a long time."

"I can already hear the taxpayers holler. They'll say the town is peaceful and we don't keep enough prisoners here to justify the cost."

"That'll change. The town's growin'."

Blessing mused, "It's just as well that Jayce got away. I have no jail to put him in now. The best I could do would be to chain him to a tree."

Flora protested, "He's a man, not an animal. He deserves a chance."

Andy said, "He had a chance, and he took it. You have any idea where he went?"

"I expect I do. Wherever Big'un goes, that's where Jayce'll go. If you want Big'un you'd better find him before Jayce does."

"I intend to try." Andy turned away from her. He found Lige standing beside the well, his arm around Scooter's shoulder. Andy said, "You know there's paper out on you."

"It'd be a wonder on earth if there wasn't. You fixin' to put me under arrest?"

Andy was aware that Lige's rifle had helped shorten the fight. "There's just one of me. I've got two wounded Rangers and two other fugitives to worry about. So far as I know the only legitimate charges against you are from Kerrville. Your take from that bank didn't amount to more than petty larceny."

"It sure wasn't what I expected. I never thought I'd be robbed by a bank teller."

"Do you suppose if I turned my back on you for a while you could disappear without causin' any commotion about it?"

"I'd bet you a hundred dollars on it, if I had that much."

"You have anyplace to go?"

"Maybe. Me and my boy talked about it some."

Scooter asked, "You takin' me with you, Pa?"

Lige bent down and hugged his son again. "I've done aplenty of thinkin'. You're a good boy. You've got a good future if you'll stay away from the likes of me. These Rangers can find a place for you where you'll grow up straight and strong and never see a jailhouse from the inside."

"Don't go without me, Pa."

"It's best this way. You may not see me again for a while, but if you ever need me I'll come runnin'. That's a promise."

Scooter cried, "I love you, Pa."

"And I . . . hell, son, you're a man almost. Men don't say things like that." He blinked a few times. "Men don't have to."

{ NINETEEN }

Walking toward the courthouse, Big'un tipped his hat to Aunt Maudie, mother of his cousin Wilbur. Her lips pinched, and her eyes flashed resentment. He wondered what kind of story her son must have told her. Damn Wilbur anyway, for deserting when he was needed most!

The reception from his aunt shook him a little. He sensed that the one awaiting him from Uncle Judd might be worse. He paused at the open door to the judge's office, summoning courage. He had imagined the scene over and over during the ride home alone. He and his cousins had managed to burn the jailhouse, but so far as he had been able to tell they had not even touched Jayce Landon or the Tennyson kid. He had seen a Ranger go down. He did not know if he was killed. The only casualties he could swear to had been on the Hopper side.

His uncle's attitude was every bit as blistering as Big'un had envisioned. Judd Hopper pushed up behind his desk and scowled like a screeching hawk about to attack. "So you're back. Why aren't you dead?"

Big'un hunched a little, bringing his arms up as if to defend himself. He was not accustomed to having to explain anything. "I done the best I could. Things just didn't work out."

"You ran off and left two cousins dead, another wounded, and one taken prisoner. If that's the best you can do, you're not worth hanging with a secondhand rope."

Big'un puzzled, "How come you already know about it?"

"The telegraph, for one thing. The word's already gone out to Rangers and local sheriffs. They'll be on the lookout for you."

"I didn't think anybody would recognize me."

"It appears they did. And by now the cousins they took prisoner have probably spilled everything they know."

"I'm not sure who they caught. I hope it's not Jaybo. He hasn't got the guts of a jackrabbit."

The judge's eyebrows arched. "Then you shouldn't have taken him along. And the others who deserted you before the fight started, they came dragging into town during the night with their tails between their legs."

"Damned cowards. I ain't real proud of this family right now."

"And most of this family is not proud of you, taking your kin out on a fool's mission. Do you know which one got killed?"

"I seen a couple of them go down. I couldn't tell which they was."

"So you ran off and left them."

"The Rangers came out shootin', and everybody ducked. They even gave Jayce Landon a gun. Can you imagine that, givin' a gun to that killer? And then some of the people from town joined in. Wasn't nothin' left but to get out of there."

"So you abandoned your kin to face it alone."

"They was of damned little use anyway. I could've done better by myself."

The judge bit the tip from a cigar and spat it halfway across the room. He lighted the cigar, his severe gaze never leaving Big'un's face. "There's one more thing I learned from the telegraph. During the excitement, Jayce got away."

Big'un was slow to grasp the significance. "Then maybe I'll get another shot at him."

"More likely he'll get one at you. You tried to burn him to death. My guess is that he's already back here among his kin. And he'll be comin' to get you if you don't get him first."

Big'un shrugged off the warning. "There's more of us Hoppers than there is of the Landons. My kinfolks won't let him come that close."

"Don't depend on your kin. You've lorded it over them for years. Now this last wild sashay . . . Everybody around here is sick and tired of that old feud. You're on your own, Big'un."

The impact began to soak in. Big'un protested, "Mostly I've just done what you told me to. You're the one who wanted me wearin' a badge in the first place."

"That was when you were useful. Lately you've been like an anvil strapped on my back."

"So you've turned against me too?"

"The stink of this will reach all the way to Austin. The Rangers will be down here like a plague of locusts, and there's no telling what they may turn up."

"I could tell them aplenty if I was of a mind to."

"You won't if you've got a brain cell still working. You'll turn tail and travel as far as you can get before the Rangers catch up with you, or Jayce does." A small knot of fear began stirring in Big'un's stomach. It burned like acid. He considered making himself scarce for a while, maybe taking a vacation in Mexico. But travel could be dangerous. The Landons would be keeping a watch on him. Jayce might catch him somewhere out in the open. Big'un was not sure he could beat him in a fair fight.

He argued, "Travelin' takes money. I ain't got any. How about openin' that safe yonder and gettin' me some, say a thousand dollars?"

Judd exploded. "A thousand dollars? You're not worth two bits." He stood up and pointed toward the door. "Get out of my office before I shoot you myself and save Jayce the trouble."

Big'un looked at the steel safe standing in the corner. Many times he had seen his uncle open it, yet he had never had reason to watch closely enough to learn the combination. Now he wished he had been more observant.

Anger churned his stomach as he moved toward the door. "You'll wish you'd done better by me."

"I wish your mother had drowned you like a sick kitten the day you were born."

Big'un was not sure what he would do. He was sure about one thing he would *not* do; he would not leave here dead broke. Uncle Judd owed him, and somehow he was going to pay. But as long as Big'un hung around here in the open, he was in jeopardy. The safest place in town would be the jail. He could bar its door from inside, and nobody would get in unless he allowed it. Unlike Tom Blessing's, this jail was of brick construction, not easy to burn down. Surely the Rangers would catch Jayce within a few days and remove him as a threat.

But what if a jury failed to convict him? Then Jayce could stalk him at leisure. Someday when Big'un did not expect it a bullet could come from nowhere and cut him down.

He had seen juries do the unthinkable, but surely they

would not in this case. Murder was murder. They would see that Jayce was hanged. They had to.

Walking down the hall, he encountered several county employees, none of them kin. He saw or imagined condemnation in their eyes. Stung, he crossed the street to a small dining room where he often took his meals. The place was operated by the widow Jones, whose husband had fallen out of a wagon and broken his neck after emptying too many whiskey bottles. She looked at Big'un as if he were a stray dog bringing in fleas. Everybody in town must know what happened, he thought.

He trusted that she liked money more than she disliked him. He said, "I'd like you to deliver me my meals over at the jail for a day or two."

She arched an eyebrow. "You figure bein' in jail will save you from Jayce Landon?"

His temper flared. If a man had said that to him he would have bloodied his knuckles. "You just fetch my meals. I'm not payin' for your opinion."

"This is goin' to cost you extra. And it'll have to be payment on delivery."

He understood her implication, that Jayce might find a way to get to him. She did not want him to die owing her money.

He said, "I'll pay you, but don't send nobody else. I won't be openin' the door to just anybody."

Stung by the unfriendly receptions, Big'un went into the jail. He locked the door with a heavy key, then put an iron bar in place. Some of the fear left him, but not all.

To himself he said, "Damn you, Jayce Landon. This is all your fault."

He sat in a chair and leaned back against the jail's office wall, staring at nothing in particular, trying to come up with an idea. There was no telling how long it might take the Rangers to get Jayce. Being shut up in here for days, even weeks, was too bitter to contemplate. His thoughts kept going back to his uncle's safe. The old man always kept a substantial amount of money locked in it. It should be enough to keep him a long time in Mexico.

Gradually he came up with a plan. It was so simple he was surprised it had taken him so long.

Rusty lay in a bed in the doctor's house, his shoulder heavily wrapped. The doctor had drugged him to sleep. Standing over him, Andy thought he had never seen Rusty so pale, so helpless-looking. The doctor said, "He's one tough rooster. Others have tried to kill him, but they never got it done. He'll survive this time too."

"How many more can he take?"

"I hope he never takes any more. Every chance I get, I'm going to tell him to go home and stick to the plow."

Andy felt guilt. "I'm the one who talked him into goin' back to the Rangers after that hailstorm hit him. I wish I'd kept my mouth shut."

Farley sat in a chair across the room. His trousers leg had been cut away, and his wound wrapped almost as heavily as Rusty's. He said, "You never talked Rusty into anything he didn't want to do. He quit followin' advice a long time ago."

And *you* never started, Andy thought.

The doctor said, "Maybe when he's stronger you can take Rusty back to his farm."

"That's where he belongs."

"And maybe you can find a wife for him. He needs one."

"I've got one in mind," Andy said, thinking of Alice Monahan. "But Rusty will have to come around to it on his own." He straightened. "When he wakes up, tell him I'll be back soon as I can."

Farley said, "You're not very good at listenin' to advice either, but let me give you a little. Wire Austin to send you some help before you go pokin' around over in Hopper country."

"Can't lose the time. I expect Big'un has gone back over there, and Jayce is probably not far behind. May even be ahead of him."

"Wait awhile and you won't have to bring back but one. Or if you're really lucky they'll kill each other and you won't have to mess with either of them."

"That wouldn't be Rusty's way."

"It'd save the expense of one trial, maybe two. And it might keep us from havin' to bury an Indian kid who's got more nerve than good sense. Gravestones come high these days." Farley saw that his argument fell on deaf ears. "Wait a couple of days and I'll go with you."

The doctor said, "Forget it, Brackett. You couldn't straddle a horse if they gave you a thousand dollars."

Andy said, "I appreciate you makin' the offer. I'll swing around and let your mother and your sister know what's happened to you."

Farley protested, "They'll just fret over me for no reason. I've had a horse hurt me worse than this, steppin' on my foot."

"They deserve to know."

Andy did not allow Farley time for more argument. He walked out into the cool of the early morning. The smell of smoke was still heavy in the air, stinging his nostrils.

He met Flora Landon walking up the street from the direction of the boardinghouse where she stayed. She said, "I was on my way to see about Rusty and Farley. How do they look this mornin'?"

"They won't be runnin' footraces for a while, but they'll live."

"I want to tell them how much I appreciate what they did. They could've left Jayce to burn. Instead they gave him a gun."

Andy started to tell her Jayce got the pistol for himself, but she was in a grateful mood. He saw nothing to be gained by disillusioning her. He asked, "Is Scooter takin' to the boardin'house all right?"

"He's still hurtin' over his daddy goin' away without him, but otherwise he's all right. Been on his best behavior. If me and Jayce had ever had a boy I'd want him to be like Scooter."

"I appreciate you lookin' after him. When we've put this trouble behind us I'll take him to some folks who will make a good home for him."

"I'd take him in myself except they burned my house down, and my husband is on the dodge. I suppose you'll be goin' after him?"

"I have to, but I'm goin' for Big'un first. I hope I can get to him before Jayce does."

"Why don't you let Jayce take care of the job for you?"

"Then he'd have two murder charges on him."

"They can't hang him but once."

"With the right judge and jury he might not hang at all for one killin'. But two of them . . ." Andy shook his head.

She said, "Be careful, then. Remember that those Hoppers aren't lookin' to make new friends."

"They won't catch me asleep."

"You've got a good reason to take care of yourself. You may not realize it, but that Bethel girl is stuck on you. She'd take it hard if somethin' bad was to happen."

Andy tried to laugh away her concern. "So would I."

* * *

His courage almost left him as he approached the Brackett farm. For the tenth time since he had left town, he asked himself whether he should ride in or skirt around and proceed to Hopper's Crossing. His sense of duty prevailed. He owed it to Bethel and her mother to tell them what had happened to Farley.

It seemed that he never brought anything but bad news to this place. The women had good cause to dread seeing him. He squared his shoulders and rode straight to the house. A shrieking peacock announced his approach.

Bethel appeared on the front porch, one hand shading her eyes. She anxiously searched Andy's face for a clue and asked, "Is it about Farley again?"

It was unlikely she had already heard. He wished he did not have to be the bearer of the news. "He's been shot."

She swallowed. "How bad?"

"Not as bad as it could've been. He was strong enough to give me a cussin' when I told him I was comin' here."

"He'll be cussin' when he draws his last breath." She made an effort at a smile, but it was stillborn.

Bethel's mother stepped through the door and joined her daughter. "What is it? Farley again?"

Andy tried to ease her mind as quickly as he could. "He'll be all right, Mrs. Brackett." He dismounted and moved closer to the porch.

Bethel said, "He's been shot again, Mama. I swear, he draws trouble like a magnet."

Andy told them, "Wasn't none of it his fault. It happened in the line of duty." He explained about the burning of the jail and its occupants' escape under fire. "Farley took a bullet in his leg. He'll be limpin' around for a while. But Rusty's the one to worry about. He got hit pretty hard."

"Where is Farley now?" Mrs. Brackett asked.

"At the doctor's house. Doc was sayin' he'd probably let him go to a boardin'house by tomorrow or next day."

Mrs. Brackett said, "He doesn't need to go to a boarding-house. Bethel and I will take a wagon and fetch him home."

"He didn't even want me to come and let you know what happened. Didn't want you frettin'. Said he'd ride over here and tell you himself as soon as he could get on a horse."

Bethel said, "I wouldn't bet two bits on that. As soon as he felt like he could travel, he'd leave without lettin' us know. He's taken a fool notion that nobody cares about him."

Andy doubted that anybody other than immediate family cared much for Farley. Even they found him a trial. He went out of his way to ruffle those who might try to get close to him. He seemed to distrust friendship as if he knew it would not last. During the war it had not. He had lost too many friends, too much family.

Bethel said, "We appreciate you coming out to tell us."

Andy said, "It wasn't much out of my way. I'm goin' to Hopper's Crossing."

"You're after Jayce Landon, I suppose."

"Him and Big'un Hopper both. I figure where I find one I'll likely find the other."

Her eyes widened. "You're goin' by yourself?"

"There ain't but two of them."

Bethel grimaced. "That's about what Farley would say."

"There probably won't be but one if I don't find them myself before they find one another."

"If they shot each other it would stop a lot of misery for both families."

"That's just what Farley said."

"But you're goin' anyway."

"It's my job."

She blinked away a tear. "Someday they'll be haulin' you here like Farley, wounded or worse. Is your job worth that?"

"The only thing I know for sure is that I have to do it. Else I couldn't look Rusty and the rest of them in the face."

"If you get killed, do you think they'll cry over you?"

"I won't know about it one way or the other."

This time she let the tear roll down her cheek, unchecked. "*I'd* cry for you, Andy."

He waited until dark before riding in to Hopper's Crossing. From across the street he surveyed the jail, remembering the night he and Farley had taken it upon themselves to guard it against a mob, needlessly, as it turned out. Through a barred window he saw a faint glow as if a lamp's wick was turned down low. Looking around to see if anyone was watching, he dismounted and walked over for a closer look. He found that cotton cloth had been tacked up on the inside. It was thin enough to allow lamplight to show but heavy enough that Andy could not see through it.

He stood awhile, watching and wondering until someone cautiously lifted a corner of the cloth. Andy saw little more than one eye, but he was almost certain: Big'un was behind that crude curtain.

He did not know what to make of it. It seemed unlikely that Big'un had come back and resumed his sheriff's duties as if nothing had happened. Yet there he was. Andy flirted for a moment with the idea of trying the door, but Big'un would be careful enough to have locked and barred it. He remembered that it was too strong for one man to break it down.

Hearing voices, he stepped into the darkness and flattened himself against the jail wall. Boots trod heavily upon the wooden sidewalk, stopping at the jail door. Someone demanded, "Big'un, open this door."

From inside came a familiar voice. "Who's out there?"

"Your uncle Judd. I want to talk to you."

"You already done more talkin' than I want to listen to. Unless you've brought me some money, that door stays shut."

"The jail is county property. As county judge I'm orderin' you to open up."

"For all I know, Jayce Landon is waitin' out there in the dark. All he needs is for me to open this door and give him a clean shot."

"Have you lost all your guts, boy?"

"Havin' guts is one thing. Bein' stupid is another. You know Jayce won't give me a fightin' chance."

"And I know why. Just about everybody in town knows." The judge cursed softly to the man who was with him. "On account of Big'un, the Hopper name doesn't mean what it used to around here. Before long every dog in town will be hiking its leg at us."

The two men walked away, the judge still grumbling.

If the situation had not been so serious Andy might have laughed at the irony of Big'un Hopper having made himself, in effect, a prisoner in his own jail.

Knowing the effort would probably be futile, he knocked on the door with the butt of his pistol. "Big'un, open up."

Big'un hollered, "I told you, Uncle, I'm done talkin' to you."

"This is Andy Pickard. Texas Ranger. You're under arrest."

Big'un did not answer for a moment. "Arrest? Are you crazy? I'm in here, and you're out there. You ain't comin' in, and I ain't comin' out."

"Give up to me and I'll take you somewhere that Jayce can't get to you."

"I ain't afraid of Jayce."

"Looks to me like you are. Else you wouldn't have locked yourself up in there."

"Go to hell."

"I'm just tryin' to give you a chance."

"I'll make my own chances. Now git!"

Andy had not expected Big'un to surrender, at least not right away, but maybe this would get him to thinking. "If you decide you want my protection, send somebody to find me. I'll be around."

Andy thought that Big'un was not likely to go anywhere for a while, not until he was sick and tired of self-imposed imprisonment. He rode down to the livery stable. The hostler showed surprise. "You all by yourself, Ranger?"

"There isn't anybody else. The other two Rangers got wounded."

"I heard about that. Good news is a long time comin', but bad news spreads in a hurry. Which one are you after, Jayce or Big'un?"

"Both. I know where Big'un is at, for now. Got any idea where Jayce might be?"

The hostler shook his head. "I've got to live with both sides. Wouldn't want anybody accusin' me of bein' a gossip. But if it was me lookin', I'd say go where the Landons are the thickest. Maybe out to Walter Landon's farm."

"Have you seen Jayce yourself?"

The hostler let the question die unanswered. "You want me to put your horse up?"

"That was my first intention, but now I think I'll go to Walter Landon's."

"You'd better either sing out loud or tiptoe like you was

walkin' on eggs. Them Landons don't appreciate surprises, and they are uncommon good shots." He paused, staring at Andy with some apprehension. "They ain't the kind that forgives easy. I'd rather you never told them you even talked with me."

"I'm not a gossip either."

There was probably not a bigger gossip in town than the stableman, but in this instance Andy felt that he would keep his mouth shut. He could not mention having seen Andy without being asked what they talked about. Andy had rather his return to Hopper's Crossing not be noised around before he had time to size up his options. He had not seen many so far.

He knew the way to Walter Landon's farm, though he lost it in the moonlight a couple of times where lesser wagon roads split off from the main one. As he began to discern lamplight in the front windows he wondered which of the hostler's recommendations he should choose: to ride in announcing himself or to sneak in and observe quietly.

His first instinct was to see before being seen, but three hound dogs took the decision out of his hands. As they began barking and trotted to meet him, the lamplight winked out. He suspected that one or more rifles or shotguns were aimed in his general direction. He shouted, "Hello, the house."

No one immediately shot at him, so he felt hopeful.

A voice answered, "Who's that out yonder?"

"Andy Pickard, Ranger. You-all remember me."

"Are you by yourself?" The voice sounded familiar, though he could not identify it.

"There's nobody but me." He rode up almost to the front porch, hoping the moon provided enough light that they could see he was alone. He raised his hands.

A match flared, and the lamp burned again. A man

stepped out onto the porch. The light was at his back so Andy could not see the face. He thought he knew the man by his shape and his stance.

He said, "Howdy, Jayce."

He heard a chuckle. "Sorry, Andy. Come closer and look again."

Moving up, he recognized Jayce's Ranger brother. "Dick?" He recalled how much the Landon brothers resembled one another. At a distance it would be difficult to tell which was which. "I thought you were still in camp on the San Saba."

"I took a leave of absence to be at my brother's trial. But it seems like you-all can't hold on to Jayce long enough for him to get a shave."

"He had a close shave at the jail. We all did."

"I know. I'm grateful that you-all got him out."

Andy suspected Dick had heard about it from Jayce. "He took care of himself. I've got no credit comin'."

"So now you're here hopin' to take him back."

Andy nodded. "Him and Big'un Hopper both."

"Just you?"

"I'm all there is."

"It might get you killed."

Andy suggested, "You're still a Ranger. You could help me."

"I already turned my brother in once. It's weighed on my conscience ever since. I wouldn't do it again for anybody." Dick jerked his head toward the door. "Tie your horse and come on in. We're all friends here."

For the moment perhaps, but Andy knew that attitudes would change in a hurry if he tried to take Jayce back to jail. He wrapped the reins around a post and went up onto the porch. He asked, "Can you look me square in the eye and tell me Jayce ain't here?"

Dick smiled. "If I tell you where he ain't, you might figure out where he *is.* My duty as a Ranger is on leave till I go back to camp."

Andy stopped abruptly in the open door. Flora stood in the front room with a couple of men, one of them Walter Landon, and a woman he guessed was Walter's wife.

Dick said, "You know Flora, of course."

Getting over his initial surprise, Andy told her, "I'm bettin' Jayce himself brought you here."

She said, "I didn't need Jayce to show me the way. My home is just over the hill, what's left of it." It was the kind of answer that said neither yes nor no.

He said, "I thought you were takin' care of Scooter."

"Tom Blessing's wife took him out to their farm. Big'un wouldn't dare do him harm out there, even if he could find the place."

Dick said to Andy, "I didn't know you-all had the boy. What're you goin' to do with him?"

"When Rusty is ready to travel we intend to take Scooter up north to the Monahan family."

"I couldn't think of a better place for him. I know you and Rusty have shared some hard times with the Monahans, and some good times too."

"I've seen them go down bruised and bloody, but they always got up and went on with their lives."

"That's like us Landons." Dick rolled and lighted a cigarette, his eyes narrowed in thought. "You're takin' on too much of a load to tote by yourself. You'd best forget about catchin' Jayce. I'd be tickled to help you with Big'un, though."

Andy wondered if anyone had told Dick of the outrage Big'un and his brother Ned had forced on Flora. It was not his place to do so. Gunning for Big'un would be legal for Dick so long as he did it within his duty as a Ranger, but to do it for personal vengeance would outlaw him, as killing Ned Hopper had outlawed Jayce.

Dick asked, "Have you got a plan?"

"Not a trace. I'm hopin' somethin' will break in my direction."

Andy had a strong hunch Jayce was somewhere within shouting distance. He ventured a few probing questions that yielded him nothing. He realized that if he captured Jayce he would have to do it somewhere else. These people protected their own.

Dick said, "It's time to hit the soogans. I've been rollin' my blankets out here on the porch."

Andy took that as an oblique invitation to stay the night. It seemed a good idea if he was right about Jayce being near. Dick accompanied him to a corral, where he unsaddled his horse and turned him loose. He removed a blanket rolled and tied behind the cantle of his saddle. Back at the front porch he lay looking at the stars, crisp and sparkling in the chilled fall air. He caught the faint odor of Dick's cigarette.

He asked, "Why do you reckon it is that so many people can't find a way to live together? If they haven't got somethin' to fight about, they'll make up a reason. I'll bet you've got no notion how the feud started in the first place."

"I've always laid it on the stubbornness of the Hoppers, but I can't truthfully say they're more stubborn than us Landons. If one of us didn't start a fight, the other one would. I remember us young'uns jumpin' on the Hopper boys and fightin' when they hadn't even done anything to us."

"Maybe a Landon and a Hopper ought to marry one another. Things might get peaceful if everybody was kin."

Dick grunted dissent. "Things would just turn meaner. You ever watch a bunch of in-laws get together?"

Andy had never seen much of family life except among

the Indians. There, just as in the white community, relationships could be fragile as glass. He said, "I get the idea that Big'un is the main one keepin' the feud stirred up."

"Him and his brother Ned. Ned's gone now, but Big'un is still a bad apple spoilin' the barrel. And behind Big'un is old Judge Hopper. He never gets his knuckles bloody, but he keeps stirrin' the pot. While everybody watches the fightin', he dips his hands into the county treasury."

"I'll bet if the Rangers got to lookin' around they could clean the judge's plow."

"Probably. But I can't put a halo around Jayce's head either. Even if he is my brother, I have to admit that he's done a lot to keep the fight goin'."

Andy thought before he asked, "Do you think Flora saw that side of him before she married?"

"I tried to tell her, but she wasn't ready to listen. After they went to the preacher it wasn't my place to tell her anything anymore. I tried to get Jayce to leave here when I did, to take her away from this part of the country and let the old fight die. But he didn't want to turn aloose. It had got in his blood like whiskey does for some people." He snubbed out his cigarette. "Flora deserves better than that."

Andy had guessed wrong. Big'un did not stay put.

Big'un was wary about going out the jail's front door, which faced the town's main business street. Even the back door could not be considered safe, but at least it was darker on that side of the courthouse square. Staying in the shadows as much as he could, he headed for the wagon yard. He had left his horse there in an open corral. He wished he could get his mount and go without the stableman seeing him, but that was not to be. The skinny hostler watched him saddling his horse and asked, "Where you goin' this time of the night, Big'un?"

"Vacation." Damn a man who asked personal questions, he thought. This nosy dickens's jaw would still be moving a week after they buried him.

"Ain't you afraid you'll run into a booger, travelin' in the dark?"

"The boogers we've got around here, they're even worse in the daylight."

Big'un tied his blankets and war bag on the saddle. As soon as he got his hands on a chunk of his uncle's money he would be gone. He was not sure how he would fit in Mexico, but if he liked it he might be a long time coming back. At least he wouldn't have to keep looking over his shoulder for that back-shooting Jayce Landon. And he would have a border between himself and the Rangers.

He reined his horse toward a quarry where workers cut building stones a few hundred yards from town. He had watched them use dynamite from a wooden shed. He had not learned much about handling dynamite beyond how to set a fuse and touch it off without blowing himself up. He figured that was enough in this case.

He had no idea how much he needed for the job, so he made a guess and tucked a box under his arm. It was about half full. He rode back to town and tied his horse to the fence behind the courthouse on the side opposite his uncle's office. Carrying the dynamite, he tried the back door and found it locked. He watched and listened before he drew his pistol and broke a pane. Reaching inside, he freed the lock. He waited and listened again until he was confident nobody had paid any attention to the sound of breaking glass.

The courthouse was almost pitch dark, but he had been to Uncle Judd's office so many times he could have found it in his sleep. He bumped into a desk on his way in, then felt his way along until he came to the safe. By feel more than by sight, he set the fuse and placed the stick back in the box with the others. He propped the box against the safe door, lighted the fuse, and moved out into the hallway to escape the blast.

The hallway was not far enough. The concussion lifted him off his feet and hurled him down the hall. His ears drummed with pain. Papers and pens and other small objects went flying. Windows shattered, and dust billowed like a dry fog.

Choking, he made his way back into what remained of his uncle's office. He saw a gaping hole in the outer wall. Glass crunching beneath his brogan shoes, he made his way to it and saw the safe lying outside. It was turned over, the door pressed against the ground. It would take several men to turn it.

Big'un did not know words strong enough to express his exasperation, but he tried all the ones he could think of. They didn't help. He could imagine his uncle Judd going into a mouth-foaming fit over this. Well, the money-grubbing old son of a bitch had it coming. It was his own fault.

Discretion told him he had better be moving before a curious crowd swarmed the damaged courthouse. He hurried out the back door and around the building. He feared the blast had frightened the horse into running away, but it was still straining against the tied reins. He patted it on the neck in an effort to calm it. As soon as he could get it to quit faunching around he mounted and set it into a long trot.

The stableman came running out through the barn's wide doors. He shouted, "What happened, Big'un?"

"Lightnin' strike." Big'un spurred his horse into a lope.

He had burned down a jailhouse and blown up a courthouse. Whatever might happen from now on, at least Hopper's Crossing would not soon forget him.

{ TWENTY }

Andy awakened from a cold half-sleep he had endured most of the night. A bloodred sun was just beginning to rise. His muscles ached from the discomfort of lying on the porch's hard floor. He felt around for his pistol but could not find it.

Dick Landon had already rolled his blanket and placed it against the wall. He said, "Don't you worry about that six-shooter. You'll get it back when we figure it's safe."

"Safe for who?"

"All of us, includin' you."

Andy sensed the reason it had been taken. "What time did Jayce get here?"

"He was here all the time. Him and Flora slept out in the barn. They're in the kitchen now havin' breakfast. You hungry?"

"Think Jayce will trust me?"

"No, but as long as you're not heeled there won't be any trouble."

Andy pulled his boots on. The air had the crisp smell of fall but not yet of frost. If Rusty had not suffered from that hailstorm he would be harvesting his fields, not lying in the doctor's house badly shot up. Andy wondered what Rusty would think of him now, about to share breakfast with a fugitive on the fugitive's terms.

Andy looked at the blazing sunrise. "I've heard them say that a red sky at sunup means there's a storm comin'."

"Only if you get reckless."

Jayce stood in the door, looking calm and friendly. "Come in, Ranger, and let Flora pour you some coffee. Eggs and biscuits are about ready. Walter's family has done et."

Andy followed Dick through the door. He sneaked Dick's pistol out of its holster and stuck it into his boot while all attention was on Flora at the woodstove. She poured coffee into an enameled cup for Andy. He thanked her and turned to Jayce. He said, "I was hopin' you'd be halfway to Mexico by now. I wouldn't have to take you in."

Smiling at Andy's show of confidence, Jayce poured coffee into a saucer and blew across to cool it. "Sorry about your friend Rusty. Hell, I'm even a little sorry about that ornery Farley Brackett."

Andy wrapped his stiff fingers around the cup, enjoying its warmth. "You got away from that jailhouse fire awful quick."

"I saw Big'un light out. Thought I could catch him, but I lost him in the dark. I didn't see any point in stayin' around, so I borrowed some citizen's horse. I wish you'd take it back to him with my thanks."

"You can ride it back yourself when I take you in."

"You don't ever give up, do you?"

Dick Landon spoke. "It's the Indian in him. Did you know he was raised by the Comanches?"

"I ought to've figured."

Flora said, "As soon as I saw that Rusty and Farley were not goin' to die and I put Scooter in good hands, I followed my husband."

Jayce said, "I'd already told her that if I ever had a

chance to get away I'd head for home. She'd know where to find me."

Both Jayce and Flora looked sleepy-eyed. Andy remarked, "After so much travelin', you-all appear sort of worn out."

The two smiled at each other. Jayce reached out to touch Flora's hand. "I take it you're not a married man."

Andy said, "Never been asked."

"When the time comes, be sure you get a girl like Flora. But not Flora herself. She's mine."

"You and her could still get away from here. There's not much I could do to stop you so long as your family has got me a prisoner."

"There's one job I ain't finished yet."

"Big'un?"

"He's done a lot of dirt to us Landons." Jayce's face tightened as he looked at his wife. "What kind of man would I be if I just let it go?"

"A live one, and free."

Andy saw something in Flora's eyes. He saw that he had reached her whether he had reached Jayce or not. She told Jayce, "If we stay here you know what'll happen. Big'un will find a way to shoot you in the back if you don't get him first. And if you get him, the law will give you a quick trial and then hang you. Either way, I'll wind up bein' a widow. I want us to go somewhere and start fresh."

"I can't forget what Big'un done to you."

"I can. Revenge isn't worth it. I'd rather have my husband alive and at my side. The law will take care of Big'un, or the devil will."

Jayce argued, "Maybe you've forgot that murder charge against me, but the law hasn't."

Andy said, "That's Texas law. But you could go someplace like Colorado or maybe California. They never heard of Ned Hopper or you either."

He could see that Jayce was struggling. Jayce said, "Before I go anywhere I'd like to have the personal pleasure of sendin' Big'un to hell."

Andy had never quite grasped the concept of an eternal fiery hell for sinful souls. It was not part of the Comanche religion. "There's hell enough right here on earth, Jayce. At the least we can send Big'un to the penitentiary for a long stretch. At the best we might be able to hang him for killin' Sheriff Truscott."

"I got a little inklin' of the real hell before we got out of that burnin' jailhouse. That's the kind I favor sendin' him to."

Andy pushed his plate away with half the bacon and eggs uneaten. "Jayce, they'd drum me out of the Rangers if they heard me say this. What if I was to turn my back for a while, and you and Flora was to slip away real quiet? I'd be so busy huntin' for Big'un that I might not even miss you for three or four days."

Flora said, "He's offerin' us the best chance we'll ever have, Jayce. We can get away from this awful old feud, away from Big'un and all the other Hoppers."

Dick said, "Listen to her, Jayce. Her and Andy are givin' you the best advice you'll ever hear."

Jayce looked across the table at Andy. "If I go, I want everybody to understand that it's for Flora and not because I'm scared of Big'un. I'd gladly meet him face-to-face, but he'd never do that. He'd lay in wait somewhere and bushwhack me."

Andy replied, "That's the way I see it. The longer you stay around here, the less chance you've got of seein' Christmas. If I was you two, I'd saddle up and git while the gittin's good."

Jayce said, "I'm bein' ganged up on. I guess I can't outargue you all."

Flora nodded at Jayce. He pushed back from the table. "Ain't got much to pack." Flora started to follow him out the door but stopped long enough to lean down and kiss Andy on the cheek.

Andy saw a wistful look in Dick's eyes as his gaze followed Flora out the door.

Dick said, "Andy, you've just violated a basic Ranger regulation. You've let a prisoner go."

"I never really took him prisoner." Andy reached down to draw Dick's pistol from his boot. He laid it on the table in front of him. "You can have your six-shooter back."

Dick dropped his hand and felt of his empty holster. "Well, I'll be damned." His eyes narrowed. "Would you really have used this?"

"I don't know. I'm glad I didn't have to find out."

Andy finished his coffee then walked outside, where Dick watched his brother and Flora lead two horses out of the corral. Dick said, "You've got me beat. I never could talk Jayce into anything. All I could ever do was wish him luck and cover his back when I could. I got so tired of it that I had to leave."

Jayce pulled his saddle down from the plank fence. As he picked up his blanket, he dropped suddenly to one knee and grabbed his leg. Andy heard the crack of a rifle. He saw a wisp of smoke in a patch of timber a couple of hundred yards away.

Flora dropped her saddle and screamed, "He's shot."

Andy and Dick ran toward the couple. With a shout of rage Flora yanked a rifle from Jayce's saddle scabbard. She threw it to her shoulder and fired, then fired again.

Dick shouted, "Come on, Andy, let's catch the son of a bitch."

Andy paused for a swift look at Jayce. His trousers leg was bloody. The wound was far from any vital spot.

Dick grabbed Jayce's saddle and threw it on the horse Jayce had been about to ride. Andy quickly caught Flora's horse and put his own saddle on its back. Dick was fifty yards ahead of him as Andy mounted, but he soon caught up.

Big'un exulted for a moment when he saw Jayce go down. Then he felt the breath of the first bullet as it passed by his ear. He turned to grab his horse as the second bullet struck. It was as if a sledgehammer had hit him in the side. He went to his knees, almost losing his hold on the reins. The air was knocked out of his lungs. He gasped desperately for breath. Each try felt as if someone were jabbing a knife into his side.

For a moment he went into a blind panic. My God, they've killed me, he thought. Slowly he began breathing, but with breath came feeling. The wound in his side began to hurt like nothing he had ever felt in his life. He knew he had some broken ribs, probably a punctured lung. He exerted a heavy effort struggling to his feet and drawing himself up against his horse. He made several tries before he was able to lift his left foot into the stirrup, then pull himself into the saddle. He leaned far forward and came near to falling off.

He grabbed the horn of the saddle and beat his heels against the horse's ribs, putting it into a long trot, then a lope. He tried to turn his head and look back, but dizziness overtook him. It threatened to make him lose his seat. He reasoned that some of the Landons must be coming behind him. They would have started their pursuit as soon as they could grab horses.

This was going to be a ride for life.

He wished now he had followed his plan to quit the Colorado River country and immediately head for Mexico.

But he had feared that Jayce would follow him no matter where and how far he went. He had to eliminate Jayce before he could feel safe anywhere.

Now he had failed in that as he had failed with the jailhouse fire and with his attempt to blow Judd Hopper's safe open. Seemed like he couldn't do anything right anymore.

He wondered when his luck had started to sour. Maybe it was when he and Ned found Flora Landon at home alone. They had grabbed the opportunity to drag her back to her bedroom. He had always thought her one of the most provocative women he had ever seen. Taking her as he had should have been pleasurable, especially considering that she was the wife of a lifelong antagonist and this represented a victory of sorts. Instead, it had left him strangely unsatisfied. It also left him with bruises and abrasions that lingered long after the fleeting moment of pleasure.

The world went by him in a blur as he rode. With each stride, pain drove through him like a lance. Tasting blood, he rubbed his mouth and saw red smeared across the palm of his hand. He knew coughing up blood was a sign that life was ebbing away. He was bleeding to death.

He felt his hand loosen on the horn despite his effort to tighten his grip. He was conscious of slipping from the saddle. Striking the ground set off an explosion of agony as shattered ribs punched into a lung. He tasted dirt and tried to spit it out. He lacked strength to raise his head. Face against the ground, he managed a few more breaths until the dirt he inhaled choked him.

His last conscious thought was, "Damn you, Flora, this is all your fault. And you wasn't worth it."

During the chase, Andy and Dick had never come close enough to catch more than a glimpse of Big'un. They had to follow tracks, which slowed them. Andy said, "We don't even know for sure that it *is* Big'un."

Dick said, "Who else would've shot at Jayce? He could be anyplace out yonder, settin' up an ambush for us."

"I don't think he's a good shot. He just nicked Jayce in the leg."

Andy was first to see the saddled bay horse grazing peacefully where the grass still contained some green. Dick said, "That's Big'un's, all right. I've seen him ridin' it around the country."

At first Andy thought Dick might be right about Big'un setting up an ambush. Then he saw the still form of a man stretched in the grass. Wind rolled Big'un's hat along the ground and picked at the loose tail of his shirt. "That'd be him, I suppose."

Dick said, "Flora must've hit him." She was the only one who had fired in Big'un's direction.

Andy drew his pistol in case Big'un might be playing possum. Riding up close, however, he could tell that Big'un was dead. He dismounted and turned Big'un over onto his back. Much of the man's clothing was soaked in blood.

He said, "That's the way the hide hunters like to hit a buffalo, in the lung. Looks to me like he bled to death."

Dick got down for a look. "The slower the better. I hope he had time to consider all his sins."

Andy closed Big'un's half-open eyes. "He's been worried that Jayce was out to kill him. I wonder if he had any idea it was Flora who brought him down."

"Seems like justice to me, seein' what he did to her."

"All the same, this could cause her some trouble if she stays around here in Hopper country."

Dick shrugged. "Nothin' we can do about that. We've got to go to town and report what happened."

Andy considered. "Maybe not. What if Big'un just disappeared and nobody ever knew what happened to him?"

Dick appeared intrigued.

Andy said, "We could tell them we lost his tracks. It should all seem natural enough. Big'un took his shot at Jayce and saw that it didn't kill him, so he quit the country. Lots of people drift away and are never heard from again. Everybody would figure after a while that he found him a safe place and decided to settle there for good."

"But what about his body?"

"All we need is a shovel."

Dick gave him a quizzical look. "That's crafty. Some of your Comanche raisin'?"

"I'm just thinkin' it would take care of several problems. If Jayce knew Big'un is dead he might decide not to leave. Then I'd have to arrest him and take him to trial. You know how that would likely come out, especially in this county."

Dick said, "I know a farmer who lives over the hill. He's not much for talkin', and he'd lend us a shovel without askin' questions. What about Big'un's horse?"

"We'll unsaddle him and turn him loose to find his way home. Folks'll figure Big'un caught a fresh horse and left for a better climate. With him and Jayce both gone, maybe the feud will die away."

They wrapped Big'un in his saddle blanket and buried him with his saddle and bridle. Andy watched the bay horse roll in the dirt then wander off, oblivious to the drama that had played out around him. Andy took a tree branch and smoothed the ground, hoping to hide the fact that it contained a grave. "It don't seem right without somebody sayin' some words over him."

Dick shook his head. "Wouldn't make any difference. He was beyond prayer a long time ago."

Scooter held the wagon team's reins, for his leg still pained him when he tried to sit on a horse. Rusty, his shoulder still bound, sat beside him on the wagon seat, restless eyes searching over the terrain. Andy rode horseback beside them, watching nervousness build in both Rusty and Scooter. The extra horses were tied on behind the wagon.

Rusty said, "The more I think about this, the more I get to wonderin' if it's right to burden the Monahans with me. I could heal all right in the Ranger camp."

Scooter asked, "What if they don't like me? And I don't know if I'll like them either." He still grieved over parting with his father.

Andy replied, "The Monahans wrote and told you-all to come, that they'd be glad to have you both. Anyway, Rusty, you've already been took off of the pay roster. Captain said anybody who's been shot up that much ought to retire before he gets himself killed. You've gotten to be a bad risk."

The captain had come near to taking Andy off of the roster too. "Look at your record," he had said. "You went off to transport a prisoner but lost him."

"It was the sheriff that lost him," Andy countered.

"Even so, he got caught a second time and you lost him again. Then there was the old bank robber, the boy's daddy. You had a chance to grab him but didn't. And that jailhouse arsonist—you ought to've caught him but let him slip through your fingers. Lord knows where any of them are now. That is not a good record for a Ranger, even a green recruit."

Andy had said, "I'll bet I can learn better, sir."

"From what I've been told you showed initiative on several occasions. That is a point in your favor even if the results were not as we might have wanted. I'll give you another chance, but you are on probation, Private Pickard."

Andy had thanked him for his generosity and then accepted leave to take Rusty and the boy to the Monahan family. Andy knew he had not followed the letter of the law, but he felt that he had served justice. That was the more important consideration.

A wheel dropped into a shallow hole and jolted the wagon. Scooter said, "Sorry, Rusty. I didn't see that one. I'll never make a teamster."

"You can make yourself into anything you want to be. You've just got to work hard at it."

"I'd like to be a Ranger someday, like you and Andy."

"You can do it if you want it bad enough. But by the time you get there things are liable to be considerable different. In my early days we mostly fought Indians. That's about come to an end. Now we're fightin' robbers and stock thieves, murderers, border jumpers, and the like. But we've got more to fight them with, like the telegraph. And they're startin' to build railroads across Texas. In a few years a Ranger will be able to put a horse on a train and take him halfway across the state in a day, then jump off ready for a chase. Show me the criminal who can beat that."

Andy said, "The way you talk, I think you'd still like to be a part of it."

Rusty shook his head. His hair that used to be red was rusty now, gray softening the color. "No, these last weeks convinced me it's time to hang up the six-shooter and take hold of a plow handle. This body has taken too many beatin's."

"The state will lose a good Ranger."

"But it'll gain a pretty good farmer."

A boy of about Scooter's size loped toward them on a paint horse, waving a misshapen felt hat over his head. He shouted, "Andy! Rusty!"

Andy pushed out a little in front to meet him. "Howdy, Billy. Still growin' too fast for your clothes, I see."

The boy rode up on Rusty's side of the wagon. "You been shot again? How many times does this make?"

"Too many," Rusty said, grinning. "How's all your folks?"

"Ready and anxious to see you."

Billy gave Scooter a critical scrutiny. "You the boy that's comin' to live with us?"

Scooter was ill at ease. "That's what everybody's tellin' me."

Billy considered for a bit. "I guess that'll be all right."

The Monahan homestead came into view. Billy said, "I'll lope on ahead and tell them to put supper in the stove."

Rusty leaned forward as if he could see the place better from the edge of his seat. "You'll like these folks when you get to know them, Scooter. They're the nearest thing to a family that I've got. I've seen happy days with them, and I've seen bitter tears."

"So I've heard," Scooter said.

Andy had told Scooter most of what he knew about the Monahans, about the tragedies they had suffered during the war because they had held to their Union sympathies, about their struggle to rebuild after the hostilities, about the loss of the patriarchs and the death of Josie Monahan, who was to have been Rusty's wife.

Rusty said, "The Monahans have been through more hell than most people ever ought to suffer. But they've always gotten up, squared their shoulders, and started again."

His face went grim. "That's what we all have to do when trouble knocks us down. Else life will grind us into the ground."

"Like it did you when Josie was killed?"

Rusty looked at him sharply, then at Andy. "He told you about that, did he?"

Andy looked away, his face reddening. He had not considered that the guileless boy would say whatever popped into his mind.

Scooter said, "He told me Josie has a sister who's a lot like her."

Rusty's expression slowly mellowed. "Maybe a little bit."

The whole Monahan clan was waiting as the wagon pulled up to the house. Mother Clemmie, limping a little from lingering aftereffects of a stroke, led the greetings. She hugged Andy, then Rusty, taking care for the bandaged shoulder. She turned then to Scooter. "This is the boy you wrote about? I'm goin' to have to fatten him up some. Like he is, he won't hardly throw a shadow."

Andy shook hands with everybody who came up to greet him, then realized he had missed someone. Alice.

She and Rusty stood on the other side of the wagon. They had shaken hands, then neglected to turn loose.

Preacher Webb gave the blessing before supper, expressing special thanks for Rusty's survival and wishing a better future for the new boy who was to share the family's bed and board. Through supper Scooter and Billy kept eyeing each other nervously.

Afterward Webb sat down to read his Bible, though Andy was sure he already knew it by heart. Billy asked Scooter to go with him out to the barn. "We've got some new puppies. Maybe you can help me name them."

"I've never had a puppy," Scooter said.

"You can have one of these for your own if it likes you."

Andy stood at the window, watching the two boys start walking toward the barn, then break into a run. He turned back to help Clemmie and her married daughter Geneva clear the table. He said, "I'd best go look for Rusty."

Clemmie caught his arm. "I wouldn't disturb him right now, was I you."

Andy saw Rusty sitting on the front porch, talking to Alice. Clemmie smiled. So did Geneva. Clemmie asked, "How would you like some more of that cobbler pie, Andy?"

He said, "Sounds real good to me."

{ AFTERWORD }

Life in Texas was changing rapidly in the post–Civil War decade of the 1870s, the setting of this story. The long and much-resented federal occupation had ended. The disenfranchised former Confederates regained their vote, allowing them to elect state and local governments of their own choosing. They adopted a new constitution guaranteeing their individual rights.

The Texas Rangers organization had disintegrated during the war years and was abolished by the federally established postwar government. One of the first acts of newly elected governor Richard Coke in 1874 was to reorganize this force, which had first been called into service by colonizer Stephen F. Austin in 1823. Though a special frontier battalion stood watch at the outer edges of settlement, guarding against Indian incursion, a majority of the state's Rangers now concentrated on suppression of crime and violence.

A vigorous army campaign in the fall of 1874 drove most Comanches, Kiowas, and other hostile Plains tribes to reservations. Buffalo hunters were systematically annihilating the vast shaggy herds, forcing the Indians into dependency on the government and opening the Plains for permanent white settlement. Apart from relatively small outbreaks, Indian trouble was over for most of the state.

The Apaches continued to roam a few more years in far West Texas, but settlement there was sparse and remained so until most of the more productive Texas land was taken.

Law enforcement was the Rangers' main concern now, and the challenge was formidable. The war had left Texas threadbare. Veterans returned to find their families in deplorable straits, often losing land and home to opportunists who flocked in to reap where they had not sown. The excesses of corrupt officials had bred a widespread contempt for law and an acceptance of violence as a means to accomplish what might otherwise not be possible.

From its beginnings, Texas had been subject to savage feuds. In one case Sam Houston felt obliged to call out the army to quell a particularly bitter fight. Other feuds flared in the combative postwar climate and required response by the Rangers to cool them down.

The border with Mexico had bred racial conflict almost constantly since the Texas revolution and would continue to do so well into the twentieth century. Border jumpers were a major problem for the Rangers in the 1870s. Captain Leander McNelly once stacked the bodies of a dozen bandits in Brownsville's town square as an object lesson. However, the Rangers had never forgotten the Alamo and were prone at times to administer punishment to Mexicans simply for being Mexicans without regard to guilt or innocence.

Cattle drives to the northern railroads were bringing fresh money into an impoverished state. They increased the value of range cattle and encouraged rustling, sometimes on a massive scale. Rustling required physical labor, however. Robbing banks was easier.

The banking industry grew in response to Texas's gradual economic recovery. Banks became a prime target for robbery by organized gangs as well as ambitious individual entrepreneurs who might rationalize that they were simply carrying on the Civil War against Northern interests.

The Rangers embraced new technology to help them meet these challenges. The spread of the telegraph meant that word of a crime could be flashed instantly across the state. Texas railroads, though few and of a limited regional nature, were beginning to plan expansions that would revolutionize travel by the early part of the next decade. That would allow Rangers and other law officers rapid transportation no outlaw's horse could outrun.

A few people were already experimenting with Alexander Graham Bell's new invention. Shortly telephone lines would be spreading across Texas like spiderwebs. A Ranger in Fort Worth would soon be able to talk to one in El Paso and others in between. Such notable outlaws as Sam Bass and John Wesley Hardin, who earlier had been able to hit, then run for the brush, would soon find themselves hemmed in by wires and rails. They could still run, but it would be increasingly difficult to hide.

Forge

Award-winning authors
Compelling stories

Please join us at the website below for more information about this author and other great Forge selections, and to sign up for our monthly newsletter!

www.tor-forge.com